THE WOMAN
IN GREEN

Jack Todd

Norman Carney SA Editions

Cover illustration and design by: Ella Mazur
Library of Congress Control Number: 2018675309
Printed in the United States of America

"You think that a wall as solid as the earth separates civilisation from barbarism. I tell you the division is a thread, a sheet of glass..."

– JOHN BUCHAN, THE POWER-HOUSE

HANNA

Montreal 1913-1914

CHAPTER 1

I t was Christmas Eve, and I was ill. I, Dr. Maximilian Balsano, had diagnosed the symptoms of acute influenza in my only patient – myself, plain Maxim, a young man both ill and far from home. The flushed cheeks and forehead, the fever, aching bones and muscles, the inability to keep so much as a dry biscuit in my stomach and a desire to sleep around the clock.

I was a twenty-four-old physician, naïve, inexperienced and newly arrived in Montreal, four thousand miles from home and so lonely that I caught myself muttering aloud to the people I had left behind in Austria: my father, my grandfather, our ill-tempered housekeeper Frau Kachelmeier, my best friend Dr. Jan Muršak and even Dr. Sigmund Freud, whose overwhelming presence had touched off something of a rebellion in me, the youngest of his protegées. I had crossed the Atlantic to work as a staff assistant to the renowned Dr. Percival Hyde at the Royal Victoria Hospital, and now my father, at home in Bad Gastein, would have only my grandfather and Frau Kachelmeier for company at Christmas, and I would have to endure my illness alone.

Everyone else in my boarding house at the corner of Milton and Aylmer Streets had gone home for the holidays. Even the landlady, Mrs. Guterson had taken the train to spend Christmas with her sister in Ottawa, and Battling Billy, the big orange tabby cat who usually patrolled the halls was nowhere to be seen. I had declined invitations to spend the holidays with new-found friends in North Hatley and Toronto, and now I was wallowing in self-pity and loneliness. Outside, the streets were deserted. Worse, there was no snow and everything seemed bare and cheerless.

The snow came at last, a huge storm that began two

days before Christmas and lasted through most of the Christmas Eve. The McGill weather station received twenty-two
centimetres of snow the first day of the storm, and twenty
more centimetres on Christmas Eve. The snow at first made
me deliriously happy, then simply delirious. It began with a
sore throat and what felt like the beginnings of a fever, but I
ignored my own symptoms. I had seen my father going about
his rounds when he was so ill he could barely stand. I wasn't
going to let a little fever stop me. I plunged into the snow,
spending nearly five hours that first day trudging through the
deepening drifts on Mount Royal until my boots were soaked
through. That evening, I did my best to dry my things near the
fire while I tried to warm myself. My throat was still sore, but
it was somewhat better after a pot of hot tea, and my temperature was no more than a degree above normal.

The next morning, the day before Christmas, my
throat was so raw I could barely swallow – but it was snowing
even harder and I longed to be outdoors. I spent part of the
day struggling with my English textbooks and at two o'clock
in the afternoon, I put the books aside and set out. The snow
was still falling heavily and the temperature had dropped. My
muscles ached and I felt much weaker than I had the day before, so I decided to head down toward the harbor, rather than
attempting to climb Mount Royal again in deep snow. First I
made my way east along Pine Avenue, and then south on Saint-
Laurent Boulevard. The boulevard had been opened that summer with the demolition of the Soeurs de la Congrégation
Notre-Dame Convent between Notre Dame and Rue de la Com-
mune, and the street now offered direct passage to the harbor
and the shores of the ice-choked river.

I dodged between the tram cars on Saint-Jacques Street
and finally reached the harbor, which was deserted. I was
alone to contemplate the ships trapped by the ice in the harbor, a long row of steamships and a handful of sailing ships
with their sails furled and their tall masts coated with ice. As
the December dark settled over the harbor, I was not feeling at

all well. My throat was worse, my limbs ached, and I could feel that my temperature had begun to climb. Now I would have to retrace my steps to get home. I couldn't face an uphill climb, so I retraced my steps as far as Saint-Laurent Boulevard, where I could catch a northbound tram.

As I waited for the tram, I began to shiver uncontrollably. The wind had picked up and seemed to tear through my clothing. My muscles ached and I felt so weary that I wanted to curl up in the snow and sleep, although I knew very well that is how people perish in the cold. It was still snowing, my clothing and boots were cold and wet, and there was no remaining doubt. I was ill. I had been a complete fool, staying out far too long the first day of the storm, then going out again for a long walk in heavy snow when I was sick. At last, the tram arrived. The conductor wished me a cheery *joyeux Noel* and I climbed aboard and stumbled to the nearest seat, not trusting my legs to carry me farther. I took the tram past my usual stop so that I could walk back downhill to my apartment; I couldn't face the thought of a single uphill step.

Once inside the door, I shed my wet clothing, stoked the fire as hot as I could get it, made myself a huge vat of piping hot tea and wrapped myself in Mrs. Guterson's thickest quilt, my feet inches from a cast-iron coal stove that was so hot it was glowing a dangerous cherry red. I was miserable, thousands of miles from home, without a soul to care for me and so feverish my teeth were chattering. I took my temperature, which was nearly 40 degrees on the Centigrade scale, or 104 Fahrenheit. On the very edge of a dangerous fever, and likely to go higher.

I picked up one of the medical texts, read the same sentence four or five times without comprehending a word, and gave up. There were a handful of tattered novels by Charles Dickens, Anthony Trollope, Arthur Conan Doyle and Wilkie Collins in the common room downstairs, but leaving my cozy room to get one seemed as forbidding as a journey on the Alaskan tundra. Instead, I went to bed, wrapped myself in all the blankets I had, and tried to sleep. I must have fallen asleep despite the fever, because I was soon dreaming of an endless, snowy slope in the mountains around Bad Gastein where I could float effortlessly downhill on my skis. Then the racket of someone pounding on the door downstairs intruded into my dream. They were calling to me in German: *Hilfe, bitten helfen Sie! Bitte öffne die Tür! Hilfe, Herr Doktor Balsano, Hilfe!* The words were repeated in English: "Help! Please help me! Please open the door! Help, Dr. Balsano! Help!"

I sat up, suddenly aware that the cries for help were not part of my dream. The pounding stopped, and I thought perhaps it was only the wind. But when I rose to put more coals on the fire, I heard it again, a woman's voice calling: "Help! Please help! Open the door!

I unwrapped the quilts from around my shoulders, pulled on my dressing gown and slippers, and made my way down the long staircase. The pounding grew louder. Someone was desperate. "Please, Maxim! Open! I must have help!"

I unlocked the inner door into the foyer with the small brass key, then slid back the cast-iron bolt and turned the heavy iron key to unlock the outer door. A blast of wind and snow came in as I opened the door. A young woman stood on the doorstep coatless and shivering in a thin dress such as she might wear to a ball, her hair matted with snow.

I leaned toward her to get a better look. "Can I help you?"

"Herr Doktor Balsano! Thank God! You are home."

"Yes, I'm home, but I'm very ill. I am sorry, but should I know you?"

"*Ich bin Hanna*, Maxim. Hanna Goss, the soprano from Vienna. Do you remember? In August, there was a reception for the medical students at McGill? I sang. We were introduced, we walked together for a time, and we talked of home, do you remember?"

I felt like a fool. Of course I remembered. The outdoor reception, held on the spacious grounds of Dr. Percival Hyde's mansion near the end of the summer, was to welcome new medical students arriving for the fall term at McGill. Hanna was introduced as the new sensation on the European opera circuit, and she had sung for more than an hour as I listened, spellbound. After the performance, I was introduced to her and we wandered the lawn at dusk, gazing down at the city from our lofty perch on Pine Avenue, watching the stars wink on one by one, happily indulging a rare opportunity to speak in German.

I recalled the occasion well enough, but I still found her unrecognizable. She was soaked through and shivering. She had lost weight since we met, there were dark circles under her eyes, and there were bruises on her neck. She seemed terrified, peering over her shoulder as though something or someone was following her. My fever-addled mind finally prompted me to act.

"Come in, come in, Hanna." I said. "We must get you into some dry clothing. I am ill with a fever, so don't come too close, I don't want you to get it."

She first removed the oversized workman's boots she had on her feet. I couldn't imagine how she happened to be wearing them, especially when she had no coat or hat. "Where is your coat?" I asked. "It's ten degrees below zero and snowing. You could have died of exposure."

"I don't have a coat," she said without explanation. I turned to lead the way up the stairs. When I glanced back, she was following me dutifully. There was something childlike in her trust. I that Mrs. Guterson would forgive me for violating the prohibition on female guests this one time. My landlady was not unkind – I felt she would understand if she knew the circumstances. In my chambers, we stood awkwardly by the fire for a few moments. She stood with her head bowed, apologetic, defeated, and (from the expression on her face) still terrified.

If she was to avoid becoming ill, we had to get her into warm clothing. To do that, she would have to remove what she was wearing – everything, because she was clearly wet through. "I have warm flannel pajamas," I said. "If you put them on you can hang up your things to dry while you sit by the fire. I will get you a towel for your hair. You must dry it carefully."

"Thank you, Dr. Balsano. Don't fuss over me. I can see that you are ill. Your cheeks are flaming red. It is I who should be caring for you."

"Don't be absurd. It's only a fever. It will pass. And please, call me Maxim, and I shall call you Hanna."

I went into my narrow bedroom, with the even narrower bed where I slept. I was thankful at least that my father had raised me to be scrupulously tidy. My bedroom was neat and clean, and so was the sitting room where poor, shivering Hanna waited. I laid out my clean pajamas on the bed and brought her the towel, then closed the door politely, sat at my work table and rested my head on my arms while I waited for her to dry and change. Despite the awkward position, I fell asleep. The next thing I knew she was tugging at my sleeve. I lifted my head to see a much different woman: her cheeks were flushed, her hair now discernibly red, her skin like the cream the maids at home used to skim from the milk pails on a spring morning. My woolen pajamas looked much better on her than they ever did on me.

"You are much changed," I said.

" I feel better. But you have a fever."

She touched my cheek. Her touch was so icy, I thought at last to check her fingers and toes for frostbite. She submitted and managed not to giggle when I examined her toes. Like her hands, they were icy as death itself, but she did not have frostbite.

Finally it occurred to me to ask: "How did you find me?"

She smiled a forlorn smile. "I have wanted to come here many times," she said, "but a young woman does not do such things and in any case I have been... busy. When we talked, you told me that you had found lodging in a pleasant yellow house at the corner of Milton and Aylmer streets. This is the only yellow house in the neighborhood. I knew that most of the students would be away for the holiday, but I hoped that you would be here. When I saw the light on in one window, I prayed it would be you and that you would hear me. I am so grateful to you for coming to my rescue, Maxim. *Vielen dank.*"

"*Bitteschön*, Hanna. All I have done is to open the door for a friend."

"Now I must lie down," I said as I handed her the towel. "The tea kettle is on that shelf next to the stove. You will find a pitcher of water there and good strong English tea in the tin. It will do wonders for you, I'm sure."

I felt that I should do more for her, but I was far too weak. I wrapped myself in the quilt again and stretched out on the divan. As I did so, I heard the clock downstairs chime the hour: It was eleven in the evening. In one hour it would be Christmas Day. A Christmas unlike any other I had ever known. When I opened my eyes I saw her in my pajamas, sitting upright on a wooden chair close to the fire. On the rack that I used to dry my clothing were her green dress and a number of those female undergarments which were an erotic mystery to me. I longed to ask her why she was so terrified, what had brought her to my door, but I was too weak and exhausted. I fell into a troubled sleep, and when I woke again, Hanna was shaking me roughly.

"Maxim! Maxim! Please wake up! Please! They are at the door!"

I sat up and looked around wildly, taking a moment to get my bearings and to remember exactly why there was a lovely, red-haired woman in my room, wearing my pajamas. Once I had regained my faculties, I heard what had alarmed her so – a heavy pounding at the outside door downstairs and rough male voices, at least two of them, shouting: "Open up! *Ouvrez la porte maintenant!* Open the damned door right now or we'll break it down!"

"Please, Maxim!" Hanna pleaded with me. "You must do something. Get rid of them! Hide me!"

I looked around the room. The only possible hiding place was the huge old wardrobe that took up almost as much space in my bedroom as the bed itself. I hurried her into it. Unfortunately, I had so few items of clothing hanging in the wardrobe that they did little to conceal her trembling body, but there was nowhere else for her to go. I closed the doors of the wardrobe carefully, pulled the quilt around me and hurried downstairs, where the pounding was only growing louder. I turned the heavy cast-iron key again, slid back the bolt and opened the door a few inches.

There were two men standing in the doorway, one huge, the other short by powerfully built. They were dressed alike, in workmen's heavy winter coats with caps pulled low over their eyes and scarves that hid the lower half of their faces. They might as well have been wearing masks, for all that I could see. My appearance seemed to have startled them. They looked at me as though they were seeing a ghost, and I supposed that's what I looked like.

"What is it you want?" I asked, trying to sound as gruff as I could. The taller one said something in strangely accented English, and then the shorter one repeated it in rough Quebec French.

"A dangerous woman has escaped," the big one said. "There are tracks to your door. We are going to come in and search."

"There's no need for that," I said. "I'm the only person here. I have not admitted anyone to this building, and women are not allowed here. Everyone is away for Christmas."

"We'll decide what needs to be done," the smaller one said. "You won't mind if we come in and search, will you?"

My feverish brain tried to come up with some way to keep them from finding Hanna. Even if I was feeling fit and healthy, I could not have stopped these two rough-looking characters from doing whatever they wanted to do, so I would have to rely on my wits. Then my illness came to my rescue; a solution occurred to me.

"You can't come in," I said. "I am a doctor of medicine, and I am going to have to put this building under quarantine. I have typhoid. I was treating patients and I must have caught the disease. I think it may be fatal in my case. As you can see, I am very ill…"

I didn't need to say more. The one who spoke French may not have had much English, but he understood "typhoid." It was a terrifying word. It had only been a short while since Typhoid Mary, the itinerant Irish cook who infected dozens of people with typhoid fever in and around New York City, had been much in the news. I am quite certain that neither of them knew the symptoms of typhus, but my appearance and the word itself was all that was needed. The big one staggered back. The smaller one retreated a step or two, but he was still skeptical.

"You're sure there is no one else here?" he asked. "We saw footprints in the snow, coming here."

"I was returning from the hospital," I said. "I had to get medicine. See, these are my boots." I held up the workmen's boots Hanna had left at the door. They were at least two sizes too large for me, but he didn't ask me to try them on. He stared as though typhoid might kill at any distance.

"Ah, to hell with it," he said to his partner. "This bastard is going to die of typhoid and we're going to catch our death out trying to find te bitch in a blizzard. But you there, if I find out you were lying, you better hope the typhoid kills you, because I'll cut your damned throat."

They seemed to hesitate then, but nature intervened to help them on their way. I had been feeling more and more nauseous, and I could hold it no longer. I flung the door open and vomited copiously into the snow, the sound of my retching as frightening as the sound of gunfire to the two thugs.

"Aw, Jesus wept!" the big man said. They turned away in disgust. I vomited until my stomach was empty, and by that time the street was as empty as I was. The thugs didn't know that vomiting is rarely a symptom of typhoid. They had vanished in the snow.

I slammed the solid oak door shut, turned the heavy key again and slid the heavier bolt into place, thanking the builders who had put such a solid impediment between the building and the street. Should the thugs decide to return, they would need fire axes to break down that door. My legs were so weak that I had to cling to the bannister to haul myself back up to the second floor. I opened the door to my flat and whispered to Hanna that it was safe for her to come out, then collapsed face-down onto the divan in my sitting room.

Hanna bent over me.

"They're gone?" she asked anxiously.

"They're gone. They're convinced I have typhoid. I couldn't have scared them more with a gun."

Hanna smiled. "That was brilliant."

"I had no choice."

"Thank you Maxim. Now you must rest. I will be grateful to you forever."

I tried to make a joke. "All I did was vomit in the snow," I said.

I was rewarded with a rich laugh from Hanna. She had such a lovely voice, singing or speaking or laughing. I wanted to hear more but exhaustion caught up to me and I fell into a deep sleep. When I woke, Hanna was again bending over me, holding a damp cloth to my burning forehead. I heard the clock chime three times. Three o'clock on Christmas morning.

"I am so sorry," I mumbled. "I'm afraid I have been a terrible host."

"It is alright, Maxim. You saved me."

I looked into Hanna's green eyes, her face only inches from mine. Her hair was dry now, but she was still wearing my pajamas. "I want to help you," I said. "Whatever it is that caused those men to pursue you, I want to help."

She put a finger to my lips. "Not now, Max. You must

sleep. We will talk later."

I was far too ill to argue. I went back to sleep. I woke once, perhaps an hour later, and saw her asleep on a chair a few feet away, her legs pulled up to her chest. The top of the pajamas had slid up and I could see, in the half-light reflected off the glistening snow on the rooftop outside my window, a patch of bare white skin on her side, from her hip-bone to her rib cage. It was the most erotic sight I had ever witnessed, but I was too weak to do more than engrave that vision on my memory forever.

When I woke again, brilliant sunshine sparkled on white snow outside. It was Christmas Day, 1913, the last peaceful Christmas for a long while.

CHAPTER 2

I rose as quietly as I could and peered at the clock. It was eighteen minutes past ten. I couldn't recall when I had last slept so late. Outside, the brilliant sunshine reflected off the snow made my eyes ache. I rose and tiptoed out into the hallway to use the lavatory. I returned to the flat and I was tiptoeing around making tea when I saw the note on the table.

Herr Doktor Balsano,

I thank you for your kind assistance to a woman in distress. You have behaved as a gentleman and I shall be forever grateful, but I must leave. I do not wish to bring my troubles to your door. Please forgive me for behaving like a thief, but I see that you have two coats hanging, so I have taken your old loden coat, an extra pair of mittens, and an old pair of pants and a worn shirt from your closet. It is fortunate that you are slightly built, because it all fits me and I shall find a way to return your clothing at the earliest opportunity.

Please do not attempt to find me, Herr Balsano. It would be dangerous for both of us.

Yours most gratefully,
Hanna Goss

I looked at the rack where she had put her clothes to dry. They were gone. In their place, hung neatly, were my woolen pajamas. I was baffled. Why would she leave a place where she had found temporary safety? The thugs had been here and left. They believed I had typhoid – surely there was a degree of safety in that? What was the danger? Who were those men?

Why were they after a young European singer? Where could her world possibly intersect with theirs? I hurried downstairs to check: the heavy workman's boots she had been wearing were gone. I opened the door and tried to focus in the glare: the snow had drifted over the walkway. There was no sign of her footprints, or of the men who had pursued her to my door.

I climbed the steps again and drank my tea. I wanted to sleep but my mind was whirling. I remembered Hanna's tenderness as she bent over me. When I sniffed the pajamas, there was the faintest trace of her perfume, the same perfume she had worn the night she sang at Dr. Hyde's mansion. It was like inhaling a summer evening.

All that day and the next, I slept and woke, slept and woke. My dreams were tormented by visions of Hanna. Twice I made toast in a pan on the stove, but I managed to eat only a few bites. Finally on the Saturday, two days after Christmas, I felt able to venture out in search of fresh air and solid food. I took the same path Hanna had surely taken when she left, down Aylmer Street to Sherbrooke. On Sherbrooke, I paused for a moment: east or west? There was a westbound streetcar approaching, so I boarded it. As always, I had forgotten the P.A.Y.E. system – Pay As You Enter. (Such an innovative system, I had to recommend it to someone at home in Vienna, which still relied on conductors nosing around to demand payment from passengers on crowded streetcars.) I fumbled in my pockets for the change, paid the fare and found a comfortable seat at the window where I could press my nose against the frigid glass and gaze out at the city. I had no clear destination but when you are young and in a city that is still new to you, that never matters.

On the seat next to mine, someone had left a copy of the Montreal *Standard,* a newspaper that was published only on Saturdays. I picked it up and glanced at the front page. In my weakened state, what I saw there forced me to grab the seat in front of me to keep from falling over in a faint. There was a precise photogravure likeness of Hanna Goss, and a headline that chilled me to the bone:

Austrian Songbird Brutally Murdered

I felt the breath go out of me, heard my lungs gasping for air. This could not be true. Surely not. Not Hanna. I read the first paragraph:

> The Austrian soprano Hanna Goss, who arrived in this city during the summer months to begin a North American tour and created something of a sensation with her voice, was found brutally murdered by a person or persons unknown at approximately ten o'clock on Christmas Eve by a man out walking his dog on Pine Avenue near McGill University.
>
> Miss Goss, whose rendition of several *lieder* by the Austrian composer Hugo Wolf was warmly reviewed by this newspaper...

The words swam before my eyes. I could read no further. "Ten o'clock on Christmas Eve?" How could that be? I remembered the clock striking at three o'clock on Christmas morning, when Hanna was very much alive. It was possible there might have been some confusion, and the witness who found her body had mistaken the time by an hour or two – but hours *after* her body was discovered, Hanna Goss was holding a cold cloth to my head in my apartment on Aylmer Street. And sometime after that, she had time to write a note before she left. I could not dispute that she had been murdered, but the time was wrong by several hours.

Back home, the old country folk would all have shared the same opinion of my visitor: She had been a ghost. *Geist*, phantom, wraith, spectre – put it however you want, they would have been certain that I had received a visitation from the spirit of the dead woman, Hanna Goss. But I, a man of science, had to demand proof. Failing that, I had to arrive at a logical explanation for the woman's appearance in my chambers several hours *after* her murder.

I swayed in my seat, suddenly dizzy, as though the fever

had returned in a rush. The truth was before me in black and white. Hanna had been murdered. She had arrived at my door, trusting her countryman for protection. I had failed her miserably, and now she was gone. Murdered, no doubt, by the thugs she was fleeing when she came to me. I stepped off the tram clutching the newspaper and bumped into a woman waiting to board.

"Watch your step, young man!" she snapped. I stammered an apology and surveyed my surroundings. I was still weak and a little dizzy from my illness. It was cold, perhaps fifteen degrees below zero, but it was sunny, and the glare off the banks of fresh snow made my eyes ache. For no particular reason, my footsteps took me west along Sherbrooke, past the row of elegant townhouses which some of the wealthiest people in the city called home, past Guy Street, and on until I was strolling by the newly built modern convent, the Mother House of the Congrégation de Notre Dame. The grey stone wall surrounding the convent appeared to cover an entire city block.

At another time, I might have taken time to admire the architecture – a field I once considered before settling on medicine. Not on this day. I felt as though I had taken a terrible blow to the solar plexus. I had difficulty breathing. My legs were wobbly. If not for the very real presence of the newspaper clutched in my right fist, I might have been able to believe it was all a dream, but the newspaper with its blaring headline would not go away: Austrian Songbird Brutally Murdered

Even as I tried to accept the reality of it, my mind posed the question: What murder is not brutal? Then I found myself asking another question: What if, in my feverish state, I had killed Hanna in my sleep? What if I was the murderer?

I thought about it for a few moments and rejected the possibility. I was not the guilty party. The night Hanna was killed, I was so weak I could not have murdered a canary. Surely she had been attacked by the thugs who came pounding on the door. They were the culprits, and I had to do something. I passed a mustachioed policeman on horseback. That was it! I had to inform the police – but of what? That the woman whose death they were investigating was in my apartment several hours *after* her supposed murder? I couldn't think of a more compromising situation. I imagined myself with my uncertain English trying to explain the inexplicable to skeptical detectives. Within minutes I would find myself in what they called the "hoosegow."

After all, what was my alibi? "Your honor, I was with the slain woman several hours *after* her death. Therefore, I could not have been guilty of her murder."

Sooner or later, I would have to go to the police. I would consider myself an utter coward if I did not. I was a witness, after all. The two men had come to my door, looking for Hanna. No one else saw them, so the responsibility was mine. It would be a betrayal of Hanna if I failed to come forward – but first I needed time to think, and I needed food.

What I didn't anticipate was that the police would come to me.

CHAPTER 3

When I felt a sudden pang of hunger, I realized that I was near a café and that the odor of hot soup, paprika and sausages with a tang of home was in the air. I located the entrance a few feet ahead along Sherbrooke Street and glanced up at the sign above the door: the establishment was called Sophie's Café. I stepped inside. I had barely eaten in four days, and the smell of real food was overpowering. I hung my heavy winter coat and hat on a peg and found a seat by the window.

I was trying to read the menu scrawled on a chalkboard across the room when a woman with a a cherubic face approached. She was as wide as she was tall, and she stood beside my table with one hand on her hip, brandishing a spatula. I thought that she was impatient for me to order, but that was not it at all.

"You do not look so very well, young man," she said. She held the back of her hand to my forehead. "You have fever, yes? And perhaps you are hungry, also? How long since you eat?"

"Four days. About four days, I'm not sure. I had some bread and tea. I had the most awful flu."

"Bread and tea! Four days! You'll be sick again if you do not eat. I have six sons. Boys must eat."

"I am not a boy, madame. I am twenty-four years old."

"Pish! You are a boy. Boys must eat."

She waddled away, and before I had time to wonder what sort of nostrum she was proposing, she was back with a steaming bowl of dumpling soup seasoned with paprika, a hunk of fresh-baked black bread and a wedge of fresh creamy butter. She put her hand on my shoulder. "Do not try to eat all at once," she said. "Take your time. There is more soup in the pot. Lots more"

I recognized her accent and the dish she had put in front of me. "*Ungarisch?*" I asked.

She paused. "*Igen, ungarisch.* From Budapest. And you?"

"*Osztrák.* From Bad Gastein, although I have been living in Vienna."

We both smiled. Here we were, a Hungarian and an Austrian, both loyal subjects of the dual monarchy and Emperor Franz Joseph, meeting by chance in a faraway land.

"*Eszik! Eszik!*" she said. "Eat! Eat! For you there is no charge, boy from the old country."

"I can't accept that, Madame."

"You must. You are a guest of Zsófia Zsitva. This is my café."

"Dr. Maxim Balsano at your service."

"Doctor? You are too young to be a doctor."

"Well, perhaps. I am twenty-four, but I have finished medical school at the University of Vienna."

"Pleased to make your acquaintance, doctor. You may call me Sophie. Everyone does."

"Well then, you may call me Max."

"Hello, Max."

I squeezed her damp, floury hand, and she left me to the dumpling soup. I buttered a slab of warm bread and tasted her soup. It was divine, all of it. Real food after four days with no appetite. It brought a tear to my eye, or perhaps it was only the paprika. After a few bites, I could feel my strength returning although my tongue was on fire. Before I could ask for it, Sophie returned with a big glass of water.

"You need water, Max," she said. "Drink. It is good for fever."

I drank, then went back to the soup. No sooner had my

spoon touched the bottom of the bowl then Sophie was back with another. I finished the second bowl of soup and mopped it up with the last of the bread and butter. I sat back for a moment, feeling content until my gaze fell on the copy of the Montreal *Standard* at my elbow. Hanna was staring out at me as if to say, "you just found out I was murdered, and here you are stuffing yourself."

Guilty as charged. I took a deep breath and read the story again, especially the most important paragraph. "Sergeant-Detective Cyril Leblanc of the Montreal police said that the body of Miss Hanna Goss was partially buried under the falling snow, leading him to believe that she had been murdered shortly after the dinner hour, at about eight o'clock on Christmas Eve. The detective said that the victim had been beaten so severely about the face and head that she was almost unrecognizable. She was identified by her long, red hair and the fur coat that she wore, and by a letter addressed to her that was found in the pocket of her coat."

Fur coat? What fur coat? She was coatless and wet when she came to me, and she had left with my plain loden coat. Surely she would not have borrowed that old thing if she possessed a fur coat?

Sophie returned with more bread and felt my forehead again. "Good," she said. "You are perspiring. You will sweat out the fever. *Eszik, Eszik.* Eat, eat."

Sophie's kindness was more than I could bear. I burst into tears. She sat down next to me, one broad arm around my thin shoulders, whispering to me softly in Hungarian until the tears had passed. Mercifully, the café was empty by then, and there was no one around to witness my humiliation. When I had recovered my composure, Sophie gazed at me with her frank blue eyes.

"What is it?" she asked. "Something is bothering you. What is it?"

I don't believe I could have told anyone else, not even my father. But Sophie was like the mother I never really knew.

I showed her the story in the Montreal *Standard.* She took the paper, brought a pair of spectacles out of her apron, and began to read. She was a slow reader, reading with her fingertip tracing the line, her lips moving silently as she mouthed the words to herself, but she got through the entire story. Then she looked at me.

"This is terrible! What monster would do such a thing? And you know this girl, yes?"

"Yes. I met her once in the summer, when I first came to Montreal. She came to me the night she was murdered. At least I believe she did. It's confusing."

"What is there to confuse? She came to you, or she did not come to you, yes?"

"Well, she did. She came to visit me."

"So! You were her lover! Why not say so?"

"No, no. Not at all. I was not her lover. In fact, I barely knew her. But we had met once, at a reception where she sang. We talked for some time, and I described the house where I have been living and told her where it was. When she came to me on Christmas Eve, she was running from something. Two men were pursuing her, I don't know why. She was very different from the woman I met in the summer, very thin. She looked frightened and she wasn't wearing a coat, even though it was snowing hard. She begged me to take her in."

"Newspaper says she was wearing a fur coat. They find a letter in her pocket."

"I know, Sophie. I know. But I know she wasn't wearing a coat when I saw her, only a very fine green dress that was wet from the snow, and a pair of workman's boots. She was frightened. Terrified, actually. She begged to come in. She was fleeing from something, or someone. A short while later two men who looked like criminals came banging on the door downstairs. They were looking for her, and they wanted to search the building. I would not allow it.

"Two men? You must be more strong than you look!"

I managed to smile. "I frightened them away with typhoid. I told them that I had the disease, and then I vomited rather profusely. Vomiting wasn't part of the plan, but it scared them away."

Sophie laughed, a deep, earthy laugh. "Go on," she prompted. "Tell me all."

"She was in my room at three o'clock on Christmas morning. I was so sick I had fallen asleep... I woke and she was at my bedside, holding a cold cloth to my head. Hours *after* they say she was killed."

Sophie crossed herself. "*Szellem!* You have ghost! Ghost of this woman comes to you."

"I don't know, Sophie. It seemed that she was real. When I woke in the morning, she was gone. She left a note. She said she was borrowing some of my clothing, and she told me not to follow her, because it could be dangerous."

"She is *szellem*," Sophie repeated stubbornly. "You have seen a ghost. It's in the newspaper, it must be true. The woman is dead, you see her after she is dead. *Szellem!* You see?"

I did not see, although I knew Frau Kachelmeier back home in Bad Gastein would believe the same thing. I didn't believe in ghosts, but what else could it be? When she came to me, Hanna Goss had already been murdered. Sophie patted my shoulder with a floury hand. "You wait, yes? Until my Jem comes home," she said. "Then you tell all to him. Every bit."

"Who is Jem?"

"Jem Doyle, who else? My Mister."

"Ah. But why would I tell him?"

"My Jem is a *policeman*," she said. "Police detective, you see? A good one. The best in Montreal. You know the judge who died with Cuban cigars shoved down his throat? Jem found the killer."

I hadn't heard of the Cuban cigars stuffed down the throat of the judge, but I couldn't imagine sharing my unearthly tale with a cop. A ghost was *szellem* to Sophie, *geist* to me, *fantôme* in French, but in whatever language, we were still talking about a ghost. I could not imagine telling a policeman such a fable.

"Please, Sophie. I can't possibly tell your Jem this story," I said. "He'll think I'm mad. Or he'll arrest me."

"No, he will not. That is why he is a good detective. Because he knows the whole world is mad."

"Thank you, Sophie, but I must go. I must get back to my books."

Sophie stood back, hands on her hips. "You must wait! Wait for Jem. And you must eat. Get strong! Books do not walk away. They will wait."

I shrugged, helpless in the face of Sophie's implacable determination. I settled in to wait.

Thirty minutes later, the door of the café opened and a giant of a man entered. He stood at least six-foot-four and boasted a black handlebar mustache. My first thought was that he must be a thug, like the two men who came looking for Hanna the night she was killed. The man scanned the room, but apparently did not see what he wanted.

"Sophie!" he bellowed. An instant later, she came running from the kitchen on her surprisingly dainty feet.

"Jem!" she shouted. "My Jem!"

Jem and Sophie embraced as though they hadn't seen one another in years, Jem lifting her off the floor as you would lift a child. Then Sophie led Jem to my table. I rose to greet him.

"Jem," she said, "this young man is from the old country. Austria. He is a doctor. Dr. Maxim Balsano, this is Jem Doyle."

I reached out to shake his hand. I could feel his hard look appraising me while his hand ground the bones in my hand to dust. Had I been a criminal, I'm sure I would have confessed.

"Dr. Balsano must tell you something, Jem," Sophie was saying. "He has waited for you, because it is most important."

Jem nodded, his eyes still on me. He pulled back a chair and sat across from me. He propped his elbows on the table and I found myself leaning backward instinctively.

"So what do you have to tell me, young man?"

I began to speak, but all that came out was a kind of strangled croak. I couldn't begin to explain it to this hard-eyed cop, so instead I handed my copy of the *Standard* to him and pointed mutely to the story about Hanna's murder.

Jem Doyle took his time, reading every line. "A young woman is dead," he said when he had finished, "and Cyril Leblanc is a pompous bloody fool."

"You know him?"

"Too well. No love lost, I'm afraid. He's lazy and sloppy, but he loves talking to the reporters, making himself out to be the bloody hero every time. If there's an easy way to close a murder file without looking into it too deeply, Cyril will find it."

"That's a shame."

"It is. It's a bloody shame. Lucky for the world, most murders are pretty easy to solve, aren't they? Dead man on the barroom floor, shot through the heart, rival for a woman's affections standing over him with a smoking pistol. Cuff him and done. Or two thieves fall out over the spoils, one crushes the other's head with a cudgel. That sort of thing. It's rare that a copper has to strain his grey matter to find the killer, though you'd never know it if you read the dime novels."

"I suppose not."

"Doctor, are you? No time for dime novels?"

"Actually, I'm here as a clinical assistant to Dr. Percival Hyde. I wish to be a psychoanalyst and I have studied under Dr. Sigmund Freud in Venice, but Dr. Hyde takes a very different approach, so I have crossed the Atlantic to work with him – unfortunately, I've scarcely laid eyes on him. Perhaps you've heard of Dr. Hyde?"

A curt nod. "I have. So tell me, young man. You're Austrian. And you know this young woman, who is also Austrian.

Or you knew her, before her death. Is that right?"

I cleared my throat. "That's correct, Sergeant-Detective."

"You can call me Jem. Sophie and me, we don't put on airs. It's just plain Sophie and Jem, alright? Unless you're a suspect, in which case you'd best call me sir."

"Yes, Jem. Sir."

"Now what can you tell us about the victim?"

"Not that much. I have only seen her twice. The first time was last summer. She sang at a reception for medical students. She has a beautiful voice. That night we talked for a while about home. She was on a tour of North America. She had stopped in Quebec City before Montreal, and she was to leave in a few days time for Boston and New York. Apparently she had already remained longer than planned in Montreal."

"Did she say why?"

"No, not that I can recall."

"Alright, you said you saw her twice, lad? What was the second time?"

I blushed and stammered when I tried to speak. Now we were getting to the hard part. I was about to explain myself when I got a reprieve, because Sophie arrived with a plate of dumplings and a pint of beer for Jem. While he wolfed down three or four dumplings and drank off half the pint, I tried to compose my thoughts. He wiped the foam off that magnificent mustache with the back of his hand and stared at me, waiting for me to go on.

"The second time I saw her was the night she was killed, but perhaps the newspaper got the time wrong by several hours, because I saw her *after* she was supposedly killed."

I expected Jem to either tell me I was daft or slap the handcuffs on me, but he did neither. He simply waited for me to go on.

"I'm quite sure that Hanna was murdered later," I said. "Much later. Two men came pounding on the door at about eleven o'clock, looking for her. I managed to get rid of them."

"You have a description?"

"I can't tell you much, I'm afraid. They were both wearing heavy coats and tuques and their scarves covered half their faces. One was very large, almost as tall as you are and probably fifty pounds heavier. I'm not very good with English accents, but he spoke with an accent a bit like yours, but different."

"Like Scottish?"

"Could be. I couldn't really say."

"And the other one?"

"Short, broad, spoke a kind of rough Quebec French."

"Eye colour? Could you see that much?"

I closed my eyes and tried to envision the men. "I believe the big one was very dark. Dark complexion, dark eyes. And I think I could see curly black hair poking out from under his tuque. The little one, green eyes and a fair complexion. I think that's correct."

"Not bad. I've had less. Anything distinctive about them? A limp, a missing arm, anything?"

"Not that I can recall."

Jem nodded. "Alright, so they left. And then?"

"I stumbled back upstairs. I fell asleep on my divan with her still there."

"Any reason you didn't go to your bed?"

"Only that I collapsed. The divan is quite comfortable for a small person like myself."

"Aye. But not so comfy for the likes of Jem Doyle, am I correct?"

"You are sir."

"So you fell asleep on the divan. Was the young woman on the divan with you?"

I blushed again. "No, no. She sat up on a chair. Wrapped in a blanket. Drying her hair, I think. I was unconscious or asleep most of the time. At about three or four o'clock in the morning, I woke for a few moments and saw her there, asleep on my chair."

"So this would been at least five hours after the time of her murder? Supposed murder? If her body was found at ten o'clock?"

"Yes. Then I fell asleep again. When I woke it was almost ten o'clock Christmas morning. She was gone. She had left a short note, begging me not to follow. She said it would risky for both of us."

"You still have this note?"

"Of course."

"Did she sign it?"

"She did. With her full name, Hanna Goss."

"Dated?"

"No. I don't believe there is a date on the note. It wasn't a formal letter."

Jem toyed with his mustache. I couldn't tell whether he believed my story or not. "Anyone else see her?" he asked.

"No one at all. I am completely alone in the building. Everyone left for the holidays. Even my landlady, Mrs. Guterson. She left me to care for things."

"Quite a job you've done," he said, "inviting a female ghost to come in and stay for a time. I'm pretty sure we have a city ordinance against entertaining attractive female ghosts."

I was about to insist that I was responsible for no such crime when I saw the faint smile playing on his lips. He was joking. He laid a heavy hand on my shoulder.

"Don't worry yourself, lad," he said. "I'm Irish. We've got to have our bit of fun or life wouldn't be worth the living. I've had a long, dreary day and tomorrow is the Sabbath, but I'll track down Mr. Cyril Leblanc first thing Monday morning and see what he has to say for himself. Like as not, he's already filed the case under "unsolved" and forgotten it, but I'll rattle his cage a bit. Where can you be reached if a fellow needs to speak with you?"

I borrowed a pencil from Sophie and printed my address. Doing so was reassuring. An actual police detective had listened to my story and had neither burst into laughter nor thrown me in jail. Furthermore, it would be hard to find another man who gave off such an air of competence and authority. I was no longer alone in this.

"That note she left?" he cautioned me, "put it in a safe place. That's a key piece of evidence, especially if we can find a sample of her handwriting to prove it was her. Don't lose it."

I nodded obediently. The note was my only link to Hanna. It was precious. I asked Jem if he had any more questions. When he said that he did not, I stood to go. Sophie tried to get me to stay but I was anxious to get home. I had much to ponder, and I needed to be alone to think.

Sophie would not let me leave without a bag stuffed of bread and dumplings and two jars of her soup for sustenance. I left just in time to catch the eastbound tram on Sherbrooke Street, which took me all the way to the corner of Aylmer Street. From there I had a walk of three or four blocks, but it was all uphill. I felt fragile, as though if a passerby were to jostle me, I might fall to the ground and crack like an egg. Away from Sophie's cheery café and Jem's reassuring strength, the full horror of what had happened struck me. A vivacious young woman was dead, beaten to death on Christmas Eve. I opened the heavy front door of the boarding house and trudged up the stairs. The apartment was freezing cold. The window was wide open and the note Hanna had left on my table was gone.

I closed the window. Was it possible I had left it open? Perhaps in a thoughtless moment because of the fever. But to have left the flat with the window open was not at all like me. I had the sensation that there was someone else in the room. There was no one, but someone had been in the room. I could sense it. Perhaps a gust of wind through the open window had blown the letter onto the floor. I searched for more than an hour. The note was gone and with it my only link to Hanna.

I started a fire in the coal stove to melt the frost, then curled up in a ball under the blankets and slept.

In the wee hours of the night, I thought I heard a sound

outside my window and woke briefly. I peered at the window
and thought I saw a pale, disembodied face watching me sleep.
I rubbed my eyes, but when I looked again, the face was gone.

CHAPTER 5

I t was crisp and cold on New Year's Eve, but not frigid. I had spent much of the day with my books to atone in advance for the evening's indulgence, so when it came time to set out for Sophie's Café, I decided to walk rather than taking the tram, because I needed to clear my mind and to work up an appetite. The walk took about an hour at a brisk pace, taking Sherbrooke all the way, past the beautiful townhouses where the servants of the rich were making preparations to welcome the New Year. It was good to feel young and strong and quick again after an illness, and the sight of the cold millions of stars wheeling over Montreal somehow gladdened my heart. We were a part of this universe, no matter how small and insignificant a part, and it was good to be alive.

Sadly, that reminded me of Hanna. She could not see these stars, and I was making no progress at all in my efforts to find out what had happened to her. Nor could I begin to unwrap the riddle at the core of it all: how was it possible that she had appeared at my apartment later that same night? Inevitably, with the note missing, I had begun to question my sanity. Could it be that she hadn't been there at all? That somehow I had either dreamt or hallucinated the whole thing, including the two brutes who came hammering on the door in the night? I had no way of proving otherwise, even to myself. After all, I had been ill and quite feverish that night, and fevers have been known to bring hallucinations – even olfactory hallucinations, which would include the faint but detectable scent of that haunting perfume, which I still could detect whenever I returned to my flat. But how, then, was my hallucination linked to a woman who had been killed that very night?

I knew that I wasn't going to resolve this on my own. I had been going round and round since the night it happened, and barring some breakthrough on Jem's part, I was unlikely ever to get to the bottom of it. It was a relief when, half a block before I arrived at Sophie's Café, I caught a mingled whiff of chicken paprikash, Spätzle, Hungarian sausages, bean soup and fresh-baked bread. I quickened my pace, eager for the feast that awaited in Sophie's café. I burst through the door and had to pause, temporarily blinded, to wipe the steam from my spectacles. While I was doing so, the boy Laszlo appeared at my elbow.

"Mama says I'm to take your coat and hat," he said, "and Father will be pleased. He has already been into the pálinka and he says he's in no condition to wrestle the Model T across town if he had to go fetch you."

I laughed. The party was already well underway, with forty or fifty celebrants in the room and midnight still more than four hours off. Jem waved at me from the midst of a circle of male drinkers, all with beer steins in their hands, every one of them boasting broad shoulders and great flowing mustaches, although none were built to Jem's scale. As he began introducing me around the circle, I realized that the men had two things in common: they were all Irish, and they were all policemen.

When the pianist took a break, Jem took me by the elbow and maneuvered me into a corner next to the piano, the quietest place in the very noisy room. "A word," he said, "before we're too far gone or it gets too damned noisy to hear ourselves think." I was anxious to hear what he had learned, but I didn't want to press him on it in the midst of this crowd. As it turned out, I didn't have to press him in the least; Jem was anxious to tell me what he knew.

"I spoke with Cyril Leblanc," he said. "The man is useless as tits on a boar. He has it down as a failed robbery. He thinks the robbers were after her coat. If it was the case, they would have snatched the bloody coat, her being dead and all, not left it on her body for someone else to find. 'Well, it could be they were frightened off by someone out for a stroll,' says he. 'On Christmas bloody Eve,' says I, 'in the midst of a bloody snowstorm, with no one about?'

"So I asks him, 'what about the bloody canvas, Cyril? How did the canvas go? Turn up anything of interest, did ye?' And Cyril looks at me like I was speaking of the dark side of the moon. 'What bloody canvas would that be?' says he. 'You mean pounding on doors and such like?' I gets up close, where I can look down at his fat stupid mug. 'Of course I mean pounding on doors and such like!' says I. 'It's what coppers do, ain't it? We goes out and disturbs people over their supper, so's to get at the truth. Where did she come from, Cyril? Think, man! Where? Dressed like that, wearing dainty shoes amidst a snowstorm, she didn't walk here from bloody Halifax, now did she? She must have come from somewhere very near. Take the spot where she was murdered and draw a circle. Say you go five blocks in every direction. Knock on every bloody door. If they ain't home receiving company, go back and knock again. If that don't turn up a witness that knows where she came from, widen it out to ten blocks and go back and ring some more doorbells. *Somebody* must have noticed she was missing from a party, or maybe someone saw her on the street. That would at least give us a direction from whence she came. A beautiful redhead in a sable coat out in a snowstorm, that tends to draw attention, Cyril. Somebody might remember!'

"So what does bloody Cyril say to all that? 'Weren't no point calling on all that manpower,' says he. 'Christmas Day, men were at their Christmas pud. Can't call them out to pound on doors, and the case is plain as the nose on your big Irish face: 'Twas a robbery. She fought, she got herself dead. That's an end to it, and I'll thank ye kindly to take your blarney back to Dublin, we've no use for it here.'

"We went a few more rounds, but that was as far as we

got. You can't talk sense to witless Cyril. Mind is shut up tight, he's lazy, and he's so crooked he could hide behind a bloody corkscrew. His real objection, he doesn't want to be out ringing doorbells when it's twenty degrees below zero, and that's an end to it. Never mind the out of doors, he couldn't even trouble himself to check the missing persons reports, and that takes no more effort than walking across the room. He resents me sticking me Irish nose into it, but I don't give a rat's arse. I scare the man to the point where he's like to wet his trousers, but we've the same rank, so I can't tell him to get off his well-padded arse and do his bloomin' job. There's nothing left but for me to keep poking around. I did manage to pry the letter out of Cyril's keeping. The one piece of evidence we have."

My heart skipped a beat. I thought for a moment that he was referring to the letter Hanna had left for me, but that wasn't it. He was talking about the letter to Hanna that was found in the pocket of the fur coat, the one that had helped police to identify her.

"The letter was from her mother in Vienna," Jem said. "Cyril hadn't figured out even that much, because it was written in German. I brought it home and had Sophie translate it. Her German is no better than fair, but it was good enough to translate this. It wasn't much, two pages about the weather and some gossip about folks they knew. But the letter was dated August 24 – which made me wonder why she would have been carrying it in her coat in December. I took it upon myself to visit the address on the envelope. It's a hotel apartment for women on Greene Avenue, not far from here. I spoke with the woman who runs the place, and she told me that Hanna had been living there with an older French woman who was her companion. They checked out in early September and left no forwarding address. Hanna gave the landlady the impression that she was going back on tour, but as far as I can tell, she never resumed her tour. It's like she simply fell off the earth in September and did not reappear until Christmas Eve. Where had she been? She didn't mention anything to you when she came to your apartment, did she? Didn't say what she had been doing since you saw her in August?"

"I was very ill, so it's possible I might have missed or forgotten something," I said, "but I don't believe so. We really talked very little that night. I'm sure I would remember if she had."

"Aye, I'm sure you would," Jem said. "I'll keep digging around, once the holidays are behind us. If we can find out where she's been keeping herself, it would surely help with the rest of it. Did she leave the place on Greene Avenue because she was frightened and going into hiding, or was there some other explanation?"

"I have no idea," I said. It was enough to give a man vertigo. The case of the woman in green never seemed to get simpler. The more we knew (and that was precious little) the more complex it became.

A couple of Jem's police buddies wandered over, then the pianist started up again and was joined by a fiddle player, and Sophie came to introduce me to a pretty young woman with black eyes and black hair tied in a long braid. Her name was Karine Vogel, and she came from Gmund am Tegernsee, a village on a lake in Germany, about two hundred kilometres west of Bad Gastein. Karine, it seemed, wanted a dance partner. I shrugged at Jem, he winked at me, and the girl and I were off with a dozen other couples, whirling around the improvised dance floor. She was a superb dancer and I was pretty light on my feet myself in those days, and I like to think that we cut a fine figure on the dance floor. After three dances we talked a bit. I found her funny and lively and enormously attractive, but when she went off to rejoin her friends, I felt oddly guilty, as though I had somehow been unfaithful to the memory of Hanna Goss.

All around me there was a merry babble of languages: Hungarian, German, English with an Irish brogue, French, Czech, Polish, even a smattering of Russian. It seemed that everyone in the neighborhood knew Sophie and they all came bearing bottles of wine and beer, more steaming platters of food, desserts enough to fill one long table. Sophie bustled through it all, beaming at her guests as she checked to see that everyone had enough wine, enough beer, enough pálinka and schnapps and Irish whiskey, enough schnitzel and sausages and bread. I have never known anyone to look happier. Sophie loved people, and they plainly adored her. This was her milieu, a crowded café filled with people, her six brawny sons everywhere at once, dancing and laughing and talking, every bit as lively as Sophie herself.

In the midst of it all, I felt a streak of sadness for Hanna, but also for my homeland, and for my lonely father, who even now was likely rising to stoke the fire before beginning his rounds, rounds he would make on New Year's Day as he did every other day of the year, even Christmas, pausing only long enough to attend mass. There would be babies to deliver, fractures to set, wounds to stitch, the elderly in need of comfort. He never took a day off.

And what of his son in Canada? I had not yet brought my father up to date on the bizarre circumstances that had plunged me into a murder mystery, in part because I had been ill, in part because I couldn't imagine how to tell him. I knew that if I began to write a full account of the events of the past week it would seem even stranger on paper, and posting it to my father would make it stranger still. In spite of his strong Catholicism, he believed just as strongly in science and that there was a reason for everything, if only we could discover what it was. If I told him about a woman who might have been a phantom visiting my chambers, he might order me home at once – and he might do the same if I had unwisely received an unchaperoned visit from a beautiful, flesh-and-blood woman. I decided on the spot that there was no reason to apprise my father of all that had happened. I would be returning to Austria for the summer as soon as the term ended at McGill. That would be the time to tell him, face to face, when he could see for himself that I hadn't gone mad.

I didn't have much time to reflect. A full polka band was setting up in the corner by the piano, and as soon as they struck up the first chords, Karine was back, wanting to dance, and off we whirled: *1-2-3-hop, 1-2-3-hop!*

Half an hour later, we all gathered around a washtub filled with cold water for an old country New Year's Eve tradition, with Sophie presiding. Beginning with Laszlo, the youngest person present, we were all given a ball of lead, which we heated in a spoon over a candle flame before dropping it into the water. Sophie, who had a reputation for accuracy in interpreting the result, would then scoop the leaden ball out of the water and, depending on the shape in which it had hardened, foretell the immediate future of each of us in turn. Halfway through the proceedings, I heated my ball of lead over the candle flame until it was entirely liquid, then let it slide from the spoon into the water. It cooled quickly into an oddly curled twist of metal. Sophie took it in her palm and turned it over and over. "You will face some very difficult times this year, Maxim," she said, "but there is cause for joy. you have good friends to see you through, and you have already met the love of your life."

I knew that Sophie was hinting that Karine would be the love of my life, but I was left to ponder the other bit, about the difficult times. Like most rational people, I don't believe in fortune-telling until someone tells *my* fortune, and then it worries me no end.

At one minute before midnight, the music ceased. Jem held up an ancient pocket-watch and counted down to the New Year. Karine held fast to my hand, and at the stroke of midnight, turned, put her arm behind my neck to pull me to her, and kissed me full on the mouth, a lingering kiss that seemed to go on and on and left me dizzy. Then she was off to her friends again, leaving me to shake hands and accept cheek kisses from strangers right and left. At last Sophie found me, and hugged me in those powerful arms until I thought I would break.

"I am so happy you found us, Maxim," she said. "Happy New Year!"

"Happy New Year, Sophie. I'm happy I found you! I hope that 1914 will be a wonderful year for you, and for the whole world."

"So do I, Maxim. Jem has to find what happened with the friend of yours that was murdered"

I agreed. No matter how jovial things were around me, I felt that I would never be able to join in fully until I knew what had happened to Hanna Goss, and why.

CHAPTER 4

I was awakened by the tolling of church bells early the next morning, well before first light. Before my eyes were open, it all came rushing back: Hanna fleeing, the two thugs in pursuit, the newspaper story, the missing note.

The theft of my one memento of Hanna, the single bit of evidence that she had visited me in the night, made me furious. Who would do such a thing, and why? My suspicions settled on the men who had been pursuing her. They had come looking for her, without a doubt, and after breaking into my chambers hoping to find her hiding there, had seized the note.

There was only one thing wrong with my theory: Surely by now, the men who had been pursuing her knew that Hanna was dead. They knew because they had killed her – and if someone else had murdered her, the story was on the front page of the newspapers. They could hardly have missed it. So why would they have been searching for a dead woman, unless they were simply being cautious and trying to erase their tracks? But there was nothing in Hanna's note connecting the men to her, so why take it? Then there was the matter of the window that opened from my sitting room directly onto the back roof of the building: it was very narrow. Even the shorter of the two men who came to my door that night was very broad through the shoulders. Had he attempted to enter through the window, he would have become firmly stuck. Then I remembered the face in the night, watching me from the same window, like a ghost. It made my head spin.

I dressed quickly. I had to see Jem Doyle and tell him about the missing letter. The trams were on their Sunday schedule. I was shivering on the street corner when a horse-drawn cab approached. I waved to him and rode along Sherbrooke Street in comfort, with a heavy fur wrapped around my legs. At Sophie's Café I paid him and rushed to the door, only to find it locked. Of course – it was Sunday morning.

I peered around the corner and saw an entrance to an apartment above the café, with a steep flight of outdoor steps that had been carefully cleared of snow and ice. Surely that was where Jem and Sophie lived. There was a bell cord at eye level, so I tugged on it and a bell jangled above me. I had to pull on it three times and I was about to give up when the door opened and Jem Doyle was glaring down at me. I feared a scolding, but he smiled when he saw me "Ach, it's you, boy. Well don't just stand there freezing your arse off. Come on up."

Jem led me into a little back room stuffed with coats and boots. I added mine to the pile and followed him into the kitchen, where Sophie was already at the stove. Coffee was perking, bacon sizzled, pancakes were piling up, and still she had time to pour a big glass of milk and set it in front of me. I thanked her and she pecked both my cheeks, felt my forehead quickly and pronounced my fever cured. "You see? You do what Sophie tells you. Eat, get strong. I feed you, one day you will be strong like Jem."

Over a cup of steaming coffee, I told Jem about the missing letter, how I had come home to find the window wide open and the letter gone, and how I doubted that I would be able to squeeze through that window, much less the two broad-shouldered thugs who had been pounding on my door the night of the murder.

Jem frowned. "And they took nothing else? Nothing at all? Only the letter?"

"Only the letter."

"Well, that's a damned shame. Now we have no proof that your Hanna was ever there. Only your word. Not that I doubt it, boy – but a fool like Cyril Leblanc would think you were telling fairy tales."

I felt that Jem believed me, but who else would? Sergeant-detective Leblanc wouldn't be the only skeptic. It was a wild tale, even with the letter to back it up. Without it, I was a lunatic, babbling about ghosts.

One by one, Sophie's sons began to appear for breakfast, in ascending order by age: the first about twelve years old, the last in his early twenties – about my own age. They were all strapping, noisy lads, speaking English with a smattering of Hungarian and French thrown in. The oldest, Joszef, was already a police officer. The youngest, Istvan, said he wanted to be a doctor, like me. As they worked their way through astonishing quantities of food, I began to warm to their boisterous ways. Having grown up the only child of a widower, I found the noise deafening, but warming to the soul.

When breakfast was over, Jem announced that we were going to my place so that he could look things over. Istvan wanted to come along and so did the next oldest brother, Laszlo, and so the four of us piled in to Jem's Model T, which was parked in a shed at the back, and Jem got the machine started, backed out, and headed east along the snowy track that was Sherbrooke Street.

It was fortunate that Mrs. Guterson and my fellow lodgers were still away, because I don't know what they would have made of our little group, the two noisy boys and the hulking police officer with the fearsome mustache. They left their boots downstairs but kept their coats on as they followed me upstairs. When we reached the door to my chambers, Jem ordered the boys to wait outside until he had a look around because he didn't want them disturbing things. I was impressed with the thoroughness with which he went through my small apartment, making a far more careful search than I had made, because he was more methodical: table and books, tea table, chairs, bed, and the armoire last.

When Jem was satisfied the letter was not to be found, he opened the window, stuck his head through and peered out at the roof. "If there was anything to be seen out there, it has vanished," he said. "We've had snow and blowing snow. If your visitor left any tracks on the roof, they are gone by now."

He called the boys in and told Laszlo to take off his coat and try squeezing through the window. The boy did as he was told and managed to squeeze through, then popped back in without much difficulty.

"So it can be done," Jem said. "A lot of these second-story fellas that make a living breaking into houses have young apprentices, agile little demons nine or ten years old, whose only task is to get through a window and open a door for the real thieves to enter. Could be that whoever took the letter used a child to get in. I noticed there's a latch on that window, lad. I suggest that in future you keep it locked."

When we were finished in the apartment, Jem led the way back downstairs and around to the back so that he could see how the thief might have gained access to the roof. There was a shed behind the house where Mrs. Guterson stored her coal and firewood. The roof of the shed was perhaps eight feet above the ground, but hard-packed snow cut the distance from ground to roof in half.

Jem turned to the boys. "Let's see ye climb, lads," he said. "See yon window? The same Laszlo just tried? That is Maxim's window. First one to get up there gets a nickel."

Istvan and Laszlo went shooting up the roof, from snow-pile to shed roof, shed roof to a narrow lower balcony barely wide enough for one man to stand, and from there onto the overhanging roof, where they kicked foot-holds in the snow as they scrambled up. In less than a minute, they were at my window. I hadn't thought it possible but if you were young, athletic and didn't mind the risk of breaking your neck, it could be done.

"It's a tie," Jem yelled to the boys. "You each get a nickel. Come on down."

They slid down, dove into the pile of snow against the shed, and came up shaking themselves like dogs and laughing.

Jem handed Laszlo a dime and told him to split it with his brother.

"So now we know how they broke into your room," Jem said, "but we have no idea who did it. If the two who came pounding on your door that night were as brawny as you say, it wasn't them but they could have hired a boy to shinny up there and grab the letter. Doesn't bring us any nearer our killers, I'm afraid."

Jem invited me back to have lunch and spend the afternoon skating in the park with Sophie's boys, but I told him that I really had to get back to my books.

"Well, in that case, you'll call round on New Year's Eve," Jem said. "Sophie will skin me alive if you don't come. We always have a party in the café. Goes on until all hours. Music, dancing, drinking and generally making a fool of yourself, so make allowances for the hangover you'll have come New Year's morning."

He called me aside while the boys wrestled for the chance to sit in the front seat of the Model T, next to Jem. Laszlo took Istvan down in the snow and they rolled over and over, punching and kicking furiously. Jem ignored them.

"Tomorrow I'll have a little chat with Mr. Cyril Leblanc," he said. "See what he really has on this murder and how much he's missed or hidden away."

"Please do. I really want to find out what happened to Hanna."

"We all do. Sophie especially. If I don't get to the bottom of this she'll wear my ears out, and half of it will be in that Hungarian goulash that she talks. And you'll be coming by our place for New Year's Eve, young fellow. If you don't, Sophie will have my Irish hide."

"Oh, that is most kind of you. I hadn't even thought... but I've fallen rather behind in my reading, so I had planned..."

Jem held up one big paw like a traffic cop in command of an intersection. "Nay, lad. No books. No excuses. You don't want Sophie all riled up and coming to your digs to haul you out by the ear. Festivities begin around nine o'clock, but you can turn up at any hour you choose. Food, wine, beer, spirits, music, dancing. Convivial folk, even the Irish cops. Better than the bloodless lot you'll find in the medical fraternity, I'll wager."

I was about to protest, but Jem was grinning and in any case, he was right – we physicians are men of science, and as such we're bound to be a rather bloodless lot – the complete opposite of the crowd at Sophie's Café, as I was about to learn.

CHAPTER 6

We were already almost four hours into 1914 when I fell asleep, wrapped in blankets on the floor of the room Laszlo shared with Istvan, with the boys sprawled on their mattresses on either side of me. My mind was whirling. I hadn't had much to drink, only a little pálinka and two glasses of beer, but I was not accustomed to drinking, and I already had a touch of headache. I thought that I could still taste Karine's kiss; I had never known a woman so bold as she. Perhaps that was the way of the New World and she had already learned it, or perhaps it was just the wine. It was exciting and I had responded as a man should respond to a kiss from a lovely woman, but I still felt guilty for allowing it to happen. I had come very near to falling in love with Hanna Goss and somehow, it was still too soon to kiss another woman.

I felt that my eyes had been closed no more than a few minutes when I woke to brilliant sunshine. The boys were still asleep and I was fully clothed, so I rose and went to the kitchen, where Jem Doyle sat alone with his morning coffee and a newspaper. After he had directed me to the water closet (which was mercifully indoors, since it was cold outside) he poured me a cup of coffee of strong black coffee and asked if I required a headache remedy.

I shook my head. "The coffee will be enough."

"Drink as much as you like," he said, "but when you are fully awake, we've a man to see."

"On New Year's Day?"

"On New Year's Day. The perfect time, as it happens. A day when we're unlikely to meet up with anyone other than

Good King."

"Good King?"

Jem winked. "You'll see, in good time."

I was baffled, but I thought my confusion might be due to a combination of Jem's Irish brogue and my own rather thick head. Jem pointed to an item in the newspaper he was reading. It was a funeral notice for Miss Hanna Goss: the funeral was to be held in three days' time at St. James Cathedral on Dorchester Boulevard, at one o'clock in the afternoon.

"I'm certain you'll want to attend," he said. "I'll come to pay my respects as well, and we should see if we can learn anything from the mourners."

As sad as the funeral notice made me feel, I couldn't help feeling a touch of pride because Detective Jem Doyle had said "we." *We* were going to see if we could learn anything from the mourners. The detective and the doctor, partners out to solve a crime.

Ten minutes later, Jem had the Model T running and we were bouncing east along the icy ruts and the tram tracks on Sherbrooke St., bound I knew not where. Either Jem didn't get hangovers or he was still drunk. He was in a wonderful mood, singing "Mother Machree" and teasing me over Karine. It was twenty degrees below zero and the inside of that automobile felt like the coldest place in town as we zigzagged south and east. I had completely lost my bearings until I realized we were on Craig Street, still headed east. We crossed St. Lawrence Boulevard on the edge of Old Montreal, where my wanderings had taken me on Christmas Eve, and came to a halt before a foreboding structure with an address above the door indicating that it was 179 Craig Street East. Before we entered, Jem had a question for me.

"Can ye stomach the sight of the city morgue, lad?" he asked.

I was taken aback. "May I remind you, Detective Doyle. I am a doctor."

"So you've been around bodies before?"

"I have. I've dissected cadavers."

"Good. This shouldn't bother you, then."

I was sure it wouldn't, but as I hurried after him, it occurred to me that if we were at the city morgue, it was surely to view the remains of Hanna Goss, not some anonymous cadaver in a laboratory in Vienna.

There was a man waiting for us. He was thin as a shaft of light, with a rake of stiff blond hair. The eyes behind his thick spectacles floated like specimens in a jar.

"Good King," Jem said as he pumped the thin man's hand. "This is the young fellow I was telling you about, Dr. Maxim Balsano. Max, meet my friend, Dr. Wenceslas Gentschenfeld."

Wenceslas. Good King. I wondered if the nickname was Jem's alone, or if the poor fellow was known by that everywhere he went.

"Dr. Balsano. A pleasure. My name is not Good King, whatever this big Irish fool chooses to tell you. You can call me Wen. Most people do. I'm the coroner here. My father was Czech-German, hence the name. I was raised by my French-Canadian mother and I've forgotten most of the German I knew in my youth, so I hope you don't mind if we stick to English, unless you prefer French?"

"Alas, I'm still struggling with my French."

"Very well then. Follow me please."

Good King led the way, walking with an odd, disjointed gait like an animated scarecrow down a stone staircase, along a dark passageway, and up another stone staircase. He unlocked a heavy wooden door and we were inside the morgue, where a partially shrouded body lay on a slab, illuminated by a single electric light.

Hanna Goss. I recognized her instantly by the shock of red hair around her head, although I saw immediately that the newspaper story was correct: her face had been beaten to a pulp. If not for the hair, she would have been utterly unrecognizable. I shuddered to think of the number of times they must have hit or kicked her to make her look like that. I had seen pugilists come out of bare-knuckle bouts looking better.

Dr. Gentschenfeld pulled down the sheet and I saw first the shock of bare breasts that were larger than I would have imagined, then the clumsy scar of the pathologist's stitching. It would have embarrassed any surgeon worth his salt, but when you're sewing up the dead, the artistry of the job hardly matters.

The coroner beckoned to me to look closer at a spot just below her left breast. It didn't look like much more than a pin prick. "You see here, Dr. Balsano? The detective, Cyril Leblanc, informed me that our victim had been beaten to death. She *had* been beaten, but I believe that the beating came *after* her death. This is how she was killed: a very thin, very sharp instrument pierced her heart. Something like a rapier, perhaps, but even thinner. An assassin's weapon."

"Good King thinks she was deliberately murdered," Jem put in. "This wasn't the act of a couple of thieves trying to steal a woman's coat. They used a weapon meant to kill."

Against my will, my gorge was rising, and I had to fight down the urge to vomit. I had indeed dissected more than a few cadavers, but I hadn't *known* any of them, much less felt the sort of connection I had felt with Hanna.

"Anything else?" Jem asked.

"Not really. Young, strong, healthy in every way, far as I can determine. She had eaten quite a bit of cake and drunk a quantity of wine before she was killed, if that means anything. Whoever stuck that needle knew what he was doing. One quick stroke, no fumbling about. Perhaps he had an accomplice to hold her – as you can see, there is heavy bruising on her arms and some around her throat, as though she had been held in a very strong grip by a man with very large hands."

I recalled the bruising I had seen around Hanna's neck on Christmas Eve, and I thought of the thug who had come pounding on my door that night, and his smaller accomplice. One to hold her, one to make the thrust through the heart. I guessed that the big one had beaten and held her, while the small one administered the death blow with a very sharp instrument. I looked Hanna up and down. My eyes took in a thatch of red pubic hair, as fiery as the hair on her head, and I looked away quickly, though not in time to keep my ears from turning red. I found myself fighting back tears.

"Why did they have to beat her?" I asked. "If they had already killed her, why did they have to beat her?"

Jem put a hand on my shoulder. "Perhaps she put up a struggle and they were just angry and took it out on her. Murder is an ugly business."

Dr. Wenceslas Gentschenfeld showed us out and we were back in the frigid Model T. Neither of us said a word, and Jem refrained from singing Mother Machree. I thought of asking him to take me home, but I didn't want to be alone. Sophie's big, noisy brood would provide ample distraction, even if all but the youngest were battling mighty hangovers.

By afternoon, I had borrowed a pair of ice skates and we were all enjoying a merry game of hockey on an expanse of ice not far from their home. I was a good skater, but I had never played the game before, and the boys had great fun dancing around me and scoring goal after goal. I didn't mind in the least. It was good to be outdoors and cold and alive.

CHAPTER 7

My landlady, Mrs. Guterson, returned in time for supper that evening, and the two of us dined alone. She thanked me warmly for taking such excellent care of the place in her absence, and I somehow failed to mention the nocturnal visit of a certain beautiful young soprano, nor the two men pursuing her, nor the fact that the soprano had been murdered that very night, nor subsequent visit of a very large police officer and his sons. As far as Mrs. Guterson would ever know, I had respected her "no visitors" policy to the letter. She was a kindly if very reserved woman whose Swedish accent was still with her, and there was no point in upsetting the old soul.

By noon the next day, all my fellow lodgers had returned to the boarding house on Aylmer Street, noisily exchanging greetings, banging doors as they moved from one apartment to another swapping news of the holidays, exuberantly babbling of this and that as young men are wont to do. Before the holiday, I had been only a year or two older than most of them. Now I felt significantly older and more mature, as well as somewhat weighted down with the freight of all that I knew. If they noticed my more subdued manner, however, none of them remarked on it. They were far too busy arguing over who had consumed the largest feast, indulged in the biggest snowball fight, or kissed the prettiest girl back home. I participated enough not to be thought a snob, then returned to my books and to brooding over the details of the murder of Hanna Goss. All in all, more than enough to keep me occupied until the day of the funeral.

The fourth day of January was mild and bright, as though God himself was mocking the gloom of the funeral. The temperature crept up near zero, and I decided to walk down to St. James Cathedral from Aylmer Street. The sun was shining, people were unwrapping mufflers and carrying tuques rather than wearing them, and a buoyant mood seemed to have struck the city. If I could have forgotten my destination, I would have enjoyed the walk enormously.

Once inside the cathedral, I had to pause for several moments to allow my eyes to adjust to the relative gloom inside the church after the brilliance of the light reflecting off the snow outside, dipped my fingers in the holy water I had not touched since the day I left Austria for the New World, and took a seat in a pew on the right side near the back, because I wanted to observe the mourners as they arrived. I had no idea what I was looking for, but if I was going to be Jem Doyle's unofficial assistant, I needed to be as keen-eyed and observant as he was, despite my spectacles.

I had never before visited the cathedral, modeled on St. Peter's in Rome but on a smaller scale. It was a lovely building, even on this sad occasion. The intersecting vaults, the paintings and gildings and especially the baldachin with its spiral columns drew my eye. I had not yet visited Rome, so this scale model would have to do for the time being. Now was not the time for a detailed study of the interior, but I had spent much time in St. Stephen's in Vienna and had often thought that if I had not chosen to be a doctor, I would have liked to be an architect.

I was chiding myself as an indifferent Catholic when I noticed a flamboyantly dressed man who had tiptoed in and taken a seat three or four pews ahead of me. He removed a long white silk scarf from around his neck and carefully folded his cashmere coat and placed it with the scarf and a wide black felt hat of the type they call Borsalino on the pew next to him, then sat with his face buried in his hands, his shoulders shaking with sobs. He wore his black hair so that it curled down over the collar of his white silk shirt, and when he glanced once over his shoulder I saw that he had cultivated a tidy spade beard and a thin, waxed moustache.

The eulogy was delivered, in French and in English, by Olivier D'Estienne d'Orves, the Parisian who had crossed the Atlantic to conduct the Mount Royal Chamber Orchestra. Hanna had performed with the orchestra on four separate occasions after she first arrived in Montreal in the late spring of 1913. The conductor clearly did not know her well personally, but he did laud her voice as a rare, soaring instrument, still unrefined because of her youth but certain to make an impact on the stages of Europe and around the world had she been allowed to go on singing.

As D'Estienne d'Orves spoke, I took the opportunity to gaze around at the mourners. There were perhaps three hundred mourners, far more than I would have expected, but on reflection it was not all that surprising. Hanna had performed in Montreal often enough to attract something of a following—and the lurid stories of her death in the press had brought out a number of curious and morbid onlookers whose appearance would indicate their musical tastes did not gravitate to the opera. Many, whatever their reasons for being there, seemed genuinely moved.

Even the most abysmal grief cannot prevent one from experiencing the beauty and harmony of a requiem mass. The smell of incense, the votive candles, the exaltation of the *Gloria in excelsis Deo* and the *Alleluia,* the fearsome chords of the *Dies irae:* The choirmaster had chosen Mozart's thrilling *Requiem* for this occasion, and I have always maintained that no greater music has ever been written, nor shall be. Listening, I was born away to the funerals of my youth, to that mingled sense of sorrow and joy that seems to accompany the Christian version of one's departure from this earth. Sorrow at the end of a life, joy at the beginning of eternity. Despite my growing doubts about the creed, I could still be moved by the celestial music, especially in a setting as beautiful as the interior of St. James Cathedral. I followed the ceremony intently, although my own Latin, I noticed as the priest spoke, had slipped a bit.

When the mourners began to line up for holy communion, I took my place in the line, shuffling along with the rest. My father would be pleased, but the communion wafer was dry on my tongue and the wine sour and far too chilled for my taste. On the way back to my pew, I noted that the well-dressed little man who had been sobbing before remained seated with his face buried in his hands. Not a Catholic, then, but a person, all the same, who was deeply affected by Hanna's death.

I must have drifted off into a private reverie after taking communion, because the next thing I noticed was that the funeral mass had ended and there was a shuffling noise as mourners rose to their feet and reached for their coats. The dapper gentleman who was so wracked with grief took his time, fiddling with his cravat, buttoning his waistcoat, carefully winding the long, silk scarf around his neck before he reached for his hat and overcoat. Now was the time. I grabbed my hat, tucked my coat under one arm and worked my way past the departing mourners to introduce myself. Although I spoke to him in English, he must have recognized my accent because he gave a tidy little bow and replied in German.

"Herr Rudolf Mayr at your service, Herr Doktor Balsano."

"Please call me Maxim. I am very sorry, but I couldn't help notice your grief for Fraulein Goss. I met her only briefly, but I would like to know more about her."

"In that case, you must call me Rudi. We are in North America, we shall be as informal as Americans, shall we not?" He took my elbow as though to steady himself. His hand was small but his grip painfully strong. His great dark eyes swam with tears. He had a strong Viennese accent that I recognized at once. Several of my professors at the University of Vienna had exactly the same accent. "Ah, Maxim, Maxim – what a tragedy this is, is it not? One so young, so talented, so beautiful. Taken from us in such a savage way. Such a horror it is."

"I take it you knew her well?"

"Knew her? I was her manager, Herr Doktor! She was my greatest discovery. I had only to hear her sing one time and from the age of fifteen, I took her under my wing. Her mother trusted me implicitly. And now this. It is tragic beyond words. I must write to her poor mother to convey my sorrow, and I have no idea where I will find the words."

"Herr Mayr," I said, "I want very much to talk with you, but I must get to the cemetery. Are you attending the burial?"

"Alas, I cannot." He waved the white silk kerchief rather helplessly in his left hand as he spoke, still dabbing at his eyes. "I have a business engagement while I am in this city, and in any case I could not bear it. Whatever am I to tell her mother? But I am staying nearby, at the Windsor Hotel. Perhaps you know it? It is convenient for my train. I shall return to Boston tomorrow, but I shall be at your disposal after five o'clock today. If you come to the hotel at six o'clock sharp, we may dine together. It will be my treat. Subjects of the emperor far from home must look after one another, must they not? I shall meet you in the lobby."

I caught sight of Jem Doyle looming out of the corner of my eye and took my leave from Herr Mayr. I thought it better not to introduce the two of them, because Herr Mayr was so small and timid that I feared a police officer as large and intimidating as Jem would frighten him off before I had a chance to find out what he knew. In any case, Herr Mayr was hurrying away already, and I followed Jem's massive shoulders out of the church and down Mansfield Street to the spot where he had parked his Model T diagonally in a snowbank.

Jem's big feet fairly danced over the three pedals on the floor of the Model T as he manipulated the accelerator level on the steering column and we shot out of the parking space and downhill at a speed approaching twenty miles an hour, before we turned onto Craig Street and took it as far as Guy before beginning the ascent up toward Mount Royal. I had my doubts about the Model T's ability to ascend such a rough, snowy track, but it was a rugged beast and only once did we bog down for a moment. Jem wrenched the steering wheel to the left and tugged the accelerator down and we were out of it, maneuvering around a heavy, horse-drawn wagon and on up the mountain.

Only a handful of the mourners from the cathedral attended the burial. It was handled by the funeral director's men, with the priest from St. James Cathedral presiding. It was Jem Doyle's keen eye that noted what I would have missed. "That's mahogany wood," he whispered as he waited, "and gold trim on the casket. Somebody paid a pretty penny for this funeral, and to get the gravediggers to open up frozen ground. They can do it, but it don't come cheap. Those are Henri Bourgie's men. I'll have a chat with him and find out who paid for this."

I cast a glance Jem's way. Big and stolid as he was, he was quick to make connections. As a doctor's son, I had attended many funerals, but I hadn't noticed that Hanna's casket was anything out of the ordinary.

The men, perspiring in the cold, lowered the coffin into the ground. The priest asked if any of Hanna's family were present. "She has no family here," I heard myself saying.

"Perhaps..." the priest gestured toward the grave. Jem gave me a mild shove in the back. I stepped forward, tears freezing in the corners of my eyes, took up one of the spades from the workmen, and heard the awful sound of frozen earth striking the coffin. I turned away, biting my lip, and Jem slung one arm around me and squeezed my shoulders. I had never felt so desolate.

Soon, we were bumping our way back downhill. Jem said little, I said less. He asked me where I wanted to go, and I said he could leave me at the Windsor Hotel. Jem raised an eyebrow. "Hobnobbing with the swells, are ye, lad?"

I blushed. "Not at all. I need to see a man who is staying at the hotel."

"The small chap ye were chatting with at the cathedral, correct?"

I nodded, embarrassed that I hadn't told him before. "Yes. He's Hanna's manager. Or was. A Viennese gentleman named Rudolf Mayr. Seemed very broken up over her death."

"I shouldn't wonder. It's always tragic when a young person is taken before her time. It's good you're showing some initiative, my friend, but please exercise a little caution. There are some dangerous folks involved in this, and until we know who they are, there's no point taking chances. Leave that to those such as myself who are paid to risk our hides."

"Yes, sir!"

Jem gave me a sidelong glance to be sure I wasn't mocking him, but he wasn't the sort of man you trifled with. The Model T skidded to a halt outside the Windsor Hotel and I jumped out into a snowbank. I was still brushing the snow from my trousers as I approached the hotel, but the doorman held the door open for me with a slight bow, and I made my way indoors, walking stiffly as though to show everyone I belonged there.

CHAPTER 8

Herr Mayr was so late that I had ample time to find a comfortable chair where I could jot down the events of the day in my journal, to admire the spacious extravagance of he hotel's rotunda, and even to read a handsomely printed little monograph on the hotel's construction and history, which mentioned the fact that the Hotel Windsor had no fewer than six dining rooms. When I had finished all that, I wandered about, trying various armchairs, until my rather odd movements attracted the attention of the hotel staff. An assistant to the concierge approached, bowed formally, and asked if he could be of help.

I introduced myself as *Doctor* Maxim Balsano, because I had already learned that my youthful appearance required the additional weight of the title when I was challenged. "I have a *rendezvous* with one of your guests here," I said. "We were to have met at six o'clock but it is well on seven and he has not yet put in an appearance."

"May I ask his name? Perhaps I can be of assistance in locating him."

I knew that his real motive was to determine whether I actually knew someone who was staying in the hotel, but I didn't mind. I have always tried to be courteous to those who are merely doing the task they have been hired to perform.

"Of course. His name is Herr Rudolf Mayr. From Austria, as am I."

"Ah, yes. Herr Mayr." He led the way to the front desk, asked for the large, leather-bound register, examined it until he found the name of Rudolph Mayr and confirmed that the guest was registered in the hotel. He smiled a rueful smile and leaned forward to confide in me: "You are not the first who has waited a long time in this lobby for Herr Mayr," he said. "He is one of those fellows who is habitually late. May I offer you something from the bar in the meantime? A courtesy."

"A schnapps, perhaps? Something against the cold?"

I returned to my seat and in a few moments, a tidy glass of schnapps was at my elbow. I drank it quickly and felt its warmth course through my veins. At home we used the drink to treat everything from upset stomachs to dog bites to melancholia. As a physician, I can confirm that it is equally effective in all cases. I was ravenously hungry. I hadn't eaten since breakfast, and it was a light breakfast of tea and toast with marmalade at that. I thought that perhaps Herr Mayr had forgotten me and determined that when the large clock in the lobby struck 7:15, I would leave and go in search of something to eat – I had already missed dinner at my lodgings, so I would have to fend for myself.

At 7:14 precisely, Herr Mayr came steaming into the lobby, looking flustered, breathless and rather the worse for wear, peering around for the young man he had invited to dinner. I stood and went to greet him and his words came tumbling out in a confused apology.

"Young man, Herr Doktor Balsano... So sorry, my deepest apologies, unforgivable to be so very late, why is it that when an *artiste* is going through a personal crisis they must absolutely talk it to death, on and on... a ballerina... represented her for some time, couldn't refuse help, she is absolutely at her wit's end ... dropped from a leading role in Swan Lake... missed too many rehearsals, understandable, of course, but she refuses to understand... Russian, Russians are always highstrung, you know... Discovered by Diaghilev, you know Diaghilev? ... Befriended him in Paris, Diaghilev, splendid chap but always rather, rather... Nijinsky too, of course, and Nijinska... But Diaghilev, special chap. Special. You must be famished?"

"I am a little hungry..."

"Yes, yes. Of course you are. Well, we are about to be well-fed, but first I must run up to my room to freshen up and unburden myself of these heavy winter clothes. I feel as though I'm in a steam bath. I shan't keep you waiting long, you have my word. ... Remind me to tell you about Diaghilev... Must go now."

He was gone only ten minutes, but when Herr Mayr returned he had changed completely for dinner. He wore a jacket with pointed collars, a white waistcoat, sharply creased trousers with a strip of silk fabric on the outside of the leg and a scarlet ascot held in place with a diamond pin. His hair was freshly pomaded and he smelled rather strongly of some expensive brand of gentleman's cologne.

He led the way and we were seated in the largest of the Windsor Hotel's six dining rooms. Marble pillars, tablecloths so white they were like fresh mountain snow, candelabra: I imagined that it was a great deal like one of the dining rooms in the Schönbrunn Palace in Vienna. I felt ill at ease in the plain, dark suit I had worn for the funeral (the only one I owned) but my dinner companion projected enough confidence and *savoir faire* for both of us. The maître d' plainly knew him well. He bowed deeply and led us to a quiet corner table. Herr Mayr muttered something about wine, and soon a rich burgundy was uncorked at our table. Before the night was over, we would work our way through three bottles, although I made do with sips. I ate, he drank. I accepted his suggestion that we order the Boeuf Chateaubriand for two, but I ate most of it.

First, we toasted Hanna's memory. Then we bowed our heads in silence for a moment. Before we began, I thanked him for arranging the concert at the reception the previous summer at the home of Dr. Percival Hyde, the only occasion when I was able to hear Hanna sing before her untimely death.

"Ah, that was the only time she has appeared in public when I did *not* make the arrangements," he said. "It was all very mysterious. She said that someone had asked her to appear at your little reception, and she agreed without asking me. I asked her please not to do that in future, not because of my little commission but because there might be a conflict in dates. She became very haughty with me and said that she would sing when she pleased, where she pleased. It was the beginning of our – shall we say, our difficulties."

"I am sorry to hear that you had difficulties with Hanna, Herr Mayr."

"Hanna disappeared perhaps a month after that reception, you know," he said. "In early September, I believe it was. After we had words and parted company. Do you know that she was so angry with me that she slapped my face? Quite hard. Left a bruise. I left after that display of violence, I am sorry to say, in a fit of pique. I took ship for Cherbourg because I had business in Paris and Lyon, and I left her here to fend for herself. I had hired a companion to help look after her on the tour, a very intelligent woman named Elise Duvernay. Since Hanna was no longer touring for me, I could not justify the expense of a companion for her, so Mlle Duvernay sailed to France with me, leaving Hanna with no one she really knew on this continent. For that I have been chiding myself since I learned of her death, but she had made it quite clear that she no longer wished to have an association with me. After all I had done for her! It was abominable behaviour." He withdrew his kerchief and dabbed at his eyes, as he had done at the cathedral during the funeral mass.

"May I ask why you had words, Herr Mayr?" I enquired.

"Please, please. If we are to be friends, you shall call me Rudi, and I shall call you Maxim. I am not all that much older than you are, you know. Alright then. The oddest thing is that I do not know. Let me amend that: I know that she wanted to cease performing for a time. What I do not know is *why* she did not wish to perform. She refused to tell me. I was angry, obviously. Her career was just beginning to attract international attention. She had been praised by Eduard Hanslick in the pages of *Neue Freie Presse!* Eduard Hanslick himself, Maxim! You spent time in Vienna, you know how important he is. For a singer in Vienna, a word from Herr Hanslick is like the blessing of the gods, and he wrote that she had a clarity of tone and a power of raw emotion such as he had not heard in twenty years! I had arranged two dozen concert dates on her North American tour, beginning in Montreal. We were to carry on to Boston, New York, Philadelphia, Washington D.C. and Baltimore before returning to Europe in the spring. There were private audiences with wealthy and influential people, soirées, interviews with the best-known music critics in North America, everything that an able manager such as myself can set in motion to enhance the career of a young and very fine soprano. Then, abruptly, it was all off. She knew how I had suffered to make all this possible, how I had laboured, the telegrams that rushed back and forth between the two continents, the impresarios I had to satisfy, the hotel arrangements, trains, our passage by ship to and from this continent, orchestras, accompanists, rehearsal rooms – a thousand details a day, you cannot imagine.

"And then, as suddenly as I can snap my fingers, the tour was off. All of it, for no apparent reason. Singers have voice problems at times, but she was in fine voice, never better. She was in perfect health. She loved singing, she loved the stage, she loved the audience – and they loved her. She was turning her back on them, and she was leaving me to cancel all that I had arranged. To contact all those individuals and institutions, to say that orchestras would not be needed, hotel reservations need not be booked, concert dates had to be annulled. In many cases, there was money to be returned, advances that had to be repaid, penalties for cancellations, all of it to come out of my pocket. I was understandably furious, especially because I could not get an explanation out of Fraulein Goss. I begged, I implored, I insisted, I got down on my knees. 'Just tell me *why*,' I pleaded with her. Give me a reason, and I shall do as you ask. But no reason was forthcoming. Ever. Not a word. I was so angry, I don't wish to conceal it from you.

I wished to strangle her, Maxim. To strangle her with my bare hands, to choke the life out of her. I actually thought of it, so deeply had she offended me."

As he spoke, Herr Mayr made a gesture as if he were strangling that beautiful neck. His face turned almost black with fury, and it was all too easy to imagine Rudi himself murdering poor Hanna. Then he seemed to become aware of how incriminating the gesture was, and he quickly hid his hands beneath the table. The damage was done, however. I felt that Herr Mayr had revealed himself in that instant as a man who was capable of murder – even if it meant strangling a woman who was, in a sense, his own creation.

"You wanted to do away with her?" I asked calmly, trying not to alarm him so that he would continue to unburden himself.

He shrugged helplessly. "I did. I admit it. You simply cannot imagine the difficulties she caused for me. And to refuse an explanation after I had made her what she was, it was unacceptable."

I was puzzled. "What did she say when you asked why she had decided to cease performing? It seems a reasonable request, after all you had done to arrange the tour."

"It is a reasonable request. But all she would say was the same thing, over and over: 'I cannot tell you, Rudi. I simply cannot. Please don't ask me to tell you, because I cannot say a word.' That was it. Nothing I could do would change her mind. Even my tears would not move the stone that was her heart."

"You must suspect something," I said. "You have some idea as to what was going on?"

"I have a suspicion, but I haven't an ounce of proof. I suspect that it all involves a man. A man she had encountered somewhere along the way, although I don't know when or where. I left her really alone only once on this trip, in Quebec City when we first arrived. She had arranged two small concerts and she insisted that she could handle those with the help of Elise Duvernay. I went ahead to make final arrangements in Montreal."

"Where is that woman now?"

"Elise Duvernay? She found employment as the companion to an older woman and remained in Cherbourg. On the voyage back to France, we talked about nothing else except Hanna, and what had caused her abrupt change of heart. I wondered about those three days in Quebec City and asked Mlle Duvernay about it several times during the voyage, but she insisted that she had never seen Hanna holding a private conversation with a man in Quebec or anywhere else. It was not uncommon for her to receive bouquets of roses after concerts from men seeking the pleasure of her company, but Miss Duvernay said there were no waiting bouquets in the dressing rooms."

I shrugged. "That would be the obvious explanation, would it not? That she had fallen for some young man along the way?"

"Yes, it would," Rudi agreed. "But if that is the case, I believe she would have told me. Or Mlle Duvernay, if she didn't want to confide in me. If somehow there was a man in her life, we saw no indication whatsoever until, abruptly, she no longer wanted to perform. If there was a love interest somewhere in her life, it would have been quite difficult for her to hide it, especially from Mlle Duvernay. For someone in her position, you understand, there is very little free time. Every moment of every day must be scheduled, or things fall apart. She would rest in the afternoons before a concert, but she was alone in her room or with Mlle Duvernay on those occasions, and we took great pains to protect her privacy."

"After you left for Europe, you were not in contact again?"

"We were not. Oh, I attempted to reach her. When we docked in Cherbourg, I sent a long letter apologizing for my hasty decision to leave. Then I posted several more from Paris and Berlin, expressing a desire to resume our working relationship when she was ready. I did not want to see that wonderful voice lost to the world. She was a singer of *bel canto,* yes? The tone, so warm and embracing. Fraulein Goss may have been Austrian and Hungarian by nationality – but as a singer, she was Italian, not German at all."

I ignored the digression into *bel canto.* "I assume she never answered your letters?"

"Never. They were returned to me in a package, with a note indicating that she had moved from her hotel and left no forwarding address. I enquired through certain acquaintances here in Montreal, but they also had no idea as to her whereabouts. I was growing increasingly alarmed. In early November, I booked passage as far as Quebec City and took the train from there, determined to find her. I searched. I went to all the places we had frequented during our stay here. I spoke with everyone with whom she had performed, and with those who had booked her concerts. Nothing. It was as though she vanished into thin air the moment I left for Europe.

"At last, in despair, I retained the services of two of those private detective chaps – one English and one French, so they could cover both communities in Montreal. They accomplished nothing except to charge me a pretty penny for eating in cafés where she had once been seen and the like, and they turned up no trace of her. After an expensive month I dismissed them and gave up the search. I left to take care of business in Boston and New York, and I tried to put Hanna out of my mind. Then came the utterly tragic news that she had been murdered. I am still shattered. And that is the end of my sorry tale."

We sat in silence for a bit, sipping our drinks, until I asked how they had met and how he discovered her talents. Herr Mayr's words came in his usual rush, and I had to exercise all the powers of my memory to retain what he said. I listened so intently that at times I found myself perspiring with the effort, and after we parted, I hastened back to my lodgings and worked until two o'clock in the morning to write down every word. I will therefore give the narrative over to him for a chapter. I reproduce it here exactly as I recalled it, and as I scribbled into my journal in the early morning hours.

CHAPTER 9

T he narrative of Herr Rudolph Mayr, as delivered in the dining room of the Windsor Hotel and transcribed from memory by Dr. Maxim Balsano on 5 January, 1914:

I have always known Fraulein Hanna Goss. Let me amend that
statement, as it is not strictly true. It would be more accurate
to say I have always been *aware* of Hanna Goss. Not from my
earliest memories, but perhaps from the age of fifteen. She and
her mother lived on my street, a matter of a hundred paces
away, where I would often look out the window and see them.
She was always on the periphery of my vision: a young tomboy racing up and down the street and throwing rocks at boys.
She was a skinny, red-haired, annoying child with powerful,
most unfeminine lungs that could destroy the most tranquil
evening. Her mother eventually became my seamstress and
tailor, but that did nothing to lessen the annoyance I felt for
her daughter.

Hanna and her mother were one of the few Christian
families living at that time on the fringe of the Leopoldstadt,
the Jewish neighborhood in Vienna. There Hanna's widowed
mother, Frau Goss, had settled with her daughter following
the death of the dashing cavalry officer she had married. I
always knew that Frau Goss had been widowed, but I only
learned the circumstances of her husband's death long after,
when I went to have a waistcoat mended. It happened that
a certain Sergeant Schama came to pay his respects to the
widow of his former commanding officer. Frau Goss went to
make alterations to the garment and I was left to make con-

versation with the sergeant. When I learned that Sergeant Schama had witnessed the death of Lieutenant Goss, my curiosity got the better of me and I persuaded him to tell the tale.

It seems that our Austrian general staff officers aimed to keep their army honed for action during a time of peace with frequent and sometimes difficult maneuvers. They were on one such exercise with elements of the German forces along the Bregenzer Ache, in Vorarlberg. It was a fine June morning, and the horses, not yet worn down by the burdens of the day, were frisky and skittish. They were cantering through a beautiful edelweiss meadow within sight of the Bregenzer when something, a marmot or a rabbit, startled the lieutenant's horse. It leapt to the side and as it did so, the saddle girth snapped and Lieutenant Goss was thrown, along with his saddle, into a thick bed of the flowers. The troop reined up smartly and some of his men, being young and in high spirits like their horses, called to him to cease idling on the job, but the lieutenant lay motionless.

I imagine the smart red trousers of the lancers caught in the tangle of green of the edelweiss plants, among the white-and-cream blossoms of the flowers – but I'm afraid that is my own fancy. You may picture the scene as you wish. Sergeant Schama, who had been riding directly behind the officer on the left side of the troop, was one of the first to reach him. Initially, he thought that his commander had simply been knocked unconscious by the fall. But when he attempted to revive the man, he saw blood and turned him slightly to discover that the back of his skull had been crushed. The sergeant turned up an odd, spherically shaped rock the size of a child's head, possibly a form of pyrite, concealed in the tangle of greenery. That single stone, quite possibly the only one of its kind in the entire meadow, had somehow found the skull of Lieutenant Goss and ended his life, for he was quite dead.

Sergeant Schama had kept the stone as a *memento mori*, a constant reminder of how quickly a life can end. He had it with him, in his saddlebags, and he went to fetch it to show me. Iron oxide on its surface gave it the appearance of metal, and it looked much like a rough sort of cannonball. It bore still the dark brown stains of the blood of Heinrich Goss, and after hefting it (I found it surprisingly light) and examining it carefully, I begged the sergeant to conceal it again in his saddlebags, lest the widow see her late husband's blood. The sergeant, a typically rough military type, saw immediately what a catastrophe that would be, and hurried out to deposit the stone once again where he carried it.

When he returned, he told the rest of his tale. It seems the young lieutenant had been very popular with his cavalrymen, who were stricken by his death. They respected nothing more than horsemanship, and Heinrich Goss had been a superb horseman, so skilled that he hoped some day to be allowed to work with the emperor's splendid Lipizzaner horses. As they stood around helplessly, trying to come to grips with their grief, a horse-drawn ambulance drew up. It had been sent by a staff officer at the orders of our beloved Emperor Franz Joseph himself. The emperor had been watching the maneuvers through field glasses from atop a height overlooking the Bregenzer Ache, and he was terribly affected by the death of one of his best cavalrymen. When he sent an officer to inquire about the lieutenant and his circumstances, he learned that the deceased had a wife and a very young daughter, and on the spot he ordered seven hundred *krone* to be paid to the widow, with an annual stipend of fifty *krone* for the upbringing of the child. Such acts of kindness, of course, are what has endeared our beloved emperor to his people through all the decades of his rule.

I thanked the sergeant for sharing what he knew; my slight friendship with Frau Goss did not permit me the indelicacy of mentioning the manner of her husband's death in her presence. I might have asked more, but just then Hanna herself came skipping in from her play to inquire, in her bold fashion, as to what we were doing in her mother's sitting room. The girl was then perhaps five or six, and annoying as only a red-haired child can be. She posed one question after another to Sergeant Schama, who plainly doted on her and indulged her every whim. For my part, I took my leave as soon as her mother finished with my waistcoat, because I simply could not abide that child.

Over the years, I learned the rest of the story in bits and pieces. Frau Goss, whose Christian name was Birgita, was of mixed Slovene and Galician heritage. She had grown up in the Kingdom of Galicia and Lodomeria, on the eastern fringes of the empire, outside the village of Stambor, between the Dniester and Strwionz Rivers. It was a difficult life, and she dreamed of escaping one day to one of the great capitals of the empire, like Bucharest or Budapest or Vienna itself. Her opportunity came when the young Fraulein Lisjak, as she was then known, met her dashing cavalryman. She was only sixteen, Henrich Goss all of twenty. Her father opposed the marriage most vehemently, but he could never resist his only daughter. He gave in at last, and shortly after her seventeenth birthday, they were wed in the village church. A few weeks after, she moved to an apartment in Vienna, where she remained with the lieutenant's aging mother while he was away, which was most of the time. She was not three months married when she learned that she was with child; after Hanna's birth, she was grateful for the help of her mother-in-law, but she was always under the woman's watchful eye and longed for the day when she would have a place of her own.

That opportunity came about in the most tragic fashion. I know from her own lips that she was devastated by her husband's death. It was a love match, and although she had spent little time with him due to his military commitments, Birgita had remained a devoted, loving wife until she found herself a very young widow. She vowed to herself that she would never marry again, but that she would keep the flame of her love burning in her heart until the end of her life.

Following the death of Lieutenant Goss which I have already described, Frau Goss's parents urged her to return to

Galicia. But in Vienna, her love of music had blossomed. She sang in a women's choir and in another choir at church, and she was learning to play the piano. With the seven hundred *krone* awarded to her by the emperor, she invested in a small but tidy house in Leopoldstadt and purchased a small but melodious piano so that she might practice at home. With her limited purse, she was still able to attend a concert almost every evening in Vienna, the most musical city in the world. Had she returned to Galicia, such concerts would have been a rare event. Returning to the village did not appeal to Birgita in the least. She wanted to bring up her child in the city, where they would be constantly surrounded by the most luminous music in the world. She had great musical ambitions for Hanna from the start, although I did not see the potential. To me the girl was simply a little ruffian with dirty elbows and knees.

Her Slovene heritage meant that Birgita prized most highly the virtues of thrift and hard work. Had she exercised great care, she might have lived on her annual widow's stipend alone, but she put her talents as a seamstress to work and was soon fashioning garments of the highest quality for well-to-do customers in her quarter of the city. With the influx of the *Ostjuden* fleeing the pogroms in Russia and Ruthenia, the Leopoldstadt quarter became more and more Jewish each year. I can tell you that the *Ostjuden* are not entirely welcome. Jews such as myself, who can look back at generations of our family tree in Vienna, feel uncomfortable with the poor, scrabbling, desperate *Ostjuden*. We are assimilated to a great degree; they most assuredly are not.

When Frau Goss found herself with a clientele that was more and more Jewish and included a fair number of the wealthier *Ostjuden,* it did not please some of her more anti-Semitic Catholic neighbors. One evening a delegation (I was a witness, and I can tell you it was closer to a mob) came to her home to inform her that it was not proper for a good Christian woman to perform such a menial task as sewing clothing for the Jews. Frau Goss faced them down on the steps of her home: With dozens of onlookers who had come out to see what the fuss was about, she listened politely to do what their leader, Gerhard Pichler, had to say. Then she turned on them.

"I should be delighted to sew for no one but my Christian neighbors," she said, "if only they would settle their bills when the orders they place with me are delivered. You, Herr Pichler, you owe me forty-two *krone*. Herr Steiner, you owe me twenty-seven *krone*, with the live goose you promised me for Christmas, and Herr Huber, you have promised on six separate occasions to settle your bill, which now amounts to fifty-three *krone* – and yet you still commission further tailoring from me, and complain if I am so much as a day late, because you resent the fact that I am also doing work for Jewish neighbors who pay in cash. So if you will be so kind as to settle your bills now, I will consider your request. But I will not abandon my Jewish customers. They are more than good customers, they are friends. Better friends, I must say, than the upstanding moral Christians who refuse to pay what is owed to a poor struggling widow."

Her tone was polite but her green eyes flashed defiance. Like her daughter, Birgita had a magnificent head of red hair at the time, and she cut quite a figure, glaring down at the mob from the height of her front steps, daring them to say another word. None did. They beat a retreat, muttering. As she told me much later, each of them later returned rather sheepishly and usually by cover of night, to settle their accounts, amidst a litany of apologies and excuses. After that she had no difficulties over her clientele, which grew more Jewish by the year until she had virtually no Christian customers left.

At the time, I was launching my own career as a manager of singers and dancers. My first client was the baritone Franz Küchler, a friend from my rather checkered career at the university, where I managed to dabble in a great many subjects without getting a degree, although I can assure you that I was a doctor of philosophy in the café society of Vienna! Franz had begun to make his mark when it turned out that his manager had siphoned most of his earnings until that time into a non-existent silver mine in Uruguay. Not only did I offer capable management to Franz Küchler, I also tripled his bookings and was able to recover a percentage of the funds he had lost. Franz told some of his fellow artists about me and soon I was representing a number of opera singers, ballet dancers and concert musicians in Vienna and I was beginning to branch out into other cities, especially Budapest. I was barely twenty-five years of age, and my career was well under way.

What I desperately longed to find, however, was someone capable of thrilling audiences not only in Vienna, but also from La Scala to the Bolshoi to the Royal Opera House – an international star. The artists I represented were all very sound, very well-trained, very talented, but they lacked that indefinable something that transcends everything else on the stage. I had not yet found my Enrico Caruso, although I was always on the lookout.

One summer afternoon, Frau Goss did not hear the shop bell when I called. I waited a few minutes, and then from somewhere in the back of the house I heard a gramophone playing. It was the aria from Act I of Verdi's Rigoletto, the *Caro nome*. You know it of course? But this version was *a capella* and exactly as it should be, the voice of Gilda, a girl of sixteen. So often we hear a soprano of forty trying to be the voice of a girl in her teens, but in this, the voice and the girl were perfectly matched. I can still hear it today, the most lovely sound I have ever heard in a lifetime in music: *Caro nome che il mio cor/ Festi primo palpitar,/ Le delizie dell'amor/ Mi dei sempre rammentar!*

I stood transfixed, motionless, listening to every note as it dropped like a ripe pear from the tree. This was extraordinary singing. I closed my eyes the better to concentrate, rocking back and forth on my heels as I listened. It was not perfect, not quite refined, but ah – the tone! The phrasing! The luscious command of the emotion! Giuseppe Verdi had been dead for eight years, and yet I felt that the great composer himself would have risen from the grave to applaud had he been able to hear that divine voice. Not until the last note had sounded did I dare to move, and then I hastened toward the back of the house, because I absolutely had to learn the source of that recording – which itself was of a quality I had never heard before. But all the rooms were empty and I didn't see a gramophone anywhere. I walked on through, opened the door onto a rear balcony, and there was Hanna, hanging sheets on a line.

But such a Hanna I had never seen before! This was not the tomboy with skinned knees I had seen pelting up and down the street. This was a girl just beginning to blossom into a young woman, a real beauty. She had wavy red hair with a gloss that made it shimmer in the sunlight. I was a mature man, she was a mere girl of fifteen, yet I was the one who became hopelessly awkward. I stammered, fumbled with my hat, dropped it, picked it up, tried to explain my reason for barging through without an invitation.

"I'm so very sorry," I said, "I am Herr Mayr, one of your mother's clients."

She curtsied prettily. "Of course. Herr Mayr. We have met many times. I am Fraulein Hanna. I have not seen you for some time."

Of course we had met many times, but I had thought so little of her that it barely registered. There was little chance that I would forget her again.

"I am so very sorry to trouble you, but I was in your mother's waiting room and I heard the most extraordinary recording of the *Caro nome*. I can't seem to locate the gramophone, and I really must know the singer."

She stared at me as if I were daft. "I fear that you are making a joke of me, Herr Mayr," she said.

"I can assure you I am not. Did you not hear it? I listened to every note."

"Of course I heard it! I sang it!"

"Now you are the one who is making a joke, Fraulein."

"I am not. I like to sing while I do the washing. It makes

the task light."

"I don't believe you."

"Believe what you like, Herr Mayr. I can assure you, it was I."

She was so self-assured, it was almost believable, but I still thought myself the butt of a joke. "Very well then," I said. "If you were the singer, then let me hear it again. You are far too young to sing like that."

"I am fifteen. Almost the same age as Gilda."

"So you are. But the voice… that is extraordinary."

"One moment, Herr Mayr. Let me finish with this and I will sing for you."

Her deft hands made short work of the last three sheets, with four clothes-pins to fasten each to the line. Then she turned, wiped her hands on her apron, took a deep breath, and began to sing: "*Caro nome che il mio cor/ Festi primo palpitar…*"

She sang it all the way through a second time. Tears coursed down my cheeks, Herr Doktor Balsano. Tears. You cannot imagine. Heard the first time, with three or four rooms to separate us, her voice was stunning. To have her standing only a few feet away with the wash billowing on the line, this girl without accompaniment, without a costume or a conductor or any of the trappings of the opera, was performing the *Caro nome* as easily, as naturally, as you or I might hum a music-hall tune. When she finished, when the last note was fading away among the overhanging chestnut trees, I fell to my knees. I wept. I thanked her profusely. I begged her forgiveness for doubting her. I thought immediately of signing her to a contract before another manager could swoop in and scoop her up. As soon as I felt it polite, I asked whether she had anyone to represent her. Hanna seemed startled by the question.

"Of course not," she said. "I've never sung on the stage at all. I sing for myself, and for my friends sometimes, and for my vocal teacher."

"And who might that be?"

"The cantor. Perhaps you know him? Herr Gideon Zelermyer?"

"Of course I know him! He is a splendid cantor. But that is a very different form of singing, my dear."

"Ah, yes, but Herr Zelermyer is a great *aficionado* of the opera as well. When there is something he thinks I really must hear, he takes Mama and me to hear it. He's a very fine teacher."

"He must be. He has a remarkable pupil."

Before I could say more, Frau Goss returned and found me talking with her daughter. I hastened to explain why I had come to the back of the house without invitation. "Your daughter has a voice from heaven," I said to her. "I have been granted the honour of hearing her sing the *Caro nome* – twice! You really must allow me to represent her. She is an extraordinary talent."

From that evening on, Hanna was my principal preoccupation. I spent many an evening in the delightful company of the mother and daughter, listening to Hanna sing while her mother played the piano, discussing the career path I envisioned for her, what roles she might now be ready to sing, how best to introduce her, first to Vienna and then to the world. Many a prodigy has been ruined by premature or clumsy exposure to the sometimes vitriolic little people who write music reviews. Herr Zelermyer often joined us, and seeing him work with Hanna I realized that she had stumbled onto a teacher who was perfect for her. He gently coaxed her natural talents to come forth, rather than browbeating her the way some bullying instructors will do.

Frau Goss was an adequate pianist, but as it happened, one of my clients was Alois Janacek, one of the best-known accompanists in the city. I arranged for the two of them to begin rehearsing, and when she was ready, I was able to insert her name onto the list of singers performing in a small, out-of-the-way concert hall, where it was unlikely the flower of Vienna's musical journalism would descend in search of a fresh lamb to skewer. I made sure only one journalist would be there, a friend who was very much in my debt.

Hanna was the seventh of seven singers who appeared that night. She sang only two numbers, the *Caro nome* and the *Batti batti, o bel Masetto* from Don Giovanni. Both would show off her vocal talents and range. In the event that she was called upon to sing an encore, she and Herr Janacek had also prepared the Puccini aria, *O mio babbino caro.* I have heard the latter too many times, but Hanna brought a freshness to it that was like snow melt in the mountains.

As I waited, I was nervous as a cat. I was sure of her singing, but I was not so sure how she would perform on stage, or how she would be received by the audience that night, some seventy or eighty music lovers who were likely to know their arias quite well. I needn't have worried. The reaction was as I expected. The encore had to be performed. The journalist gushed that even if he were not indebted to me he would have written the most splendid review. In the midst of all the adulation, Hanna remained the simplest, most unaffected, most natural young woman you could imagine. She had only to turn a certain way in the light and she would again be that urchin pelting down my street with a rock in her hand, alternately climbing trees and terrorizing the boys of the neighborhood.

After that debut, we were together constantly. I was very careful with her career, perhaps too careful. We kept the audiences small, the performances relatively brief. Her first appearances on the opera stage were in lesser roles, with smaller companies, where less would be expected. She was chafing under such artificial restraint, certain that she was ready to take on any role in the opera canon, but I thought it better to expose her a bit at a time, and I wanted to take great care of her voice. Many a young voice has been destroyed by overwork, many a prodigy ruined by too much attention early in a career. Hanna received good notices, conductors liked working with her, soon she was known by the best companies in Vienna and given an opportunity for any of the lesser roles that might suit her.

Then, at nineteen, she was asked to sing Gilda in Rigoletto at the Vienna State Opera. This was the role and the setting for which she was born. Hanna was perhaps the finest Gilda Vienna has ever seen, and her career was fairly launched. The rest, until the day we arrived in Montreal on our North American tour, was a blur, Herr Doktor. A blur. Concerts and rehearsals, fittings and notices, trains and new concert halls, new opera companies, offers for roles pouring in from all over the continent, even from La Scala in Milan.

To my great sadness, Hanna did not perform at La Scala. She was to have made her debut there in the next opera season, again in Rigoletto, but it was not to be. Ah, Maxim – if only I had not set out to conquer the New World. If only I had been content with Europe, which after all was more than enough. But fool that I was, I had to bring Hanna to this continent, and now she is dead, a great voice stilled, a young life nipped in the bud. I shall never forgive myself, and now I must take the long journey home and attempt to console her mother, when I cannot console myself.

CHAPTER 10

When he had finished his tale, Herr Mayr leaned back in his chair and took a generous swallow from the cognac that had appeared at his elbow. He offered me one of his Virginia cigars. I refused, but he lit one and sat back, lighting it carefully, and blowing a series of tidy smoke rings in the air when he had it going to his satisfaction.

I tried to phrase my question as delicately as possible. "I have the sense that you were in love with Hanna Goss, were you not?"

He guffawed, so loudly that the only remaining diners in the cavernous room glared at us in irritation from a table a hundred feet away. He laughed until tears ran down his cheeks. "My dear boy," he said, "I thought you knew? I loved Hanna, certainly. She was a delightful person, a good friend and a wonderful singer. But I was not *in love* with her in the least, for the oldest reason in the world." He leaned forward and lowered his voice. "I have rather different inclinations, you see, with an unfortunate penchant for slightly built blond Austrian men who possess a certain quality of lithe beauty. Do I make myself clear?"

I was aware of my pale winter face turning a most disagreeable shade of red, along with my ears, which habitually turn redder than the rest, so that they look like a couple of beets attached to my head. Rudi Mayr was talking of a physical type entirely like myself. I glance around at the waiters working the dining room. I had the sense that they were all watching us, assuming that I was Rudi Mayr's young companion. I am ashamed to say that I did not react well. As soon as I could politely take my leave, I did so. I offered to pay for half the meal, albeit in a half-hearted fashion. Had he allowed me to do so I would have had to write to my father to beg for more funds to see me through until the end of the term, because I could live for a month on the cost of that meal. Herr Mayr waved me away, as though it were no more to him than the cost of a bowl of soup at Sophie's Café. Before we parted company, he left me his address in Vienna, with strict instructions that I was to keep him informed on the investigation into her murder, and to visit him without fail the next time I was in Austria.

I left him with mixed feelings. He was entertaining company, and I didn't doubt the sincerity of his affections for Hanna, but the man was so extravagant in his emotions that I found it a little wearing. Mercifully, the night was not as cold as it might have been that time of year, and I had much to contemplate. The moon was at the quarter, but its path through a silken web of cloud was as lovely as any full moon, and despite the lights of the city I could make out the skein of far-flung stars overhead. All this chilly beauty was a spectacle that Hanna would never see again, a constant reminder of the task I had set myself – to find who was responsible for her death, and to see that individual or individuals prosecuted for their despicable crime.

Back at my table at last, I dipped my pen in the inkwell and began. Two hours later, I had most of it down, as much as I could recall, but my mind was still racing. Herr Mayr's narrative, of course, told me much about Hanna's life before we met, but it offered little in the way of clues as to how she met her death. What I found most troubling was her disappearance for a period of more than three months between early September and the evening she turned up at my door, fearing for her life and begging me to hide her. Where had she been? What had she been doing? What mysterious person or persons had come into her life to make her cancel a tour that was so important to her career, to break with the manager who had done so much for her and to go into hiding? Had she been in prison for some bizarre cause or another, Herr Mayr would have found her. Rudi had hinted that she might have a man, but a lover would have no reason to hide her away for months.

We did not even know for certain that she had remained in Montreal, but I sensed that she had been in Montreal all along. Moreover, I felt that she had not been far from my apartment. After all, she had appeared at my door without a coat, indicating that she could not have gone far. But when did she get the coat? And why had she appeared at my door without it, then acquired it before she was murdered? And how could we explain a time discrepancy between the hour when Cyril Leblanc said she had been murdered and her actual death?

Once again, more questions than answers. I was proving very adept at turning up new questions, rather less adept at answering them. I retired for the night, willing my mind to shut down long enough to permit a few hours sleep. As I have done throughout my life when I found it difficult to sleep, I returned to Bad Gastein, to the pleasant white house where I had grown up, to the mountains I had hiked, the streams where I had finished, the waterfalls cascading down a cliff face, the snails and grasshoppers I collected on my walks. It was home, and home has rarely failed me, nor did it on this occasion. I was soon fast asleep.

When I woke, the sun was streaming through my window. I rolled over and was on the verge of going back to sleep when I recalled that it was the first day of the new term and that Dr. Percival Hyde, the very man whose presence here had convinced me to cross the Atlantic, was delivering a lecture at nine o'clock sharp. As a staff assistant, I was not required to attend his lectures, but one of the other assistants had warned me that Dr. Hyde took a dim view of assistants who missed a lecture. I looked at the clock: I had twenty minutes to make it to the lecture room, and Dr. Hyde was also famously intolerant of tardiness. I rushed to the lavatory, dove into my clothes, ran through the snow to the campus, and arrived with two minutes to spare.

I took a seat in one of the upper rows, still surreptitiously catching my breath, and settled in with my fellow staff assistants, a scattering of interns and students, all of whom were awaiting a lecture from the great Dr. Hyde. At nine o'clock precisely he came striding in, a tall, elegant figure in a beautifully tailored dark suit. There were more than the usual number of females attending, as there were in all his classes. I'm sure it was only the course material that interested them, but the fact that he was wealthy, handsome, and famous may have influenced them slightly, even though he was married. He had a doctorate in anthropology and a doctorate in medicine, and he was doing groundbreaking work in psychiatry (which was what had enticed me to Canada in the first place) and if ever a man had been touched by the favor of the gods, it was Dr. Percival Hyde. He was the most popular professor on campus. You would see him between classes, trailed by a group of acolytes of both sexes, striding from building to building or pausing under a particularly picturesque tree to deliver a brief, impromptu lecture.

Sometimes I trailed after Dr. Hyde like the others, but I felt somewhat detached from these scenes. I had experienced some of the same fervor during the single year I spent attending Dr. Sigmund Freud in Vienna. Although there were men of powerful intellect who could and did challenge Dr. Freud (and on occasion broke rather spectacularly with his doctrine) I was put off by the disciples around Dr. Freud, and I think "disciples" is the right word. They hung on every nugget from the master, scribbled down every remark as though they were transcribing the Ten Commandments, and brooked no dissent. I valued independent thinking above all else, and there were in Dr. Freud's circle those (not necessarily the good doctor himself) who treated any diverging point of view as apostasy – especially when it came from a young physician such as myself who had the misfortune to look as though he were still in his teens. Youthfulness is not a quality the Viennese esteem highly, in any profession. It was in part to escape this combination of prejudice and straitened thinking that I sought a different university, a different teacher, and a different country, only to find the degree of adulation heaped on Dr. Hyde not at all unlike what I had observed in Vienna with Dr. Freud.

Not that Dr. Hyde didn't have a great deal to teach me, but I was not born to be anyone's acolyte. Despite my skepticism, I was as entertained and enlightened by Dr. Hyde's lectures as any of my fellow students. He had the gift of an agreeable baritone voice and he was a masterful orator. He knew how to coax his audience in by lowering his voice, how to build a crescendo, how to inject self-deprecating humor to put himself on a more equal footing with his audience, how to build his points one by one so that they could lead in only one possible direction.

On this January morning, Dr. Hyde was at his finest. His best-known book, called *Assistance, Not Analysis,* had first brought him to my attention, and the series of lectures he was delivering that winter went under the same title: "Assistance, Not Analysis." His theme, as always, was that those suffering from illnesses of the mind who turn to psychology or psychiatry for help need just that – help. Immediate help, not simply a lengthy process of probing deep into the psyche that may eventually lead insights but does not provide the kind of on-the-spot care that patients suffering profound ailments really need. Dr. Hyde did not dispute Freud's theory that psycho-neuroses were at the root of most of what were called "nervous" conditions. Instead, he thought that a great deal of time was wasted attempting to unlock these neuroses from the subconscious, when what was needed was immediate and effective treatment. Dr. Hyde believed that there was a biological cause for most forms of mental illness and that biological treatments could be found, including something as simple as brisk daily exercise. He also embraced the use of a variety of substances ranging from morphine to paraldehyde to penicillin and thiamine to control and influence a patient's behavior over time.

While I concurred with exercise as a first step in therapy, I knew that even a walk in the Alps or the Dolomites does not cure everything. Yet drugging patients, in my view, was a less useful solution because when the drugs were removed, you would be left with the original problem, exacerbated by withdrawal from the prescribed drugs.I had not yet heard him lecture on the subject, but I knew that he had also conducted experiments in hypnosis, which I found odd given that Dr. Freud had tried and rejected hypnosis years before.

Dr. Hyde's target on this chilly January morning was a book Dr. Freud had published the previous year, a book I had acquired just before I left Austria and had read three times during the crossing to North America, published in English as *Totem and Taboo, Resemblances Between the Mental Lives of Savages and Neurotics.* I had many unformed doubts about the book that I could not quite express, even to myself. Dr. Hyde had read it in the original German, as had I, and his keen nose for the absurd had quickly sniffed out the ridiculous elements of that discourse. He quoted a passage, freely translated from the German, that I had found particularly off-putting: "We surely should not expect these poor naked cannibals should be moral in their sex life according to our ideas, or that they should have imposed a high degree of restriction upon their sexual impulses."

"If you will notice," Dr. Hyde said, "the good doctor of Vienna has already, in just a few words, disposed of his subject by reducing them to *poor naked cannibals.* Since they are impoverished, nude and prone to eating each other, then, we can say whatever we wish, no matter how offensive it might be if we said the same of barristers in London or fashionable society women in Paris. His theory is that we can discover our own neuroses in their root form by studying the *poor naked cannibals,* even though our modern urban neurotics are not, in any way, descended from or related to the aboriginals of the

Australian Outback.

"I'm not certain whether Dr. Freud is telling us that all primitives are neurotics, or that all neurotics are primitives," Dr. Hyde went on, "or that all neurotics are cannibals. Such offhand remarks, characterizing all the aboriginals of Australia as cannibals, based on the rituals of a handful of tribes, are typical of Freud. He is a master at drawing on a great many sources to build a gaudy castle of theory – but that castle, I would suggest, is too often built on a foundation of sand, airy fantasy and speculation that, while it may strike a useful point here and there, is the farthest thing from modern science."

As he warmed to his subject, I found myself watching his audience more than I watched the speaker. Their faces rapt, eyes shining, many of them trying to take down every word. I wondered: What if Dr. Hyde was as wrong as Dr. Freud? What if neither of them had a monopoly on truth? What if we were all clumsy seekers in the darkness, stumbling over one another as we fumbled toward a light we could glimpse but never quite reach? I did not pretend to be close to Dr. Freud, but I knew the man well enough to know that he was hardest on himself, that he worked harder and with more dedication than any of us, that he submitted his own theories to the most rigorous scrutiny and he did not hesitate to reject them if they turned out to be wrong. I did not believe that the same could be said for Dr. Hyde.

When the lecture was finished, Dr. Hyde gave a slight bow and exited quickly by a side door before I had the opportunity to accost him, but by the time I put on my coat and made it out of the building, I saw him walking alone on a path through the heaps of snow on the Lower Field. By a deft maneuver that involved circling onto a different path, I managed to cut him off and make it look as though we had met by chance.

"Dr. Hyde," I said as he approached, "I wonder if I might have a word with you?"

He paused, looking somewhat startled, and blinked

down at me as though I were some strange species of animal that had wandered into his path.

"Dr. Balsano?" I prompted. "Dr. Maxim Balsano? We haven't seen much of each other, but I'm one of your staff assistants. We met several times during the last term."

"Ah. Yes, yes. Balsano. What may I do for you, young man?"

"Sir, I am very sorry to trouble you, but I wonder if you learned of the death of Miss Hanna Goss over the holidays – the singer who performed at your residence before the beginning of the last term?"

"Why yes, I did hear something about it, though I'm afraid I was away skiing through the holidays. What a tragic event! Wait – wasn't the young lady Austrian, like yourself?"

"Yes sir, she was."

"And did you have some prior acquaintance with her?"

"No sir, I did not. Although we did have an opportunity to chat at some length the night she sang at your reception."

"Lovely voice. Lovely voice. What a pity she's gone!"

"It is. Sir, I wonder if you can tell me how it was that you came to retain her services at your residence that evening? I've spoken with her former manager, and he says she made the booking without his knowledge or consent, which was rather unusual."

Dr. Hyde shrugged and I could sense his impatience with all this. "I have no idea," he said. "All I do for these events is to make my residence available, because I am fortunate to have the space to accommodate a crowd. The arrangements, I believe, are made by the secretary of the medical school."

Just then a great bear of a man came breezing up to us on feet as dainty as a ballet dancer's. He was as elaborately dressed as Herr Mayr, but in a very different way: in a pale suit, delicate brown shoes and a straw hat that might have been suited to the Riviera in July but not to Montreal in January. He had a boutonniere in his lapel, he carried an elaborately carved walking stick and, in his only concession to the climate, he had an enormous dark cape draped over his shoulders.

"Ah, there you are!" Dr. Hyde said, somewhat in the tone of a man grateful to his rescuer. The big man kicked his heels, swept off his hat and offered an elaborate bow. "Count Ottavio Respighi," he said.

I shook his hand. "Dr. Maxim Balsano."

"Ah, a countryman, are you? Another son of Italy, far from home?"

"Among my distant ancestors, perhaps, but I am Austrian."

"Ah." The count, if indeed he was a count, wagged his finger at me. "Most unfortunate for you. You realize that Italy must have the Trento, do you not?" Then he laughed, a great fountain of a laugh, as though he had made the best joke in the universe.

"You will excuse the count," Dr. Hyde said. "He is my liaison to my business interests here and elsewhere. I'm afraid I haven't the time to manage a large shipping concern. I have men to do it for me, and I have Count Respighi to watch them and keep me informed. Now, young Dr. Balsano, I'm afraid we have a luncheon at the club that can't be avoided."

And they were off, as odd a couple as I have ever encountered, the perfumed count and the rather starched professor, striding over the university grounds as though they owned the place, and perhaps they did. I made a note to myself to check with the department secretary about the arrangements that had been made for Hanna Goss to sing at the reception in late summer, in a time that already seemed as distant as my boyhood.

CHAPTER 11

In the early afternoon I returned to my lodgings for a brief nap and some much-needed time with my books. At four o'clock I went downstairs and used the house telephone to call Sophie's Café, because I wanted to compare notes with Detective Jem Doyle. Sophie answered and told me that Jem was working evenings on the three-to-midnight shift, so if I wanted to see him, it would be best if I could come on Wednesday – not that I wasn't welcome at the café any time I pleased.

On Wednesday morning, I observed a new surgical procedure at the hospital, then returned to my lodgings to pull together my notes. It was a haphazard process, because my mind kept drifting to Hanna and to the events of the past that had turned my world upside down. Nevertheless, I resolved to work until the evening, when I could dine at Sophie's Café and have a delicious meal from home while reviewing the case with Jem. The prospect of the cheery warmth of the evening was enough to keep me focused, and I did not cease until five o'clock, when I put the books aside, donned my coat and boots, disdained the tram and made the walk in one hour, with a light, cold rain falling.

The café was filled with the dinner crowd, including many faces I recognized from the New Year's Eve festivities. Sophie greeted me with an effusive welcome and showed me to a narrow table, where fresh-baked bread and butter appeared almost before I sat down. Sophie would have fed me right away, but I preferred to wait until I could dine with Jem. Sophie agreed, but only if I had the soup with a slab of bread while I was waiting. As it happened, I was still waiting for the day's fiery concoction to cool a bit when Jem stalked in, dripping water and cursing the foul weather.

"If I wanted rain in January, I'd have stayed in bloody Dublin, where it rains three hundred and sixty-four days a year and pisses on t'other! At least in Ireland, we don't have to deal with rain atop snow. In this fecking bog, we get both in the same hour, and the first lot freezes before the second lot starts to fall, so we bust our arse to smithereens!"

Jem tugged off his dripping coat and hat and hung them on the rack, then pulled out a chair at my table and sat rubbing his hands to warm them. "I'm pleased as punch to find ye here, boy," he said. "Saves me a trip to that university where you hide out. McGill makes me break out in hives, all them bloody smart fellas couldn't find their arse with a lantern and a compass – present company excepted, of course."

I wanted to ask what he might have discovered since the funeral, but Jem silenced me before I could get a word out. "I've been on the track of master criminals the day long, boy!" he bellowed. "Will ye leave a man in peace until I've had an ale or three and a wee bite to keep starvation at bay? Will ye do that?"

I laughed. As if on cue, Sophie arrived with a brimming pint of a dark ale and another slab of bread, and in a moment she was back with the same fiery soup I had in front of me.

"Had a fellow today," Jem said after he had drained half the pint at a single gulp and wiped the foam from his mustache, "bloke tried to steal the harness off a draft horse full seventeen hands high, and that in broad daylight. I don't believe he'd seen a bloody harness before, or maybe his fingers froze up, because he couldn't get it unbuckled. Seems the animal got annoyed with the whole process and nipped a chunk right out of the thief's shoulder, then kicked him in a place that will leave him unable to procreate from now till kingdom come. Which is the Lord's mercy, because a man of such surpassing stupidity ought not to have offspring."

He went on through the soup, and two more pints, and wienerschnitzel and roast potatoes that Sophie had made especially for me, with a steak and kidney pie she always made for Jem on such foul days. It was not until the last plate had been polished off and he was sipping an Irish whiskey that Jem began to tell me what he had learned.

"First, I spoke with Monsieur Henri Bourgie, him that runs the funeral parlor. Sort of chap you hope not to meet too soon, in the course of things, but he's a helpful sort. Useful to know, in my line of work. I paid a call on Henri, and asked him who broke the bank to pay for that casket. Henri didn't have to think about it for an instant. First, a gentleman calls him up on the telephone. He speaks a queer sort of French, like they speak t'other side of the pond. Good French, but odd. Anyhow, the chap wants to know what it will cost to give a friend of his the royal sendoff. Best casket Henri Bourgie has available, the works. Henri thinks on it, remembers that he's had an elaborate sort of coffin on hand for three years, too pricey for the folks in his neck of the woods, just waiting for such an occasion as this. Henri, he supposes they're going to do a little bartering, so he tosses out a price that is way up on the high side, double what he would accept, thinking the caller will start low and they'll meet in the middle. The gentleman on the telephone doesn't miss a beat. 'Very well,' he says. 'The money will arrive in the morning.' Then he gives the name of the deceased, Hanna Goss. The body is to be found, he says, at the city morgue on Craig Street. Henri is to make the arrangements to have the body transferred to his parlor, and the chap knows exactly what he wants in the way of a funeral. She's to have a horse-drawn hearse to carry her up to the mountain, none of these noxious, wheezing, motorized things. Make it real dignified like, and the horses must be black."

"Very specific," I put in.

"He was. Down to the details. Mark my words, the fella who made that call, he's behind all this. Maybe he wasn't the one that knocked her down in the street, kicked her in the face and jabbed that little needle into her heart, but he's involved in some way. And he's a right bastard, he is. *Go ndéana an diabhal dréimire do chnámh do dhroma!*"

I thought for a moment that Jem's brogue had gotten too thick for my ears. He must have seen the puzzled look on my face, because he translated for me. "It's an old Gaelic curse, lad. *May the devil make a ladder from your spine.*"

Jem's grin was devilish indeed. He winked at me and went on with his narrative. "Old Henri, he calls the morgue, speaks to some flunkey who works for Dr. Good King, finds out there is indeed a Mademoiselle Hanna Goss in residence. Henri makes arrangements for the body to be transferred to his care. Then he calls it a day and goes home for the night, thinking that may be the end of it. If the promised payment doesn't arrive next morning, he'll have no more to do with it. But when he turns up for work, don't you know that someone has stuck an envelope under the door, addressed to Henri Bourgie. Sure enough, inside is the payment. Cash money. Every penny, in advance, and it's a considerable sum.

"Now the coffin and the undertaker's work, that's only part of the job. There has to be a place for the coffin to, are ye with me? Henri knows this as well as the next man, so he checks with the Mount Royal Cemetery, it's the same story: The anonymous call, the precise instructions, payment received in cash and in full. And at the cemetery, extra was paid for the grave-diggers to work in winter, and on a Sunday at that. I had a chin-wag with the cemetery folk, 'cause I don't like to take another man's word for what I can learn myself, and it was just as Henri said. Then I made one last stop and spoke to the priest at St. James Cathedral. Same story: anonymous call on the telephone, asking the price of the service. Cash money in an envelope, more instructions. The bastard was thorough, if naught else."

I had barely time to think it over, but of course *some-one* would have had to pay for Hanna's funeral, or she would have been dumped into a pauper's grave in a plain pine box, and that only after the ground had thawed. I felt a twinge of guilt, because I had not offered to pay for it myself. I would have made the offer, had I thought of it, but I could not have afforded a casket at all on a par with the one in which Hanna was buried.

I had another thought. "If this individual sent notes to the funeral parlor, the cemetery and the cathedral, then we have copies of his handwriting, don't we? Did he sign the notes?"

Jem reached into an inner pocket of his suit, withdrew all three notes with a flourish, and laid them on the table. "The typewriter," he said, "is naught but another instrument of the devil. If you must type what you have to say on one of these machines, it's because you're up to no good, and you don't want to be discovered at one nasty business or another."

Jem grinned as he said it. He was fooling, but there was a kernel of truth in his fooling. Whoever had written these notes did not want to be discovered, and he most certainly had not signed them.

"There's one last bit that might interest ye," he said. "When I returns to the station house, there's an almighty fuss. Seems a couple of items have gone missing from the evidence room. The keeper of the room, who is as honest as the day is long, went out for his lunch hour precisely at twelve, locking the door as he always does. When he returned at exactly one o'clock, the lock had been picked. Two items were missing – the fur coat belonging to our victim, Mlle Hanna Goss, and the letter that was in the pocket of said coat. Nothing else. Some dark-hearted bastard has made off with the evidence. I suspect the motive was to sell the coat, and the letter was a coincidence. But here we've got a mystery inside a mystery."

"That makes two vanished letters in this case," I said.

"The one found in Hanna's coat, and the one she left at my apartment."

Jem nodded thoughtfully. "Like someone is trying to erase the young woman's very existence, ain't it?"

At that moment, Sophie appeared with slices of Sachertorte for us, each slice decorated with a large dollop of freshly whipped cream, along with a demi-tasse of coffee for me and another Irish whiskey for Jem. For herself, she had only a wee slice of the Sachertorte, just enough to be sure it was up to her standards. With the supper crowd thinning, she sat with us for a time, a plump arm draped over her husband's brawny shoulders.

"Have you gentlemen finished your business?" she asked.

"I've told as much as I have to tell," Jem answered. "This young fellow, I guess he's spent all his time since last we talked gazing at some young filly's ankles, because he has nothing to tell me. Is it that young Karine, lad? She was quite keen on you, although I'd think the lasses would find you a little scrawny."

My curse descended on me, and my ears turned bright red from embarrassment. To change the subject, I told them most of what I had learned about Hanna from Herr Rudolph Mayr. It was a long story, but they hung on every word. Everyone should have friends like these two. Especially on a January night, when the weather is foul and spring is far away.

CHAPTER 12

It was a fine night at Sophie's Café. Near nine o'clock the establishment began to fill again. A friend of Sophie's started tinkling on the piano, and Jem sang Mother Machree, and someone else played the accordion, and Sophie sang a Hungarian tune from her childhood. The waiters and bartenders were all Sophie's sons, and they couldn't pour the beers fast enough. I was persuaded to have a pálinka, and then another, and then a third, which was over my limit. It was a small-scale version of the New Year's Eve festivities, except that this time, the party began to break up around eleven o'clock.

I said goodbye and dashed out just in time to catch the westbound tram on Sherbrooke Street. I was feeling a bit dizzy from the pálinka, and I dozed on the journey, waking just in time to get off a block beyond my stop. I crossed the street and trudged homeward, my mind now fixed on a warm bed and a good night's sleep.

I was walking with my head down, paying attention to nothing except the somewhat icy sidewalk in front of me, when I heard a voice from a dark lane that veered to the left off Aylmer Street, a passageway between two apartment buildings so narrow I had barely noticed it before.

I couldn't make out whether the voice that called to me was that of a man or a woman, it was so faint. "Help me! Please help me. I'm badly hurt!"

I thought that someone must have fallen on the ice and broken ankle or hip, something that made it impossible for the victim to walk. I did not hesitate. I am a doctor, and the son of a doctor, and the grandson of a doctor, and I grew up in a place where the dangers were from avalanches and stampeding horses, not one's neighbors. When someone needed help, you helped, to the best of your ability. I peered through the darkness, feeling my way along, trying to locate the voice.

I was about twenty paces along the dark lane, far enough so that I could scarcely see my hand in front of my face, when they struck. The first blow, so powerful that it must have come from a baseball or cricket bat, caught me in the back of the knees and dropped me to the ice. The next was a boot to the face that shattered my nose, followed by another thump from the bat that caught me in the small of the back. I suppose that I must have screamed or shouted, I don't recall. I flailed out with my arms, trying to strike one of my attackers, but they seemed to be coming from all directions at once. They were merciless and thorough. I could hear them wheeze and snort as they drove one blow after another into my body. Only once did they pause long enough for one of them to growl: "Maybe now you'll keep that Kraut nose of yours out of other people's business after this!"

My hat had fallen off, and one of them tangled his fingers in my hair (which badly needed cutting) and held my head while he punched my face. He seemed to have heavy, sharp-edged rings on every finger, and each blow opened new cuts on my face. One of them caught me full in the mouth, and drove my two upper incisors back so that they were touching the roof of my mouth, without quite knocking them out entirely. I felt kicks from steel-toed boots that broke my ribs, and one that caught me between the legs, eliciting a scream. One leapt into the air and came down with his knee on my broken ribs, and I screamed again. Then it was back to the rhythmic punches to my battered face.

It probably lasted no longer than a minute or two, but it seemed to go on for hours. After the first onslaught, I became two people: the poor, huddled chap down in the snow, curled up in a ball as the kicks and blows rained down on him, and the watcher, somewhere up above and comfortably detached from the scene, looking on dispassionately and wondering if this was what it was like to see a man beaten to death. It was a wonder that I didn't black out, but I did not, and I was still conscious of every blow when I heard a policeman's shrill whistle, felt a last kick in the ribs, and heard my attackers pelting away.

Then, at last, I did lose consciousness. When I woke, the only part of my body that didn't hurt was the soles of my feet. My eyes were swollen shut and I couldn't see, though it seemed there was light in the room. My broken nose could still detect the sharp medicinal smells, so I knew that I was in a hospital room. I moaned and asked for water, and a nurse came to help me. I managed to ask her where I was. "You're in the Royal Victoria Hospital, Dr. Balsano," she said, "and you are very fortunate to be alive."

I was back in the very hospital where I had witnessed a surgical procedure only a few hours before the attack. I lost consciousness again, and the next voice I heard was that of Sophie Szitva. I sensed the warmth of her plump body hovering near, and felt what it must have been like to have the mother I had never known. Her warm hand touched my forearm, somehow finding a spot where I wasn't bruised. I tried to speak, but with my battered mouth, I couldn't form words.

"Rest," Sophie said. "You must rest. I will be here, or one of my sons. You are now my seventh son, Maxim. We must look after you."

I slipped away again. The next time I woke, I caught the heavy scents of shag tobacco and Irish whiskey. "Jem," I managed to say.

"At your service, my boy. Seems to me you ought to be dead, but since you're not, I suppose we'll have to listen to ye. If ye can talk."

"I can, I think."

A nurse brought me water. I sipped at it, unable to take in more than a few drops at a time.

"Easy, lad. You're lucky to be alive."

I gurgled something that might have sounded like 'yes'.

"First question: Did you get a look at the bastard that done this?"

"Bastards," I whispered. "More than one."

"Men always say that when they take a beating."

I ignored his jibe. "Three of them, unless it was a man with six arms and six legs."

"Oh, a wiseacre, are ye? Well, at least you're sounding like ye might survive after all. You recognize any of them? Get a look at them?"

I gestured for more water. "I couldn't see a thing. Dark."

"Yes. A convenient dark alley. Why in bloody hell did you go there anyhow? You were a hundred yards from your door."

"Somebody. Needed help."

"Calling for help, were they?"

"Uh-huh."

"Old trick and a nasty one, that. Did any of them speak?"

I held up one finger. "Said keep my Kraut nose out. That's all."

"Out of what? I guess we know. Five will get you ten it was the same lads what sent Hanna Goss to the next world. A good thing our beat copper happened to wander by. He scattered them and whacked one with his billy club as he ran by, but he couldn't nab any of them and he didn't get a good look either. There were four of them, so you know. Not three. Now Sophie says I have to let you rest. I don't think they meant to kill you, or they'd have brought that needle through the heart into play. But they damned near did the job anyhow. You're busted up everywhere, do ye know that? I didn't care for a look, but I'm told that your testicles are solid black and the size of grapefruit."

At that I felt a stab of pain that made my stomach do a backflip, and I remembered that heavy boot in my groin. I had once been hit there by a football off the toe of the best player on our side, and I thought that was the ultimate in testicular pain. It didn't come close.

I heard Jem getting to his feet. "Alright, Max. These lads will meet up with Jem Doyle sooner or later, and they'll rue the day. However many it might be, I'll have them all in worse shape than you're in this moment. They'll not get away with this, not on my turf."

Jem's place was taken then by Sophie. I caught a whiff of chicken soup with paprika, and soon she was spooning the heady broth between my swollen lips. I could feel my strength returning with every spoonful. I tried to tell her how grateful I was, but she was having none of it. She told me to hush and have some more broth, and I did, thinking that if heaven had a taste, it would be Sophie's soup.

Sophie had also brought raw steaks from the café, and the steaks were applied to my eyes to bring down the swelling. Slowly, my eyes began to open, and on my third day in hospital I could see well enough to peer into the mirror Sophie held up for me. The wreckage was impressive. What caught my attention first was my ears. The ears that turned bright red when I was embarrassed would not be turning red for some time: they were so bruised they were black, and they stood straight out from my head, like black flags on a doomed ship. Other than my ribs, nothing, not even my swollen testicles, caused me more pain than those ears. I couldn't lie on my side, or turn my head in either direction, because if one of my ears brushed the pillow I felt a jolt of pain. In appearance, however, the ears weren't the worst part. I couldn't see my heavily bandaged nose, but my face was a crazy quilt of stitches. One hundred and seventeen stitches, the surgeon who had sewn me up told Sophie, all of them the result of that ringed fist striking me over and over. I also had five broken ribs, bruised kidneys, a fractured clavicle, and contusions over much of my body.

Still, I was alive. When the pain eased with judicious doses of morphine, I felt absolutely buoyant. I was young and strong (at least for a man who weighed less than sixty kilos) and I had the resilience of youth. From one day to the next, I could monitor the recovery: The diminished swelling, pain beginning to fade, mobility in some of the joints stabilizing, less blood in my urine.

During my fourth day in hospital, I received an early-morning visit from Dr. Percival Hyde himself. Two of my fellow lodgers from Mrs. Guterson's had been by, and most of Sophie's family, but I expected no other visitors. Then a tall figure in a dark suit slipped through the door.

"Dr. Balsano, I am so pleased to find you awake," he said. "I am often in the hospital in the early morning hours, so I looked in on you twice previously, but you were quite unconscious. I wanted to convey my sympathy to you, and to apologize on behalf of the university for this dastardly attack. You must think we are a nation of thugs. I was appalled, but they tell me you are expected to recover fully. A little the worse for wear, perhaps, but you shall recover."

I mumbled my thanks. Until that moment, I had found Dr. Hyde reserved, stuffy, even somewhat cool – especially considering that it was his letter inviting me to spend a year as one of his staff assistants that had brought me to Montreal. Now I was seeing a different side of him, a side that reflected genuine human warmth and sympathy. I felt ashamed that I had sometimes thought the worst of him.

Before he left, Dr. Hyde asked about my injuries and how they were being treated. He knew about the fractured tibia, the fractured wrist, the fractured clavicle, the bruised kidneys, the entire catalogue, and he had been over the treatment with the doctors who had treated me. I had no concerns about their work, but I felt enormously gratified by his personal attention. Before he left, he apologized for not having spent more time working with me.

"I hope you will understand, there are enormous demands on my time," he said. "Each day is a high-wire act: lectures, patients, hospital visits, fundraising efforts, board meetings for the shipping business in which, willy-nilly, I am still involved. There are times when a man does not know which way to turn, and I'm afraid that I can seem rather cross and abrupt. If that sounds like an apology – it is. But I am going to do my best to make it up to you. In fact, the Count and Countess were saying last evening that we must invite you to dinner as soon as you are ambulatory. Now I must be off. I'm certain the pain is all you can bear at the moment, but you are on the mend. The advantages of youth – if I had your injuries, I would be flat on my back for months."

At that, Dr. Hyde patted my shoulder in a fatherly fashion and took his leave. Watching him go, it was hard to imagine that tall, vigorous man flat on his back for more than a few hours sleep. He was as dynamic as any man I had ever met, as intelligent, as ambitious. I could do worse than to take him as a model for my own career. We Austrians, I'm afraid, tend to like our coffee, our wine, and our café society a bit too much. North Americans, like our Prussian friends in Germany, drive themselves harder. I resolved to be more like them.

After ten days in the hospital, I was released. Jem and Sophie came to get me and drove me straight to their home. Jem had explained the situation to Mrs. Guterson, and two of her boys had fetched my things from my apartment so that I could finish recuperating at Sophie's house, where there would be someone to look after me constantly.

As soon as my fingers could grip a pen again, I wrote to my father. I told him, falsely, that I had gotten the worst of it in a bout of pugilism with a classmate, and thus had been unable to answer the letters that had piled up while I was in the hospital. I knew that would alarm him, but it was better than saying that I had taken a terrible beating at the hands of a group of murderous thugs. *That* sort of news would have alarmed the old man to the verge of a stroke, and at least now I had prepared him for the sight of me, next time we met.

At least we would meet again, I was now sure of that. During the restless nights in the hospital, I worried that I would contract an infection or that in some other way my in-juries would put an end to my short life before it had fairly begun, and I would never see Papa again, never hike the hills around our home again, with him showing me all the places where he had seen the beloved Emperor Franz Joseph, who was in the habit of spending his summers at Bad Gastein. Incredibly, the emperor was still on his throne and it was impossible to imagine the world without him. Even while languishing in a Montreal hospital, I felt comforted by the great and enduring Habsburg Empire of which I was such a tiny particle.

CHAPTER 13

On the ninth day of February, a Monday, I returned to McGill University to hear another of Dr. Hyde's lectures, and I received two letters by afternoon post. Karine asked if I would join her the following Saturday for a Valentine's Day skate, and Dr. Hyde invited me to a dine at his Westmount mansion the day after. I quickly replied in the affirmative to both invitations. There was little I would enjoy more than an afternoon outdoors with Karine, and I was aware that my remaining time in Montreal was growing short, and that if I wished to make the most of my brief acquaintance with Dr. Hyde, I had to spend every possible moment in his presence.

Had I realized how difficult it would be to skate, I should not have accepted Karine's invitation. It was not the fractured tibia; it had healed nicely, as had my clavicle. The ribs were still tender, but not terribly so. The problem was my physical conditioning, which had suffered terribly during my convalescence. I labored around while Karine flew over the ice. I kept at it for no more than ten minutes before I had to sit and watch Karine leap and twirl, but she did not last long either. Montreal was in the throes of a bitter cold snap, with thirty-two degrees below zero at night, and I had no trouble persuading her that we should take a cab back to Sophie's Café for supper. Karine ate quickly and left because she was expected at home. I offered to accompany her, but she said that I'd had enough exercise for a man who was still recuperating. Sophie busied herself looking after the usual Saturday night crowd, and I was left with Jem. When he asked how I planned to spend my Sunday, I told him about the invitation from Dr. Percival Hyde.

"Well, ain't you among the swells!" Jem kidded me. "Be sure you mind your manners, now. I wouldn't want to hear that you've misbehaved in society, lad."

I asked what he knew of Percival Hyde. Jem claimed that he knew nothing at all, but it turned out that he knew quite a lot, as a good policeman should. "Percy Hyde is a bit of a mystery hereabouts," he said. "He's the heir to Hyde Brothers Shipping, which I believe is second or third largest in the country."

"He has a brother?"

"Not Percy. He was an only child. It was his father who had the brother, Dougal. Father's name was Declan. Twins, they was, from Aberdeen. Dougal and Declan. The two of 'em came with money, founded the shipping firm, made so much more money they didn't know where to stow it all. Declan was Percy's father. Dougal was a bachelor, never married. All a bit of a fairy tale existence, I suppose, except that Percy was only seven years old when his Mum and Dad were drowned in a yachting accident in heavy weather off Cape Cod. The two of 'em were lost, and Percy was left a wealthy orphan. Old Dougal had no idea what to do with Percy, so he shipped him off to a private school in England. No one in these parts saw Percy again until Dougal died of a stroke. Percy was twenty-four or twenty-five years old by then, a grown man. He'd been away almost twenty years, and there was almost no one around here who had ever laid eyes on him. It took a few weeks but they tracked him down in Italy, told him Dougal had passed and that left Percival as the heir to one of the biggest fortunes in Canada. Percival didn't want to have much to do with it. He had a medical degree from Cambridge (or maybe it was Oxford, I can never keep them two straight) and he wanted to press on with his work. He took possession of the mansion, delegated the shipping business to some folks who knew how to run it, and started climbing the rungs in the medical world."

Jem paused, stroking his mustache. "There was one thing that got the tongues wagging. A man like him, a wealthy, good-looking, youngish bachelor, you know he was a prime target for socialites looking to marry off their daughters. But about two years ago, Dr. Hyde married a young woman, Eleanor Porter, who was thought to be well beneath his station. Her father was a mere clerk in his shipping business. The marriage was very abrupt and the girl was only nineteen when they tied the knot, while he was forty if he was a day. I've not laid eyes on her, but from the photographs in the press it seems she's a great beauty. Had she been the daughter of one of the prominent families of the city or European royalty, no one would have minded. But a clerk's daughter? That was a scandal, good for an entire season. Still and all, your Dr. Hyde seems to know what he's about in the medical business. Is that true?"

"You could say he's an eminent psychiatrist," I said. "There aren't more than five or six in the entire world with his stature. Dr. Freud in Vienna, whom I studied with for a time, Dr. Carl Jung, perhaps three or four others. Dr. Hyde is the reason I came to Montreal. His fame had reached all the way to Vienna. He has a theory about the biological origins of mental disturbances in humans..."

"Yes, yes," Jem cut me off. "All that is Greek to me anyhow. Folks like Percival Hyde are far above me, lad. That's well and good. Sometimes it's better not to question the things we can't change."

I laughed. "Alright, Jem. No more medical talk. But speaking of the social register, what about this Italian friend of Dr. Hyde's, Count Respighi? Have you heard of him?"

"Aye, that I have, but I can't tell you much. He came here shortly after Percy Hyde. He's meant to be the liaison between Hyde and the shipping people, apparently, but he doesn't seem to do much work. They say he's there only because he rescued the good doctor from some sort of scrape in

Italy when Dr. Hyde was a young man. Apparently the gratitude of the eminent physician is bottomless. But I don't begrudge the Count any more than I begrudge the doctor. Truth to tell, I can't imagine havin' all the stuff Percy Hyde has to his name. A copper doesn't make much if he's on the up and up, but it doesn't matter. Sophie and me, we got all we need. Friends and kids and the café, and that's plenty for any man."

"I know what you mean. My father is just a country doctor. Half the time, he gets paid in prosciutto and sauerkraut, wine and schnapps, but he's more than content with his lot."

We sat thoughtfully for a time, not saying much. "You're staying here tonight, or I'm taking you home," Jem said at last. "It's your choice, but you ain't taking the tram."

"I've imposed on you enough," I said. "I should go back to Mrs. Guterson's."

"Then I'll drive you."

"I know better than to argue with you, Jem. I'll stay. I don't want you to have to go out on a winter's night. Besides, it's Valentine's Day, and you should be with your valentine."

"Ach, that's my Sophie. She's got me hooked by the stomach, and that's a powerful hold for a woman to have on a man."

Sophie was busy on the far side of a noisy room, too far away to know that we were talking about her, but she looked up at that moment, and blew a kiss at Jem, and I thought I saw the tough old bird blush a little. Love is a beautiful thing when you get it right.

CHAPTER 14

The next day, I took some time over my appearance before departing for the Hyde Mansion. I shaved with care, brushed a suit that had been freshly cleaned and pressed, polished my shoes and tied my cravat with care. I was appalled to see that I had a small blemish on my forehead; like most young people through the ages, I failed to see what I had (youth and health, in abundance) and focused on what was wrong (a barely visible blemish on otherwise flawless skin.) The care I was taking was a source of enormous amusement to my fellow lodgers, who could not be convinced that a young lady was not the object of all the fuss.

It was a relatively short stroll from my lodgings on Aylmer Street to the Hyde Mansion on Pine Avenue in the Uptown area of the city, but it was like walking from a poor nation to one that was unimaginably wealthy. Despite the bitter cold, I almost wished that it was farther to give me more time to steady my nerves. After a ten-minute walk, much of it steeply uphill with my galoshes slipping on the icy sidewalks, the great mansion came into view.

The structure was meant to awe the onlooker with the wealth of its inhabitants, and in that it succeeded admirably. The Scottish Hyde brothers, Dougal and Declan, had commissioned a Scot named George Aitken to build it, but I fancied that the brothers had demanded more elements in the design than any architect could successfully incorporate. Like many a wealthy man with a great deal of money and very little knowledge of art or architecture, they had borrowed in the most eclectic fashion from the Middle Ages, the Renaissance,

Antiquity and (especially) the Second Empire, and if you cared to peer closely enough, you would see Greek pillars, Gothic arches, Renaissance windows and Baroque decorative touches all scattered throughout more or less at random, with an overall theme that Baron Haussman might have used in the redesign of Paris. It was built mostly of a reddish stone (and I wondered what it could be, and where and at what expense they had quarried such material) and the feature that first caught your eye was the turrets at all four corners, with the sort of high, narrow windows from which Rapunzel had once let down her hair. I counted seven bay windows on the front of the mansion alone, a feature common to every mansion I had seen in Montreal.

If the amateur student of architecture in me recoiled at much of it, the casual tourist was over-awed, as I was meant to be. The central entrance was of similar design, with doors a dozen feet high and as many feet wide. A doorman bowed as he opened a single black walnut door for me, and I entered for the first time a vestibule (set off by pillars of Florentine marble and an elaborately carved mantle) that was, by itself, larger than my entire apartment. I would have lingered to admire the mantle, but I was relieved of my hat, coat and galoshes and ushered into the drawing room, where Dr. Percival Hyde awaited with his young wife and his friend, Count Respighi.

When I had attended the reception at the same address during the summer, I had arrived with a group of students from the medical school and led onto the spacious terrace and lawn in back of the house, and it seemed far less intimidating. Now, a single guest arriving on foot on an absolutely frigid day in winter, I felt such panic that for a moment all I could think was to flee. The greeting from my host was so effusive that I felt as though the luncheon was being given in my honor. I was introduced to everyone, including several other eminent physicians from the hospital and their wives, a financier or two, executives of the shipping company – and finally to the lady of the manor, Madame Eleanor Hyde. She was, as

Jem had warned me, considerably younger than her husband –
and, with the exception of the late Hanna Goss, quite the most
beautiful woman I had ever seen, even in Vienna, where some
of the jewels of Europe are on display. She was tall, taller than
me by at least three inches, with a long, elegant neck, raven
hair, blue eyes and a sprinkling of freckles across a very pretty
nose. She was wearing a long rose-colored gown set off by a
string of white pearls and the effect she had on everyone, male
and female, was immediate and noticeable.

Something about her, however, was not quite in focus.
As I took her hand and bowed, I detected a faint whiff of whis-
key. M'lady had been drinking already, and it was barely noon.
I had no experience at all of Canadian high society, and even in
Austria I had observed it only from a distance, but I was pretty
certain that it wasn't common for the very young wife of a
prominent and wealthy physician to be drinking alcohol on a
Sunday morning.

As she greeted the arriving guests, I noticed that
Eleanor Hyde was under the constant scrutiny of both her
husband (who kept those cool grey eyes on her even when he
was making small talk with others) and Count Respighi. The
Count seemed to be able to do several things at once while
still watching the host's young wife: He spoke volubly, greeted
the wives of the arriving guests as though they were all international beauties (saving his most lavish praise for those
corseted matrons who plowed through the drawing room like
battleships, chins and bosoms thrust forward, wearing the
expression of a person visiting a filthy lavatory rather than
one of Montreal's three or four most stunning mansions.) The
Count fairly danced through his greetings to all the women,
all the while petting a grey kitten that he held prisoner in the
crook of his arm. Even the most formidable of the ladies were
charmed, and I marveled again at the way someone with his
height and enormous bulk could move so smoothly, on feet as
dainty as a ballerina's. I was many inches shorter than Count
Respighi and I weighed less than half as much, but I am quite

certain that I could not have slipped my feet into his tiny shoes. No aspect of his performance, however, could deter this huge man from keeping watch over Eleanor Hyde. He never seemed to divert his gaze from her, and I wondered if it was possible that he was in love with her.

We were plied with drinks and canapés by uniformed staff of both sexes, and invited to admire the paintings all around us: a Rubens, a Frans Hals, a Vermeer, even one of the lesser works of Rembrandt. The collection seemed a bit stuffy for a man as modern as Dr. Percival Hyde, but there were newer works by Camille Pissarro, Gustave Doré, Edgar Degas and Austria's own Gustav Klimt. Even with my limited knowledge of European art, I could see that Dr. Hyde (or someone near him) knew his artists well and collected their work relentlessly. The Hyde brothers who were responsible for the architecture may have been artistically naïve men of wealth, but the present owner had more discriminating and even *avant-garde* tastes.

At last, we were led to the dining room and seated. I took the opportunity to make a hasty count, and determined that we were forty souls around that table, and there was space for more. I was seated near an eminent professor of laryngology, who took the opportunity to question me about the famed Viennese laryngologist Dr. Johann Schnitzler and his son, the dramatist and novelist Arthur Schnitzler (who was also, almost by chance, a doctor.) The professor of laryngology seemed more interested in the erotic content of the younger Schnitzler's work than in the medical achievements of the father.

To my right was the wife of an executive in the Hyde Shipping Company who toyed nervously with her food and giggled at every remark I made, no matter how banal. Seated across from me was a woman who introduced herself, rather oddly, as Celeste Townsend – now the Countess Respighi, an Englishwoman of opulent build who was married to the count. As the count watched Eleanor Hyde, the countess watched him, but with a different intent. At one point when the count was plainly looking about for a fresh bottle of wine, the countess jumped to her feet, located one of the servants, and saw to it that a bottle was brought to the count immediately. He thanked her graciously, but something in his manner made it clear that he expected no less.

All in all, I found the conversation at Dr. Hyde's enormous dining table less enlightening and far less entertaining than an evening at Sophie's Café. Even the food was not up to Sophie's standards, although perhaps it simply wasn't to my taste. The wine was very good, even heavenly, so I drank a trifle more than I should and nibbled at what was put in front of me. I was relieved when the meal had finished. There remained only the ordeal of the library, where the men retreated to smoke, and then I should be free to return to my lodgings, away from an atmosphere I found stifling despite the size of the room.

Before joining the men over their cigars, however, I had to use the lavatory. I discreetly asked the butler for directions. It was a fair distance straight down the hallway and then a left turn down another hall. I had drunk a fair bit of both water and wine during the meal, and I thought my bladder might burst before I located the facilities, but I found it at last. I washed and dried my hands with great care, a habit taken from the surgery, and had just emerged when I bumped into Eleanor Hyde, who was wandering along the hallway like a guest who had lost her way, when she was the lady of the manor.

"Pardon me, madame," I said, and offered a slight bow.

"Well, aren't you the pretty one," she said. "Where has Percy been hiding you?"

Her hand was on my arm in a way that was altogether too familiar. Up close, I caught the mingled scents of wine and Irish whiskey. The lady had been drinking.

"I'm afraid I'm not a student," I said. "I'm a visiting doctor, from Austria."

"A doctor? You can't be more than twenty!"

"I'm twenty-four, madam."

"Twenty-four? With blond hair, blue eyes and rosy cheeks. Well, they don't grow them very big in Austria, do they? Small but pretty, is that more the style?"

I bowed again. "Madame, I'm afraid I must go. I was to meet the men in the smoking room."

"Oh, of course you must go, you pretty, pretty boy. Can I tell you a secret, pretty boy?" She leaned in close to my face, and the smell of alcohol was almost overpowering. "Unspeakable things. That's my secret. There are unspeakable things afoot, but I must never, never tell."

I took a firm step backward. She quickly closed the distance between us and brought her face up to mine again. "Do you know what unspeakable means? Do you understand me?"

"Of course I do. But I don't think it's appropriate for us to be talking like this."

She grabbed my lapels and brought her face to within an inch of mine. "Unspeakable," she repeated. "Unspeakable things. Do you understand?"

She was tugging me to and fro with the force of her emotions as she spoke. "Madame, please!" I said, taking her wrists rather too firmly to lift her hands away from me. "That is not the sort of conversation one has with a stranger! Please!"

"Oh, Percy won't mind," she said. "He doesn't care. Nobody cares. It's unspeakable!"

Eleanor was blocking my path and there was no easy way to escape her without making a scene.

"Madame, please let me go my way," I said.

She tittered. "You *look* shocked," she said. "I didn't mean to shock you. It's just that you have the face of a man who would understand. I thought I could trust you." She ran her finger-tips down my cheek, like a blind woman exploring a face. She looked around quickly, as though to see if anyone was eavesdropping on this bizarre conversation, then leaned into me again. This time, I felt the pressure of a full breast against my forearm and drew back as though I had received a jolt of electricity, but she took both my arms and drew me close. As appalled as I was by what she was saying, I was even more horrified to discover that the heat from her body was causing a stirring in my groin.

"Madame!" I broke away firmly this time and brushed past her. At that instant, Count Respighi rounded the corner on his little cat feet. I was certain from something in his manner that he had been listening.

"Ah, Dr. Balsano," he said. "We are awaiting you. Are you quite alright?"

"Fine, yes. Fine," I stammered. "Just going now."

The count stepped deftly around me and took Mrs. Hyde's elbow. "Now Eleanor," he said, "I believe it's time for your nap. You're getting a little unruly and you really must nap."

The poor woman crumpled. Her legs seem to go all at once, and the count had to support her limp body as he began leading her off in the other direction as one would lead a child. She stumbled along at his side, barely able to move her feet, bowing to his authority. She glanced back at me once and I thought she was crying, but I could not be certain. I went off in search of the smoking room before I could become further entangled in a bizarre situation.

I found my way back to the library, where I wished that I had the time and the solitude to peruse the hundreds of volumes that lined the walls, but the talk among the gentlemen was of war – or rather the impossibility of a European War, despite tensions on the continent. To a man, the financiers and physicians present blamed Prussian militarism and the German Kaiser Wilhelm for creating tensions. (No mention was made of my native Austria or the aging Emperor Franz-Joseph, but at least we were not blamed.) No sooner had I seated myself and declined a cigar than my host, Dr. Hyde, asked my opinion of the Kaiser and the situation in Europe. I hesitated, but I felt that I had to say something.

"The German Kaiser is not well-liked in Austria," I said,

"in fact he is generally despised as an ignorant lout, a braggart and a bully. But I don't believe that he alone is responsible for the tensions. The Czar in Russia, the Serbs, the French, the English – even the Italians are equally to blame. It seems that everyone wants something from someone else, usually territory."

Count Respighi joined us as I was speaking. The count, still holding the grey kitten captive in the crook of his arm, lit an enormous cigar and amused himself by blowing smoke in the kitten's face. The kitten would squint its eyes and bat at the smoke with its tiny paws, and the count would chuckle and blow more smoke in its face. Dr. Hyde asked the count what he thought of my statement.

"Of course Dr. Balsano is quite correct," Count Respighi said with a slight bow in my direction, "the Germans are not solely to blame for the difficulties in Europe. We must look at the Habsburg Empire of which Dr. Balsano is a dutiful subject. Your Emperor Franz Joseph knows very well that there are territories that ought by rights to belong to Italy, yet he stubbornly withholds them."

I could feel anger getting the best of me, but I asked politely which territories the count had in mind.

"Why, the Trento, of course," he said, with an airy wave of his cigar. "And Trieste, Fiume, the Alto Adige..."

The list of Austrian territories that should be handed over to Italy went on and on. When he finished, I remarked that Italy seemed to want the entire Habsburg Empire, at least as far as the borders of Hungary to the east and Greece to the south.

"Yes, yes," the count replied. "It's a legitimate claim. Historically, we Romans held all that and more."

"Roman?" I dared to ask. "From your accent, Count Respighi, I thought you were a Neapolitan."

There was a ripple of laughter in the room, and for an instant the count looked at me with such hatred that I thought he might inadvertently crush the poor kitten. He recovered quickly, however.

"All this is moot," he laughed. "There will be no European war in our lifetime. It is unthinkable, given the peak we have reached in the history of civilization. Our machines of war are too effective, our abilities to think rationally too advanced. We shall achieve agreement by diplomatic means, nothing more. Europe shall perhaps need an adjustment of its borders, but it shall all be done without the loss of a single infantryman."

"I hope you are correct, Count Respighi," I said. The talk moved on, from the horrible weather and the thickness of the ice on the St. Lawrence River (ice that threatened to delay the opening of the Montreal harbor by two weeks or more in the spring) to the steps being taken to avoid another Titanic disaster on the North Atlantic shipping lanes.

As the sun set and the fading light in the smoking room made it necessary to light more lamps, some of the men excused themselves and went in search of their wives. I rose to take my leave, but in an instant Count Respighi was at my elbow, saying that Dr. Hyde wished to have a private word with me before I left. The count led me to the doctor's private office, where I was left to peruse more works of art and the countless medical texts on the bookshelves. At last Dr. Hyde entered and asked me to take a seat opposite his beautifully carved desk.

For the next hour, we talked about medicine – what I had learned during my stay in Montreal, whether I was still determined to pursue a career as a psycho-analyst, what expertise I had developed in Vienna, what direction I saw for my work in medicine in the future. Before I left, Dr. Hyde surprised me with an offer.

"I know you intend to return to Europe after the university term ends in June," he said, "and we shan't try to stop you. However, I would like to offer you a permanent position on my staff, beginning in September. You would be one of three associate physicians working under my direction. In the future, there might be also the possibility of a professorship. I am working hard to persuade the directors that it is time to open a department of psychiatry within the McGill Medical School. If I succeed, you would have the opportunity to become a lecturer in the new department."

"I don't believe I am qualified, sir. I am still far too young."

"Not at all! We know your academic record, Dr. Balsano. You are considered a prodigy, with boundless potential, and you have one great advantage over the rest of us – you have been a staff assistant to Dr. Freud, you have attended his weekly *soirées* in Vienna, and you are able to discuss his work on the basis of an intimacy which none of us can claim."

"I can't claim any sort of intimacy with the doctor."

"He knows who you are? He calls you by name? You have worked with him directly?"

"Of course. But…"

"Then you are qualified to discuss his work."

"But I am not in agreement with a great many of Freud's ideas."

"Nor am I. But we need someone who can discuss his theories from your perspective. Please tell me that you will at least consider it. We can iron out the details later. The salary, I can assure you, would be far better than anything you would receive in Vienna, possibly through a chair that I will personally endow."

"I would be a fool not to consider such an offer," I said at last.

"That's all I ask. I am quite sure you will say yes in the end. It will be a delight to have a young physician of such intelligence and accomplishments on our staff." I felt neither intelligent nor accomplished, but if he wished to claim that I was both, it was not for me to dissuade him.

"I must fill the position, so I shall need your answer within a month," he went on. "Let's make it by St. Patrick's Day – the seventeenth of March. An easy date to remember."

After further pleasantries, the great doctor and the count escorted me to the entrance. All the other guests had departed and it was quite dark outside already. Waiting outside was a Peerless Model 48 limousine, complete with driver.

"My driver will see you home," said Dr. Hyde.

I wanted to refuse; I had planned to walk back to my lodgings. It was mostly downhill and I still needed to walk a certain distance every day to rehabilitate my injuries. Then I recalled the strict instructions I had received from Jem Doyle. I was not to wander about by myself, especially after dark. The foot man opened the door of the automobile, I said my goodbyes to Dr. Hyde and Count Respighi, and I was whisked home in luxury.

CHAPTER 15

I did not see Jem Doyle for a week, and when I did I described the luncheon at the Hyde Mansion only in the most general terms, but I did give Jem a detailed description of the conversation with Dr. Percival Hyde at which he had offered me a permanent position on his staff.

Jem winked at me. "Not for long will you be supping with the likes of Sophie and myself," he said. "Soon you'll have your own mansion up there on the hill, and we'll have to visit through the servants' entrance."

I bristled at that. "Never!" I said. "Even if I lived in a castle, you and Sophie would be honoured guests. And rest assured, I have eaten far better meals in the café than what was served at Dr. Hyde's mansion." Then I noticed the grin behind the mustache. Jem loved having his little laugh at my expense. Once he'd had his fun, the big detective turned serious.

""So which way is the wind blowing, lad?" he asked.

"Excuse me?"

"What do you think will come of it? Will you stay or will you go?"

"I have no idea. I had promised Papa I would be away for only a year. He's old and lonely. But even if I were in Austria, I would be working in Vienna, not in Bad Gastein. He has always envisioned me taking over his practice, delivering babies and setting fractured limbs from skiing accidents, but I have bigger ambitions."

"Is it a long journey, Vienna to Bad Gastein?"

"It's not really far, but it takes about six hours by train. You must travel west through Linz as far as Salzburg, then change trains for the journey south to Bad Gastein. It's far enough that during my student years I went home only at Christmas and during the summer breaks."

"Ah. Well, I'll not say a word to influence you one way or t'other, my boy. Just remember that family is the biggest ambition a man can have. The rest of it fades with time. I regret that I have no children of my own, only Sophie's six boys – but I'd not want to see any of the six of them on the far side of the world."

Jem tipped his empty beer stein in Sophie's direction, and she brought him a fresh ale. The interruption gave me time to think about what I wanted to say. By the time she had bussed her husband on the cheek and left, I had made my decision.

"I think I must remain here, at least for one more year," I said. "I don't know what else I could possibly do to help this investigation along, but I would go home with a clearer conscience if the men who killed Hanna Goss were behind bars. I'll return to Europe in June, as planned, but I'll return in late August. That will give me more than two months with Father. A generous span of time."

Jem raised his glass. "Here's to another winter freezing your arse in Montreal," he said.

I laughed. "It's a frigid place, indeed, but it grows on you."

"Like icicles on your mustache."

"I can't grow a proper mustache."

Jem raised his glass to that, leaving foam on his own elaborately grown mustache. As to the investigation itself, he had nothing to report. He had his hands full trying to catch a jewel thief responsible for a series of diamond thefts downtown, and he had little time to devote to a case that had been written off as a theft gone wrong. He did suggest one task with which I could occupy myself, which was to go back to all the Montreal newspapers published since Hanna had first arrived in Montreal and to read all the accounts of her concerts. Perhaps something in there might suggest a new direction for inquiry.

"There are a number of periodicals in this city, French and English," I pointed out. "That's a great deal of reading."

"Not necessarily," Jem said. "Every newspaper has what they call a morgue. Not like the sort of morgue where Good King works – a morgue where they keep clippings of every story they run. All you have to do is ask for the clippings pertaining to Hanna Goss and they'll hand you the lot. They're good chaps, most of them. And if any of them refuse, a word from me will suffice to open their files."

I thanked Jem and resolved to read through every file I could lay my hands on. Before I could begin the rounds of the city's newspapers, however, I decided that I had to visit the medical faculty at McGill. It had been some time since I put in an appearance, mostly because I was embarrassed to show my face before the bruises healed. When I did return, it occurred to me to speak with the secretary who had made the arrangements for Hanna to sing. She was a pleasant, cheerful person from the Canadian prairies who had helped me with all the arrangements when I first arrived. When I looked in on her, however, I found that she had been replaced by an older and more formidable woman. I introduced myself and asked where I might find Miss Ingrid Stevens.

"She was dismissed over the holidays," the woman snapped.

"May I ask why?"

"You may not. I am not at liberty to discuss such matters."

"Very well. In that case, can you tell me where I might locate her?"

"Why would you be interested in locating a person who has been dismissed from her position here?"

I decided to turn the tables on her. "I am not at liberty to say," I replied.

"I'm told that Miss Stevens has returned to her home

on the prairies," she said. "That's all I know. One of those god-forsaken places where they burn buffalo feces to keep warm, I suppose."

I tried to recall the names of Canada's prairie provinces. "Which one? Manitoba, Saskatchewan or Alberta?"

"One of those." She waved her hand dismissively. "Now if you don't mind, Dr. Balsano, I have work to do. I'm not about to waste my time fussing over an incompetent woman who has been sacked."

"Actually, she was terrifically competent," I felt compelled to say, "but I wish you a good day, Madame."

I bowed my way out. It was typical. It seemed that when it came to Hanna's death, every possible avenue of investigation turned into what the English call a blind alley. As I was about to leave the building, however, when a clerk from the department caught up to me at the door.

"I heard you asking about Ingrid Stevens," she said. "I was her best friend in Montreal. She has gone back to Saskatchewan, but here is her address if you wish to contact her."

The young woman, whose name I did not know, pressed a slip of paper in my hand and hurried back to the office. I glanced at the address, printed in neat block letters: Ingrid Stevens, C/O General Delivery, Mortlach, Saskatchewan.

Before the day was out, I had posted a letter to Miss Stevens in Mortlach, asking if she could enlighten me as to the circumstances under which the soprano Hanna Goss was hired to perform at the medical school reception in August. As a postscript, I added that I had always found her competent and helpful, and asked whether she would care to provide details of her dismissal from the department.

Over the coming weeks, I did as Jem suggested and visited the Montreal newspapers, one by one, asking to see their clip files relating to the life and death of Hanna Goss. Most were very helpful; the one or two newspapers where the staff was reluctant to provide clippings to the general public were quickly brought round by a call from Sergeant Detective Jem Doyle of the Montreal Police Force.

In some cases, I was able to purchase back copies of the newspapers, which I assiduously clipped and filed. Most of the stories I kept were reviews of her performances. The reviews were uniformly glowing; given what I knew of the tendencies of the press in Vienna, that was unusual in itself. Even the great Sarah Bernhardt received unfavorable notices from some publications when she spent a dozen nights performing before some of the most glittering crowds in Europe. Reviewers, as a group, were a dour, jealous lot, resentful of the applause bestowed on those who took to the stage, more resentful still of their rivals in the trade. If one reviewer lavished praise on a particular artist, you could be sure that his rival would find fault with the same artist, simply for the sake of disagreement.

No such rivalry seemed to interfere with the reception accorded Hanna Goss. She was young, she was fresh, she was marvelously talented. Her voice was heralded as a rare treasure, the emotion she poured into each number carried the audience away and occasioned tears even from hardened critics. One rapturous reviewer, who heard her at a performance devoted solely to the *lieder* of the composer Hugo Wolf (one of my father's favorites) said Hanna possessed a voice straight from heaven, and that the combination of her voice, Goethe's words and Wolf's compositions was unlikely to be rivaled in our time. She would be, another reviewer said, "an enduring star of the opera stage, destined to receive plaudits from the Metropolitan Opera to La Scala, from the Royal Opera House to the Bolshoi."

Reading such notices, I was moved to tears myself. So much had been lost when Hanna was murdered. All the thousands, tens of thousands of people who might have heard her sing, whose lives would have been enriched by that rare voice – that had been taken from us, and it could not be recovered.

The accounts of her death were uniformly alike, in

both French and English, and they added little or nothing to what I already knew. For a week or two, the murder had been big news. It had all the elements that attract the press – a beautiful and talented victim, nefarious murderers, a whiff of international scandal. But either the reporters weren't that enterprising or there wasn't much to be found, because the stories had a dreary sameness. It took me a while to realize what was behind it: they all quoted the same police officer, Cyril Leblanc, who emerged in story after story as a singularly dull-witted detective. When his clumsy investigations yielded nothing new, the newspapers lost interest and the story ran out of steam, faded from the front pages to the back, then vanished altogether. I was unable to locate a single story on the murder written in the month of February.

After struggling with a French dictionary to translate some of the items, and ruining my eyesight no matter what the language, I was on the verge of giving up when I came across one seemingly insignificant notice, not in the news pages but in the social pages of the Montreal *Gazette*. The newspaper was dated July 7, 1913, and the item concerned a performance Hanna had given at a "cottage" in North Hatley owned by an executive of the Canadian Pacific Railroad. The date of the performance was July 5, a Saturday. The newspaper provided a complete guest list, and the names of two couples caught my eye: Dr. Percival Hyde and his wife, Eleanor Hyde, and Count Ottavio Respighi and his wife, Countess Respighi.

I read the item three times to be sure I had not misinterpreted something, and checked again the date at the top of the page. When I had asked Dr. Hyde how it was that he came to hire Hanna Goss to perform at our reception, he said the arrangements had been made by the departmental secretary, and that he had no role in selecting the singer. Yet some seven weeks earlier, he and Count Respighi and their wives had attended a function in North Hatley at which Hanna had performed.

I tried to recall the details of that conversation with

Dr. Hyde. He had, after all, not denied any previous knowledge of Fraulein Goss, and it was entirely possible (given the attention guests at such functions tend to offer the performers) that he had not even noticed the singer on either occasion. Yet it was curious. Hanna had performed twice in a single summer at functions attended by both the count and the doctor, at a time when she was already something of a sensation in Montreal, and yet Dr. Hyde seemed to have barely taken note of her.

I decided that I would share this item with Jem Doyle. I was able to purchase three back copies from the newspaper, and I lugged all three back to my lodgings, where I tucked them away carefully at the bottom of my armoire.

LOVE & WAR
EUROPE 1914-1918

On the sixteenth of March, one day before Dr. Hyde's deadline, I visited his palatial office to inform him in person that I had decided to accept his generous offer to join his clinical staff and to lecture (provided I was permitted to express my skepticism) on Dr. Sigmund Freud at the medical school. I would sail for Europe in early May, because I had no real reason to remain in Montreal for the end of the term at McGill, but I promised to return to Montreal no later than the last week of August for the beginning of the next school year. While in Austria, I would attempt to meet with Dr. Freud in order to bring myself up to date on his most recent theories. It was possible that he would be too busy to meet, but I had always found the man very accommodating when it came to discussing his constantly evolving work.

When I went to announce my decision to Dr. Hyde, I was surprised to find Count Respighi in his office as well. Was Dr. Hyde never without his shadow, in the person of the corpulent count? I had to resist the impulse to wipe my hand on my trousers after shaking the man's tiny, moist hand. He had such an adverse effect on me that I wanted to plunge into a hot bath after every meeting in order to wash off the taint, and yet Count Respighi had given me no real reason for such an intense reaction. I wanted to ask why he was in attendance at the medical school: He had nothing to do with medicine, and you would have expected him to have his own offices with the Hyde Shipping Company, yet here he was.

In any case, both men greeted me in the friendliest manner, and Dr. Hyde expressed his delight that I would be returning to work with him. He even offered to secure a state-room for me on one of the Hyde Shipping Company vessels en route to Liverpool in May. I had to decline. I explained to him that Liverpool as a destination would be inconvenient for me, because I would then have to take the train at one of the ports on the English Channel and a ferry to Calais before boarding another train to Salzburg or Vienna.

I had other reasons for declining the offer, however. First, I imagined that on one of the Hyde ships I might be spied upon by one of Count Respighi's minions. He struck me as the sort of fellow who would spy on a man for no reason at all except to have information that he might be able to use in some way in the future. I could afford my own passage (that was one blessing of my father's post as spa doctor, where during the season he was paid exorbitant fees for looking after the largely imaginary complaints of the wealthy and powerful) and I had reasons for choosing another route to Europe.

Each fortnight, like clockwork, I received a letter from Rudi Mayr, the former agent to Hanna Goss. Mostly, the letters were simply a plea for me to keep him up to date on the investigation into her murder. I did so, within limits. I did not tell him all that I knew, I never betrayed anything Jem Doyle told me in confidence, and I didn't say anything that might give him false hope that we were about to solve the case. From Herr Mayr, however, I learned that Elise Duvernay, once hired as companion to Hanna, had remained in Cherbourg, where she was now companion to a wealthy heiress, and that she would be delighted to tell me all that she knew if I cared to return to Europe by way of Cherbourg so that we could meet face to face. I contacted Mlle Duvernay directly with a list of my questions concerning Hanna. I received a prompt reply, but the Frenchwoman declined to discuss my concerns by post. She would be pleased to oblige me but only if it were possible for us to speak in person. Her condition only piqued my curiosity, and I wrote back immediately saying that I would come to France to meet her on my return voyage to Bad Gastein –

after which I immediately booked passage to Cherbourg from Montreal.

I concluded my conversation with Dr. Hyde and Count Respighi without mentioning the performance they had both attended in North Hatley. I had no real reason to avoid the subject with them, but neither did I have a reason to share what I knew with them.

As spring came, there was a sense of emerging from a nightmarish winter in every sense, and, inevitably, a process of letting go of the mystery I was no closer to solving than I had been on the day Hanna was murdered. On April 19 it was 23 degrees, and I felt as though I had been released from prison. Karine and I went for a stroll on Mount Royal, and it seemed as though the entire city was out walking, faces up-turned to the sun, smiles everywhere. There were still dirty banks of snow everywhere you looked and you had to be on the lookout for the calling cards left by the city's numerous dogs as the snow melted, but the sun was shining and buds were full on the trees. I had never waited so long for the green-ery to reappear, but it promised to be a delightful show.

Karine had news for me: she was returning to Gmund am Tegernsee in Germany with her family and they were embarking for Hamburg a week before I left for Cherbourg. Gmund am Tegernsee was not more than two hundred kilo-metres from Bad Gastein, so we made vague plans to meet at some point during the summer months, and exchanged ad-dresses, but there was a sadness in her kiss when we said good-bye. I believe that Karine, an intelligent and sensitive young woman, understood by intuition that I could never give her the love she deserved. What she did not know was that the ties that bound me were to a dead woman.

When I returned to my chambers that day, I found a letter addressed to me from Saskatchewan. At first I was taken aback, until I recalled that I had sent an inquiry to Miss Ingrid Stevens, seeking to learn whether she had made the arrange-ments for Hanna Goss to sing at the reception. I read the following with great interest:

Dr. Balsano,

It is a pleasure for me to answer you and to provide what information I can. As I remember you quite well, simply because you have such beautiful manners. I think of them as "Old World" manners, although it may be only that you were exceptionally well brought up. So many of the medical students and the younger doctors I had to deal with are arrogant children; they come from wealth, for the most part, and they tend to treat persons such as myself as though we were clumsy chambermaids who had broken a vase. I did not at all understand the reasons for my dismissal; it was very abrupt and the circumstances were never explained to me in the least, although I was well compensated by way of severance.

Now, in reply to your question: Although it was one of my duties to plan all department functions, on this occasion I was told that either Dr. Hyde or his wife, Mrs. Eleanor Hyde, would take care of the arrangements. I had nothing to do with it. I did not contact the singer who performed that night, nor indeed had I ever heard her name until I read of her scandalous murder. I do not know who contacted her, or anything else about the details of that reception. Alas, I can tell you no more. I thank you again for your exemplary behaviour and I wish you well in all your endeavors.

Yours truly,

Ingrid Stevens

I pondered the letter from Miss Stevens for some time. I believed that she was telling the truth, but if that was the case, why would Dr. Percival Hyde tell me that she was responsible for hiring the entertainment for the reception? The only possible explanation was that he was quite busy, and that someone else had done the hiring – most likely his wife, Eleanor, since Miss Stevens said that Eleanor and Dr. Hyde were in charge of the arrangements. It would have been useful to pose the question to Mrs. Hyde, but I was in a great rush to prepare for my voyage back to Europe. I made a note myself to find a way to meet her and to make my inquiries when I returned to Canada in August. Meanwhile, I had to pack.

I did not wish to take all my things for a stay of three or four months in Europe, so with the help of two of my strongest fellow lodgers, I moved my heaviest trunk with all my winter things into the storage space in Mrs. Guterson's basement, a decision I would have cause to regret. I spent the last day before I left at a party in my honor at Sophie's Café. Sophie clung to me like a mother. "I feel like I am losing a son, Maxim," she said. "Please come back, safe and sound. And *write!* Do not forget us!"

"I could not forget you, Sophie. Or Jem, or your café. Ever. I will be back before you know it."

After that, we drank and danced and sang into the wee hours of the morning. I slept no more than two hours before Jem roused me for the drive to the port. Sophie rode in the rear seat of the Model T with my suitcases and Jem drove. On the way, he gave me the bad news he had avoided the night before, because he didn't ruin my party. "I'm afraid the investigation into the murder of Hanna Goss has been shut down. We're not to pry further, on pain of provoking the severe displeasure of the chief himself. The case is shut up tight: Murdered by unknown assailants. Motive: robbery, unsolved. Never mind that she was wearing a sable coat when they attacked her and it was still on the body when she was found. Some robbery."

"Why would they shut it down?"

"The excuse is that they don't want our time wasted on a case that can't be solved. The truth is that somebody don't want pesky detectives sticking their noses in. Somebody has something to hide and don't want the likes of us pokin' around. Even Cyril Leblanc is off the case, and they can lead him around by the nose like a pet poodle."

"But who has the power to do this? The mayor? The chief of police?"

Jem snorted. "Not the mayor. He dances to their tune. The chief as well, though half the time he's too drunk to follow what tune they're playin'. No, there's bosses in this town, Max. The big boys. They don't even bother to see the mayor in person, they just send a flunky over to give the mayor his orders. Then the same flunky pays a visit to the chief, whispers a word or two in his ear, hands him a bottle of good Scotch whiskey and a wink, and we're left to hold our peckers and whistle Danny Boy for all the good it will do us."

I didn't always follow Jem's brogue, but I got the sense of it alright. There was to be no more official investigation into Hanna's murder. But I knew Jem: He would be cautious, but he would pay no more attention to that directive than he would pay to the direction of the wind. Our investigation might be on hold for the summer, but I would be back in less than three months time, and I was determined not to let it rest.

I embraced Sophie one last time, accepted a rough hug from Jem that rattled my bones, and dragged myself up the gangplank to board the SS *Marsellaise* for the voyage to Cherbourg as one of the five hundred second-class passengers – sad to be leaving but anxious to be home and even more anxious to visit Elise Duvernay in Cherbourg. In half an hour there was a great blast of the ship's horn and the tugboats began easing us out into the river. I remained on the deck with many of my fellow passengers, waving until my arms grew tired and even Jem's tall, broad-shouldered figure vanished from sight. I had tears in my eyes, but I would have wept a great deal more had I known what was to come.

LOVE & WAR

EUROPE 1914-1918

CHAPTER 17

The wind was fair, the sea was calm, the daily excitement provided by schools of dolphins and flying fish, the occasional albatross, an enormous pod of right whales off the southern tip of Greenland. The company at dinner was witty and varied, the fare excellent, my cabin more than satisfactory, the Milky Way at night an enchanting blanket of stars. In other circumstances, I would have savored every moment of the voyage across the Atlantic.

Instead, I spent my time wishing there was a more rapid way to cross the ocean, and on the final day I was on deck from the moment the sun rose, straining my eyes, hoping for that first glimpse of the coast of France, so anxious was I to reach Cherbourg, to meet Elise Duvernay at last, and to learn what she might know. After all, during the final months of her life, Hanna had no close companion other than Elise. Her mother had remained in Vienna, Rudi Mayr was busy making tour arrangements, but Mlle Duvernay had shared her stateroom and her hotel room, helped her dress and to prepare for concerts, listened to any confessions she had cared to make, offered consolation when she was upset. Herr Mayr believed that it was impossible for Hanna to meet strangers during the tour, but I wanted to hear it from the only person who really knew. I also had some questions I wanted to ask Mlle Duvernay concerning Herr Mayr himself.

I knew that Mlle Duvernay had found employment as a companion to Madame Liais, a woman from a prominent Cherbourg family who made few demands on her apart from her companionship. Her only real tasks were to read to the lady and to accompany her on long morning walks. As the sea voyage came to an end, all I wanted was to Mlle Duvernay and to learn all that she could tell me about Hanna's life.

We debarked at the Transatlantic Maritime Terminal in Cherbourg, a wondrous Art Deco affair, and went through the mercifully brief customs formalities there. Without my heavy trunk, I had little to declare, only a few small gifts. Outside the terminal, I was able to hail a fiacre. I gave the driver directions to a small hotel, where I had reserved a room for a single week. I sent my card to Mlle Elise Duvernay as soon as I was settled, asking when it would be possible for us to meet. I was tired from the crossing and wanted to sleep, but my curiosity got the better of me. It was two o'clock in the afternoon and my legs longed to stroll on solid ground. I have always delighted in new places, and no sooner do I arrive in a place where I have never been (or even an old haunt revisited after a lapse of many years) then I must be out and about, exploring, inhaling the sights and sounds and odors of a new place.

I have always believed that there are two occasions when we humans are most alive: when we fall in love, and when we arrive in a foreign setting. Travel, like love, brings out our best, but to experience either fully, we must be open to all the new and unfamiliar sensations that bombard us. I have known people who travel because they must, and despise all they encounter that is either inconvenient or foreign to their senses, just as I have known individuals who marry because they feel they must, and despise every new thing they discover about the person whom they have chosen. For a traveler as for a lover, everything about the new world or the newly beloved stimulates the senses, excites the mind and gratifies our deepest desire, which is to be profoundly alive.

I wandered first along the promenade facing the Harbour, thrilling in the scent of the salt-sea air. As an Austrian, I had been landlocked most of my life: neither Bad Gastein nor Vienna is anywhere near the sea. During the voyage, I was constantly fending off seasickness, but in Cherbourg, with my feet on solid ground, I was free to revel in every sensation. It was a chilly, blustery day for that time of year, with low-hanging grey clouds fleeing inland from the sea, and the occasional gust of wind forcing me to close my eyes against the blowing sand. Nevertheless, I revelled in every step, and in the dark swells booming in from the sea.

After drinking in the sights, sounds and scents of the magnificent harbor, I turned my steps inland and, following no particular path, soon found myself at the Basilique Sainte-Trinité, a narrow but elegant Gothic structure, with beautiful stained glass windows and elaborately painted pillars in the nave. I could not be there without thinking of the last occasion when I had set foot inside a church, at St. James Cathedral in Montreal, for the infinitely sad funeral of Hanna Goss. It was on that same day that I had met with Herr Mayr at the Windsor Hotel, and received his account of Hanna's life, an account that had eventually brought me here, to this small city at the tip of the Cotentin peninsula in Normandy, in the perhaps forlorn hope that a young woman who had once been a companion to Hanna might shed further light on the events that had led to her death.

That thought cut short my visit to Sainte-Trinité. I retraced my steps back along the Harbor to the narrow street where my rather nondescript hotel was situated in mid-block. When I went to retrieve my key from the plump madame at the desk, I was handed a note on very fine stationery. I hastened up the stairs to my room and sat on the rather saggy brass bed to read it. It was from Elise Duvernay, written in surprisingly good English for a young Frenchwoman:

> Dr. Balsano,
>   I regret that I am unable to meet with you today. Ma-

dame Liais requires that I dine with her each evening, and that after dinner we read for some time before retiring for the night. However, according to our arrangement, I am free each day from one to four o'clock in the afternoon, when she takes her siesta. May I suggest that we meet at the statue of Napoleon Bonaparte near the Basilique Sainte-Trinité at a quarter past one tomorrow? I shall carry a parasol and a book so that you may recognize me.
Kind regards,
Elise Duvernay

I had just come from the Basilica, and I had barely taken notice of the rather grandiloquent statue of Bonaparte on horseback located almost directly outside the entrance. Even then, I was repelled by the statues of bellicose military men strewn all over the continent, celebrating these murderous old thieves who led tens of thousands of young men to violent deaths. Better to celebrate our scientists, our composers, our painters and sculptors and musicians. They represent the pinnacle of our civilization, not the generals who left such a trail of blood, sorrow and destruction in their wake.

I was eager to learn whatever Elise could tell me about Hanna, but I was also tired and famished and looking forward to a good night's sleep on a bed that was not rocking to and fro to the rhythm of the waves. After the sort of simple but exquisitely prepared meal you can find only in France and at Sophie's Café, I took another long walk that evening and retired early. The next morning I spent walking again and scribbling in my journal, and I was at the statue thirty minutes before the appointed time, pacing around it, finding that my disgust with Napoleon and all his works did not improve through closer acquaintance with his statue, then trying out various perspectives on the Basilique Sainte-Trinité to see which a painter might prefer.

I was still engaged in this activity when I noticed a young woman with erect bearing standing almost within the shadow of that bronze Napoleon. She wore a long dress the color of *café au lait,* trimmed on the sleeves and lapels with a shade like burgundy wine. On her head was perched a gay straw hat. She carried a parasol and a book, and she had a long braid of dark hair down her back. There was no other woman in sight, and we had reached the appointed time, so I approached her, removed my hat, and bowed. "Mademoiselle Duvernay?"

She extended her hand. "Dr. Balsano, a pleasure to make your acquaintance. I saw you looking at the *Basilique* from a number of angles, and I thought perhaps you were an artist."

"Alas, I am not. I would require the assistance of a five-year-old to draw a proper stick figure. But I do love architecture and the *Basilique* is a fine example."

I noted that the title of the book she carried was *Du côté de chez Swann,* by the French writer Marcel Proust. I had heard vaguely of the novel, which had been published the previous year, but I hadn't read it and I did not expect to see it under the arm of Mlle Duvernay. It was the first time she surprised me. It was not destined to be the last. As the young do when they meet an eligible member of the opposite sex, I took in many details at once. She was tall, taller than me (which is common, even among the female sex) and with a dark complexion, such as you might expect to see in a woman from Spain or Greece. The English, in that politely nasty way of theirs, would refer to as "plain." Her eyebrows were heavy, her nose rather too thick, her teeth uneven, her chin rather too strong for a woman. But the eyes – the eyes were what drew and held you. They were dark and frankly beautiful, lit by an unusual and sympathetic intelligence. I thought at once that we would be great friends, given half a chance, and that there was no one I would trust more if I were seeking a companion for a young woman traveling abroad. In that sense, at least, Herr Rudi Mayr had judged well. I guessed her to be not yet thirty years of age, enough older than Hanna to act as a chaperone.

After exchanging a few pleasantries, we strolled the length of the promenade along the harbor and back. By the end of that time, most of my conceptions about Hanna Goss, and especially her relationship with the impresario Rudi Mayr, had been altered significantly. It is said that witnesses to the same event will offer radically different versions of what they saw; so also will our impressions of a particular human being differ dramatically from one person to the next. You will hear someone spoken of as disagreeable and unpleasant to be near, and then you meet that person and you are surprised and charmed; or the opposite may occur. In this instance, I had taken away a generally favorable impression of Herr Mayr from our lengthy dinner in Montreal, although I was unable to quite let go the possibility that he might have been capable of Hanna's murder. When I mentioned to Mlle Duvernay how devoted Rudi had been to Hanna Goss, I received a cool glance in return.

After gazing out to sea for some moments as though deciding how much to confide in me, Elise posed a question of me instead. "Do you mind explaining to me first how you were drawn into all this? I understand that you are also Austrian, and that the two of you were both in Vienna at the same time, but how did you become so caught up in this investigation? Surely that is not a doctor's normal line of work?"

"It is not. And I shall be more than happy to tell you all that I know. I will not hold back. But I have waited such a long time to hear your story. Can you not first enlighten me as to what you learned during your time with Hanna? I am interested in her relationship with Rudi Mayr, especially the way he doted on her. He seems to feel that he created her from raw clay."

"I am sure that is how Herr Mayr saw the services he rendered to Mlle Goss," she said, "but what I saw was different. I was employed as a governess in Vienna when I first answered an advertisement for a companion to a young singer about to depart for a tour of North America. The children in my care were nearly grown and no longer had need of a governess, and I longed for adventure. I thought the position would be perfect for me, and Mlle Goss and Herr Mayr seemed to feel the same, because I was hired on the spot.

"From the beginning, I found Hanna in a very nervous condition. Understandably so. She had never really traveled, and here she was, about to set off on a voyage to another continent, a mysterious place where she would be expected to perform at her best while constantly on the move from city to city and concert hall to concert hall, always in unfamiliar settings and with unfamiliar orchestras and conductors. She had never been farther than one hundred kilometres from Vienna, she had never been away from her mother for more than a night, she had never performed outside Austria. So there was an obvious reason for her nervousness, but she seemed in such a constant state of anxiety that I thought there might be another cause. As I got to know them better, I concluded that the real source of her unease was her manager, Herr Mayr.

"You met him, surely you noticed that he is a very nervous man. Nervous and driven – obsessed, actually. And Hanna had the misfortune to be the object of his obsession, not in the romantic sense, but in the sense that her career was the entire focus of his energy, even though he represented many other clients. To be around him is enough to induce a state of agitation, but when you are his constant focus, as poor Mlle Goss was from the start, it is something more serious. I could see her flinch each time he knocked at the door, feel her cringe whenever he began to list all the tasks and obligations she would face in Canada and the United States, sense the way she recoiled at his habit of always crowding too near her person.

"Gradually, Hanna began to confide in me. From the start, she had never wanted anything more than to sing for the pure joy of singing. She would have been quite content never to have ventured onto the stage. Left to her own devices, I think, no one but her family and friends would ever have heard her sing. You can say that would have been a waste of the extraordinary gifts she had as a singer, but it would also have resulted in a far happier life for Hanna.

"I know that is not how Herr Mayr sees it. He believes that he had to restrain her, that she was very keen to have a spectacular career on all the stages of Europe, but I can assure you, that was not the case. The truth is that she was pushed, and pushed hard, by Herr Mayr. I have no doubt that he appreciated her talent, but Hanna had the potential to garner international fame. Had she succeeded, she would have considerably enhanced both Herr Mayr's prestige and his wealth. Hanna really should have spent at least another two years touring in Europe before visiting the United States, but such is the wealth of America that in cities like Boston, Philadelphia and (especially New York) she was able to command fees that were many times higher than she might have earned in Vienna or Budapest or Milan.

"Rudi never let her forget it for an instant. He was constantly at her, hounding her about rehearsals and concerts and possible future bookings and recording sessions. I can attest that he visited her hotel rooms and her stateroom aboard ship many times a day, always bursting in with papers to be signed, concert schedules, rehearsal schedules – always the schedules. It was as though he couldn't bear to allow her a quiet moment to herself. No wonder the young woman was a mess of nerves, with such a creature hovering about day and night.

"As a result, by the time we reached Quebec, Mlle Goss was not well. I would wake in the night and find her standing at the porthole in her shift, staring out at the darkness. I knew that she was homesick, that she wanted more than anything to simply cut all this short and return to Vienna, but she felt she could not disappoint Herr Mayr. When I found her like that, I would take her back to bed, and crawl into bed with her, the poor thing shaking like a leaf, and at last she would fall asleep with me stroking her hair and holding her tight. Still, she did not sleep enough, she did not eat enough, she was losing weight and losing her strength, and I feared for her voice."

When she paused to gather her thoughts, I took the opportunity to remark on an incongruity I had noted in her version of events and those I had received the day of Hanna's funeral. "Herr Mayr told me that she was virtually never out of your sight," I said. "He thought that perhaps she had become involved with another person, but he did not understand how it might have been possible, when she had little time to herself."

"That is untrue, although I can understand how he might have thought that. There was a degree of deception involved. And a degree of self-deception on his part, I think, because he was never quite as attentive as he thought."

"What do you mean by deception?"

"We were deceiving the man, Hanna and I," she said. "Midway through the voyage, I spoke to her of my concerns. She was too nervous, she needed to get more sleep, she wasn't eating properly, she wasn't taking care of herself. I told her frankly that I was afraid for her well-being, and that I felt we had to act."

"How did she react?"

"She collapsed in tears. She buried her face in my shoulder, she called me her greatest friend in the world, she thanked me for noticing that things with her were not as they should be. But she also begged me not to inform Herr Mayr. She was mortally afraid that he would think her ungrateful, or that he might believe she was not up to the tour. She knew that he had put himself out for her, and she did not want to disappoint. It's been my observation that women often behave thus: they would rather suffer themselves than disappoint a man who has in some way believed in them. There was no romantic connection whatsoever between her and Herr Mayr, their relationship was entirely a business relationship, yet she did not want to disappoint the man."

"Herr Mayr does give the impression that he might have a nervous collapse if you were to let him down in any serious way."

"In any case, Hanna did eventually begin to see a doctor in Montreal. She did not say what manner of doctor he was,
nor did I ever hear his name, then or later. I didn't press her
terribly hard on the point. I thought it a good thing that she
was seeing someone who might help her, and I left it at that. I
don't know why she never told me the name of the person who
was treating her; I thought at the time it was a little odd, but I
never raised the issue. Now I very much regret that I indulged
her, but at the time it seemed the right thing to do. Do you
agree, Dr. Balsano?"

"I do. Part of the difficulty with any nervous condition
(or mental illness, if you will) is that a stigma is attached to
it, and thus the person suffering is afraid to seek help, for fear
they will be singled out as fit only for the madhouse. She told
you that she was undergoing treatment, but perhaps it was
difficult for her to divulge more than that."

Mlle Duvernay agreed. "That was my fear exactly. I did
not want to add to the burdens Hanna already felt, quite the
opposite."

We walked along in silence for a time, watching the sea
and the wheeling gulls. She began to say something, but as she
did, a noisy automobile went past. I leaned in closer to hear
what she was saying, and I detected a faint but enthralling
scent that instantly conveyed me to an August evening on the
lawn of a mansion in Montreal.

"Mlle Duvernay," I said, "pardon me for asking an intrusive question, but could you tell me the name of the scent you
are wearing?"

She smiled. "You noticed? It is a perfume by Jacques
Guerlaine. Quite new, actually. It is called l'Heure Bleu for that
time at dusk when it is neither day nor night."

"It's enchanting. I seem to recall that Hanna was wearing it the night we talked after she sang – and again at my lodgings. Very faint on the second occasion, but even after she had
left, the scent lingered."

"It does. That is part of the loveliness. Someone gave it to Hanna as a gift. Two bottles of the perfume, two bottles of the eau de cologne. It was not like her to keep such things to herself, so she gave one of each to me. I could never afford such a scent, so I use it only a tiny drop at a time."

"I am grateful to you for enlightening me," I said. "It is well-named, this perfume. L'Heure Bleu. Scent has an odd power. It can erase time. It transports you to another time as none of the other senses do. A familiar scent, and you are overcome with nostalgia. Have you noticed?"

"I have. And it's quite true. Each time a drop of this perfume touches my skin, I am again with Hanna. She is still vital and filled with talent, the future stretches in front of us like a magic carpet, all is well."

We looked away from each other, both troubled by the same bitter thought, of Hanna's future, the hours, days, months and years that had been snatched away from her, by a person or persons unknown. To hold the most painful memories at bay, I brought us back to the topic we had been discussing when I caught the scent of l'Heure Bleu. "So she began seeing this doctor?"

"Yes, she began seeing him in Montreal, three afternoons a week. They were booking a very heavy schedule because she had to prepare for her American tour, but that was good for her – she became lighter, less worried. Then something else happened. I am ashamed to say this of the dead, Dr. Balsano, but I fear it is true and it may be important to your investigation. I believe that she took a lover."

"A lover!"

"I believe so. She claimed that she was having still more appointments with this doctor, but they were at irregular intervals. Early in the morning, late in the afternoon. It was all very unpredictable and I don't believe doctors work that way, do they?"

"Not at all," I responded. "We are the most predictable of men. Of necessity. There are always too many patients, too many demands. We must schedule ourselves very tightly. There is rarely time to see patients at odd hours."

"That is what I thought. She never confessed it to me, but I could tell by the state she was in when she returned to our room. Her face flushed, her hair mussed, the buttons on a dress not properly aligned. One afternoon when she returned to the hotel and began to change for her concert, I noticed that her shift was on backwards. I knew she had not left the hotel with it in that state, because I had helped her dress. With these irregular hours, it became harder and harder to hide her absences from Herr Mayr. But she was eating again, she was sleeping better, she seemed to be bubbling with happiness. I felt less worried for her, but at the same time I wondered about the lover, although I understood why she would keep him a secret. If he knew she had a lover, Rudi would not have taken it well. And I believe it may have been a tenor with whom she performed in Montreal. A handsome young fellow, but to Rudi, that would have been absolutely forbidden. He often said that affairs among cast members can destroy an opera company – or a young singer's career!"

"May I ask the name of this tenor?"

"He is André Lafleur. Handsome, dark, robust. Very attractive to women, I think. Well-known in Montreal but not outside the city, I believe."

I made a note of the name. I would ask Jem Doyle to pay a call on M. Lafleur to see if there was any information to be gained from that quarter.

I pondered what she had told me, watching the gulls turn frantic and descend in squadrons as a child tossed bits of bread into the water. "You are absolutely certain she had a lover?" I asked, trying to stifle any note of jealousy in my voice.

"I am. There were three nights when she did not return to the room at all until shortly before dawn. Very rash behaviour, given Rudi's need to control her life. The first time it happened, I spent a sleepless night, and we had words when she returned. I told her that I had been on the verge of summoning the police to report her disappearance, and in that event it would have been impossible to hide her absence from Herr Mayr. On the latter two occasions, she informed me in advance that she would not return until morning. I know that I ought to have been less accepting of her behaviour, but she had been so very unhappy and now she was so very happy. It would have been wrong to interfere. Knowing Hanna as I did, I am certain she would not have become involved in an affair had she not assumed that she would eventually marry this person. Hanna was not a person to do anything in a light or casual way. She put her heart into loving, just as she put it into her singing. If Rudi had not been so obtuse about such things, he would have noticed: she was radiant."

We found a small café at the end of our walk, took a table facing the sea, and ordered (appropriately, given the book she was reading) tea and madeleines. It was a fair day, much milder than the day my ship docked in Cherbourg, and we sat contentedly, sipping our tea and watching the passersby. We chatted about other things for a time, the tensions in Europe, my father, what I planned to do on my return to Montreal, and then I asked her opinion on a question that had been troubling me.

"I want to ask you about Rudi," I said. "He did a very odd thing when we dined together in Montreal. He was talking about how angry he was with Hanna after she canceled the rest of her tour. He mimed the gesture of strangling her – and at that moment, from the expression on his face, I thought he might be capable of doing such a thing."

Mlle Duvernay did not answer immediately. She replied with care. "I think we are all capable of murder in the right situation. Given enough stress, the means, whatever it takes to bring a human to such an extremity. When she first told Rudi that she was abandoning the tour, he was so angry I thought he might do something terrible. His face turned almost black, he paced back and forth, waving his arms and shouting at her. Rudi carries an elegant walking stick. He took it up and for a moment, I thought he was going to strike her with it – then he brought it down, broke it over his thigh, threw the splinters aside, and stormed out. In ten minutes he was back, begging her to forgive him for this display of temper. Hanna was very upset and she did not want to talk to him, and when he grabbed her by the arm, I'm afraid she slapped him quite hard. She never looked it, but she was a strong young woman. Rudi was black with anger and I feared the worst, but I was able to get between them and persuade him to leave.

"Rudi had a fearsome temper, but could he have battered her face to the point where she was unrecognizable? I don't know. With men who regularly lose their temper, it's impossible to say. He threw tantrums I found quite frightening, especially coming from such a seemingly mild little man, but that is well short of murder. If he killed her, he would have destroyed a woman that might have earned a great deal of money for him, but perhaps he knew she would never work with him again and he had nothing to lose."

I had to agree. Elise Duvernay knew the man and the situation far better than I did. I had the sense that Herr Mayr, although a man of keen intelligence, was not half so perceptive as Elise Duvernay – certainly not where Hanna was concerned. He had failed to see what was ailing her, or indeed that she was ailing at all, and hadn't noticed that he was the direct cause of the nervous condition that had driven her to seek help in Montreal. He was hardly the first man to refuse to see what was in front of his face (especially when it came to dealing with the opposite sex) and he would not be the last. But Herr Mayr's dealings with a fragile young singer, and the violence with which he treated her,

might have led to catastrophic consequences.

My thoughts went back to my chosen profession: If I wished to learn how to heal the human mind, I would have to display a sensitivity and a sagaciousness in dealing with patients; qualities I was not at all sure that I possessed. Elise Duvernay, on the other hand – Elise should have become a psycho-analyst. She had the rare gift of instinctive perception. On the basis of our very brief acquaintance, I knew already that I had much to learn from this astute Frenchwoman.

CHAPTER 18

I should happily have spent the evening with Mlle Duvernay, but the hour had come for her to return to the company of her employer, Mme Liais. The elderly woman, I was told, was not strict about much, but punctuality was something of an obsession with her, and she would be miserable for a week if her schedule was thrown off by as much as ten minutes. We still had much to discuss (I had told her virtually nothing of what I had learned from my investigations in Montreal) so we made plans to meet the following day at the same hour, again at Napoleon's statue. I must confess that I watched her walk away, intrigued by this self-possessed woman with the long braid striding along the quay with such insouciance. I had left one exceptional female in the young German Karine, and met another wonderful friend in Elise – or so I hoped, because I did not wish to presume that we would be friends, although I sensed it already.

Back in the hotel before dinner, I found a comfortable writing desk in the lobby, complete with stationery and a fountain pen, and began a longish letter to Jem and Sophie, telling them of my voyage to Cherbourg and of the perception Elise Duvernay had of Hanna Goss and her relationship with her manager, Herr Rudolf Mayr. I thought it very significant that he had threatened Hanna, and I emphasized that Mlle Duvernay's understanding of the situation differed so dramatically from that expressed by Herr Mayr during our conversation at the Windsor Hotel in Montreal. I told Jem that I was unaware of Herr Mayr's whereabouts at the moment, but that if he should return to Montreal, there was surely reason enough for Jem to question him. I filled several sheets of paper recapitulating what I had learned from Mlle Duvernay, and I asked Sophie to please kiss all her children for me, and I asked Jem to write at his earliest convenience, in care of my father's address at Bad Gastein, to enlighten me on any further developments in the investigation in Montreal.

The letter posted, I noticed an elegantly dressed older man in a cream-colored suit and a scarlet cravat seated not far from me, playing chess against himself on a small portable chess board he carried with him. He was tall and very lean, with flowing white hair and what was called a Van Dyke beard (after the 17th century Flemish painter) and when he sat back to survey the board after putting himself in check, I happened to catch his eye. He smiled and gestured to the board, inviting me to play. I knew myself to be a clumsy and inadequate chess player, but I had spent many pleasant evenings in Bad Gastein thrashing about on the board in the company of my father and his friends, two of whom ranked as chess masters, and I accepted his invitation more for his company than for the game. He bowed and extended his hand. The initial conversation we had was almost comically European, as we switched from Italian to English to German and back to Italian.

"*Bon soir, monsieur. Sono Signore Fulgencio Traversini,* at your service ..."

I switched to Italian. *Buonasera, signore. Sono Dottore Maxime Balsano.*"

"*Ah! Sei Italiano!*"

"*No, sei austriaco.*"

"*Ah, si, si. Vengo da Bolzano. Bozen.*"

"*Vengo da Bad Gastein! Siamo vicini di casa. Scusami. Il mio italiano non è migliore. Parli tedesco?*"

"*Si, si... Ich kenne Bad Gastein sehr gut. Ich ging dort wandern, als ich ein Student war.*"

And so on. Unlike Montreal, where the French and English factions seemed almost to take pride in refusing to learn the other's language, in that section of Europe where empires collide, it seemed completely normal to switch languages from one speaker to another, from sentence to sentence, even from word to word. After a few such pleasantries, Signore Traversini suggested that he would play the black pieces. I bent over the table, made my moves only after careful consideration, and was mated in a dozen moves. I switched to black, essayed the King's Indian Defense with which I was somewhat familiar, and managed to survive for perhaps twenty moves, although my fate was sealed after ten.

"Perhaps you are tired," Signore Traversini suggested. "I believe it is only today that you arrived, is that correct?"

"No, I arrived yesterday. In the afternoon. But I was not about much."

"Ah. So it is. And you came by sea?"

"I did, thank you. From Montreal."

"Ah, yes. I understand it is pleasant but very cold. Alas, I have never been able to visit. Perhaps you will join me for dinner? I would like to learn more of this Montreal."

I bowed my acceptance. Nothing (except perhaps to dine with Mlle Duvernay) would have pleased me more. Signore Traversini had the superb manners of another age, and the air of a man who has read many books. I was certain I would enjoy his company. We moved to the dining room, where we were seated in a spot near the window. Signore Traversini said that he would order, because he had been two weeks at the hotel already and knew the menu thoroughly.

On his recommendation I had first a light *sole meuniere* with parsley and lemon as a first course, washed down with a glass of Chablis. Then he ordered a filling *pot au feu* with potatoes for two, with a rich Burgundy. We finished with a Calvados and cheese and then, against my better judgment, a second Calvados. The food was splendid, the company even better. Signore Traversini explained was a poet and a professor emeritus of literature at the University of Perugia. He had traveled widely, read more widely still – and gained wisdom from his travels and his reading, which is not always the case.

"I hope you will not draw the wrong conclusion from the fact that I am both Italian and a poet," he said. "I assure you that I am not in the least like that bombastic fraud Gabriel D'Annunzio. I am a mere cobbler of words; I have no wish to set fire to the world."

"I should like very much to read your work, Signore. I haven't much time for poetry, but I do enjoy reading Heinrich Heine and Rainer Maria Rilke when I have a few hours to myself."

"Excellent choices. If you wish to read my work, I shall have a book sent to your room. My collections are slender; it is no burden to carry them with me."

"*Mille grazie, signore.*"

"*Prego.* Perugia is a lovely city. You must visit some day to see the Etruscan gates. I will be your guide. Eight or nine months a year, you will find me in Perugia. Summers, when it's hot, I travel north to my ancestral home in Bozen. Bolzano – almost your namesake. If you can't make it south as far as Perugia, you must visit me in Bozen, although I can't promise scenery more beautiful than you will see in Bad Gastein."

We exchanged cards. I apologized because the only permanent address I had was in Bad Gastein, but I assured him that I could always be reached through my father's address. Signore Traversini asked many questions about my background, my home, my father, my time in Vienna and Montreal, my future as a physician.

On the whole, he was a circumspect, softspoken man. Only once did he reveal something personal about himself: He was in the hotel, he said, because he had an assignation with a young woman of fifty.

"I am eighty-two," he said. "There are many years between us, but it is a great love nonetheless, the last of a full and fulfilling life. Unfortunately, she is chained to a brute of a husband many years younger than herself. She was to meet me here when she is able to escape, but I fear she has been detained. I may have to return to Italy and challenge the man to a duel."

I raised my eyebrows at that. "I jest," he said. "I'm afraid I'm past the age for dueling – but not past the age for lovemaking."

We left that romantic subject to discuss the world at large, specifically the Italian irredentists of whom Gabriele D'Annunzio was merely the most repugnant example. These were the very noisy nationalists who wished to expropriate great swathes of the Habsburg empire for Italy. As I suspected, Signore Traversini was not in sympathy with men like D'Annunzio and Count Respighi.

"The irredentists are fools," he said. "Virtually all the lands they want are more German than Italian – or Slovenian, or Croatian. Every day it is something new. They want the Trento, the Alto Adige, Trieste, Fiume... They want, they want, they want. And they would be happy to sacrifice any number of the lives of other men to get what they want."

I told him about my conversation with Count Respighi in Montreal, when the count had presented the grocery list of Austrian territories to be handed over so that there would not be conflict between our nations. My companion chuckled at that. "They always assume it will be so easy," he said. "They forget that we are dealing with an armed and powerful empire. You don't simply demand something and have it handed to you. Much blood would be spilled before a square metre of Austrian land became Italian."

It occurred to me then that this cultivated Italian might know something of the count who had made such an unfavourable impression on me. "Perhaps you know of an Italian individual I encountered in Montreal," I said, "Count Ottavio Respighi. A man in his late forties, I believe. Very large and very heavy. Claims to be Roman, although from his accent I think he may be Neapolitan."

"I have heard of a young composer named Respighi," Signore Traversini replied. "I believe he is from Bologna. I have not heard his work performed, but he is quite esteemed."

"Count Respighi has nothing to do with music, except that he dances very well for so bulky a man," I said. "He resides in Montreal at the moment."

"I don't believe I have heard of your Count Respighi," he said, "but that does not mean he does not exist. We Italians manufacture counts the way we make wine. What we lack in quality, we make up for in quantity when it comes to our nobility, such as it is. Too many are noble in title, rather less noble in deed. Respighi's title may be centuries old, or he may have acquired it when he had new visiting cards made up. Count Respighi... Count Respighi. There was someone of that name involved in a tragedy," he said. "Count Respihi and a young Englishman man who was his friend. The count came to his rescue in some way. Some Englishmen on a yacht somewhere in Italy – Lake Como, perhaps? A person was washed overboard and drowned, there were suggestions of foul play, the count stepped in... Please excuse me, I cannot tell you more. The difficulties of an aging mind. I can recall the names of all my classmates when I was nine years old, but I cannot remember where I had breakfast this morning."

"The Englishman who was his friend, could that be Dr. Percival Hyde?"

Signore Traversini shrugged. "It may be, or it may be something else entirely. I cannot recall. It was one of those scandals that blew up quickly and vanished just as quickly, and though my mind is still alert enough for chess, I do forget things."

"Do you recall approximately when it happened?"

He stroked his beard and gazed out the window, as though looking into a past that was, for him, a very long time. "I believe it would be around 1900," he said. "The turn of the century, as they say. That would be it. Perhaps a year before or a year after. I can recall no more."

I thanked him. By the time we finished our second Calvados, it was nearly eleven o'clock and my companion was anxious to get to his bed. I promised to dine with him again before I boarded the train for home, and he insisted on paying for the meal.

As it happened, we were unable to dine together again. When I opened the door the next day, I found a nearly wrapped package addressed to Herr Doktor Maxim Balsano. I opened it and there was a slender volume of poems by Amedeo Traversini, titled *La donna delle rose*. Inside, it was beautifully inscribed to me. I read a few poems, but alas, my Italian was not quite up to the complexity of his verses – although it was clear that he was a serious poet, with an ear for the beauties of the Italian language. I hoped to be able to thank him at breakfast, but he was not there, so I wrote a note of thanks and sent it to the room of Signore Traversini. When next I saw him, he was arm in arm with a buxom blonde woman of fifty who clearly doted on him. He raised his walking stick, gave a slight bow, and winked at me as we passed, but as he did not pause to make the introductions, I gathered that he wished to keep to himself and said no more. His paramour, I guessed, had been able to elude her brute of a husband. We were to meet again, under very different circumstances, but I did not encounter them again during my stay in Cherbourg.

Signore Traversini had raised the question of Count Respighi's background, and now I was genuinely troubled. What sort of scandal had involved a Count Respighi and an Englishman (who may or may not have been Dr. Hyde) and was it the same Count Respighi I met in Montreal? Dr. Hyde, of course, was Canadian – but he had been educated in England from the age of eight, he had a pronounced English accent, and he would have been taken as English by anyone who met him.

I wanted to mention it to Mlle Duvernay when we met at Napoleon's statue, but I refrained. However repugnant I found Count Respighi, whatever scandals lay in his murky background, he had nothing to do with the fate of Hanna Goss. Instead, I spent my second afternoon with Hanna's former companion telling her what I had been able to learn about

Hanna's death. What shocked her most was that the cause of death was some very slender object that had pierced her heart.

"So it was quite deliberate, then?"

"I believe it was. I have the word of the coroner, and I saw the wound myself. I don't believe one receives such a wound by accident."

Mlle Duvernay bit her thumb as she walked, a gesture I had noted previously: it meant she was thinking. "That means someone wanted her dead," she said.

"I believe so."

"Did you tell this to Herr Mayr?"

"I did not."

"How did you come to learn of this?"

I told her then about the friendship I had struck up, quite by accident, with Sophie Szitva and her common-law husband, Sergeant Detective Jem Doyle, and how Jem had been able to open doors for me I could never have opened for myself, especially the door into the morgue. Then I came to the most difficult part: I told her about the nocturnal visit I had received (or thought I had received) from Hanna on the night of her murder.

"I was very ill and feverish," I said, "and of course it was very improper of me to have her in my lodgings. But I was too weak to say no, and in any case I was very sympathetic to her and there was no one about to know that she was there. The impression I had was that she was utterly terrified; I don't believe I have ever seen anyone so frightened. Sometime after, two men, one very large and one very short, came pounding on the door to the apartment building. I was able to get rid of them by saying that I was quarantined with typhoid. I happened to vomit just then, which made the lie more believable. They left, but Hanna was still terrified. I am quite sure she was still there at three or four o'clock in the morning, but when I woke to find sunlight streaming into the room, she was gone. She had left behind a note, begging my forgiveness."

"May I see the note?" Mlle Duvernay asked. "I can confirm whether it is in her handwriting."

"Unfortunately, the note was taken. I came home one frigid night to discover that my window was wide open and the note was gone. It had been taken off my table."

Elise gave me a long, appraising glance. I could see what she was thinking: it was quite a story, a nocturnal visit from a ghost and the thief in the night who conveniently stole the note, so that there was no way of confirming that Hanna had ever been there. I was asking her to take a great deal on faith.

Something in my open, rather naive countenance must have convinced her, because she gave a brisk nod and said, "I believe you. But I don't believe in ghosts, so the detective who was investigating her death must have gotten the time of death wrong."

"I believe that is possible," I said. "Jem says that detective, Cyril Leblanc, is the most incompetent on the force. Leblanc still believes the murder was simply a robbery gone wrong, even though the sable coat she was wearing was not stolen."

"The sable coat!" Mlle Duvernay said.

"Excuse me?"

"The sable coat. I had forgotten it entirely. The coat arrived at her dressing room one night after a performance in Montreal, with a single red rose, a few nights after she received the perfume, also with a single rose. There was no note, but Hanna seemed to know who had sent it, although she would not tell me. She was blushing and she appeared to be acutely embarrassed that I had seen it. She loved the coat, however. She loved to lie in it, even when she was in bed. It is not difficult to believe that she would have put up a fight if someone tried to take it from her. It was the most valuable thing she owned."

"Presumably a gift from her lover?"

"Perhaps. Or an extravagant admirer who wished to *become* her lover."

Mlle Duvernay paused to admire year-old triplets in a pram, out for a stroll seaside stroll with their nanny. She and the young woman exchanged a few words about health and diapers while I walked on a little. When she caught up to me, she asked about Cyril Leblanc.

"How could a person as incompetent as this man be a police detective?".

"I have no idea. I know there is corruption in Montreal. But there are incompetents in all walks of life, even medicine. In any case, he's no longer in charge of the investigation, because there *is* no investigation."

Mlle Duvernay came to an abrupt halt. "No investigation? What are you saying?"

"Jem says the investigation has been called off. The police chief claimed that it was a waste of manpower, and that it was simply an attempted robbery gone wrong."

"But we know that's not true! Hanna was murdered! It was no accident."

"I believe you are right, and Jem would agree. He will go on probing, but he has to be careful. He could be dismissed from the force if he steps on the wrong toes. But a new mayor was elected in April, a chap named Médéric Martin. There was an inquest five years ago, and Martin was accused of misusing public funds. Now he's back."

"What a place!" Elise said. "Blocking murder investigations, stealing from the public. I thought only Europe could be so corrupt. You are returning to Montreal in August, Dr. Balsano?"

"Yes, late August."

"You must find a way to keep this investigation alive. Perhaps a journalist, someone to put pressure. Insist that the men who killed Hanna be found and punished."

"I will try. I must."

"Thank you. I don't believe I will sleep well until I know these men have been caught. It is so horrible, so horrible. Such a violent world, doctor. We must learn where Hanna was."

"Excuse me?"

"If we knew what happened to Hanna when she vanished, we would have the killers. I'm sure of it. Where did she go? Herr Mayr hired a detective and still he could not find her."

"I don't believe he was a very efficient detective."

"Nonetheless." Mlle Duvernay fixed me with that intelligent, unwavering gaze. "*We* must be efficient. I wish I could be there. It is maddening not to be able to act. But a woman alone, without a fortune at her disposal, there is little I can do."

"You can use your mind," I said. "It seems to be a smoothly functioning instrument. Anything you can remember, anything you can suggest. I will give you my address in Bad Gastein. When I return to Montreal, I will keep you informed."

"Please. Please do. I couldn't bear it otherwise." She turned away and reached into her bag, then handed me a beautifully wrapped gift.

"I have something for you," she said simply. "Please accept this as a token of my thanks."

I looked at her quizzically, then opened the little package with care. Inside were two ten-inch discs containing concert recordings from the Deutsche Gramophone company. One was a recording of Hanna Goss singing the Hugo Wolf lieder "Vergeborgenheit", the other the "Caro Nome" from *Rigoletto*.

"Hanna made these in a studio in Vienna two months before we left for Canada," Elise said. "Only a few copies were made, because she was not yet well known. They are about three minutes long on each side, but you will need a gramophone on which to play them. The quality is quite good, if you wish to hear her voice."

I was all but speechless. "I am so very grateful," I said. "It never occurred to me that recordings might exist. Thank you, Elise. Thank you profoundly. But surely you don't want to part with your copies?"

"I have others. Hanna gave me three copies of each recording. I will keep the others."

I had tears in my eyes. "I can't imagine... her voice. I will be able to hear her voice!"

"You will. And it is a very beautiful voice, even on a recording."

"Why did Herr Mayr not tell me about these?"

"Perhaps he forgot to mention them? Or perhaps he wanted to keep his copies for himself? After news of her murder appeared in the newspapers in Vienna, the remaining copies of the discs sold very quickly."

"I will never forget this, Mlle Duvernay. I will treasure these forever and guard them with my life."

She touched my arm. "I know you will. That is why I wished to give them to you."

CHAPTER 19

The hour had come for Elise Duvernay to return to caring for Madame Liais. I bade her a fond farewell. I might have lingered a while in Cherbourg, but my poor old father would be waiting anxiously in Bad Gastein, and I had a long journey ahead. I walked to the train station to make the arrangements, and found a round little man with thick spectacles who was very helpful. I purchased a ticket for the Paris train departing at six o'clock the next morning; it would take me from Cherbourg to the Gare du Nord in Paris, and three days after, I would board another at the Gare de l'Est, bound for the München Hauptbahnhof. I could not fail to see Paris. I had never been there, and it was impossible to say when I might return. I found a modest pension near the train station and spent three happy days tramping the streets, gazing up at the tour Eiffel, wandering the Rive Gauche, marveling at the gargoyles atop Notre Dame.

As it happened, my last day in Paris was June 5, 1914 – my twenty-fifth birthday. I could not think of a better place to celebrate a birthday. Like Vienna but on a grander scale, Paris was the symbol of a supremely confident Europe, where the possibilities of human existence were soaring in all directions. After forty years of peace, we were making a new world where national borders would wither away, where science and rational thought ruled the day, where young people were no longer bound by the strictures that so impeded their ancestors. I knew that I had to return to Montreal for a time for Hanna's sake, but my future was here, on this brilliant continent, perhaps even in the City of Lights.

On that last day, I wired Papa from Paris to tell him when I would arrive in Bad Gastein. I told him that I was perfectly capable of hiring a cab to take me to our home, knowing that he would be there to meet me, no matter what I said. Then I treated myself to an excellent dinner at an outdoor café within sight of the Eiffel Tower, and toasted my birthday and my future with two glasses of a superb burgundy.

The tenor of my voyage (indeed, the direction of my entire life) began to change after I boarded the train for Munich. There seemed to be blue-coated *poilus* everywhere, French soldiery on the move. At the German border, the customs formalities appeared to be far more brusque and suspicious than usual, and as the train rolled into Germany, the *poilus* were replaced by soldiers of Kaiser Wilhelm's *Landwehr* in their field grey and spiked helmets. So many soldiers mobilizing, so much tension in the air. Like most Europeans at the time, I was certain the tension would dissipate without violence, but already Europe seemed very different from the continent I had left less than a year before. Now I longed to get home to the peace of Bad Gastein and away from all this bellicose tramping to and fro.

I spent much of the trip writing letters, including brief notes to Karine Vogel in Gmund am Tegernsee, Elise Duvernay in Cherbourg and my closest friend, Dr. Jan Muršak, who was working at a hospital in Linz. I spent a much longer time composing a long letter to Jem Doyle, telling him what I had learned from Elise. I stressed that while Hanna was in Montreal, she had begun seeing a psychiatrist (or a physician who was counselling patients, at the very least) that Mlle Duvernay was quite certain she had taken a lover (possibly the tenor, André Lafleur, who ought to be questioned) and that she had received at least two expensive gifts from her lover, the perfume and the sable coat in which she had been found the night she was murdered. I stressed the odd dissimilarity between what I was told by the Frenchwoman and what Rudolf Mayr had said during our dinner at the Windsor Hotel. According to Mlle Duvernay, Hanna had been in a very nervous state before her tour began, and contrary to what Herr Mayr said, she was a reluctant opera star who had been all but hectored into a career she did not want.

Finally, although I did not wish to suggest a line of inquiry to a detective as clever and experienced as Jem, I ventured that perhaps it might be possible to interview those psychiatrists and physicians in Montreal who treated women with nervous conditions. The list, surely, could not be a long one, not after the French side was eliminated, because I had learned from Elise that Hanna's French was virtually non-existent. It was possible that such an inquiry would turn up nothing at all, but we could not afford to overlook any possibility.

When I had finished discussing our business, I wrote a separate letter to my dear friend Sophie Szitva, who had sustained my soul during one of the most difficult times of my life, thanking her once again for all she had done for me, and promising to bring a taste of the old country with me when I returned to Montreal in August. As soon as I had found a suitable small hotel near the Munich Hauptbahnhof, I posted both letters in the same envelope, after adding a postscript meant for Sophie's younger boys.

I spent a peaceful evening in a beer garden in Munich, dining on huge sausages with mounds of sauerkraut and potatoes washed down with beer from a stein so large I could barely carry it to the table. Children tumbled and hid under the tables, apple-cheeked waitresses hurried from table to table, a cheerful accordion played polka music and a handful of couples danced under the linden and chestnut trees. It was hard to imagine a more peaceful scene within any large city. Early the next morning, I was ready for the journey to Salzburg, and from Salzburg to Bad Gastein. I arrived in the afternoon and found Papa standing on the platform, hat in hand, his blue eyes watery. He was nearing sixty, and his hair was beginning to grey, but his back was still straight and his gait as sprightly as ever. We had a long embrace on the platform, both of us fighting back tears, and Papa scooped up both my heavy valises and carried them to his fiacre, which was waiting outside with two prize black horses, a present from a duke whose life he had saved while treating the wealthy guests at the spa. We went off at a great speed and covered the eight kilometres to our home in an impossibly short time, while I took in the subtle changes in these familiar surroundings. Then I was home.

To my embarrassment, our cranky and deeply religious housekeeper, Frau Kachelmeier, fell to her knees at first sight of me and began noisily praying, thanking God for bringing me safely home. I found her theatrical prayer ironic, given that she had always treated me as an unbearable nuisance, the biggest single obstacle to a perfectly tidy home. She had come to work for my father a year after my mother's death, and terrorized us both for two decades. Not once could I recall eating a meal that was hot at breakfast or dinner, because it was Frau Kachelmeier's habit to say grace for ten minutes or more while the dishes she brought piping hot from the oven cooled on the table, but my father was far too tender hearted a soul to send her packing, so he put up with the unending prayers, the cold meals, and the scoldings because his hat was wet and had to be brushed, or he had left a trace of mud on the floor. I told him he was a saint for enduring Frau Kachelmeier, but in truth I would have been no more capable of sacking the woman that he was. She was part of our lives in Bad Gastein, like the stone fireplace or the rack of old snowshoes at the back door. There was, however, a lightness to the place when she was away on one of her pilgrimages to Fatima and other shrines or, on one occasion, all the way to Jerusalem.

Over our cold supper that evening, Papa listened in silence as I told him everything – or almost everything. I left out the details of the beating I had absorbed and the time in hospital, but I told him about Hanna's murder, the nocturnal visit she had made to my lodgings, my friendship with Sophie Szitva and Jem Doyle, the invitation from Dr. Hyde to return to Montreal as a member of his staff at the clinic and a lecturer at the university, the meetings with Rudi Mayr and Elise Duvernay. Those kindly blue eyes showed nothing but concern for me. He made his only comment when I revealed my intention to return to Canada: I had not mentioned that agreement in my letters, because I wanted to tell him in person.

"You're quite certain you want to go back?" he asked. "I had hoped you might remain in Austria. In Vienna, at least, if not in Gastein."

"I'm quite certain, Papa. In part because I have much to learn from Dr. Hyde, in part because it is the only way I can help to find the men who killed Hanna. Eventually, though, I shall return to Austria. I feel such optimism for Europe now. It is my home, and it is beautiful."

"It is beautiful. I've lived here so long that I forget that myself at times. But for an ambitious young doctor like yourself, it is Vienna that is the attraction. I understand. I was ambitious like you, but your grandfather was not so understanding. He ordered me to come here and work in our surgery alongside him, and I did not dare to defy his wishes."

"How is grandfather?" I asked.

"*Streitsüchtig*," he said. "Cantankerous. He has always been cantankerous, but he is more so these days. He hikes constantly in the mountains. Wears out the young men who try to walk with him. Treats the occasional patient from the old days, assists me a little when things get busy. You know how he is. He doesn't know how to stop."

"We must go to visit him."

"Yes. Tomorrow. I told him we would set out first thing in the morning."

My Popi, Grandfather Balsano, lived only three kilometres from us, but his cabin (which he had built with his own hands) was on a meadow halfway up the side of a mountain, a difficult hike from our home, but one I looked forward to with joy. I was still not entirely fit following my recovery from the beating I had absorbed during the winter, and I planned to regain total fitness by hiking these mountain trails where I had spent so much of my boyhood.

I also wanted to listen to the gramophone recordings Elise Duvernay handed to me in Cherbourg, but Papa still did not possess a gramophone. At the earliest opportunity, I planned to take the fiacre into Gastein and to locate a store where I could purchase one. Papa would cluck over the expense, but his birthday was coming; I would insist he accept it as a birthday present, and we would listen to Hanna together.

When we retired for the night, I placed the recordings carefully on the bedside table in my old room, took down a worn copy of *novellen* by the writer Friedrich Halm, and tried to read myself to sleep, but I found that I could not concentrate. Even in Bad Gastein, the images of Hanna pursued me in an endless sequence, as they had in Montreal, aboard ship on the Atlantic, in Cherbourg, on the train. Hanna on a summer evening, framed against the greenery in the fading light, accompanied on a grand piano dragged out of doors for the occasion, her incomparable voice soaring into the night as the tapers were lit, one by one, and night birds answered her song. Walking with her on that spacious lawn, happily chatting with her in our Austrian dialect, inhaling the dusky notes of l'Heure leu, stealing glances at the elegant curve of her neck and the rise and fall of her bosom. Then Hanna in that emerald green dress, at my door because she was running for her life. Hanna in my apartment, sitting up while I slept, the merest glimpse of bare skin before I faded away again. And finally Hanna, naked on a slab in the Montreal morgue, her face beaten to a pulp, the ugliness of the pathologist's clumsy stitches, her breast pierced by the narrow instrument that had killed her. No matter how far I traveled, no matter how much time went by, I would see Hanna on that table for the rest of my days.

By the time I had settled into the country routine of

Bad Gastein, I had begun to accept my fate. I loved Hanna Goss. I had loved her, almost certainly, from the night we met at the reception, perhaps from the first moment I heard her sing. I was too intent on my career, too absorbed in a new city and a new life to realize it fully, but she had made an enormous impact on me from the first moment I saw her, one hand on the piano, the other gesturing gracefully as she sang. I had loved her still more, despite her plight and my illness, the night she came to me. I loved her with a kind of hopeless bitterness on the day I saw her body. I loved her, and I would not be able to stop loving her, and there was nothing I could do for her except to find her killers. And here I was, an ocean away from the one place where I might discover what had happened. At last I fell asleep, telling myself that in two or three months time I would be back in Montreal, back in Dr. Percival Hyde's clinic, back at Sophie's café, back on the hunt for her killers.

CHAPTER 20

The summer of 1914 was like a ripe, sun-warmed peach. Even the old folk like my cantankerous grandfather (who had seen more than eighty summers with his own eyes) conceded that never had the sky been such a brilliant shade of blue, the occasional clouds so fluffy and white, the breezes from the south more like a lover's caress, the meadows more fragrant and green, the woods more alive with new growth. To this day when I hear the word (Sommer in German, l'estate in Italian, l'été in French, poletji in Slovenian) I think of that flawless, golden summer in Bad Gastein, a time long since swallowed whole by the galloping horsemen of history.

The early part of the summer passed quietly, as I had hoped it would. I spent my days hiking and fishing and sometimes helping my father in the clinic, setting a fracture or suturing a wound. I was happiest when hiking under the impossibly tall Swiss pines, some of which had were three hundred years old, seeing marmots dive out of my path, nodding at goatherds, dodging the cow flop, as even Emperor Franz Joseph had to do when he hiked these same trails in his plain green loden coat – a coat exactly like the one Hanna had borrowed from me the night before she left. I took frequent detours from the main trail up the goat paths, occasionally picking the deep purple gentians, yellow arnica and white edelweiss along the way, seeking always those tall, slender waterfalls where I could splash in icy water to cool myself.

Evenings I spent with Papa and Frau Kachelmeier, or I ventured out to visit old friends. Twice I slept at my grandfather's cabin after long hikes during which I had to work to keep up with him, answering his prickly questions about Canada, never once bringing up the murder of Hanna Goss in his company because I didn't wish to upset him.

At the first opportunity, I found a shop in the village and purchased a gramophone so I could listen to Hanna's recordings. I took the recordings with me to be certain that I found a machine that would play them. It cost more than I could afford, but I came home with a wind-up gramophone, a large brass horn mounted on a wooden base with a crank handle. The base even had a pull-out drawer in which you could store your recordings. That evening my hands shook as I took the first of the discs out of its protective cover, placed it on the spindle, cranked the handle and began to play. Papa sat in awe and even Frau Kachelmeier ceased her complaining as Hannah's voice filled the room. In the coming days, I listened so many times that I knew every note of both recordings. I had only to close my eyes and I was back on the lawn of the Percival Hyde estate in Montreal, it was August 1913 again and we were all listening, spellbound, as the living Hanna enchanted us with her voice. I wished that I could wind back the months as easily as I wound up the gramophone; I could not, but as long as these recordings survived, I would have Hanna's voice as near as the gramophone.

I had planned to visit my crazy Slovenian friend Jan Muršak in Vienna, but Jan visited us at the summer solstice and stayed four days, to my father's delight. Papa had always been especially fond of Jan. He enjoyed practicing his Slovenian with my friend, and he found the sight of the two of us together a source of endless mirth, merely because, while we were equally thin, Jan was an entire foot taller.

During my first week back home, I wrote to Dr. Freud, reminding him that I had been one of his clinical assistants before I left for Canada. I explained that I was to lecture on his theories at McGill University in Montreal beginning in the fall, and that I wished to meet in order to bring myself up to date on his work, if that might be possible. Dr. Freud said that he would be pleased to make himself available to me, but it would not be possible before mid-August. He suggested Monday, August 17, if I could appear at his clinic at seven o'clock in the morning we would have at least an hour for a discussion. I responded immediately. The timing was ideal. I would take the train from Bad Gastein into Vienna on the Sunday before, spend the evening with Jan Muršak and stay overnight with him and be at Dr Freud's address at the appointed time. From Vienna I would travel by train to Hamburg, where I would embark for the return journey to Montreal.

Soon I had settled into a routine built around my daily hikes. Sometimes I took a sleeping roll, sometimes I was content to choose a route that would bring me home in time for Frau Kachelmeier's cold supper. Most of June went by like that, and on the last weekend of the month I took an especially long hike, my longest of the summer, far up into the mountains. I left before daybreak on Friday, slept rough in the mountains for two nights, and planned to make it back by Sunday evening. My plan, however, was interrupted by a sudden, violent thunderstorm with odd flashes of red lightning such as I had never seen before. I found shelter in a hay-shed and by the time the storm had passed it was getting dark, so I decided to spend the night where I was.

The next morning, I dawdled along on the way home. My father would be at mass in Bad Gastein because it was June 29, the Feast of St. Peter and St. Paul. It was a Monday morning, but the cathedral would be more crowded and airless than usual, and the mass a long one. God would forgive me, I thought, if I chose to spend His glorious summer day out of doors rather than cooped up in a cathedral going through the familiar ritual, sitting and standing and kneeling and sitting and kneeling again. I would rather be hiking, feeling the sun on my shoulders, breathing in the fragrance of new-mown hay, scuffing up dust, keeping an eye out as always for likely waterfalls where I could wash away the sweat and dirt from the hike.

By the time I reached the end of my walk, it was very hot, my back was bathed in sweat from the pack, the walking staff I had cut from a branch early in the summer had chafed my hands, and I was anxious only to get home. I was striding up the path to our house when I was overtaken by a bicycle messenger in a great lather, who muttered *"der Prinz... der Prinz..."* under his breath as he cycled up to the house, leaned his bicycle against a bush and began pounding furiously at our door.

"Dr. Balsano! Dr. Balsano! *Aufmachen*, Dr. Balsano!"

"I am Dr. Balsano," I said as I caught up to him, "can I help you?"

"No, I mean the *real* Dr. Balsano," he said.

Just then my father, who had been shaving, opened the door, still wiping shaving cream from his cheeks. "What is it Anton?" he asked. "Are you trying to raise the dead? It's a feast day, lad! Show a little respect!"

The messenger, who would normally have shown the greatest respect to a citizen as prominent as my father, instead ignored what he had said. *"Der Prinz, der Prinz!"* he shouted. "He is dead! The Archduke! Franz Ferdinand, with his wife. Murdered in Sarajevo by the bloody Serbs. It happened yesterday, but we are only just learning the news today. Such a tragedy!"

"Calm yourself, Anton," Papa said. "How did you come to know this, boy? Did the angels tell you?"

Anton shook his head furiously. "No angels. The telegraph master got the news. They have posted the telegram outside the station and at the city hall for all to see." According to Anton, even the band that played in the park on Sundays and feast days had ceased playing and the musicians had put away their instruments.

"So what then?" Papa asked the boy. "The telegraph master told you to come pelting out here to bother me with this wild tale?"

"It is not a tale, sir. It is true. In the village, they are talking of nothing else. He told me I should tell everyone I can reach. I have been riding for two hours."

"Has the telegraph master not heard of the telephone? You could have done all this without leaving the office."

"*Nein*. Out this way, not everyone has a telephone, and in any case, he says this is the sort of news you must deliver in person. Such a tragedy! There will be war!"

"Yes, you said that, but there will be no war. People aren't fools, and the Archduke was as unloved as any man alive. This is no cause for war." Papa stood with the razor dangling at his side. For an awful moment he looked as though he wanted to slash the boy's throat. Then he lifted the razor to wave the boy away. "Go," he said, "go on your way. Spread your madness. That's all we need, some crazy story to get everyone agitated over nothing. Mark my words, this will turn out to be untrue."

Anton climbed on his bicycle and rode off, muttering something about ingratitude. Papa turned back to the house and I followed. The razor clattered to the floor and Papa sat heavily on his kitchen chair, stunned. "*Das zweite Mal*," he muttered to himself. "The second time. First Crown Prince Rudolf, now this."

I did not have to ask what he was talking about. For Austrians of my father's generation, the suicide of Crown Prince Rudolf at Mayerling in 1889 was the defining event of a lifetime, a sorrow cast over the nation like a shroud. The much-loved crown prince, the great hope of liberal and progressive thinkers in the Habsburg Empire and throughout Europe, had joined in a suicide pact with his young mistress, Baroness Mary Vetsera. He shot her and then shot himself at his hunting lodge. The brightest jewel in the empire was dead at thirty and his father, Franz Joseph, was left without an obvious heir to the throne. For months, Vienna was wrapped in black. Franz Joseph was admired and respected, but his son was loved by men and women alike.

The death of the Crown Prince had brought with it a

much greater sorrow for Papa. My mother was just getting back on her feet after my birth the year before, a trial that had sent her into a mysterious depression for months. She was better, almost her old self again, and then the Crown Prince killed himself, and she went back into the depression and never came out of it. My beautiful mother died the following winter, still two years short of her thirtieth birthday. Papa himself listed the official cause of death as pneumonia, but he knew it was something else, an incurable desolation of the heart. It was because of her death that I had decided, very early in my medical career, to attempt to do what my father could not: to cure the despondency of the human soul that no forceps or scalpel can reach. He tormented himself with his failure to cure my mother for years, but he didn't have the tools. In Vienna and elsewhere, we were just learning to recognize ailments of the mind, and were fumbling toward cures we had yet to discover.

Now, as Papa said, it was *das zweite Mal,* the second time. Franz Ferdinand was not loved, not at all like Rudolf. He was abrasive, arrogant, completely lacking the common touch. The people accepted him as they might accept a bad harvest or a flood. Whether the archduke was loved or not, the dual murders were a dangerous provocation on the part of the Serbs. We felt it, even in this tranquil place, where the bees buzzed around the hay mows, the goats clambered up the hillsides, waterfalls spilled down from the mountains in rainbow arcs of spray. A storm was coming, and it would shake even this isolated valley to its core.

"Perhaps it's untrue, Papa," I said. "We can't be certain. Anton is just a boy."

"No. I'm sure it is true. I should not have chased him off, but it's disturbing news. I didn't want to discuss it with him. Let us see how things unfold, Maxim. It doesn't have to mean war, as long as we don't link our fate to that bloody Prussian fool Kaiser Wilhelm. We need cool heads now. If only Rudolf had lived..."

He trailed off. I wondered how many times that had been spoken in the twenty-five years since the death of the prince. *If only Rudolf had lived...*

Papa looked at me sharply. "When were you to leave for Canada?"

"The end of August," I said. "I am to meet with Dr. Freud in Vienna on August 17, then I plan to spend a day or two in Vienna before taking the train to Hamburg. The ship for Montreal sails on August 22."

"That is just as well," Papa said. "If this foolishness takes hold, I want you well away from here. Armies need doctors to sew up the broken bodies. I don't want you caught up in this."

"But it's as you said, cooler heads must prevail. Surely our leaders can see that."

"They may see it, but will they have the strength to act? Our Crown Prince has been murdered, apparently by a Serb, if we're to believe that boy. There will be enormous sentiment for war to teach those bloody Serbs a lesson. Then the Russians will come in on the side of their Slav brethren, and we will be in the maw of Hell."

Despite the terrible news, I slept well that night, exhausted from my hike. It was advice I have given to hundreds of patients over the years: wear out the body, and the mind will follow. My subconscious mind, however, would not sleep. I had wild dreams of Hanna: erotic dreams, violent dreams, peaceful dreams in which she sang to me in the shade of one of the hay mows, disturbing dreams in which she stood naked under a mountain waterfall, her chest and abdomen still bearing the pathologist's clumsy sutures. When I woke the next morning, she was still with me, and it was not until I had ground the beans and made myself a pungent and powerful coffee that I was able to climb out of a state somewhere between waking and sleeping and accept a new and dangerous reality: the world we knew was about to change in profound and unpredictable ways.

As soon as Papa was awake, he harnessed the blacks to the fiacre while I dressed and we drove quickly into town. It was not yet eight o'clock on a Monday morning when we arrived, but the square in Bad Gastein was already filled with people milling restlessly about, looking at the headlines pasted on buildings all around. There was not the sentiment for war that Anton had promised and my father feared. They trusted our leaders, especially Franz Joseph. He was old and wise, he would not go storming off to war for no reason at all. They trusted the leaders of the other nations: England, France, the Russians, the Italians, the Serbs, even Kaiser Wilhelm, although they despised the man. There would be peace. Everyone agreed. Who, after all, would start a war during such a glorious summer as this?

CHAPTER 21

The month of July was agonizing, like watching a pile of dinner plates fall in a dream. At first, it seemed, no one outside my family even noticed what was happening and yet the plates were falling, slipping off the table and crashing to the floor. One by one they tumble and shatter, until the dining room is a shambles of broken crockery, and there is nothing you can do to stop it.

The routine in our quiet valley remained much the same, except that each morning we rode into the town of Bad Gastein to catch up on the news and to buy the newspapers from Vienna and Salzburg as they came in on the train. Some days were hopeful, some days oppressive, some days you could almost smell the acrid scent of gunpowder. There was talk that all young men my age had been conscripted; many were already joining the colors, afraid the war that had not yet begun would be over before they got there. I had already spent my year in the army. As a young medical student, I had been assigned to treat venereal diseases among the troops, a thoroughly distasteful task. I was still in the reserve, and subject to a call-up in the event of war.

Each day there was a new assortment of headlines in the newspapers. The dual monarchy (embodied in the single person of Franz Joseph, also known as the All Highest) issued an ultimatum to Serbia. The Serbian response was unsatisfactory. Count Leopold Berchtold, our famously vacillating foreign minister, had tumbled off the fence. Now he had gone over to the side of Conrad von Hotzendorf, the bellicose chief of the general staff, and was pushing for a "full and final reckoning" with Serbia. Berchtold dispatched one of his advisors, Count Alexander Hoyos, to Berlin, to consult with our German allies. Hoyos returned with a blank cheque from Berlin: Austria-Hungary would have Germany's support if it decided to invade Serbia.

On the twenty-eighth of July, the Empire declared war on Serbia. We were officially at war, and still the plates kept crashing. The following day, Austrian artillery shelled Belgrade, the first shots of the war. On the last day of July, the French socialist Jean Jaurès, an advocate of *rapprochement* with Germany and thus of peace, was shot and killed in Paris days after he had returned from Brussels, where he had traveled to try to persuade German socialists to strike in order to prevent a war. The assassination of Jaurès removed one of the major impediments to the coming conflict. The next day, August 1, Germany declared war on Russia. On August 3, Germany declared war on France. The day after, Great Britain declared war on Germany. If Britain was in it, its dominions had been dragged into the war as well, meaning that Germany was now at war with Canada. As Germany's ally, so were we.

And so it went. Reservists were called up, changed hurriedly into the pale blue uniforms and peaked caps of the Austro-Hungarian army, and tumbled into awkward formations in the street, where pretty girls kissed their cheeks and weeping mothers pressed cakes into their hands before they were loaded onto trains and shipped east. Bands played. Politicians gave warlike speeches, newspaper columnists vied to see who could express the most hatred for the enemy. Everyone was certain they would be home for Christmas, after they had given the Serbs a proper spanking.

Everyone except my father, who kept muttering "*Narren... Narren...*" under his breath. "Fools ... fools." I agreed, except that like most young men, I was not immune to the martial music and the sight of pretty girls fawning over soldiers. When the *Radetzky March* began to play, I wanted to board those trains with the rest, but Papa would not hear of it. I was to go ahead with my plans to depart for Canada.

All around us, the fever for war mounted almost hour by hour. Few of us knew what it was. Austria had not been in a shooting war since 1866, and that had been a distant three-week conflict against Prussia. We were about to learn.

On August 12, Austro-Hungarian troops under General Oskar Potiorek crossed the Drina River into Serbia. Not for the last time in this war, an incompetent general sacrificed his troops in a catastrophe. At the Battle of Cer, Gen. Potiorek lost twenty-three thousand men. After four days, he was forced into an ignominious retreat. That same day, I received a note from Dr. Freud, saying that his plans had been changed due to the war, and that he would be unable to meet with me on August 17. He said that he would be willing to meet with me as soon as the war was over.

I had to make a decision. Papa wanted me to catch a train to Hamburg and board the ship for Canada. Already passenger trains were being commandeered for troops. My friend Dr. Jan Muršak, as peaceful a soul as I have ever encountered, had volunteered already and was working as a surgeon in Vienna, treating the wounded. I received a letter from Jan, pleading with me to join him. There were already too many wounded, he said, and too few doctors. Canada and Austria were now on opposite sides of this conflict, even if we were not directly at war, and I was not at all sure what sort of welcome I would receive in Canada, as the subject of an enemy monarch.

A letter from Jem Doyle removed any doubt. Amid the general war hysteria, a group of German seamen aboard a ship docked in the Montreal harbor had been arrested and marched off to jail. They were reservists, so they were considered enemy combatants. I would be in the same position if I traveled to Canada – or to France, for that matter. In the short time since I left Elise Duvernay in Cherbourg, we had become citizens of warring nations. I cancelled my passage to Montreal on the ship out of Hamburg and received a full refund for the price of my ticket, but the money was little consolation for all that had already been lost to the war.

Apart from the news about the German seamen, Jem had little news for me. He and a trusted partner had interviewed all the doctors and psychiatrists in Montreal who were known to treat women with what were known as nervous conditions. They had even held a brief interview with Dr. Percival Hyde, and checked appointment books for 1913. They turned up nothing. Hanna's name did not appear in any of the books, nor did any of the physicians recall treating her. Jem had also attempted to pay a call on André Lafleur, but the tenor was performing in an opera in San Francisco and was not available.

Papa did not expect a short war, but I was more optimistic. Austrian boys, some of them friends and neighbors, were being killed and wounded. I had a skill the wounded desperately needed. I could not remain on the sidelines, and in any case as a reservist I knew that I could be called up at any time. I anticipated that it would be for no more than a few months, no matter what the outcome. I wrote to Jan Muršak to say that I wished to join him, and to ask how I should go about volunteering in such a way so that we could work side by side.

Before I could receive a reply, the decision was taken out of my hands. I was conscripted. I learned the news when Papa and I made our morning journey into the village. We found a crowd milling around city hall where the new conscription lists were posted on the front of the building. There were no names – the lists went according to birth years. Young men scanned them, found the year of their birth, and learned when and where they had to report: I had seven days to join my regiment, the Landwehr-Infanterieregimenter Linz No. 2 in Linz, two hundred and thirty kilometres from Bad Gastein.

Papa was devastated, convinced that he would never see me again and that our nation had embarked on a ruinous folly. Before I left, I wrote letters to Dr. Percival Hyde, explaining that due to circumstances beyond my control I would not be able to accept his offer of a staff position at his clinic until such time as the war was over, to Jem and Sophie, thanking them profusely for everything they had done for me in Montreal, to Elise and Karine and to Rudi Mayr to provide them all with my military address.

Almost before I had time to say my goodbyes, I was donning that blue tunic with the peaked cap and practicing the time-honored technique for polishing my boots by mixing lamp-black with lard and spit and applying it with a cork. As an officer with the rank of lieutenant, I was given five hundred krone in bank notes and silver when I arrived, and billeted with a charming family in their home not far from the camp, which made it possible to maintain the illusion that I remained a civilian. Once at the camp, however, I was subject to all the degradation and nonsense the military visits on its own. I rose at five o'clock each morning, donned my uniform, had breakfast at a café in town and reported in time for parade at seven o'clock. I maintained this routine for three weeks, worrying that the army bureaucracy would ignore the fact that I was a Doctor of Medicine and assign me to march as a regular soldier with the infantry. On the Monday of the fourth week, however, a genial major called me in to inform me that I had been reassigned to the Medical Health Service, and that I was to report to a field hospital that had opened in an elementary school in Linz.

In late November, Jan Muršak arrived from Vienna by train. He had been reassigned to the same field hospital in Linz, and for most of the rest of the war, we would work in close proximity. His tall, dark, lugubrious presence and dry wit were a constant comfort to me, and when there was time we were able to discuss our theories of psychoanalysis. We were everywhere together, the tall Slovene and the short Austrian, and I think it's fair to say that we kept each other sane through the darkest days of the war.

In those early days of the war we had work and we had wounded to treat, but we never felt overwhelmed. Linz was a good distance from the two fronts on which Austria-Hungary was fighting, in Serbia to the south and Galicia to the east. Casualties arrived, but by the time they reached us they had already been treated, first at a dressing station near the front, then at a field hospital closer to the fighting than we were.

Still, some of the wounds we had to treat were ghastly. A young Bosnian soldier arrived with his face melted from the heat of an explosion. His nose was a blob, the skin around his eyes like the raw dough for strudel when it has been folded over, eyes and mouth and nose reduced to slits, all of it giving off a stench that made experienced nurses blanche. It was not uncommon to see amputees walking on the grounds with two legs and two crutches between them, arms around one another's shoulders, hopping along in unison, the Siamese twins of war. We saw and treated almost everything except the gas attack casualties that would emerge later in the war, refined our techniques and learned to do everything quickly, so that when we were moved closer to the front we were both as prepared as surgeons can be for the unimaginable flow of casualties.

As long as I was stationed in Linz, Papa was able to come for regular visits, usually twice a month. Austrian civilians were already feeling the pinch of the war, especially in the working-class districts of Vienna where food was scarce, but my father was still making his own sausages and prosciutto, pickling sauerkraut and making *apfelstrudel* from our own apples. Papa brought bags of everything, including fresh apples, on every trip, and we shared our *largesse* with orderlies, nurses and patients alike. With his insatiable curiosity, my father followed us on our rounds, making comments, asking questions about the latest techniques, chatting with patients. He was already treating at least a dozen long-term casualties at home in Bad Gastein, men whose wounds were too serious for them to be sent back to the war. He confided in me that one of his most serious problems was treating them for depression, especially two *Landwehr* soldiers who had lost their sexual organs when they were wounded. No wound terrified a soldier more. Papa was grateful for any advice I could give on treating the resulting depression, but I had little to say. One could commiserate, but that did little good for a soldier whose penis and testicles had been shredded by shrapnel.

As it happened, Papa had just made one of his visits in mid-December when we were granted ten days leave. At the last minute, I decided to go first to Vienna, then to Bad Gastein. I would call at Dr. Freud's clinic but the real purpose of my visit lay elsewhere. Rudi Mayr had provided the address of Frau Birgita Goss, Hanna's mother. I would pay her a visit and bring some of my father's provisions. I felt that a gentleman bearing cured ham, sausages and apples would not be turned away in a time of privation.

CHAPTER 22

No sooner had the locomotive huffed into the station at Linz than I realized that the journey to Vienna might be more difficult than I anticipated. The throng of passengers waiting on the platform surged toward the train even before the passengers debarking at Linz could climb down. There was pushing and shoving and cursing and two or three fistfights broke out on the platform, as passengers who were trying to get off panicked, thinking they might be knocked under the train or forced back into the cars, while those attempting to storm the train feared that they might miss the train and be forced to wait hours for another. I was heavily burdened with packages for Frau Goss and my own effects, but most of the passengers were carrying more than I was and it helped that I was slender. I was able to slip between two bulky gentlemen and board.

As I looked desperately for a place to sit, a muscular young soldier who looked vaguely familiar beckoned to me. He slid over to make room and helped me find a place to stow my packages, and before I could thank him, he thanked me. He was one of the wounded men I had treated. He had an infection that had developed in a wound in his knee and I was able to drain it and treat it with penicillin. Now he was able to walk again, albeit with a heavy limp because he had suffered multiple fractures to his kneecap.

Fortunately, he made a good traveling companion, because a voyage that ought to have taken three hours took nine hours to complete. There had been heavy snow on the tracks the night before, and we had to stop repeatedly and wait for the snow to be cleared from the tracks. Twice we were shunted onto a siding and apparently forgotten to make way for troop trains barreling through, bound from Salzburg or Linz to the front in Galicia. As they passed in a thunder of noise and clouds of snow, I couldn't help thinking that some of the soldiers on those trains would someday be on my operating table, waiting for me to heal their wounds. And they would be the lucky ones.

We talked and dozed and tried to forget about the time. The compartment was freezing cold and the benches on which we sat were hard. I had to remind myself that the privations of the soldiers at the front were so much worse during this first winter of the war. The cold was as much an enemy as the Russians or the Serbs – I had already treated a dozen cases of frostbite, some sufficiently severe to require amputation, usually of the toes. There would be more.

In Vienna there was the same scene we had experienced in Linz, with some passengers battling to disembark as others tried to board the train. I wedged myself behind the frame of the young soldier and followed him. We parted ways on the platform. We were going in opposite directions. I wished him luck, and I told him that I hoped not to see him back on my operating table again. He laughed, a deep, rich laugh: such fine, strong young men we were pouring into this killing machine.

I was not familiar with the neighborhood where Frau Goss had her modest home and her tailor's shop. It was on the fringes of Leopoldstadt, a Jewish neighborhood, not far from Prater park. I had visited the Prater many times but I did not know the rest of the area at all, and from the tram I first walked the wrong way a considerable distance in the cold. A kind stranger pointed me in the right direction, but I had to fight my way back against a stiff wind with all that I was carrying. By the time that I arrived at the correct address, I was half-frozen. A warm light glowed in a window and I took that as I sign that the welcome inside would be warm. It was not.

I had to knock three times before the door opened a crack and a woman's face peered out.

"Good evening, Frau Goss. I am Dr. Maxim Balsano. I was a friend of your daughter's in Montreal. I wrote to you once to express my condolences for your loss, and I wonder if I might come in for a moment."

"*Warum?*" Why?

I was taken aback. I didn't expect to have to explain why I had come. "Well, because I would like to talk with you about Hanna, and because I have brought you some things."

"*Warum?*" Again, the same question: why.

"Because I know that life is becoming difficult in Vienna now. I am a surgeon at the military hospital in Linz, and my father brings me more than I need from our home in Bad Gastein. I thought since it is nearly Christmas, you might be in need..."

There was a very long pause. I was shivering from head to toe as she looked me up and down. Finally, she gave a brisk nod. "*Ja, ja. Komm herein.*"

The door creaked open and I stepped into a pleasant ante-room. She closed the door behind me and introduced herself. "Birgita Goss."

"Frau Goss. I am pleased to meet you." Then I repeated what I had said in the doorway, in case she hadn't understood. "I was a friend of your daughter's. I wrote you a letter some time ago, from Montreal..."

"*Ja, ja. Ich erinnere mich.*"

She remembered, but she did not seem in the least pleased to meet me. She turned abruptly and led the way into a room that was part sitting room and part fitting room. The house was much as Rudi Mayr had described it, except that it was not summer, and there was no beautiful young soprano singing as she hung out the wash in back. Frau Goss turned up a kerosene lamp and faced me. The resemblance to Hanna was breathtaking: It was as though the young woman I had known had aged twenty-five years overnight, while remaining very attractive. Frau Goss had the same mane of red hair, except that hers had no lustre and was streaked with grey and her face was thin and careworn.

"You have something for me?" she said, and in that question I could detect a barely concealed desperation. The wartime shortages were already biting deep in Vienna.

"I do." I reached into my bag and drew out my packages, one by one. A sack of polenta flour. A cured ham. A long string of sausages. A jar of sauerkraut. Sugar. Tea.

As I handed her each package, Frau Goss looked it over and muttered, *"Danke, Herr Doktor. Danke, Herr Doctor. Danke, Herr Doktor."*

She said little, but her hands were trembling. She gathered up the things I brought to her, one or two at a time, and took them into another room, which I assumed was the kitchen. Only then did she invite me to sit, but she said nothing at all, only stared at me as though waiting for a more complete explanation as to why I had come bearing gifts.

"As I said in the letter I wrote to you, I am very sorry for your loss. The loss of Hanna. It must have been heartbreaking."

She gave a curt nod, as though what I said was too obvious to merit comment. Even as she sat, she was a bundle of nervous tics, brushing at a wisp of greying hair that kept falling into her eyes, compulsively flattening her dress over her thighs, looking anxiously back over her shoulder as though she expected to be assaulted from behind in her own home.

"Before the war began, I was working with a police detective in Montreal," I said. "We were trying to solve the mystery of your daughter's murder."

"Yes. You said in your letter. Why?"

"Well, because her killers have not been caught. They must be found...justice ... surely you must want justice for the men who murdered your daughter?"

"I want nothing. You are not a policeman, why do you do this?"

"Because I cared for Hanna. I thought she was a wonderfully talented singer. And I may have been the last person to see her alive."

"Ja, ja..."

She looked away, avoiding eye contact. Those green eyes, Hanna's eyes, looking at anything but me. I might as well have been a door-to-door salesman, trying to sell her something she didn't want. I was taken aback. I had expected to be welcomed because of my efforts to find Hanna's killers, but I had also taken the trouble to arrive bearing gifts, yet she was clearly impatient with my presence and anxious for me to go. She was barely polite, and nothing in her manner or her words betrayed any hint of welcome or gratitude. We sat in an uncomfortable silence while I wracked my brain for something to say. I was cold and hungry and I would have welcomed a cup of hot tea, but I didn't feel that I could ask for one.

"I had a letter from Herr Rudolf Mayr about a month ago," I said. "He's still in New York. It seems he feels he would be safer there for the duration of the war."

"Rudi!" she said. She spat his name. "If not for Rudi..."

"If not for Rudi, Hanna would be alive?"

"It is true!"

"He said that he visited you twice since her death," I said.

She looked up. "Rudi? Here?"

"Yes. That's what he said."

"He's a liar. Rudi was never here. He sent me a telegram. From Montreal. *I am so sorry to inform you, your daughter is dead.* Someone told me later that he was in Vienna, but he didn't visit me. Not since they left for North America. Two telegrams and one letter. That is all. I know why – he is afraid I will ask for the money from her concerts. Rudi kept all the money. He was supposed to invest it for her. If he did, all she ever got was money for her expenses. He said he would take ten per cent, but he took ninety per cent, maybe more."

She sat stiffly, glaring at me, as though I were responsible for the actions of Rudi Mayr. I was baffled. I could not understand why Rudi would have failed to visit her, or why he would lie about such a thing. Perhaps his failures accounted for the rather hostile reception I was receiving from Frau Goss. She associated us with her daughter's death. Who was I to object? I who had never had a child, much less lost one, the victim of a brutal murder on another continent?

"If I may, I would like to ask you one question," I said. "Do you think it is possible that Rudi may have killed her?"

She shrugged. "Who knows? He shouted at her, he struck her – anything is possible.
He wanted the money! It is always that, is it not – the money? When she did not want to go on with the tour, she wanted him to give her the share she had earned from all her performances. He did not want to give! Not a *krone*! He never cared about Hanna. It was always a pretense."

She stood then, a clear sign that she wanted me to go.

"Frau Goss," I said. "A strange thing happened the night your daughter was murdered. I cannot explain it. Your daughter came to my lodgings. I thought you would want to know what happened…"

"Why?"

"Well, because you are her mother, because I saw her, because…" I trailed off. Her manner had become more nervous and agitated the longer I remained. When a blast of wind shook the windows, she jumped as though she had seen a ghost. She seemed disinterested in my explanation, disinterested in anything I had to say.

I saw no reason to bother the poor woman any longer. She had lost a husband and her only child. I took my leave, as graciously as I could. She was so relieved that she could not hide it. She led me quickly to the door, pointed the way back to the tram when I asked, said *guten abend* and stopped just short of slamming the door behind me. I stood for a moment on the street, staring at the house, baffled.

The wind had picked up while I was struggling to explain myself to Frau Goss. I walked away without looking back, winding my scarf around my neck and over my face. Halfway to the tram I saw a workman's café that was open and entered. A dozen conversations were interrupted as hard-looking men stared at me from their tables. I found a seat by the window and they went back to their conversations, but I had the feeling that I was being watched all the while. The surly proprietor brought me sauerkraut, potatoes, and sausages. The atmosphere was unfriendly but the food was decent and plentiful. Dining in this cold, cheerless place made me long for the warmth and cheer of Sophie's Café. I wondered if I would ever see it again. When the war began in August, we were assured it would be over by Christmas. Now it was nearly Christmas and there was no end in sight.

The next day I tried to visit Dr. Freud early in the morning, but he was away from Vienna. I caught a crowded train to Salzburg and a less crowded train to Bad Gastein, and spent a few restful days at home before my war began in earnest.

CHAPTER 23

J an Muršak and I felt that we had been at war since August of 1914, but in truth we knew little of the war. We treated the wounded at the hospital in Linz, but we did so in relative comfort. We had heat and light and sterile conditions in which to work. Had we remained there for the duration, we could have had no complaints, but on May 23, 1915, Italy declared war on the Austro-Hungarian Empire. It was an act of unimaginable cynicism at a time when the horrific consequences of modern warfare were evident on every front. If the other powers went clumsily to war in the blind belief that it would be a short, decisive conflict, Italy entered the conflict with its eyes wide open. The Italians wanted Habsburg land, just as Count Ottavio Resphigi had warned during our unpleasant encounters in Montreal. They wanted the Dolomites, they wanted Fiume, they wanted Trentino, they wanted Trieste. Given the chance, they would seize all of it, as far as Dubrovnik on the Adriatic coast and, if possible, Vienna itself.

The Italians had convinced themselves it would be easy to defeat an aging empire already pinned down on two fronts, in Serbia to the south and in Galicia to the east. General Luigi Cadorna, the Italian commander-in-chief and as repellent a monster as you will find in the annals of warfare, had convinced the weak Italian government that the war would be as easy as a "walk to Vienna."

Had Cadorna's men not faced the natural barrier of the Julian Alps, it may have been so, but Cadorna seemed to think that the dedicated, highly trained troops of the Habsburg Empire, skilled at fighting mountain warfare from a defensive position, would present no obstacle to his brave Italians. His doctrine of war boiled down to one simple word: *Attack*. And if the first attack fails, attack again, with more élan. And if the second attack fails, and the third attack fails, and so on, then find a pretext to decimate your own men: have them chosen at random from various units and taken out and shot, on the theory that firing squads somehow improve morale.

The Austrian generals were only a bit wiser. Jan and I arrived at the front three weeks after Italy declared war. Our troops desperately needed surgeons at the dressing stations and field hospitals nearer the front. They wanted us as close as possible to the fighting, where we could perform the sort of brutal triage the military expects from doctors in a war zone. Sew up the lucky ones, give the others morphine and a priest and wait for them to die.

The promise and optimism of Europe in the early years of the century was bleeding to death in the mountains and on the Karst, in the mud of the Eastern front and on the endless plains of Galicia. All around us, the most destructive instruments man could invent were being employed, night and day, to pierce, explode, break and shatter the fragile human bodies that were brought back to us on litters, flung across the backs of the ponies, propped inside motorized ambulances. It was our job to bring these broken soldiers back to life so that they could be flung into another battle and another after that, until their luck ran out and they were buried under a few rocks in a shallow grave, or have their bodies pushed off the mountain to plunge hundreds of feet into a makeshift ossuary. It was madness.

I won't bore you with the succession of battles. They were all different and yet utterly alike, because they were all driven by the unending slaughter of tens of thousands of young men on both sides of the conflict. In the space of two and a half years on the Italian front, there were twelve Battles of the Isonzo alone. The same blunders were repeated dozens, hundreds of times.

Wounded Italian soldiers were often brought to me, side by side with the Austrians, sometimes in the same ambulances. Croats. Slovenes. Ruthenians. Galicians. Bosnians. Poles. Czechs. Slovaks. Hungarians. Even Serbs, some of whom had remained loyal to the empire. All so unlike in their culture and their beliefs, so alike when they were wounded, sobbing for their mothers in all the languages of the empire. All sharing cigarettes and the same bitter jokes, sharing danger and death, not understanding for a moment why they were here. In the mountains, we operated in surgeries that were little more than makeshift huts tacked onto a mountainside. In the mayhem of an ill-lit operating theatre, we would sometimes toil for thirty hours without stopping. When I could not go on, I would find an unoccupied stretcher, collapse onto it face down, and fall into a sleep so profound that it was like death. A few hours or a few minutes later, I would stumble to my feet when another wave of the wounded was brought in. If I was fortunate, someone would hand me a tin mug of bitter black coffee, and if the gods were smiling on me that day, it might even be hot coffee with a pastry.

Sometimes, to maintain my sanity, I would write down a few thoughts about Hanna. Random memories, lines of investigation we might follow if I survived the war, speculation as to who might have wanted to kill her. I didn't know why I felt compelled to write, except that perhaps I might one day get back on a trail that was by now very cold.

CHAPTER 24

By the time we had slogged through three years of war to what is known as the Battle of Caporetto in October of 1917, the war had reached a state where peace seemed unimaginable. We would go on killing and being killed for this hill or that, grabbing a piece of high ground that would be taken back the next day, always at great cost. The Battle of Caporetto was also known as the Twelfth Battle of the Isonzo, the twelfth time the troops had fought over the same stretch of the river, known as the Isonzo to the Italians and the Soča to our side, a river only one hundred and forty kilometres in its entire length, along which 1.7 million soldiers died in two and a half years of fighting.

The Battle of Caporetto was the greatest triumph of the war for our side but for our overextended troops, it would lead to catastrophe and our exit from the war, the last gasp of an Empire that had stood for six centuries. It began on 24 October 1917, and by the time it was over it would enter the Italian language as the term for a complete disaster. Our troops (now working in tandem with forces from our German allies) moved so quickly that our forward dressing station was moved three times in ten days as we struggled to keep up. Because of the haste of the advance, each station was more crude than the last. The last was an old hunting lodge perched halfway up the side of a mountain near the Tagliamento, where German troops fighting with us had established a bridgehead. The makeshift dressing station was on a track that could just barely be navigated by ambulance. Most of our gear was transported by the hardy little Bosnian ponies that moved hundreds of thousands of tons of equipment for our army during the war, while the surgeons and orderlies rode toward the front in motorized transport, sometimes in ambulances that reeked of blood, feces, sweat and gasoline, more often in the small, wooden-wheeled *panje* carts pulled by the same ponies.

The front itself was no more than five hundred metres away, and we knew the Italian gunners might fire at us, despite the hastily painted red cross on the roof of the lodge. We had barely time to set up our equipment before the *panje* carts and the ambulances began to arrive, each loaded with moaning, screaming, praying, cursing wounded men, sometimes with Austrian and Italian soldiers packed together, bitter enemies only moments ago, trying to help one another survive until they reached the dressing station. They had all been picked up by the stretcher bearers, slid onto ground sheets, lifted onto stretchers, carried over the roughest ground (often under fire) and finally dumped onto a cart or (if they were lucky) into an ambulance for transport.

The speed of the advance meant that we had outdistanced our supply lines by many kilometres. The troops were short of everything: gasoline, food, ammunition, endurance. We medical officers were short much of what we needed, especially ether and sterile dressings. Even when we were fully supplied, our means of administering anesthetics were primitive: We would place a mask over the wounded man's face and drip ether onto it until he was no longer conscious. If he turned blue or stopped breathing, we knew we had given him too much. Now we were so short of supplies we often had to amputate limbs without anaesthetic.

During the battle, even the surgeons were hungry and exhausted. The weather was miserable, cold and foggy and rainy, half the troops were sick and more than half the doctors. We had barely arrived at the hunting lodge when I began to shake with fever. I was ill but I could not take to my bed and sweat it out. There were only three of us to handle an endless supply of the wounded.

Jan and I had been sent to separate dressing stations, so of the other two "surgeons" working with me, one a second-year medical student when he was conscripted, the other a dentist just beginning his practice. I was the senior medical officer in rank and experience. I had no choice but to remain at my post until I collapsed.

Our equipment was wretched. We were short of every-thing. We had no ether. We were sometimes forced to use crepe-paper bandages to dress wounds, which was not unlike wrapping an injury in toilet paper. We had no cotton wool, so we used cellulose paper. It soaked through almost imme-diately with blood and pus so that when you went to change the bandage you pulled away a rotting mass that reeked of the stench of death. Rubber was in such short supply that for the most part, we had been operating without surgical gloves for more than a year, and to scrub before surgery we had only what they called "sand soap," a mixture that was two-thirds sand to one-third soap. Under these circumstances, it's mi-raculous that any of the wounded we treated survived, but many did – a tribute to the toughness of the human spirit more than to our skill.

For the first time, we were fighting alongside our allies, the Germans. They were superb soldiers and they excelled at the arts of war (no one who has faced them in any conflict would argue otherwise) but being forced to live in constant company with them, I had noted that we had little in com-mon except our language. On the first night in the hunting lodge, I was led along the row of wounded by a German master sergeant, who barked at his men to lie at attention. Many had fractured limbs, some would not survive the hour, but the ser-geant expected them to lie with their arms and legs perfectly straight while I walked through to examine their wounds. Not wanting to dress him down in front of the men, I took him outside and made him understand that my surgery was not a parade ground. I told him that if I saw him talking to wounded men like that again I would have him removed and sent back into the fighting. His beefy face turned red and I thought for a moment he was going to strike me, but he thought better of it, saluted briskly and stalked away.

There was no way I could shake my illness under these conditions, with far too little sleep and only the thinnest soup and an occasional wedge of the bread made from ground turnips and sawdust for nourishment, but I had no choice. I could operate and give them a chance to live, or collapse and let them die. So I went on amputating and stitching and setting, removing shrapnel fragments where I could, leaving some for surgeons working in better conditions farther from the front lines.

Around dusk on All Souls Day, November 2, 1917, four nurses arrived at our outpost. It was rare to see females this far forward, but not unheard of. Our entire army was on the move, pursuing the fleeing Italians. The nurses, with a group of ambulances, had been caught without shelter on the road down below with the chilly early November night settling in, so the officer in command of their transport brought them halfway up the mountain, on the assumption that they could be of assistance in the field hospital and find shelter at the same time.

The women caused something of a stir among the wounded men, some of whom had not seen a female in weeks, but I barely noticed. When I glanced up, they were like any of the thousands of other nurses I had seen during the course of the war, clad in the usual plain grey smocks with the red cross symbol on the left sleeve, their hair covered with matching grey scarves. I saw two squarish women who might have been forty or fifty or sixty, and gestured weakly at them to take their place where they chose. I was too exhausted and weak to give orders, or even to welcome them to the surgery. Fortunately, they were all experienced, and soon they were making themselves useful, bringing water to the wounded, fetching forceps and scissors and such bandages as we had, sometimes suturing a wound as I moved on to the next wounded soldier.

We worked well into the night. Around midnight there were no more wounded who had not been seen, although there were many for whom we could do nothing except try to ease their suffering. I was about to put down my implements and collapse on the nearest stretcher for a few hours of sleep when one of the nurses called out that a man was choking on a sliver of shrapnel that was lodged in his throat. I gestured to two orderlies to bring him to me and they did so, although their legs were almost as weary as mine.

The soldier was young, not more than eighteen. His eyes were wide and desperate. He had been quiet all evening, but now I saw that he couldn't speak without fear that the shard of metal in his throat would do more damage than it had already done. The shrapnel had just missed his carotid artery, but now it was lodged against his windpipe. I had two choices, to make a wider cut so that I could extract the shrapnel without slicing through his windpipe, or simply to try to pull it straight out. The desperation in his eyes told me what I had to do; if I took time to open him up, he might suffocate before I got to the shrapnel. I took a deep breath, trying to steady my shaking hands. I was about to begin to remove the shrapnel, when I glanced up at the nurse who was attending me, the one who had called attention to the wounded soldier's plight.

The nurse gazed back at me with a look of surprise on her face. I nearly collapsed. My legs wobbled and I had to grab the operating table to keep from falling. I was looking into the green eyes of Hanna Goss, and she was staring back at me. Even with the surgical mask covering her face, her eyes were unmistakable.

"Hanna," I managed to croak. "Hanna!"

I saw the alarm in her face and thought for a moment that it was because she didn't recognize me. "Maxim!" I said. "I'm Dr. Maxim Balsano. Montreal... years ago... before the war... you came to my lodgings..."

She shook her head violently and pointed to the wounded man on the table. I understood. For the moment, there were more important things to attend to. I bent to the task, concentrating so fiercely that I barely noticed the movement around me. I got a secure hold on the sliver of shrapnel, held my breath, and eased it out of the soldier's throat a millimetre at a time. When it was free, the soldier and I caught our breath in the same instant. I saw the look of gratitude in his eyes as he took great gulps of air, stood back to wipe my brow, gazed across the table expecting to see Hanna and saw in her place one of the older nurses.

"The nurse who was here," I said, "where did she go?"

The woman pointed vaguely to the door. I tore off my mask. "There's only a very small wound," I said to the nurse. "Can you suture it for me, nurse? Two stitches should do it."

She nodded and began sponging away the trickle of blood from the wound. I stepped away and staggered toward the door on exhausted legs. The beefy German master sergeant was standing outside the door, smoking a cigarette. When he saw me, he flung it down and saluted.

"The nurse," I said to him, not bothering to return his salute. "There was a nurse in here before. Did you see where she went?"

"The young one? She went down there," he said, and pointed at the narrow, rocky road that descended the mountain. "She asked me where she could find transport. I told her it's down on the road. The way she came, she ought to know that."

I thanked him and hurried down the steep path. Within fifty meters I had twice stumbled and cut my hands on sharp edges of granite. It was only partly cloudy and there was a sliver of moon to light the way, but still the path was narrow and dangerous. I had to pick my way. If I tried to hurry, I risked a terrible fall. As I worked my way down, I kept calling to her: "Hanna! Hanna! It's me, Maxim! Please, I have to talk to you! Wait for me, please!"

I was halfway down when a bombardment commenced from our lines. Shells from the big guns whistled overhead. I gave up shouting, because there was no way she could hear me over that. I could barely hear myself. I hurried on down the mountain until I came to the encampment where the motorized ambulances had stopped that afternoon. There was only one left. I found a lieutenant who was awake and asked what had happened to the others.

"They just left," he said, "headed for Tolmin – or maybe it was back to Gorizia."

"Which was it?" I said, shouting to be heard over the din of the bombardment, "don't you know?"

"It's none of my business. A captain gave the order to move out, so they moved."

"Why? It's the middle of the night. I have wounded men up there who are going to need transport in the morning."

"We were told there were more ambulances on their way, and these were needed somewhere else."

I was so exasperated, I wanted to scream. "Did a nurse go with them?" I asked.

"Maybe. I didn't notice."

"A red-haired nurse. Very pretty."

He shrugged. "If I saw her, I would have noticed," he said.

I looked down the road toward Gorizia, and back up the road toward Tolmin, but I could see nothing at all, and with the bombardment going on there was no way to hear the engines of the ambulances. I had the absurd thought of running desperately in one direction or another, but I had used up the last of my reserves hurrying down the mountain after the nurse I thought was Hanna.

I explained to the lieutenant that I was a medical officer, that I had been operating in the surgery up the mountain, that I was exhausted and ill and needed a place to sleep for a few hours. He led me to the tent where the ambulance drivers had been sleeping before they were roused and given orders to move on. There were still a dozen blankets inside, and the tent held the warmth of their bodies. I crawled into it, piled blankets atop my shivering body, and in a moment I was fast asleep.

My last thought before I lost consciousness had the crystal clarity of a fever: *It was Hanna. I saw her eyes. I saw red hair under that grey scarf. I saw the way she looked at me. It was Hanna. She is alive and she is here – somewhere.*

It was another ten days before I could shake the fever, days of the most intense dreams I have ever known. The dreams always began the same way. I would hear a voice, a male voice I could not identify, saying the same thing, over and over: *Sie war es. Sie lebt. Sie war es. Sie lebt.* "It was her. She's alive. It was her. She's alive." Sometimes the dream would turn into a bloody horror, a hideous stew of the things I had seen in the war. Other times, something would shift and the dream would become frankly erotic: Hanna in her nurse's uniform, covering my face with kisses, lifting her frock, mounting me right there on the operating table where I had seen her. Somehow, although I was at the time the oldest virgin I knew, my subconscious could imagine the entire scene in the richest detail, right down to the warmth of Hanna enveloping me, the sensation of her bare breasts on my chest. At the moment of my dream climax, she would whisper in my ear: *Ich war es. Ich bin am Leben, Max. Ich liebe dich.*

It was me. I am alive, Max. I love you.

To which I would reply, fervently, *Ich liebe dich, Hanna.*

Of course it was absurd. Hanna Goss was *not* alive. She had been dead almost four years now, murdered in Montreal on Christmas Eve, 1913. I had seen her body with my own eyes, on a table in the morgue. I had attended her funeral. I had seen her coffin lowered into the ground on a frigid January day. It could not be otherwise. When the war was over, I would delve into my dreams, I would take into consideration the state I was in (the fever, the exhaustion) and I would find the cause of my hallucinations. Freud said that dreams are wish fulfilment, after all, and I had no more powerful wish. The circumstances were very different, but the state I was in varied little on the two occasions Hanna had come to me. I was very ill each time, I was exhausted, I was suffering from a high fever, and the visit had come at night, when we are all of us prone to see and hear things that are not there. The *why* of it, that was a proper task for a budding psycho-analyst, which was what I still hoped to become once this ghastly carnage had ended.

The other explanation that occurred to me was that I had encountered a ghostly apparition – that perhaps we see most acutely when we are something other than our everyday alert, healthy, sober selves. Perhaps, I thought, it is only under the most extreme conditions that we are able to really *see* what is before us. We know the rest of the body well but the mind remains a mystery, even now. I had "seen" Hanna three times. Was it possible that the night she visited my apartment and again in a mountain surgery I had seen not the living, breathing Hanna but her spirit?

I wished that it were possible to discuss the intense dreams I had with Dr. Freud. He believed that he must delve into our dreams in order to explore the subconscious in order to better understand the conscious mind. Even now, I believed in my waking hours that Hanna was dead. My subconscious, however, clearly had other thoughts.

Mercifully, perhaps, I was working sixteen, eighteen, sometimes twenty hours a day, so the erotic torments of my dreams were necessarily confined to the brief periods when I was able to snatch a little sleep. Then I received new orders and I was able to leave the front, never to return. My war was almost over.

CHAPTER 25

fter the Battle of Caporetto, I was transferred to the military hospital at Bozen, or Bolzano as it is now called, a facility on the outskirts of town with three thousand beds. It was meant to treat the less significant casualties – less significant, it must be said, only in the eyes of the generals, not to the surgeons or the wounded. I welcomed the move. Next to the madness of a mountainside dressing station near the front on a windy All Souls Night, the hospital was a bastion of order, cleanliness and calm. The wounded still screamed for their mothers, the amputated arms and legs still piled up outside, the dying went on, but at least the surgery was immaculately clean, we had almost enough to eat, we had at least some of the equipment we needed, most of the patients survived – and Dr. Lorenz Bohlen himself was there, the great pioneer in treating fracture wounds with surgical methods, which meant that I was able to absorb as much as I could learn about his techniques. I emerged from the experience a much better surgeon than I had been at the beginning of the war.

The most gratifying thing about the hospital in Bozen was that, after more than three years of almost constant labor, I finally had some time to myself. I used it to stroll the town, to read, to write letters, to begin to recover fragments of myself. By degrees, I was easing back into civilian life.

On a sunny, pleasant Saturday in late March 1918, a day when the arrival of spring made the war seem all the more absurd, I was released from my duties at lunchtime and had the entire afternoon and evening to myself. I went for a lengthy stroll in a town I was coming to love, despite the wartime privations. My steps led me to Piazza Walther, the main square in Bozen, where I came across a pleasant row of shops, including a *chocolaterie* and a dress shop. The *chocolaterie*, sadly, had nothing to offer because of the shortage of both sugar and chocolate caused by the war, and the dress shop, for obvious reasons, did not interest me.

I strolled on, trying to ignore the sudden craving I felt for chocolate, and paused in front of a bookstore window. There were half a dozen slender volumes of verse by Amedeo Traversini displayed in the window, and a placard that said the poet would be reading from his work in both Italian and German that very evening. I had all but forgotten Signore Traversini, the gentleman I had encountered at the hotel in Cherbourg before the war. It seemed an impossible coincidence until I recalled that Bozen was his summer home; it was not summer, but the amiable poet was here nonetheless. I noted the time of the event, and by exchanging shifts with another surgeon, I was able to get the evening free.

When I arrived, I was surprised to see more than a hundred lovers of poetry waiting eagerly to hear Signore Traversini in a town afflicted by the strictures of wartime. They had to make do with candlelight because there was no electricity or kerosene, and the owner of the bookstore apologized profusely because he was unable to provide coffee, wine or cakes, but those in the audience clearly forgave him.

Signore Traversini, elegant as ever, made a dramatic entrance, seated himself on a high stool, and began to read by candlelight, a long poem about a lover lost to the war. His manner was dramatic, his voice commanding. I was startled. The soft spoken man I met in Cherbourg was capable of dramatic contrasts from thunder to whispers and back again. From the first line, he had the audience wrapped around his little finger. They hung on every word. I saw tears glistening in the eyes of some of those nearest me, and when he finished the last poem of the night, they rose as one, whistling and applauding as he bowed his magnificent white head.

I had to wait another hour to speak with him, while he signed copies of his books for those who could afford them and chatted with his adoring fans. When the last one had turned away, I stepped from the shadows, thinking that it was highly unlikely Signore Traversini would recognize me.

I could not have been more wrong. "Herr Doktor Balsano," he thundered, using his stage voice, "you have come at last to Bolzano!" He laughed uproariously at his own joke, embraced me with surprising strength for a man his age, and kissed me repeatedly on both cheeks. "I am so happy to find you well!" he said. "I was afraid the war would have treated you as it has so many others. How is it that we find you in Bolzano?"

"I am a surgeon at the military hospital," I said.

"And how did you find me?"

"Purely by coincidence. I was wandering about today, and I saw the sign in the window. I am happy to see you doing well, and I adored your performance."

He bowed. "*Gracie, gracie.* Now you must say hello to my wife Carlotta, or she will become jealous. Carlotta, Carlotta, *dolcezza,* I want to introduce you to Dr. Maxim Balsano. He was a most wonderful companion to me for a night or two in Cherbourg while I waited for you."

"Of course, you told me about the brilliant young physician who played chess with you. Dr. Balsano, how nice of you to come to hear Amedeo read his poetry." Carlotta, her bosom quivering, approached us in a cloud of perfume and offered her cheek for a kiss. I turned to Signore Travesino to ask for a clarification. "You said your wife?"

"Yes, yes. We were not married at that time, except on the hotel register. You should know that when the war began, that brute of a husband who was married to my darling Carlotta immediately volunteered to serve. Because he was more than forty years of age, he was assigned to guard prisoners of war. He got hold of a bottle of grappa and got drunk on duty one night, passed out too near the prisoners compound, and his head was split like a cantaloupe by a spade wielded by a Bosnian prisoner. The Bosnian liberated the keys from the brute's pocket, fifty prisoners escaped, and Carlotta's nightmare was over. We were free to marry, but we waited until May of 1916 to allow a decent interval for the grieving widow. Because there was a certain scandal attached to our names in Perugia, we decided to come here to live out our days at my home, a house that has been in my family for a hundred and fifty years. You will of course come with us tonight to sample our wine cellar? I will not hear a refusal."

"You have wine?" I said rather stupidly. Except on the rare occasions when our soldiers stumbled on a cache of wine and got blind drunk, I had rarely encountered wine since 1915.

"Of course I do," he smiled. "We are an old family, centuries old. It is a very old cellar. It was old when I was a babe. Our stocks are vast."

Signore Travesino possessed a motorcar, but he could not obtain gasoline, so we walked rather steeply uphill to his villa. Once home, Carlotta busied herself lighting candles, bustled around in the kitchen and emerged with wine, prosciutto, cheese and actual bread. I wanted to weep with joy. When the table was set, Carlotta joined us, snuggling up to her husband. He called her *topolina,* meaning "little mouse," and she called him *polpetto,* for "meatball." I might have been embarrassed by their flirtation, but they were so plainly in love that I could do little but smile at each fresh endearment. As soon as it was polite, I dove into the food. Every mouthful tasted like the finest meal I had ever eaten and the wine (which would have been magnificent even if I had not been deprived for years) was like the nectar of the gods. When I had eaten what I thought was my fill, Carlotta disappeared into the kitchen again and returned with platters of spaghetti smothered in a tomato-and-cheese sauce. To my surprise, I discovered a second appetite and dove in like a starving sailor.

When I could eat no more, we sat back and talked of everything but the war. After dinner, Carlotta brought *caffè corretto* or *caffè corretto alla grappa* in the Venetian fashion, cups of real coffee "corrected" with a healthy dollop of grappa.

It was past eleven o'clock and I had to be on duty at the hospital at seven o'clock in the morning. I was about to thank my hosts and depart, when the poet brought up a topic that hadn't crossed my mind in years: the incident on a lake somewhere in Italy that had involved my erstwhile mentor, Dr. Percival Hyde, and his friend, Count Ottavio Respighi. I had forgotten that we ever discussed it, but Signore Traversini had not. Thanks to the caffè corretto, my drowsiness vanished. We sat on the comfortably overstuffed chairs in his parlor, surrounded by towers of books and sketches of Bozen and the Dolomites, while I gave him my full attention.

"I have always been a very poor excuse for a scholar, because I lack discipline," he said. "I set out to find one thing, and then I become curious about something else, and then something else again, and days or hours later I discover that when I set out to find a certain line in a verse by Petrarch, I have ended up learning instead about miniature Japanese figurines or the Napoleonic wars, and found myself far from my destination. After Carlotta and I were married and left Perugia for Bozen, I had time on my hands. I was in the library in pursuit of one thing or another when I came across a reference in *Corriere della sera* to an incident involving your friends Count Ottavio Respighi and Dr. Percival Hyde. That caught my attention. The newspaper happened to mention it because it was the anniversary of the Regatta on Lago di Garda. I believe I may have told you the incident happened on Lago di Como, which is north of Milano. It did not: It happened on Lago di Garda, which is about a hundred and fifty kilometres south of here.

"The incident became something of an obsession for me. I combed all the newspapers I could find. I tracked down the investigating magistrate, who in the interim had been conscripted into the army, wounded at the Third Battle of the

Isonzo, and returned to practice law in Verona. I found the two medical examiners involved and interviewed two or three of the yachtsmen who were participating in the regatta that day."

Signore Traversini paused for a sip of his brandy. "Now none of this will make any sense to you unless you know of Mr. Adrian Howell. Have you come across the name?"

"I have not."

"I thought as much. According to the *Times* of London, Adrian Howell was a bad seed. He and Percival Hyde were once very close, the best of friends while they were students at Cambridge University. They had met as seven-year-olds at the boarding school they both attended, where they were subjected to the usual sadomasochistic behaviour of teachers at those institutions, with frequent ritual canings. Howell and Hyde grew to be fast friends long before they reached Cambridge. Howell was poor and Hyde was rich, but apart from that, they had much in common. They were both orphans (albeit one with a fortune, the other with little to recommend him apart from his own brilliance) they both wished to become physicians, and they were both fiercely competitive. They rowed and fenced for Cambridge and they were enthusiastic amateur yachtsmen, although Percival had to supply the yacht. Perhaps inevitably, for young men who were such fast friends in that milieu, rumors circulated that they were more than friends, but no one seems to have known the exact nature of their relationship except that they were very close.

"Their differences were more obvious in their academic life. Howell was a scholarship student who had made it as far as Cambridge through sheer intelligence. He was the type who shines at everything, almost without visible effort. His professors extolled his brilliance as did his peers, although they seem to have had some reservations as to his character. No one knew quite what he was going to do, but whatever he did, he was sure to do it well. Hyde, on the other hand, was something of a drudge. He had to work hard to achieve even middling marks, but he obeyed the rules, wrote his exams, and progressed accordingly while Howell's high spirits kept landing him in trouble. He was a prankster, he loved parties, he was adept at sneaking out at all hours of the night. And with the opposite sex, well – you know the effect men like that always have on women. They are irresistible."

At that point, Carlotta interrupted. "You are only saying that, *cuore mio*, because you were that way when you were young. The very devil, if your old friends are to be believed, with lovers in every nook and cranny of the town."

"My old friends exaggerate wildly," Signore Traversini smiled, "and in any case, very few of them are left alive to tell the tale. I am almost the last. Now where was I? Ah, yes, the irresistible Adrian Howell. Unfortunately, his attractiveness to women was his curse. It got him into one scrape after another, until finally he was caught embracing a seventeen-year-old girl from the town in his chambers at Cambridge. This would have been near Christmas in the year 1898.

Howell was expelled from the university immediately, and with no compelling reason to remain in England, he decided to head south by unorthodox means: He would walk from London all the way to Sicily, except for that portion of the journey which took him across the English Channel. He borrowed money from Percival and set out in January, spending some frigid nights sleeping in barns before the weather warmed. Howell apparently aspired to be a writer since he could no longer become a physician, so he kept a number of journals which the *Times* of London later acquired and quoted rather liberally. He had an entertaining if somewhat florid style, a curiosity about everything, and an ability to make friends everywhere he went – a useful trait when you are travelling. Howell spent time in whatever city took his fancy – Amsterdam, Paris, Lyon, Zurich, Milan, Marseille, Barcelona. He had friends everywhere, some in high places, some even in the criminal element. He had a gift for languages and picked them up as he went, as a sponge soaks up water.

"In Italy, he made friends with your Count Ottavio Respighi. He was invited to stay as long as he wished at the Count's villa on the shores of Lago di Garda and he appears to have remained several months at the villa. He was constantly out on the water, sailing a small three-ton yacht, usually by himself, but occasionally in the company of Count Respighi, never anyone else. Apparently he had thought of competing for England in one of the lighter sailing classes at the Olympics in Paris in 1900, where the sailing events for the smaller boats were held on the River Seine, but nothing came of it. In May or June of that year, Percival Hyde, now a Doctor of Medicine, joined Howell at Count Respighi's villa. There was a regatta on Lago di Garda in July, and they immediately made plans to compete.

"Shortly before he arrived in Italy, Dr. Hyde had learned of his inheritance. He would no longer have to get by on a fixed annual income, however generous. His uncle had died and Percival had inherited the Hyde Shipping Company in its entirety, along with many millions of dollars – is that correct?"

"Yes, it is. I learned that much years ago, before I left Montreal."

"According to the *Times* of London, Dr. Hyde thought of canceling the trip to Italy in order to accept his enormous responsibilities in Canada, but he decided to have one last light-hearted fling before the weight of adulthood descended on his shoulders. The fling seems to have consisted mainly of sailing on the lake. Howell and Hyde were out at dawn every morning, no matter what the weather, just the two of them. Those who saw them confirm that they were very able sailors and that had they been able to sail in the regatta, they would have done very well indeed.

"As it happened, the race itself was threatened by weather, a series of heavy thunderstorms that made the waters choppy and difficult to navigate, accompanied by powerful winds and the constant risk of lightning. Most of the sailors, even those planning to compete in the regatta, stayed off the lake. Not so Dr. Hyde and his friend Howell. The day before the race, they were back out on the lake in a three-ton yacht called the Phoebus. The weather kept getting worse, but they sailed on. The sky was black, there were six-foot waves on the water, there was a driving rain that made it almost impossible to see. To make the task of navigating in such conditions even more difficult, Count Respighi, who was no sailor, was out with them. I'm no sailor myself, but I'm told that a three-hundred pound passenger can make the job of handling a small sailboat difficult, because each time he shifts his weight, the boat tilts one way or another.

"They had sailed from a harbor at Riva del Garda, on the north end of the lake, but they were perhaps fifteen miles to the south, nearer Limone sul Garda on the west side, when the Phoebus was swamped by a single enormous wave. The boat was turned upside down and all three were dumped into the water. Count Respighi, the only one of the three wearing a life jacket, bobbed quickly to the surface. Howell and Dr. Hyde were not wearing life jackets, but both were excellent swimmers. Dr. Hyde, who suffered a blow that cut his scalp when the boat turned over, testified later that he was trapped for a few panicky moments underneath the boat, but when he was able to swim to the surface, he located a life preserver from the Phoebus and managed to slip it around his waist. He looked around for Howell but could not locate him on the stormy surface. Still, he was not overly concerned, because Howell was such a good swimmer and the shore, visible during breaks in the storm, was no more than five hundred metres away. Dr. Hyde apparently tried very hard to right the Phoebus, but the boat was dragged down by the weight of its water-logged sail, and he was unable to do so.

"Responding to Count Respighi's cries for help, Dr. Hyde managed to secure a rope to the count's life jacket and set out to tow him to shore. It was exhausting work under those conditions, but he swam and rested, swam and rested, and they reached the dock at Limone sul Garda at about eleven o'clock in the morning. Dr. Hyde found a *carabinieri* station and the count was taken for medical attention at a small hospital, because he was having difficulty breathing. Dr. Hyde expected to see Adrian Howell there waiting, because Howell was the better swimmer and he didn't have the burden of towing the count, but Howell was nowhere to be seen. Hyde paced the dock, waiting, and witnesses said later that he appeared increasingly desperate and frantic.

"By two o'clock in the afternoon, the *carabinieri* had alerted their posts up and down the coast, but no sighting of Adrian Howell had been reported. They sent out two boats and by late afternoon, with the wind dying down and the lake calming, fishermen and even tourist boats had joined the search. The regatta the next day was postponed so that the search for the missing Englishman could go on, but nothing was found. After three days, the search was called off. A week after Howell's disappearance, a body was found by a fisherman, washed up against a dock on the coast just off the town of Bassanega, four kilometres to the south. The body was grotesquely swollen after a week in the water, but there was no doubt: it was the body of Adrian Howell. Dr. Hyde and Count Respighi both made a positive identification. The young assistant coroner, substituting while his boss was away, did a quick examination and pronounced his verdict – accidental death by drowning.

"Of course, nothing is ever simple here in Italy. The investigating magistrate reviewed the verdict and called Count Respighi and Dr. Hyde in for some very sharp questioning, despite the count's pleas that he wasn't up to such an interrogation so short a time after his terrifying ordeal in the water. But the magistrate persisted, and he spent several hours questioning the two men, separately and together. As he told me years later, he found many small inconsistencies in their stories, but then it is common for two witnesses to the same event to give varying accounts. It's when their version of events is identical that investigating magistrates become suspicious.

"In the end, the magistrate agreed with the coroner's verdict: accidental death by drowning. Their passports were returned to Dr. Hyde and Count Respighi by the *carabinieri*, and they were told that they were free to go. Dr. Hyde left the country the next day in order to meet one of his firm's steamships in the port at Genoa. From there, he sailed for Montreal and a new life as one of the wealthiest men in North America. A week after, Count Respighi left to join him, at Dr. Hyde's invitation.

"As it happened, the day after the count left for North America, the coroner returned from his holiday in Switzerland. The body of Adrian Howell had been packed in ice and held for burial, pending his return. After his initial examination of the body, he was ready to sign off on the verdict reached by his assistant, but then he noticed something – a very small hole, so small it was easy to miss, inside the left thigh. Adrian Howell's femoral artery had been penetrated by a thin, very sharp object. The wound was to no great depth, but it had pierced the artery. As a physician, you will understand how quickly such a wound could cause a man to bleed to death."

I felt the room sway and the lights seemed to dim. I saw very clearly Hanna's corpse lying on the table in the morgue in Montreal, the tiny perforation that seemed too small to have killed her, heard the voice of Dr. Gentschenfeld pointing out the wound that had killed her. I didn't have to be told that it does not take a deep wound from a sharp object to kill a human being. I had seen it so many times during the war, a piece of shrapnel three centimetres long that penetrates into the heart, the liver, the femoral artery.

The connection was tenuous, perhaps, but I found it dizzying nonetheless: Lago di Garda in 1900. Montreal in 1913. Two victims, both healthy young people, the athlete Adrian Howell and the singer Hanna Goss. And only two individuals who could in any way be linked to both: Dr. Percival Hyde and Count Ottavio Respighi. I was so stunned that it must have looked as though I would faint, because the next thing I knew, Carlotta was standing over me with a fresh brandy, looking worried. I took a deep draught and felt it burn down my throat.

"*Grazie, grazie,*" I said. "I am fine Signora Traversini. *Grazie.* I knew someone who died in the similar fashion, except that her wound was to the heart. She also knew Dr. Hyde and Count Respighi."

After that, there was no help for it. I had to tell the whole story, from the August day when I first met Hanna to the night she came to my door, the entry of Jem and Sophie, the body on the morgue table, the beating I had taken, my dinner with Rudi Mayr, the uncomfortable meetings with Dr. Hyde's wife and the count, the time spent strolling and chatting with Elise Duvernay in Cherbourg.

When I had finished, it was my turn to ask questions of Signore Traversini again. What had happened after the wound was discovered? If one of the two other men on the boat had stabbed Adrian Howell, why had they not been charged?

Signore Traversini turned first to his wife. "*Un altro* brandy *per favore, pasticcina,*" he said. For a man in his mid-eighties, the poet could drink, and he could do so without visible effect. Once the brandy was warming in his hand, he turned to me.

"I asked the same questions myself," he said. "The investigating magistrate, Signore Cavalcanti, wanted to pursue the investigation, but he had some difficulties. The evidence was almost nonexistent. He had only that little hole in the victim's thigh, and there was water in the lungs, so Howell was breathing when he entered the water. After a week spent washing around the lake, there was no way to determine whether he died from drowning or from the wound to his thigh. There were so many ways he might have suffered that wound. He might have been caught by a fish-hook, by a nail on a wharf, by any sharp object. Or he might have been stabbed, but there was no murder weapon and there were no witnesses, other than the two possible suspects.

"Now consider those two men. One was Count Respighi. He is a real count, by the way, from a very old family, although his father had squandered much of his inheritance before he was born. Nevertheless, he is a man of the nobility with many powerful friends. As for Percival Hyde, he was above suspicion. His inheritance made him one of the wealthiest men in Canada, and an internationally famous psychiatrist. Against all that, we have only one almost invisible hole in the leg of a man who most probably drowned before his thigh was pierced."

"Did the investigating magistrate think of any possible motive, if it was a murder? Dr. Hyde and Adrian Howell were the best of friends."

"They were, and he had only one possible explanation: blackmail. Dr. Hyde had just come into a fortune. There had been whispers of a homosexual affair between the two men. Adrian Howell was a poor man who had been involved in some shady business in the past. Perhaps he saw his opportunity and threatened to expose Dr. Hyde. So Hyde enlisted the help of Count Respighi to eliminate his rival."

We sat in silence, sipping our brandy. I had to admit that there was every possibility that the wound that had pierced the femoral artery of Adrian Howell was accidental and its resemblance to the stabbing that killed Hanna a mere coincidence, but it was tantalizing nonetheless.

The clock chimed. One o'clock. I rose to go, intending to walk back to my quarters at the hospital, but my hosts would not hear of it. There was enough gasoline in the car to take me that far, and Signore Traversini had a black-market connection where he could get more fuel. I would sleep now, and he would take me to the hospital in the morning.

Ten minutes later, I was slipping between the cool sheets of a narrow but comfortable bed in a room next to theirs. Around three o'clock in the morning, I woke suddenly to the sound of a woman crying out, as though she were in pain. In my confused state, I thought at first that it was Hanna. Then I heard the furious squeaking of the bedsprings from down the hall and understood. It was not Hanna but Carlotta, in the throes of passion rather than agony, in the arms of her husband, the octogenarian poet Amedeo Traversini.

I smiled, slipped a pillow over my head to cover my ears, and went back to sleep.

LOVE & HUNGER

VIENNA 1919-1920

CHAPTER 26

I was able to live a quiet life in Bozen for the last year of the war, alternating shifts at the hospital with delightful hours in the company of Carlotta and Amedeo and many of their friends.

The war dragged on, but the Battle of Caporetto marked the real end for Austria. The rest was mere survival, until the empire formally surrendered on November 3, 1918, eight days before the guns fell silent on the Western Front.

That day, November 11, I was taken prisoner. The experience was brief but alarming. A unit of ragged, scavenging Italian troops burst into the hospital, aimed their rifles at the staff and the wounded, and announced that we were all prisoners of war. The scene, initially frightening, quickly turned comic: by that time several hospital trains had already taken most of our casualties back to hospitals in Linz, Vienna, and elsewhere, and the beds in the hospital were mostly filled with wounded Italian soldiers, who began cursing their countrymen in half a dozen different dialects. The filthy sergeant who had been prodding me in the back with his rifle barrel apologized, but when he learned that I was Austrian, he announced that I was a prisoner of war anyway. When he informed his captain that he had captured one of the enemy, the captain reminded him rather sharply that the war was over, and that the Italians were in need of every surgeon they could muster.

After that, my imprisonment was of the strictly technical variety. An Italian medical unit took over the hospital, and I was ordered to remain to help care for the wounded and to organize the transfer of our remaining casualties to Austria. My tenure as a prisoner of war was so lenient that I spent much of my time playing chess with the captain (who played so badly that it was almost impossible to lose to him) and three or four evenings a week at Signore Amedeo Traversini's villa with the poet and Carlotta.

It was not until January 1919 that I was released. I said farewell to Signore Traversini and his wife through a long, wine-soaked dinner at their villa, amidst many promises to meet again at the earliest opportunity. The next afternoon, I left by train to travel from Bozen through Innsbruck to Salzburg. It was a journey of some three hundred kilometers, and yet it required seventeen hours to complete. I had not understood how badly the war affected my homeland until I rode on that dilapidated train, with the wheels squealing for lack of grease and the engine running on brown coal that supplied so little power that every uphill grade was a lengthy test of its endurance.

There was no light at all in the car, not even an oil lamp. We left Bozen at two o'clock in the afternoon. By the time we left Innsbruck it was dark, and we rode in absolute darkness on a moonless night. Despite the discomfort and the privations, the train was crowded, and after Innsbruck people were riding everywhere – seated in the aisle, crouching between seats, even clinging to the steps that led up to the carriages.

There was no question of checking baggage. Everything that wasn't on your person was liable to be stolen, and you would be lucky if the clothes weren't taken from your back. I had taken the advice of the Italian captain and armed myself with a long Italian bayonet. I rode with all my things in an army field pack between my legs, my medical bag held in the crook of my arm. I was fortunate to have the window seat next to a massive soldier who said not a word. I heard sharp struggles going on elsewhere in the car, but the soldier was large enough to discourage anyone from bothering us.

We arrived in Salzburg at first light and I had to fight to get off the train with my bags. I hurried into the station hoping for warmth, but there was no warmth to be found there either, although at least the wind was not blowing through. Finally, after a six-hour wait, a nearly empty train departed for Bad Gastein. I slept through the two-hour journey, and by the time I arrived the sun was setting.

Without telephoning ahead to warn my father, I hired a motorized taxi at the station to take me home. I arrived just as he was sitting down at supper in the company of my grandfather, with Frau Kachelmeier hovering over the two of them. It was only the third time I had been home since the Italians attacked in May of 1915, and the first time in two years. Frau Kachelmeier was surprised into silence. My father hugged me so tightly that I feared he would break a rib, mine or his. My grandfather did not get up, but took my hand and would not let go.

It was an almost wordless reunion. None of us knew what to say. I was home. I had survived the war. Amid so much dying, we were still alive. I took my customary seat at the kitchen table. Frau Kachelmeier set another place for me. I noticed how meager the fare was, although it was far worse in many parts of the country: there was stewed rabbit, a few turnips that had likely had the frost scraped off them, bread that seemed to have at least a little wheat in it, carrots and beets that she had canned in the fall. I had eaten worse, or not eaten at all.

Although they had already begun to eat and had surely said the customary prayer before I arrived, Papa began to say the Lord's Prayer again. I took the hands of my grandfather and Frau Kachelmeier in mine, bowed my head, and spoke the words of the old prayer, with feeling: *Vater unser im himmel, ge-*

heiligt werde dein Name...

When he had finished, Papa dabbed at his eyes with his napkin. "Do you remember Anton?" he asked.

I shook my head. "Anton?"

"The telegraph boy. The day of the Feast of St. Peter and St. Paul, the boy who brought the news that Franz Ferdinand had been assassinated?"

"Ah, yes. Of course. I remember."

"He was killed on the Piave during the last campaign, when we thought he had survived it all. Anton and so many others. So many. They say that Austria lost eight hundred thousand men killed, for nothing. So many sacrificed, and yet the empire is shattered. Finished. There is talk in the village of putting up a memorial to the dead, but I don't think anyone wants to be reminded and there is no money."

I wondered if I might have been able to save Anton, if he had been wounded in my sector. There was no way of knowing. So many had died, in so many different ways. Gas, explosives, disease, frostbite, snipers, machine guns. I remembered the parades, the laughing girls handing flowers to the soldiers, the Radetzky March.

Papa had sold the beautiful black horses, purchased an automobile and learned to drive at the age of sixty-five. "I have been driving for one year," he said proudly, "and I have had only three accidents."

I told them about the Italian poet and his wife, how gracious they had been to me, how well they had fed me, how I wished to invite them to Bad Gastein during the summer. I knew that he wanted to ask, but Papa did not mention what I might do now that I was free of the military. I knew he was hoping I would stay at home, but I had to get back to Vienna. I wanted to resume my work in psychiatry, but more than that, I had to resume the mad search for Hanna. Even in Bozen, there were stories of how bad things were in Vienna, of people trapping rats for the dinner table, genteel women selling themselves for the price of a meal, salaries paid in krone that were more worthless by the day. I would have to see it for myself, but I had no idea how. I didn't even know where I might stay.

As Frau Kachelmeier began the washing up and grand-father went to relieve himself outdoors, my father squeezed my arm. "I am so very happy to see you alive," he said. We held on to each other, putting aside for once the reserve that had always made us shy about such things. I imagined that all over Europe, families were going through the same things. Some were deliriously happy, others completely shattered. It was a lottery, and there was no explaining it. There had to have been a thousand times when I could have been killed by a sniper, a stray shell, a gas attack. I had made it home.~Chapter 27~

The next morning, I was awake so early that my father and grandfather, both early risers, were not yet up. I decided to take advantage of the quiet in the old house to listen to the recordings given to me by Elise Duvernay in Cherbourg in May of 1914. I listened to both, three times each, then I took up the neatly wrapped piles of letters left for me by Frau Kachel-meier and began to read. First was a letter from Jem Doyle.

Montreal
11 December 1918

My dear Maxim,
I hope that this letter finds you alive and well. One never knows in these times. Sophie has gone and got religion on me, because her boys all came home – safe if not exactly sound. Our second-born, Lukacz, was hit in the knee on the first day of the Battle of the Somme, when that damned fool General Douglas Haig had our boys kicking soccer balls into the teeth of machine-gun fire. Lukacz won't be kicking soccer balls, but he's fit otherwise. Tamas was hit while driving a truck with a convoy taking supplies to the front lines. Their entire column was bombed by an aeroplane; we keep inventing new and terrible ways to kill one another. Tamas lost

his hearing in his right ear and they plucked a fair lot of shrapnel out of him, but he hasn't lost his sense of humor. Joszef's wound, suffered at Passchendaele in 1917, was the worst of the lot, because he got gangrene in that festering mud. But they saved his leg, and he's home. That's the best tonic Sophie could have.

As for this old Irish cop, I'm muddling along. They made me a lieutenant-detective, over my noisy protests, because half our coppers went off to the war, leaving only us incompetents behind. Speaking of incompetents, our old friend Cyril Leblanc is behind bars, serving a five-year sentence for theft. Seems he turned up at the Policeman's Ball, of all places, with a youngish girlfriend in tow. The foolish lass was decked out in a sable coat. The fellow who runs the property room recognized the coat as the one that belonged to Hanna Goss – the one that was once stolen from our property room – I think you will recall that incident. The property chap was able to prove the coat had been stolen by a tag sewn inside one sleeve. The girl was arrested and charged with theft, but she protested that Cyril told her he bought it with his gambling winnings. I had the pleasure of interrogating Cyril myself. My Irish temper was up, and he grew fearful for some reason and confessed the whole thing. The prisoners at his gaol were delighted to welcome Cyril into their midst, given that he had sent a few of them to prison in the first place.

Unfortunately, the coat does not bring us any nearer to solving Hanna's murder. Barring an unlikely break, I'm afraid that we will never get to the bottom of it. The two thugs who likely murdered Hanna have never surfaced. We've been unable to learn who paid for Hanna's casket and the funeral, we still can't explain how her body was found several hours before she arrived in your chambers, we still don't know her whereabouts from September to December, 1913.

I know it's a long journey in difficult times, but it would bring much joy to our Sophie if you could visit us again. one day; she had taken you in as one of her sons, and it would be devastating to her if she were to learn that we've lost you. If I could trouble you to pen the briefest of notes to assure her that you're alive and well, I

would be grateful.
   Now I must go. War or no war, crime goes on.

                              As ever,
                              Jem Doyle

Next was a letter from Jan Muršak. We had become separated before the Battle of Caporetto and I had not heard from him since. Jan was working as a surgeon at the Vienna General Hospital. He had rented rooms, and there was space for me should I want to join him. He warned that life in Vienna was a daily struggle and that merely finding enough to eat was a daily challenge, but he added that it might be easier if we faced it together. He added that I would have no difficulty finding employment. The hard part, he said, would be getting *paid* for the work I did. The salary physicians received for their work at the hospital was in krone, obviously, and our currency had lost most of its value. Jan had discovered that the only way to survive was to offer his services outside the hospital, on a barter basis – trading an appendectomy for prosciutto and cheese or setting a fracture in exchange for a loden coat. Sooner or later, I was bound for Vienna, because if there was a trail that would lead somehow to Hanna, it was in Vienna that I would be able to pick it up.

I took time to jot a note to Jan promising that I would join him without saying when, then worked my way through moree letters until I came to one from Elise Duvernay that raised my spirits.

Cherbourg
January 7, 1919
My dearest Maxim,
   They tell me that the mail is once again flowing across our borders in a world without war, so I must attempt to assure myself that you are alive and unhurt. So many are not. Such horrors, such privations, such an absurd war. Please write at the earliest oppor-

tunity to let me know how you have fared.

My address remains unchanged, but my circumstances are much altered since last we spoke. I fear that I have become independently wealthy, through no fault of my own. It seems that Madame Liais took a great liking to me during the last years of her life. Upon her passing in November of 1917, I discovered that she had no living relations, and thus had left to me her sizable home and a much larger personal fortune, except for the endowment she had left to fund a home for indigent women. I have increased that endowment and have taken it upon myself to get the home up and running, an activity that has kept me occupied night and day.

Not for a moment have I forgotten you or my dear Hanna, or your noble quest to learn what happened to her. I know that much time has passed since her death (more than five years – is it not scandalous how quickly time slips away?) but I want to do anything I can to assist you in resuming your quest. I am being presumptuous in thinking that Hanna remains on your mind after all that has happened, but if I know my friend Dr. Balsano, you have not given up. Should you have need of any financial assistance to move things along, you have only to ask and I shall provide. If you are ever to discover who killed Hanna and why, it will be necessary for you to return to Montreal. I have only one favor to ask: if you take ship for Canada, you must depart from Cherbourg, and I beg you to allow me to come along as your traveling companion.

At the earliest opportunity, I hope that you will let me know that my young friend Maxim has survived.

Your friend always,
Elise

The letters read, I dug my old wooden skis out from the shed behind the house, gave them their first waxing in four years, put on a sweater and the tuque I had brought from Quebec in 1914, and went happily *schussing* under the tall Swiss pines. Their branches bowed under the weight of the snow, and when a bird landed on a branch directly above me, it sent a cascade of snow hurtling down the back of my neck. I didn't mind. It had been so long since I had been out skiing that every stride was a pleasure. We had fresh snow overnight, and it was still snowing, those large, plump flakes that decorate Christmas cards. It was cold, but the sort of cold that you can easily balance by traveling at a brisk pace. I knew that it would take weeks of such skiing to recover the strength and health I had once possessed without thinking about it, but one had to start somewhere, and nothing I have ever done has made me feel as alive as skiing on a bracing winter day.

When I returned home, I found Frau Kachelmeier preparing lunch, and Papa going through two scrapbooks full of newspaper clippings he had made while I was away. He read a half-dozen different papers, cutting out items that caught his interest and pasting them into enormous scrapbooks. There were stories on battles, on advances in medical science, social notes concerning old friends from around Bad Gastein, black-bordered newspaper pages reporting the death of Emperor Franz Joseph in November 1916. It was well, I thought, that the old gentleman had not lived to see the end of the war, nor what happened to his beloved country.

I perused those pages with interest, but what really caught my eye was a two-year-old item about the remarkable success the Austrian impresario and manager Rudolf Mayr had achieved in America. I read the story all the way through. It was not until near the end that the writer mentioned a lawsuit that had been filed against Herr Mayr in a New York court in 1915; the suit was brought by a Swiss pianist who charged that Rudi had absconded with the lion's share of the money from an American tour. The lawsuit had been settled out of court and apparently had not damaged Herr Mayr's reputation, because he was now the foremost representative for European musical talent appearing in American cities from Boston to New York to San Francisco.

I noted the name of the pianist and the date. The slippery Herr Mayr had been neither fair nor honest with Hanna and at the first opportunity, I resolved to take it up with him. At the very least, her mother was entitled to Hanna's share of the money and Rudi's success Hanna had earned during the time Herr Mayr represented her as her agent, with interest. His current success made it well within Rudi's means to settle an old debt owed to a poor widow.

It took nearly two days for me to catch up with my correspondence and by the time I came to writing a letter to Rudi, I was rather short with him. I informed Rudi that Frau Goss had disputed his account of his visits to her in Vienna and insisted that no such visits had ever taken place, and I informed him of my intention to see to it that his debt to Hanna was settled in full with a payment to her mother. If it was not, I would make it my business to pursue him through any possible means.

Having completed that unpleasant task, I settled down to a peaceful country routine. I skied daily, I helped Papa from time to time in the surgery, I spent hours reminiscing with him and my grandfather around the fire, I listened to Hanna sing on the gramophone. I knew that this life could not go on forever, but in some ways I wished that it could. Why, after all, did I require a life so much different from that enjoyed by my father and grandfather? They lived in a beautiful place where they were known and respected, they lived well and lacked for nothing. What had made me so restless and ambitious, so incapable of accepting a life as a country doctor in Bad Gastein? It was a question I couldn't answer.

CHAPTER 27

I was still wondering whether Dr. Percival Hyde would invite me to return to Canada when a very different offer reached me in Bad Gastein. Dr. Freud wished to see me in Vienna. He had been very active in a new field, examining the war traumas suffered by combat troops and felt that, in view of my battlefield experience, I might have something to contribute..

"We were able to hold the international congress of psychiatrists in Budapest in September last year, the first time it was held since 1913," wrote Dr. Freud. "Official representatives of the Austrian, Hungarian and German governments, which have ignored us in the past, were present. They have begun to appreciate the part war neuroses must necessarily play in military calculations. A great many soldiers are utterly incapacitated (as you know far better than most) by such trauma, and we understand very little about it; indeed there are not even reliable statistics as to the numbers of men affected, although they are considerable. I would like to discuss your observations of war neuroses in the field and to hear what solutions you might care to advance for treatment.

"I can offer no illusions as to the situation here. We are forced to work in bitter cold indoors because of the lack of heat. There are no funds to be had for any purpose and there are privations we must all endure in what has become a daily struggle for the basics of life, but there is important work to be done here in the field of war trauma and you would be in a position where you would be able to apply your skills and experience to that work."

I was thrilled and flattered. My view of Dr. Freud was rather altered since I left Vienna for Montreal in 1913. I had always admired the man even when we disagreed, but the fact that he had remained in Vienna through such difficult times meant a great deal to me. He could easily have sat out the war in America, or established himself in Zurich in competition with his former disciple turned rival Dr. Carl Jung, but he had chosen to stay in Vienna. I knew that Dr. Freud worked hard to get at the truth. When he had been wrong (as he was about the uses of hypnosis in therapy, for instance) he was quick to admit his error and move on. I was not at all certain that Dr. Percival Hyde would so readily acknowledge his own mistakes.

I wrote immediately to accept Dr. Freud's offer and to tell Jan Muršak that I would join him in February. I was eager to meet with Freud but I was even more anxious to resume the search for Hanna. While in Bozen, I persuaded a high-ranking nurse to search the records of the nursing corps for Hanna Goss. There was no such name in the records. If Hanna had enlisted, she had done so under an assumed name. The only remaining possibility was through her mother in Vienna. I would visit Birgita Goss and see if she was more forthcoming than she had been on the previous visit.

As it happened, grandfather was in the kitchen when I told my father I was leaving for Vienna in a few days' time. He rose and put on his coat as soon as I had finished writing my letters. "Come with me, Maxim," he said. "You'll need snowshoes."

I had things to do, but my grandfather so rarely issued such instructions that I felt I had to comply. I looked to my father for guidance, but he merely shrugged and winked. I followed the old man's lead, dressed warmly and strapped on my snowshoes. By the time I got out the door, he was already a hundred metres away and moving fast, bound for his cabin.

The cabin was buried under nearly two metres of snow, and we had to take shovels and dig our way in. While I shook the snow from my coat, Popi got a fire going in the coal stove, and we stood as near to it as we could while we warmed our hands. When he judged the room was warm enough, he poured us each a tot of brandy and we drank it down.

"I made a trip to Zurich during the war," he said. "Perhaps your father told you?"

"He did not."

"Just as well. I didn't want it to become public knowledge."

Now my interest was fully engaged. My grandfather did not like to travel. He had traveled as far as Salzburg only three times in fifty years and Zurich was more than five hundred kilometres away.

"As you know, I did not support the war," he said. "I despised the whole thing. We were fools for going to war, and now we are suffering the consequences."

I could only nod.

"Go in any direction in the valley," he said, "and you will find dozens of people who invested their life savings in war loans. All those who did are ruined. Even those who were not wiped out by the war loans will find that the fifteen thousand krone they had in the bank before the war is worth a single krone today. Our currency has no value."

Again, I nodded. Apparently, I had been marched three kilometres up a mountain on snowshoes to get a lecture on currency and wartime investment.

"I have never been an especially farsighted man," he went on, "but I do read the financial pages. At the start of the war, I knew that Switzerland was neutral and was likely to remain so. The Swiss have always been masters of banking and investment. They would not be ruined by the war. Even if we had won, we would have been left deeply in debt, with our resources exhausted."

He paused and took his time lighting one of his long pipes.

"Your father, as you know, had some quite good years before the war, after he began working as a physician at the spa. He was paid in a variety of currencies from all over the continent and sometimes even in American dollars, and he was good at hanging on to what he earned. The Balsano family has always been thrifty. I was never so well-off as your father, but I have lived on almost nothing since your grandmother died, and I had a fairly substantial nest egg of my own. When the war began, I knew what had to be done. We quietly withdrew our money from the banks. I took it all to Zurich with me and there I deposited it in Swiss francs. There are four different accounts – one in my name, one in your father's name, and two in your name. I also brought back a sum in francs to take care of our basic needs. The collapse of the krone means that these francs will last a good deal longer than I foresaw.

"The reason I am telling you all this now is that you have plans to live in Vienna. That can be nearly impossible with worthless krone. With Swiss francs, you can at least buy food when it is available on the black market – and many other things, which you are best doing without."

He puffed a black cloud of smoke to the ceiling of the cabin and winked at me again. Then he went to the wall behind the stove, removed a length of one of the rough-hewn pine boards on the inside of the wall, reached into the hole, caught a long leather cord, and pulled it up. It was fastened to a rather heavy metal strongbox, which I helped him to place on the table. He took a key from his pocket and opened it. The box was stuffed with Swiss franc notes, with heavy silver five-franc coins and smaller denominations: half-franc and franc coins, 5-rappen pieces, 10-rappen pieces, 20-rappen. It took us thirty minutes to count it all, but it came to an impressive sum.

"All this is yours," he said, "although I must insist that

you find a safe place for it once you reach Vienna, and I would not trust any Austrian bank in these times."

"I can't accept all that, Popi," I said. "What are you to live on?"

"Me? I have little need for money. Your father takes care of most of my needs. And I'm afraid I'm not much longer for this world."

"But you're in wonderful health! I had difficulty following you in the snow."

"I am, Maxim. But when you are nearing ninety winters on this earth, your time could come at any moment. Now, help me get this into a case for you. You may take it all if you wish, but I suggest you take the banknotes and only a few of the coins. They are very heavy to carry. Those I'll leave in their hiding place, and you will know when it's time to retrieve them."

He reached under his narrow cot, pulled out a small leather case, and began packing it with Swiss francs for me. I thanked him as best I could, slipped the little suitcase inside an ancient army pack for the trip back down the mountain. I knew that he had done me an enormous favor, but I had no idea at that time how enormous it really was. Had grandfather invested in war loans and left our money in Austrian krone, we would have been impoverished, and all my efforts for the next several years would have been concentrated on mere survival. Instead, my Swiss francs would see me and some of my friends through a time when life in Vienna was almost unimaginably difficult – all thanks to the foresight of an old Austrian country doctor and his skepticism toward a ruinous war.

CHAPTER 28

I would like to believe that Jan Muršak was deliriously happy to see me when the dilapidated train pulled into the Wien Westbahnhof station. He was not. Not because we weren't still the greatest of friends, but because it is very difficult to be deliriously happy when you are cold and tired and hungry. Like me, he was always thin, but now he was almost skeletal. His dark hair and solemn features always made Jan look lugubrious, but his appearance normally concealed a quick wit and a cheerful disposition. Now his sorrowful face was completely in tune with his mood. Still, we embraced, and he led me quickly through the crowded station and out to where the taxis normally waited.

One look at the emaciated nags and half-wrecked automobiles outside the train station and we decided to take the tram to Jan's modest apartment, which was within easy walking distance of the hospital. We had to climb four flights of stairs to reach his lodgings, and I was only too happy to let him carry half the weight of my bags. When he opened the door and ushered me inside, the first thing I noticed was that his sitting room was almost as frigid as the outdoors. He showed me to the room that would be mine, which was already equipped with the sort of narrow camp bed I had become accustomed to during the war, and he directed me to the lavatory down the hall. While I was settling in, Jan put a few lumps of brown coal in the stove and got a fire going. Then we sat facing each other, taking stock of the ways we had changed since last we met.

"I'm pleased you are here," he said at last, "but you're a

lunatic. No one comes to Vienna voluntarily these days. We're starving. We can't even get drunk to forget how hungry we are."

His words reminded me that half the weight of my luggage was in food supplies lugged from Bad Gastein. I opened one case and began taking things out, one after another. Wedges of cheese, a side of prosciutto, real bread and *špeh,* the lard Jan loved to smear on bread, a dozen potatoes that weren't moldy, even two jars of pickled beets. Without waiting for an invitation, Jan took out his pocket-knife and began to eat. As I watched (and cut off an occasional wedge of cheese with my own knife) he devoured bread and *špeh* and cheese, like a man who hadn't seen actual food in years.

"You are a prince," he said when the worst of his hunger had been sated. "No, that's not good enough. You are a king. An emperor. Divine. Any man smart enough to bring food to Vienna now is a friend for life."

"I thought we *were* friends for life."

"That depends," Jan said, licking butter off his fingers. "Before you got out the food, I was noticing how they fattened you up at home. I could get five or six good meals out of you, if I wasn't greedy."

I laughed, but it was a macabre laugh. "It's that bad?" I asked.

"It's worse. It's a bleeding mess. Krone worth nothing, no supplies coming in, people trying to survive on rats and pigeons. You can't buy or steal enough coal to stay warm. The hospital is cold, the restaurants are cold and have no food anyway, home is cold. Spring can't come soon enough – for some people, that's the only way they're going to survive. They can't last much longer in this cold. People are freezing to death all over the city, and we have this damned Spanish flu epidemic to contend with on top of that. The hospital was overloaded before – now it's hopeless. We can't keep up."

To cheer him a little, I opened another case and drew out two five-litre bottles of the schnapps my grandfather had made in the fall. "*Tristo kosmatih medvedov*," Jan said, uttering one of his favourite Slovenian oaths, which translates roughly as "three hundred hairy bears." "The man has brought the elixir of the gods!" He darted into the kitchen, came back with two almost clean glasses, and waited impatiently while I poured a thimbleful for myself and filled his to the brim. Jan downed the fiery liquor in three gulps, filled the glass again himself and downed that one before he settled down to nurse a third glass.

"Did I mention that you are a prince?"

"I believe you did..."

"So, my Austrian friend. What are we going to do for our second act?"

"I don't know about you, my Slovenian friend. I must try to find Hanna."

"Hanna? That songbird you keep babbling about? The one who was murdered in 1913?"

It was only then that I realized I hadn't told Jan about the strange encounter on the mountain on All Souls Night, 1917. At first he was a little angry that I hadn't mentioned it before, but I was able to say that I didn't want him to think me a fool.

"*Kristusove gate!*" he swore. "Christ's underwear! I already know you're a fool. You're crazy, or you wouldn't be here. But to come back to a dead city looking for a dead woman, that is inspired madness."

Jan raised his glass: "*Zivio!*" he bellowed. "Let us drink a toast to madness!"

"*Zivio!*"

I told Jan the whole story of what happened during the Battle of Caporetto – the fever, the wounded, the nurses, the soldier with the shrapnel in his throat, the sudden recognition that the nurse on the other side of the table was Hanna, her flight and my fruitless pursuit down the mountain in the darkness.

Jan had seemed at least half-drunk, but now he was

fully alert. "So that's why you've come back to Vienna. *Naj te kaklja brcne!* May the chicken kick you! It has nothing to do with Dr. Freud. You're here to chase a ghost. And all these years I thought I was the crazy one."

"I know. I'm crazy. But she was there, I tell you. Hanna."

Jan rolled his eyes. "So now you will pursue her in this place where you can't tell the living from the dead. You are magnificent, my friend. Magnificent! Magnificently mad! You make Don Quixote himself seem like a man of eminent sanity. This is one to tell the grandchildren!"

"But you said you weren't going to have children. You can't have grandchildren without children!"

"Oh, no. I must have children now. Maybe a dozen. And they can have a dozen children each, and I will gather them all around, a gross of snot-nosed grandchildren, and tell them the story, how my great and wonderful friend Maxim saw a ghost on a mountaintop and set out to find her! This is romance! This is love! This is madness!"

Jan was in fine form. I let him go on about my magnificent madness, sprinkling almost every phrase with more Slovenian curses without repeating the same one twice. Finally he asked a practical question. "Where will you begin?"

"Her mother is still here, so far as I know. She is a seamstress. She has a house and a tailoring business near Leopoldstadt. I saw her right at the start of the war and she was strangely unfriendly, as though she was anxious to hurry me out the door. I brought food and I thought she would be grateful, but if she was, she hid it well. I will go to pay her a visit in the morning."

"Then you shall not go alone! Like Don Quixote tilting at the windmill, you shall have your Sancho Panza at your side!"

"You're too tall to be Sancho Panza."

"True, true. And you are too short to be the Don. So I shall be the magnificently mad Don Quixote de la Mancha, and you shall be his runty friend Sancho, the skeptic mounted on his donkey. We ride at dawn!"

Neither of us saw the dawn. We woke at ten o'clock to the racket of the Sunday morning church bells up the street and crawled out of bed, groaning and frozen, our heads pounding from an excess of schnapps. Still, Jan was game for an excursion to Hanna's former home – once we had something in our stomachs to counter the effects of the alcohol. I sliced some more of the bread and smeared it with *špeh*, Jan's favourite breakfast. After two slices of that washed down with glasses of yellowish water, Jan pronounced himself ready to go.

I still had a headache and the brilliant Sunday morning sunshine outdoors hurt my eyes, but the crisp air made the headache lift. We took one dilapidated tram between two long walks and arrived at the home of Birgita Goss just at noon. There was no sign of life and no one responded when we knocked and rang the bell. We waited half an hour, then strolled over to the Prater. We watched children squeal on the ferris wheel, visited the flea circus ourselves, decided that our stomachs weren't settled enough to try the *achterbahn,* a kind of roller coaster, and tried to convince ourselves that things were normal, although they clearly weren't. Everyone was too thin, clothing was frayed or patched, most of the adults and too many of the children had that pinched look of the hungry, and although they walked around and looked hungrily at the few treats on sale or coaxed for rides on the merry-go-round, most people had no money to spend. After two hours, we walked back and tried the doorbell again, and again there was no response. I think Jan was more discouraged than I was. I had told him that Birgita was also Slovenian and he wanted to meet her.

We walked to a café, drank something that tasted vaguely of coffee, and returned one last time. There was still no answer when we pounded on the door and rang the doorbell, so we wandered disconsolately back toward the tram. We were halfway there when I thought I saw a familiar figure and a quick flash of red hair rounding a corner a block ahead of us. "Hanna!" I shouted. "Hanna!"

She did not look back and I took off in pursuit, like a sprinter launched from the starting blocks. After fifty strides or so, I heard Jan panting after me, his long legs gaining ground with every stride. As I hit the corner where the woman had turned, I also hit a patch of ice. My boots had once been good army boots, but there was no tread left on the sole. I went flying through the air and landed heavily on my side.

Jan caught up and bent over me anxiously, instantly the emergency surgeon at work, but when I was able to speak, I told him that I didn't think anything was broken. He helped me slowly to my feet and I stood, gasping for breath, poking gingerly at my ribs. It appeared nothing was broken, thanks to my relative youth and my heavily padded winter greatcoat.

"Did you see where Hanna went?" I asked Jan as soon as I was able to speak.

"I didn't see anyone at all," he said. "One moment we were walking along like sane Viennese, the next moment you were off like a magnificent madman. *Je bela cesta!* The road is white! You really are crazy."

"I would know that red hair anywhere. I want to know where Hanna went."

"Hanna, Hanna, Hanna. My friend, you were in the war too long. So was I, but you went really crazy. I didn't see a red-haired woman and even if there was one, if you're going to chase after every redhead in Vienna, you're going to be a busy man. I like redheads too (and blondes, and brunettes) but I don't run after every one I see."

I looked up and down the street in both directions, but it was getting colder as the sun went down and we were the only people out. The houses on both sides of the street were ordinary, dilapidated, lower middle class homes. The woman I saw could have vanished into any one of them, or perhaps I didn't see her at all. "There was something about the way she walked," I said. "I just caught a glimpse of her, then she was gone."

Jan sang it back to me, as though my words were the beginning of a song. *"I just caught a glimpse of her, then she was gone... la-da-di, la-da-da!* That seems to be the story of you and this Hanna: you catch a glimpse of her, and then she's gone. She's a phantom. A figment. A ghost. You are a rational man until it comes to this Hanna, then you are crazy as a kangaroo. Come on, my crazy Austrian friend, let's get you home and have some of that lovely schnapps. It warms my heart, and it will be good for your bruises."

"You think I'm a fool, don't you?" I asked Jan over another supper of bread and cheese and grappa. "You don't believe that Hanna is alive, do you?"

Jan shrugged his bony shoulders. "What does it matter what I believe? *You* believe she's alive. That's all that matters."

CHAPTER 29

"Of course, your Hanna does not exist," said Dr. Freud. "Not in the present. We are men of science, I am sure you know that the Hanna you believe you saw is a trick of the imagination. What you experienced is somewhere between dream and hallucination. The conditions each time were extreme: extreme fatigue, high fever, sleep deprivation, the unparalleled stress of war. This Hanna is not real. Whether we call it hallucination or dream, the impetus is the same. It is wish fulfillment. I have been clear on the nature of dreams. They represent fulfillment of a wish, although not always in ways that are obvious or easy to interpret. You said that you have the most intense erotic dreams involving this woman, did you not?"

"I did. And that I feel the most terrible guilt afterward, as though I had violated her."

"That is normal, my friend. Entirely normal. There is nothing out of the ordinary here. You experience profound erotic and romantic desire for this woman, Hanna. You are unable to fulfill those desires in any way during your waking hours, so your subconscious, unfulfilled desires break through in the form of dreams. You need not go searching for this young woman. She does not exist. You saw her dead on the pathologist's table, you saw the wound that killed her, you saw her buried. We are men of science, doctor. We do not believe in life after death."

Like Dr. Freud, I wore my overcoat indoors, along with a scarf and a heavy woolen sweater. We were in his office at Berggasse 19 in Vienna, and we were freezing. I was seated on a plush red couch against the wall, Dr. Freud on a matching chair. It was February, three months after the end of the war, and the privations the Viennese had endured during the war were getting worse. Coal was so scarce that my host rationed it a few lumps at a time, and the scant heat that emerged was not enough to fend off the cold outside, where it was eleven degrees below zero.

It was our second meeting. At our first meeting, Dr. Freud had been more than welcoming. Initially, he wanted to know everything I could tell him about Austrian prisoners of war being held in Italy. Possible courses of treatment for men dealing with war neuroses would have to wait. Freud's son, Martin, had been taken prisoner with his entire unit by the Italians *after* the war had ended, and Freud had reason to fear that Martin had been wounded. Despite his international stature and his energetic efforts on Martin's behalf, he had been unable to get further information, and anxiety as to Martin's fate would troubled his mind day and night.

All I was able to tell him was that we had been well-treated by the Italians, to the point where I had been free to visit a poet friend in Bozen most evenings. As a surgeon who was needed at the hospital, however, I received special treatment. Regrettably, I knew little or nothing about the fate of combat troops held prisoner in Italy, but I had made some friends among the Italian officers and I promised to make inquiries to see if more could be learned about the whereabouts of Martin Freud.

Most of our first meeting had been taken up with a detailed discussion of the phenomenon of battlefield trauma. It was an issue that had troubled me since early on in the war, and I was pleased to know that it had drawn the attention of the eminent Dr. Freud. I had seen dozens of cases, although the men typically passed through my hands so quickly that I was rarely able to offer anything at all in the way of psychiatric treatment. When Freud urged me to write a paper on the subject and offered to help shepherd it into print, I jumped at the chance.

At our second meeting a week later, however, I brought up the story of Hanna Goss and gave him a brief outline of events from the night we first met in August 1913 until the encounter in that converted mountainside hunting lodge during the Battle of Caporetto on All Souls Day, November 2, 1917. I told him also, in some detail, of the intense erotic and romantic dreams I had of her, and how the dreams had become more frequent since that last meeting. Freud listened with great interest, with that gift of attention that made it possible for him to attend to what a patient was saying with every molecule of his being. I wish to stress that I was speaking to him as a colleague, not as a patient, but I welcomed the opportunity to discuss the mystery of the murder and apparent reapparance of Hanna Goss.

Freud was no great aficionado of the opera, but he had twice heard Hanna perform during the winter of 1912-1913, before she left Vienna for Montreal, once when she sang the "Mein Herr Marquis" aria in a performance of the Johann Strauss opera *Der Flierdermaus*, and again in a recital during which she performed "Chacun le sait" from Donizetti's *La Fille du Regiment* and the "Vedrai carino" from Don Giovanni.

"I had the impression that she was both a wonderful singer and a delightful human being," he said, "but we must not let our impressions of her carry us into the realm of fantasy. Her death is tragic, but we must not allow sorrow to sweep away what we know to be true."

It was my inclination to disagree. I was not a patient unwrapping his inner world for Dr. Freud, and yet I felt that resistance so common among those who are undergoing analysis, when the tendency is to put every possible obstacle in the path of both the analyst and oneself. It is a phenomenon that Freud himself had noted, even in patients who very much want to participate in the process, and who are making every effort to get at the truth. I knew all that, and yet I wanted to insist that my last encounter with Hanna had not been a dream.

"We cannot always immediately locate the rational explanation," said Dr. Freud, "and yet we must not conclude from our failure that such an explanation does not exist. We must constantly separate what is mere fantasy from what cannot be proven in any scientific way. I believe you told me once that your mother died when you were very young, is that not so? And that you were able to recall nothing of what she was like?"

"I remember shadows," I said. "A shadowy figure over my bed. A scent like cinnamon. That is all."

"A shadowy figure. Yes, quite. That is what she would be to you. So that when you become attached to another female figure, the attachment is quite intense, is it not?"

"I suppose it is."

"The woman you described sleeping in a chair in your rooms in the middle of the night, the nurse who appeared at the operating table as you were removing shrapnel from a soldier's throat. Shadows."

I wanted to dispute Freud's conclusion that Hanna was a mere shadow, a figment of my imagination, wish fulfillment expressed in a dream, but I hadn't the strength, physical or mental. Those probing, intelligent, questioning eyes were on me, and I simply froze. I made no reply, because I had nothing more to say, but he had not shaken my faith.

I left the house at Berggasse 19 with much to ponder. Dr. Freud had one interpretation of the intense dreams I had of Hanna. I had another. I did not wish to argue with his view that dreams represent wish fulfillment, but Hanna was not a shadow. The very intensity of my dreams was proof of her existence, as though she was talking to me through my dreams when she said *Ich lebe, Maxim.*

In a city of half-starved shadows, ghostly Hanna was more alive to me than the people I met on the street. I had barely left Dr. Freud's office when I was accosted by a young woman whose only resemblance to Hanna was her reddish hair. Still, I felt drawn to her, by pity if nothing else. She was clearly hungry, like most Viennese, but from her shabby clothing it was clear that she had known better times. I could not see her clearly in the gathering darkness, but I understood her proposition clearly enough. She wanted me to follow her into a laneway for a sexual act. I declined her offer, but I reached into my pocket, found some Swiss francs from my grandfather's cache, and pressed them into her half-frozen hand, knowing that they were worth many times our Austrian krone. She looked at them in astonishment, burst into tears, and fell to her knees in gratitude.

"It's not for me," she said, "I must buy food for my girl. Her father was killed in the war."

"Then buy for both of you," I said, and found more Swiss francs to give to her. "Because if you are too weak or ill to care for your daughter, the child will perish too."

I walked away rather hastily. I felt that if I looked back, my heart would break. In a starving city in the harshest times we had known, this solitary widow forced to take to the streets to survive was the symbol of our time.

CHAPTER 30

The balance of the winter passed. Spring arrived, and with it some minor relief for the suffering denizens of Vienna. We were still hungry, but at least we were no longer cold. Even with my Swiss francs, Jan and I found it difficult to survive. Jan once waited all night in a very long queue outside a butcher's shop, only to find when the shop opened in the morning that the butcher had sufficient meat for only the first thirty people in line. The remainder were sent home with empty hands and empty stomachs.

At least once a week, I visited the home of Birgita Goss to ring the doorbell. I tried to arrive at various hours of the day and night in the hope that I would catch her at home, but I was not successful. Once I noticed that there were fresh flowers growing in front, but they might have been an annual variety. On one chilly evening, I thought I saw smoke rising from the chimney, but there was no answer when I knocked and rang the bell.

There were no more sightings of Hanna. I scrutinized the face of every red-haired woman I saw on the street, without success. I did manage to learn something about Birgita Goss, although it was not the news I wanted to hear. After another fruitless visit, I stopped to purchase a copy of the afternoon edition of *Neue Freie Presse* from the elderly Jewish woman who ran a little stand at the corner. She did a brisk business. Vienna might be starving, but the Viennese needed to have their newspapers several times a day.

"Madame," I said to her, "I wonder if you might answer a question for me?"

I had tipped her handsomely, and she answered in the affirmative.

"There is a woman who lives near here; I have attempted to visit her several times, without success. She is a tailor, so I would expect her to be at the shop in her home, but I can never seem to catch her there. Her name is Frau Birgita Goss, do you know her?"

"Of course I know her! We were good friends. *Sie ist tot*, Frau Goss. She died in winter, of *der spanische Grippe*. And no wonder, it was freezing in her house, she didn't have much food. So many, so many carried away. These are evil times."

So Frau Goss had died of the Spanish flu. The epidemic was hitting Vienna hard. Jan talked of little else. He was especially troubled by the fact that so many of the victims were young and healthy, unlike other flu epidemics that seemed to affect the old and infirm. Now it had taken Frau Goss.

I was stunned. "And her daughter?" I asked. "Her daughter, Hanna?"

The old woman shook her head sorrowfully. "*Die Sängerin Hanna*? She is also dead," she said. Without prompting, she offered details of Hanna's death: "Before the war. She was only twenty years old. Beautiful voice. She was raped and stabbed in the throat by a gang of Gypsies in Montenegro. She was traveling alone. You try to tell these young modern girls it is dangerous to travel alone, but they do not listen. I have three daughters. Do they listen? Never. Never. They are the sorrow of an old woman, like this girl Hanna, *die Sängerin*, killed with her legs open for the Gypsies."

The old woman's words left me shocked and angry. I couldn't stop myself from trying to correct her. "I think you will find that she was killed by two men in Montreal, Canada," I said. "and they were not Gypsies, nor was she raped."

"Believe your fairy tales if you wish," she said with contempt. "I know what I know."

The tram arrived and I hurried to board it with my newspaper. I had to get away, before I was seen cursing an old woman on the street. I returned to the apartment feeling so burdened with sorrow that I felt unable to eat. But a schnapps or two and a few of Jan's cheerful oaths restored my spirits, and that evening Jan and I decided that we would spend a few weeks that summer at my home in Bad Gastein. I was still working with Dr. Freud on the treatment of war neuroses, but Freud himself intended to spend a month in Bad Gastein, although he was living in straitened circumstances like everyone else. We would be able to continue our weekly meetings to discuss my work, Jan and I would have enough to eat without standing in line all night to buy nonexistent meat, and the sunshine and fresh air would do us good after a brutal winter we had endured.

Shortly after we arrived at my home, I received a letter from Jem Doyle concerning a development which, while it did not concern Hanna Goss directly, nevertheless cast Dr. Percival Hyde in a somewhat different light. I should say "Sir Percival" now that he had been knighted by the king, but somehow I could never get accustomed to that.

Montreal
June 27, 1919
Maxim,
I trust you are enjoying your summer at home in Bad Gastein with your Slovene friend, Dr. Jan Muršak. We'd love to share a bottle of pálinka with you and this fellow, so you must spirit him across the Atlantic one day.

I have a bit of news to share with you, nothing that bears on the investigation into the death of Hanna Goss, but perhaps you will find it of interest. It appears that Mrs. Percival Hyde, once the beautiful Eleanor Porter, has been confined to a private hospital near McGill, one that is apparently affiliated with Dr. Hyde in some way, though we have not been able to find out exactly how. We haven't even been able to learn the name of this institution, although it is handsomely endowed and appears to cater to the very wealthy. I had heard rumors for years that Mrs. Hyde has been drinking heavily. She has disrupted several parties, where she has the habit of becoming seriously inebriated and telling folks that "terrible things" are afoot at the Hyde mansion, although she never specifies exactly what "terrible things" she has in mind.

We had a report about six weeks ago that a woman was found wandering on Pine Avenue "in a state of undress." In fact, she was completely nude and barefoot. The woman was Eleanor Hyde, and she was quite intoxicated. Our men bundled her in a blanket and took her home to her husband. Then there was word that she had disappeared, but another detective, on an unrelated assignment concerning another woman who had vanished, visited this asylum and saw Mrs. Hyde among the patients. He recognized her from the many photos that have appeared in the newspapers over the years. Apparently she is taking the cure, and it's all very hush-hush. Poor woman. So wealthy, and yet so troubled.

All here are doing well. Sophie is a grandmother, thanks to Joszef and his wife, Julie. A bouncing baby girl, named Marie-Anne Silvie Yolande Marguerite Beatrice Szitva, under the prevailing French-Canadian theory that you can never burden a child with too many names.

We await your first visit, young man.

Yours,

Jem

I was deighted by the news of the grandchild, burdened with names or otherwise, but appalled by the fate of poor Eleanor Hyde, now confined, most probably against her will. Apparently the unspecified "terrible things" she had once mentioned to me were still going on, as was her drinking. I was surprised that in this instance, that silken bully Count Respighi had not been able to manage her in such a way as to keep her from wandering the streets naked. The more actively involved I became in various forms of therapy and psychoanalysis meant to deal with human neuroses, the less I could support confining patients, especially against their will. In most of the institutions I had visited, confinement itself was a way of driving people mad. When that confinement was combined with some of the more grotesque solutions, such as straitjackets, insulin shock, electric shock therapy and lobotomies, the results were the opposite of the cure we sought. Healthy humans suffering from some sort of treatable neurosis were reduced to babbling, incoherent beings. I didn't know whether that was the case with Eleanor Hyde, but it was disappointing that a better solution could not be found in a case in which her spouse was an internationally known psychiatrist.

What troubled me most was that I knew Eleanor would have no control over her fate. If her husband sought to have her committed, she would be placed in an institution on his testimony alone. Given that her husband happened to be a famed psychiatrist, there would be no questions asked. Public or private, the institution would do his bidding where his wife was concerned. I made a note to myself that night on a topic for future research. What role did the sheer powerlessness of women play in their neuroses? If any person lacks the freedom to make even the most basic choices about life, what effect does that have on the mind? Surely that is a kind of prison, even if you are not technically confined. We know that there are other sorts of confinement that do not involve prison walls; I thought of Emma Bovary, so tightly restricted by her nonentity of a husband and the conventions of the small-town *bourgeoisie.* How many tens of thousands of women lived such straitened lives? Was Eleanor Hyde one of them? Was that behind her drinking and her eventual breakdown?

Dr. Freud was a sturdy, rapid walker who enjoyed setting out for quick tours in the company of someone who knew the area thoroughly, as I did. We would walk a dozen kilometers, with Freud firing the occasional question while I did my best to respond without making a fool of myself. When we returned to Vienna, he wanted to set up a thorough clinical study of combat veterans who were still suffering from war neuroses. He wanted a good number of subjects, and they were easy to find. You had only to set out the door, even on the Ringstrasse, and you would encounter them everywhere, men with missing arms, missing legs, missing their senses, reduced to begging. The wounded who could not function at all were still being cared for, but those with mental traumas were simply cast out into the street to fend for themselves. Dr. Freud wanted me to recruit as many as I could and to begin assembling a comprehensive list of their symptoms and the way they responded to treatment. I was so keen to get started that I wanted to return to Vienna, but I lingered because the summer was golden, there was almost enough to eat in Frau Kachelmeier's kitchen (where even Dr. Freud occasionally stopped for lunch) and because there had been a development that made the summer of 1919 especially memorable.

A few days after we arrived in Bad Gastein, Karine Vogel came from Gmund am Tegernsee for a visit, and to put aside the sorrows of her widowhood through travel. She seemed older and rather drawn, as most of us did after the war, but she was still a very energetic, attractive young woman. I feared that she might want to rekindle something of the affection we had for each other in 1914, but I was spending a great deal of time talking and hiking with Dr. Freud, and Jan Muršak stepped in to fill the void. Karine and Jan had much in common. They both loved to hike, swim, ride bicycles, drink wine and talk – especially talk. I knew that something was going on when I noticed that Jan had dropped the Slovenian oaths with which he sprinkled every sentence but I did not realize how quickly it was progressing until he confessed that he had fallen in love with Karine.

In the past, Jan had always insisted that the only woman he would ever love was all of them, and he had industriously spread his affections around when we were in university and after, but this was different. Jan was smitten, and after a lengthy preamble, he apologized to me and asked if I would be offended if he proposed to her. I assured him that I would not be in the least offended. I was delighted. Jan valued intelligence and energy, and Karine had both in abundance. She had experienced hardship during the war, but so had he. They were perfectly suited.

Within a few days, everything was settled. Karine accepted Jan's proposal and they decided to get married immediately, before the end of the summer. On our last day in Bad Gastein, we all attended the wedding. Karine returned to Germany and Jan made a brief trip to Vienna to pack the few things he owned for shipment to his new home, and then I was alone in the stricken city, without Jan's bawdy jokes and frequent oaths to keep my spirits up, with another hungry winter looming, a great deal of work to me done on the important but depressing issue of war neuroses, and my fruitless quest to find Hanna now at an end, because without the faint hope that I might find her through her mother, there was no way to carry on the search.

CHAPTER 31

I found salvation in my work. I threw myself into it in earnest now that Jan was gone, and I found it easy to put in twelve or fourteen hours a day, six days a week. Sunday mornings, I attended mass at St. Stephen's, where I went to collect my thoughts and to admire the architecture. In the afternoon, if the day was fair, I roamed the city. If it was not, I did the same thing I did the other six days of the week – I worked. I began assembling case histories of war neuroses, talking with the men for several hours every morning, alone and in groups and writing up my notes in the afternoons. I met frequently with Dr. Freud to inform him of my progress.

Like everyone else, I spent too many hours of my spare time trying to find enough food to survive. I had plenty of Swiss francs thanks to my grandfather, but there was little to buy and I hadn't the time to stand all night in a butcher's queue. Twice Papa sent packages of supplies from Bad Gastein, and both times they vanished en route, stolen by starving postal workers or the men who worked the trains. I felt guilty turning to the black market, but there was nowhere else to go: if I didn't eat, I couldn't work.

Out of habit more than hope, I still watched the faces of young women on the tram and on the street, always searching for Hanna. Once or twice, I stared so brazenly that a woman took offense, but for the most part, my beardless face and harmless-looking appearance kept me out of trouble. Just as well, because I had reached the point where I could no more stop searching than I could stop breathing.

Life might have gone on like that forever – working too

much, eating too little, absent-mindedly scanning the faces in the crowd for Hanna everywhere I went. The fall turned crisp and cold, winter and more hardship was in the air. I was aboard the tram on my way to the hospital early one morning, reading letters mailed in the same envelope from the happy newlyweds, Karine and Jan, when I noticed the throngs on the street. It was All Saints Day, November 1, the day all of Catholic Vienna, rich and poor (and now mostly poor) made its way to the cemeteries, bearing candles and flowers, colored lanterns and holy images to decorate the graves of their loved ones. Many Viennese would spend the entire day adorning family graves. Before the war, the *Neue Freie Presse* and most other newspapers ran detailed critiques of the floral displays on the tombs of some of our more celebrated citizens, such as the composers Beethoven and Schubert and numerous captains of industry whose sole accomplishment was to make themselves very rich. I didn't know whether the newspapers had maintained the practice, but I smiled to see that at least one of our traditions had survived.

Many of those on their way to the cemeteries carried baskets of food. They would spend the night in the cemeteries, maintaining their vigils. Those who could afford it hired substitutes, usually old women dressed in black to take their places. If you didn't know what was taking place, it was frightening to enter a cemetery and see a multitude of these wraiths moving in the darkness. The crones would spend the night nibbling bits of bread and bacon and mumbling liturgies from their prayer books, and at dawn they would scuttle away like roaches in the light.

I was halfway to the hospital when I had a sudden inspiration. I jumped off the tram at the next stop and onto another. In ten minutes I was at the news kiosk where the old Jewish woman who had told me of the death of Birgita Goss sold her copies of *Neue Freie Presse.* She had angered me with her talk of Hanna being raped and murdered by Gypsies in Montenegro, but I was prepared to forgive her. To my relief, she was still there. I waited for her to complete her transactions with two other customers, bought my own copy of *Neue Freie Presse* and tipped her extravagantly.

"Madame, we spoke in the spring," I said. "I enquired about Birgita Goss, and you told me that she had died of *der spanische Grippe*, do you recall?"

She looked at me rather sharply, but she nodded. "Yes, I remember you."

"You know so much about the neighborhood, I thought perhaps you could tell me where Frau Goss is buried?"

She hesitated. I guessed correctly that she was waiting for another tip and pressed another Swiss franc into her palm. "*Der Kaiser Juberlaum,*" she said. "*Franz von Assisi.*" The Kaiser Jubilee church, as it was sometimes known, was the Church of Francis of Assisi on the Mexikoplatz. Because of my passion for architecture, I knew it well. The cathedral itself was no more than twenty years old, but the cemetery was much older. I thanked the woman and hurried away before she could start telling me about the attack on Hanna in Montenegro again.

It was a final gamble. If Hanna was alive, if she was not buried in an elaborate coffin in a grave at the Mount Royal Cemetery in Montreal, then I was convinced that she would visit her mother's grave on this night of all nights. She was Catholic, she was Viennese, the tradition was so deeply ingrained in her soul that she would not be able to do otherwise – *if* she was living, *if* she had not moved far away, if, if, if... It was the one time, the one place when I would not be searching for a needle in a haystack. I would join the rest and keep the All Souls vigil in the cemetery. I would go to the house of the dead to search for the living. If at the end of this night she had not appeared, I would give up the quest and find a way to resume the hunt, not for the living Hanna, but for the men who had murdered her.

I was impatient all day. My mind drifted when I talked to patients in the morning, in the afternoon I could not concentrate on my notes, and at three o'clock I gave up and left for my apartment. All Souls Day fell on a Sunday, so I would be able to take the next day off, which was just as well, because I planned to stay awake the entire night. I rushed home, assembled a basket of provisions, put on long underwear, three pairs of socks, two sweaters, my Quebec tuque, my army greatcoat, and two pairs of gloves.

By the time I arrived at the cemetery, it was dusk and a great party was in progress. Jugglers juggled, musicians played, hawkers sold hot drinks and tiny cakes. At that hour, the cemetery was so crowded, it was difficult to make my way through the throng. After searching without success for nearly an hour, I found a caretaker who was able to direct me to the grave of Frau Birgita Goss. I bought two cakes, a hot drink of some unnamed but potent origin, and the largest bouquet of flowers I could find – white asters, the favourite flower at this time of year because of the way the white blooms seemed to burst through the darkness.

There were many elaborate headstones in the cemetery. At the larger mausoleums, footmen stood guard with torches, as they had before the war, but hers was simple, a small grey stone in the northwest corner of the graveyard, bearing the inscription: *Birgita Goss, 1872-1918*. My pulse quickened when I saw that someone had left a candle and a small bouquet of flowers at the grave, but then it occurred to me that it could have been any friend, acquaintance or relative who left those flowers. I placed my own flowers at the grave and looked for a place to wait where I could see the grave clearly without being noticed. I found a spot, up against a tall pine tree, between two other graves ten paces away. There was no one keeping a vigil at either one, so I could sit with my back to the tree and keep watch.

At first, the wait didn't wear on me too much. The moon was at the quarter and mainly visible through a scattering of cloud, the stars were out, the musicians played on. Entire families were holding their All Souls picnics at the grave of a young one. Strangers found our customs bizarre, but

I liked that we turned All Souls night into a festival. It was better to remember the dead this way than through the wailing and gnashing of teeth.

After midnight, clouds hid the moon and it turned colder and darker. I got up and thrashed my arms around to keep warm, then went to purchase another hot drink and roasted chestnuts from the vendors outside the cemetery before hurrying back to resume my post. Most of the family groups had departed and the brightly decorated graveyard was left to the stones and the old women, shrouded in black, keeping their paid vigils, reciting their liturgies. Now and then, I could hear the crunch of boots on gravel approaching and someone would leave asters at a grave and depart, but never at Birgita's grave.

An hour after midnight, it began to rain, a light, cold rain. Even under all the clothing I had worn, I felt the chill. It seemed to rise from the ground to clutch at me, like the hands of the dead. I dug into my basket and found some hard biscuits and a few bits of bacon, which I nibbled under the illusion that they would keep me warm. *Look at you,* I taunted myself. *What a pathetic figure you have become. Haunting the grave of this dead woman, on the very tiny chance that her equally dead daughter might somehow appear. You are half-mad, Maxim.*

I wasn't aware that I had drifted off to sleep but I must have, because when I opened my eyes, an old woman was walking directly at me, her shoes crunching on the gravel path. It was still raining, and the rain made it hard to see. She was shrouded in black, and hunched over, and she was walking very slowly, looking at each grave as she came to it. She was carrying a spray of white asters. She peered at grave after grave in turn, until at last she came to the grave of Birgita Goss. There she came to a halt, dropped to her knees, lay the asters very carefully at the foot of the stone, and drew her dark cape around her. I watched for a time as she remained there motionless. I thought I heard the sound of someone sobbing very softly, but it might have been the wind. I tried to decide what to do. If the crone was here, it was because someone had paid her to keep the vigil – and perhaps that someone was Hanna. I had to find out.

I approached her carefully, circling around so that I would not come up behind and startle her. She was bent over the grave, so I knelt three or four feet away, and spoke as softly as I could.

"Excuse me..." I said. She looked up. The clouds parted for an instant and the moon lit her face, which was streaked with tears. But it was the face of a young woman, not an old crone paid to keep a graveside vigil. I went on with the little speech I had rehearsed in my mind, not quite able to take in what I was seeing. As I attempted to explain myself, something between a groan and a shriek escaped from her lips, and she leapt to her feet with surprising agility for one so old. An instant later she was off, but not before the hood of her cape fell back, releasing a cascade of blonde hair. The hair confused me. I was very tired, and my brain was not processing things in the usual fashion. But the face, the face...

"Hanna!" I shouted, but I had hesitated too long. She was already thirty feet away, a very agile young woman darting around the sleeping crones, the empty food baskets, the gravestones. I had the absurd impulse to return to my post to recover my basket, but then I realized that she would be long gone if I did. I set off after her, but the wet greatcoat was enormously heavy, as were my old army boots, and the gravel was slippery and dangerous. There were obstacles everywhere, abandoned baskets, gravestones, shrubbery, more huddled old women. She was already ten paces ahead of me and gaining. I wanted to throw off the greatcoat, but I knew that if I did it would be lost and I would never find another as warm. But the thing was too large for me, so long it fell almost to my ankles, and I was constantly tripping on it.

Still, I managed to keep her in sight until she reached the cemetery gates and turned left, overturning a chestnut vendor's cart as she did so. I leapt over the cart, shouting an apology at the cursing vendor as I did so, and kept up my pursuit, past the façade of St. Francis of Assisi, out onto the slick and dangerous cobblestones of the Mexikoplatz, then an abrupt right down a sidestreet. I managed to keep her in sight, but only by running as hard as I could. Already, my thighs were burning and my lungs felt as though they would burst. The street we were on was deserted except for us, and so dark that at times I was following her by sound more than by sight.

We made two more quick turns, a left and then a right only a dozen steps later, and I was completely lost. If I couldn't catch up with her I would be trying to find my way out of this maze until dawn. When we came to a wider street that was lit by a single electric lamp, she lengthened her stride and began gaining ground again. I strained to keep up, but it was hopeless. She was a really fine runner and I was exhausted. Even if I threw off the coat, I knew that I would not be able to catch her.

I was about to give up when she caught her toe in a crack in the sidewalk and stumbled. She ran on for three or four strides, her arms windmilling as she fought for balance, and then she fell hard on both knees. When I caught up to her, she was still struggling to get to her feet. I helped her up and stood holding her sleeve while she brushed at her knees.

"Please," she said. "Why are you running after me? Let me go."

"No," I gasped. "Two years... the mountain... The Battle of Caporetto... You were there, Hanna, across the table. Looking for you... Every face. Please, Hanna. ... Let me help."

"You have the wrong person. I am not Hanna. My name is Claudia. Please. Let me go. I am not who you think."

"Perhaps you are using the name Claudia. And you have dyed your hair blonde. But you are Hanna. I know your face. Since Montreal, your face has been with me. Day and night."

"No, sir. I have never been to Montreal. You have made a mistake."

"Then why did you run? You were at your mother's grave. Your mother has only one daughter. I waited all night. I thought you might come. I am Maxim. Six years ago, you came to my apartment in Montreal..."

"No! It's not true."

"It is. It was Christmas Eve. There was a snowstorm. You were frightened. I was very ill. Two men came looking for you. I told them I had typhoid so they would leave. I fell asleep. I saw you once in the night, asleep on a chair, but when I woke you were gone. You left me a note, saying that you did not want to put me in danger. A few days later, I was on a tram and I saw the story in the newspaper. It said you were murdered. ... It was terrible. I blamed myself for letting you go. The story in the newspaper said your body was found on Christmas Eve, but I knew you were with me at three o'clock in the morning on Christmas Day. It was a mystery that drove me mad. ... I tried so hard to find out what happened..."

I was rambling, trying to tell a complicated story to a woman who might be a stranger in the middle of the night. I was beginning to think that perhaps I was wrong after all when she burst into tears and buried her face in her hands. I put my arms around her and she sagged against me. I let her sob, on and on until I thought she would never stop. At last she caught her breath and looked up at me, her face streaked with tears.

"Ah, Maxim, Maxim," she said. "You have found me. What are we going to do?"

CHAPTER 32

"First, we must get warm," I said. "It's terribly cold now. I have been out all night, waiting, hoping to see you."

Hanna peered at my face. She had that same open, lovely countenance I had first glimpsed on a late summer night in Montreal, now somewhat altered by privation but more beautiful than ever.

"Then come with me," she said, so softly I could barely hear. "We will go to my mother's house. It is not far."

She turned to go, but I clung to her sleeve. "You don't have to hold onto me," she said.

"Yes, I do. I have waited too long. And you run very well."

She took my arm. "I won't run away from you again. I promise. Whatever made you wait for me there, in a cemetery?"

"I know the Viennese," I said. "I learned from an old news vendor near your home that your mother had died, rest her soul. The woman told me where she was buried, and I knew that if you were alive you'd want to keep the vigil for your mother on All Souls Night. I didn't have much hope, but I had to try."

We walked on in silence, arm in arm. Every few steps, I had to pinch myself. Here I was, after all these years, walking arm in arm with a living, breathing Hanna. She was neither a ghost nor a figment of my imagination. Tonight I was very cold, but I had no fever. My head was clear, and Hanna was with me. We walked several blocks without saying a word, then we rounded a corner and I recognized her home, even in the darkness. We made our way up the steps, and she withdrew a key from under her cloak. A moment later we were inside, but the temperature in the house was almost as cold as outdoors.

"We have one bucket of good coal I have not used," she said. "I will get it." When she started toward the back of the house, I almost went after her, but then I realized that at some point I would have to trust her and I let her go.

She came back with the coal, lit a stub of a candle and got a fire going in the stove. I was shivering, but I took delight in watching every smallest gesture of the living Hanna.

"It has been two years tonight since I last saw you," I said. "The night on the mountain."

She smiled a rueful smile. "Yes, it is, isn't it? Two years. And almost six years since..."

"Yes. Since you died."

Hanna sat on the same divan where her mother had sat when I visited before the war. She motioned for me to sit next to her. "Yes. It was all very horrible," she said. "The worst time of my life. But I cannot talk of it now. Perhaps I will try to explain it to you, but another time. Just sit with me now and let us try to get warm. I am cold, Maxim. Sometimes I think I am cold to my very soul."

I knew what she meant. I felt that way in the mountains at times, as though the cold had seeped into my bones and marrow and that I would never be warm again. Hanna was still wrapped in her cloak, I in my greatcoat. We sat watching the hypnotic glow of the goals in the stove, listening to the groan of metal as the stove heated. Like all coal stoves, this one heated your face to burning while your backside froze, but we were grateful for any heat at all.

Around us, the tailor's dummies Birgita had used in her work kept watch, shadowy figures in the darkness. I had often thought of all the things Hanna and I might say to each other if we could ever be together like this, but now we sat in silence, content simply to be indoors, watching the fire. Hanna leaned against me, and I put my arm around her. We sat like that for perhaps an hour, then she got up and put on a pot to make tea from herbs her mother had collected in the forest. There was no milk or sugar, but the tea warmed us and when we had finished, Hanna asked me to help drag her mattress down so we could sleep by the fire. We placed it on the floor as near the stove as we dared, and lay down side by side, wrapping my greatcoat and her cloak around us.

"It was you on the mountain during the Battle of Caporetto, wasn't it?" I said when we were settled. "You called my attention to the man with shrapnel in his throat. Then I recognized you. You ran away down the mountain. I tried to catch up with you then, but when I reached the place where the ambulances were parked, you had gone. ... But I'm sure it was you."

"*Ich war es*," she said softly. "It was me. I ran because I did not want to put you in danger. I did not want anyone to know that I was alive. ..."

"Why not, Hanna?"

"Because if they know, they will kill us."

"*Who* will kill us?"

"I cannot tell you... I don't know who. ... Someone. Very dangerous people. I can't explain now. Perhaps later. Now we should sleep, or you will be ill again."

"I am not sickly," I told her. "It is only coincidence that I was ill when you saw me."

Hanna smiled. "Two times I saw you, two times you were sick."

"You forget the first time."

"Not the first time in the summer, no. It is true. The first time, I thought you were a beautiful man."

A beautiful man. What an odd thing for her to say. Never once in my life had I thought of myself as a beautiful man.

"I tried to find where you were through the records of

the nursing corps," I said. "But they had no one by the name Hanna Goss."

"That's because I have taken the name Claudia Lisjak. Lisjak was my mother's maiden name, and Claudia is my middle name. I was very frightened of the people in Montreal. I didn't want them to be able to pursue me."

"Even here?"

"Even here – as long as they thought I was dead, I felt safe."

"And you dyed your hair."

"Yes. I had to. My hair – it was too obvious. I thought that you would not have known me if not for the hair."

"Possibly not. But surely your neighbours must know you are living at your mother's?"

"Oh, but I'm not living here. I still have the key to the house. I came back only for tonight. I have been living in Bratislava. I was there when my mother became ill. The trains are so bad that it took me two days to get home after I got the telegram that she was very ill with the Spanish Flu, and the next morning she died."

"I am so sorry, Hanna."

"We live in evil times," she said. "I want to sell the house and my mother's business, but it is difficult. What is worth one hundred crowns today will cost two hundred next week. Nothing has any value except coals for the stove, something to wear, food to eat."

"Love has value," I said. I don't know what made me say it. It just slipped out, then I felt foolish for saying it, but Hanna reached out to me in the darkness and stroked my face.

"Yes," she said. "Love has value."

I don't believe that we let go of each other once that night. At first Hanna lay on her side with her back to me, and I was pressed up against her, my arms around her, my face in her hair. Later, I woke to find myself on my back, while Hanna was turned to me, one leg over mine, her head on my shoulder. I knew from her soft and steady breathing that she was asleep, and I lay caressing her hair, watching her face in the light of a waxing gibbous moon glimpsed through a high window.

She woke once, and looked at me, and ran her fingers over my face again, as though making certain that I was real. "Maxim," she said, "I have dreamt of you. Many times." Then she fell asleep again without saying more.

The next thing I knew, I heard the old clock in the hallway strike nine times. It was nine o'clock. We had slept the night away in each other's arms and this time, Hanna was still there, her blonde hair on my shoulder, her breathing soft on my neck. The room was suffused in a pale November light, and the tailor's dummies in the shadows no longer looked like ghosts.

Hanna managed to get the stove going again and make more tea. Without discussing it, we were both eager to get outside. Hanna disappeared into her room for a few minutes and when she came out she had changed into a dark green dress – not a gown such as the one I had seen her wearing in Montreal, but the sort of dress a woman might wear to work in an office. She was also carrying something I never thought I would see again – my plain green loden coat, the one she had taken the night she left my flat in Montreal.

"I'm sorry I didn't return this right away as I promised I would," she said. "I was going to bring it back the night I went to get the letter from your flat, but it was very cold and I needed it."

"Thank you for the coat – but what did you say about the letter? You took it?"

"I thought you would have guessed. I went back when you were not home and slipped into your apartment through the window. It was foolish of me, I suppose, but I was afraid the letter would fall into the wrong hands if they came back looking for me again."

"They? Who are they, Hanna? Who were you running from that night?"

Her face grew flushed and she waved a hand as though

she was brushing away invisible cobwebs. She shook her head violently. "I can't talk about it. They are dangerous. They hurt people and they kill people. Please let's not talk about it. I don't want you to be in danger because of what you know. It frightens me terribly. Perhaps one day, but not now."

I changed the subject by asking Hanna if she would like to walk with me to my flat, so that I could change clothes and perhaps we could pack a basket for a picnic. I had some food in my apartment and we could find a sunny park near my lodgings to have lunch. She smiled the loveliest smile, and I thought that I could endure virtually all the privations of this city, if only I could see that smile every day.

We set out. The weather was fair. Vienna by daylight was filthy. Once the tidiest of cities, it was now a place where papers blew everywhere: rival political philosophies, manifestos, advertising flyers, entire newspaper pages. Everything was cast aside, nothing was picked up. Our footsteps led us through Augarten Park, along Berggasse past the home and office of Dr. Freud (which I pointed out to her) then right on Wahringer Strasse to the side street where Jan had rented lodgings near the hospital. I thought Hanna might be reluctant to enter a gentleman's apartment, but then it occurred to me that it was not the first time that she had been in my home. She waited patiently while I changed, and then I packed a picnic basket and we went out to find a sunny place to have our picnic. I asked Hanna where she wanted to go, and she chose the Stadtpark, so we walked another half an hour and arrived with healthy appetites.

I was bursting with questions, but I kept them to myself. The first was the most urgent. Since it was obviously not Hanna who had been murdered in Montreal on Christmas Eve, 1913, who was it? *Someone* had been murdered, because I had definitely seen a woman's body on the pathologist's table. Did Hanna know who it was, or was it perhaps a complete stranger whose death was completely unconnected to Hanna?

My questions would have to wait. What mattered now

was caring for Hanna. Although she seemed very relaxed as we sat on a bench in the Stadtpark watching mothers play with children while fathers read their newspapers, Hanna was a very frightened woman. She had been frightened in Montreal, frightened when she ran away on the mountain, frightened the previous night at her mother's grave, frightened even now, sitting beside me in the light of day. She would unburden herself when she was ready, not before.

I was in love with Hanna but I still did not know her, nor did she know me. I told her about Bad Gastein, about being raised by my father after my mother died when I was very young. Mention of my mother reminded her of the mother she had lost to the Spanish Influenza.

"She always wished to see you again so that she could apologize," Hanna said.

"Apologize for what?"

"For the way she behaved the day you came to visit us at the beginning of the war. You brought food, and she was enormously grateful, but when the doorbell rang I hurried upstairs because I didn't want anyone to know I was alive. I had a bad cold and she was afraid my cough would betray my presence in the house. In trying to get you to leave, she behaved in a way that was entirely unlike her. She can no longer apologize to you, so I must apologize on her behalf."

I hastened to tell her that no apology was necessary. Still, it was stunning news> I had been that close to Hanna in 1914 without dreaming that she was only a few steps away.

"You didn't know it was me?" I asked.

"I heard a voice, but nothing distinct. People often came by because my mother still ran her tailoring business. I always hid, but on this occasion the client seemed to stay longer than usual."

Fate takes such strange twists. Had Hanna's cough betrayed her presence, I might have found her five years before I did – but the war would have pulled us apart anyway. Now

I had found her at last, and I was determined that we would never be separated again. When we had finished eating, we wandered around the park, fed bread crumbs from our meal to the ducks, and speculated on when the first snow might fall. On this sunny Sunday, it seemed far away indeed. On the way back to Hanna's home late that afternoon, I found a telegraph office that was open and with Hanna's permission sent off two telegrams, one to Jem in Montreal and one to Elise in Cherbourg. They bore identical messages:

HAVE FOUND HANNA ALIVE AND WELL. LETTER TO FOLLOW. – MAXIM

After we returned to the apartment, I wrote the promised letter to Jem and Sophie. Aside from the fact that Hanna was alive, I could add little to what Jem already knew but I promised to keep him informed of anything I learned. Hanna wanted to write to Elise herself – she had felt guilty for years about leaving her friend and chaperone in the dark as to what had happened, and she wanted to apologize herself.

I'm afraid that at every opportunity, I found myself staring at Hanna, drinking in every detail of her appearance from the sprinkling of freckles on her nose to her creamy skin, her wide mouth, the prominent dimples and the green eyes that seemed to glitter when she smiled. And that hair, that magnificent hair, now blonde. One day, I hoped, she would let it revert to its original colour, but she was a beautiful woman no matter what colour her hair. There were perhaps a few fine lines left from war and worry but the biggest change in Hanna was that she was so gaunt. She had always been a slender woman, but now she was much too thin, as were so many in Vienna. I had vowed to care for her mind, but I also had to look after her body, even if it meant weekly trips home to Bad Gastein to procure enough food.

That night, I brought up the subject of the mysterious thugs who had been following Hanna in Montreal – not to ask questions, but to convince her that she was safe in Vienna. As far as anyone in Canada knew, she was dead. We were six years and an ocean away from all that had happened in Montreal. She was now a nurse named Claudia Lisjak, not the soprano

Hanna Goss. It took some persuasion, but I was able to convince her to remain in Vienna rather than returning to Bratislava, where she had been sharing a cramped flat with a nurse she met during the war. If she was uneasy in her mother's home, then she was welcome to stay in Jan's old room.

We made two trips that first week, one by horse-drawn cab to her mother's home to get some of her things, another by train to Bratislava to pack the few items she had left there. Her friend had already found another woman to share the flat – all over Europe, there were war widows in difficult circumstances in need of a place to stay.

I felt uneasy when I returned to work at the hospital, half-expecting her to have vanished again, but when I returned to the flat Hanna was dressed in a simple nurse's frock for lack of anything else, reading my copy of Dr. Freud's *Die Traumdeutung – The Interpretation of Dreams*. She appeared to have spent the entire day cleaning and tidying my apartment. The floors were spotless, the glass sparkled, the windows were flung open to let in fresh air.

"Does this Freud know anything about women?" she asked before I could take off my coat. I laughed. "Well now – there we have a topic that should last us a month or two."

Hanna soon found a job in the pulmonary ward of the hospital. We settled into life in Vienna and into our domestic life at home. I would have been content to have her sleep in Jan's bed, but she wanted me with her. Nothing happened – we didn't even kiss, although we did hold onto one another very tightly, night after night. She wanted the warmth of my body, the reassurance of my presence, nothing more. I was more in love with her than ever, but she needed a friend and confidante, not a lover.

I wanted to draw her out, to get her to discuss the events in Montreal that had so changed our lives, but I thought it better for her to open up when she felt ready. Hanna was warm and friendly toward me, but she said little. She was a quiet person by nature, and on certain topics she said nothing at all.

Her nights were more revealing. She would occasionally cry out and thrash back and forth in her sleep as though fending off blows, and I would hold her until she calmed. Sometimes she would sit staring at the wall, her legs up and her arms wrapped around her knees, rocking to and fro. It was hard not to step in and ask what was wrong, but I still felt that was the wrong approach. When she was ready, I would know.

On November 21, the third anniversary of the death of Emperor Franz-Joseph, the school children were given the day off and I was given an appointment with Dr. Freud for half an hour to review some interesting cases of war neuroses, I brought up the fact that I had indeed found Hanna. "*Ist das so?*" he said, one of the few times I have seen him ruffled. "*Am leben?*"

"Very much alive."

"How is that possible?"

"I'm still trying to understand that. I believe that she has been traumatized by the events in Montreal. She seems deeply fearful." I described some of her behaviour to Dr. Freud. When I had finished, he nodded.

"It seems to me that she fits in very well with your study of the war neuroses, does she not?" he asked. "She has suffered a great trauma, like the *zitterers,* no?" The shell-shocked veterans wandering our streets often trembled – thus they were called *zitterers,* or shakers. Hanna did not tremble physically, but I had no doubt that she had been shaken to her core – yet I still did not know or understand precisely what had happened to her, or why.

Hanna's story did not come spilling out all at once, like water from a burst dam. At first, it was a mere trickle. It was painful for her to dredge it all up again. As she talked, I played many roles: friend, confessor, scribe, psychoanalyst. For as long as it took for her to tell her story, I tried to put my love for her aside and to be as objective as I would be with a stranger. More than anything, I strove to be the blank page where her story could be engraved.

We talked in the kitchen, we talked on long walks, we talked in the bed we shared. I took no notes as she spoke, but as soon as possible I wrote down everything she said. There was a great deal that Hanna either did not know or did not understand about what had happened to her, and she was careful to avoid speculating about events she did not understand.

Hanna spoke with many hesitations, corrections, detours that ended in unexpected places. She would often stop talking all together, sometimes for as much as an hour, and I would simply wait silently for her to resume her narrative. She slept frequently, and she seemed to need sleep after we had talked, so I would take advantage of her naps to write down all that I could recall of what she said. What I offer here is a version distilled from my notes of our conversations, which ran to several hundred pages, with many repetitions and detours. I cannot produce here her speaking voice, as lovely as her singing voice, or the way I was sometimes mesmerized by this lovely, haunted face as she pried loose her secrets and shared them with me, one by one.

CHAPTER 34

I t began when I told Hanna about the day I learned of her alleged death, and my poor attempts to unravel the mystery. I told her of the tram ride, the newspaper, the headline announcing her death, my initial encounters with Sophie and Jem. I omitted only the New Year's Day visit we had paid to Dr. Good King, the time I thought I had seen her body, naked and shattered, on an autopsy table.

Finally, I mentioned my dinner in Montreal with Herr Rudi Mayr, and the delightful time I had spent in Cherbourg with Elise Duvernay. I noted the shadow that passed over her face when she heard Rudi's name, and the happy way she responded when I brought up Mlle Duvernay.

"I hope that we hear from Elise very soon," Hanna said. "She was so kind to me, one of the kindest persons I have ever known. I feel very guilty for not telling her sooner that I was still alive, but I didn't know where to reach her. It never occurred to me that she might have remained in Cherbourg."

"You seem to like her very much, as do I."

"I do. I wish I could be more like her. Wise and calm."

"You were very young then. You are wiser now."

"I will never be like Elise. I am a woman in fragments. Always. Like a mirror that is broken. I know that. I can't pretend to be other than what I am." Hanna smiled ruefully. "If only I had remained in Vienna and never traveled to the New World... But then I wouldn't know you. You are so very kind, like Elise."

"That is kind of you to say so."

Hanna was quiet for a long while. She wiped her hands

over her face several times, as though trying to wipe something away.

"Elise gave me the recordings you made before you left," I said. "I bought my father a gramophone so that we could play them. They are very beautiful."

Hanna blushed. That was something we had in common, we both had very fair skin and we both reddened at the slightest provocation. "It seems to me now that all that happened to someone else," she said. "All that singing part of my life, from the day Rudi first stepped into the yard where I was hanging the sheets until... until the end. I have often thought that for a girl of sixteen, finding myself the focus of such intense interest on the part of a man like Rudi was like waking to find that you are in the path of a hurricane. Rudi *is* a hurricane. He has so much energy, it spills off him. He must have a hundred ideas a day, and they are always going off like firecrackers, and you are always afraid that the next one is going to be a big explosion that carries you away.

"One moment I was hanging sheets to dry on the line, and the next moment I was in this hurricane, and so many things were happening at once that I didn't even have time to talk. At first, I was very excited when a famous person such as Rudi said wonderful things about my voice. Anyone who loved to sing would have appreciated the attention and flattery he showered on me. I didn't know if I should believe him. Even then, I knew that you can't just take a girl and put her on the stage, it takes years of training. But Rudi was convinced that the training I had received from Herr Zelermeyer was excellent and that with only a little polishing, I would be ready. He said that I had a great deal of power for a singer with a very slender frame, and that I would be like a magnet for all those who loved great singing once I was on the stage.

"We started the training right away, and after that first concert I was more confident, and I thought, 'perhaps I can do this.' My mother thought I could, Herr Zelermeyer thought I could (though neither of them trusted Rudi entirely) and of course, Rudi himself believed in me. Until he decided to make this North American tour, we were okay. If we stayed in Vienna, maybe it would have been different. But when he started talking of Montreal, New York, Boston, Philadelphia – I started to feel some fright. I never had what they called stage fright before. That began later, with the tour. I was frightened of everything, a little. I had been outside Vienna only to visit my grandmother in Galicia. I spoke German and Slovenian. But New York – somehow the name of it was frightening to me. I had seen pictures of the tall buildings, I had seen news-reels with all the people in the street. So many! I thought, 'I cannot sing there. Montreal, yes. Perhaps Boston. But not New York.'

"I tried to tell Rudi of my fears, but he would never listen. He would interrupt, wave his hands and say, 'it is not a problem, it is not a problem, you will be wonderful, they will eat out of your hand in New York City.' I wanted Mama to come along for the trip, but we were going to be away for nine months. She could not leave her business that long. But she insisted that I have a female companion, because already she did not trust Rudi. He argued that it wasn't necessary, but even he could see that I was feeling more and more nervous, so finally he agreed. We interviewed three women. The first two were the most frightful old gorgons. The first one prattled on for half an hour about how she would see to it that I got some discipline in my life, that spoiled young women were the devil's tools and all that. The second one promised never to let me out of her sight. Listening to them, I was feeling more miserable by the moment. Then Elise walked in and I knew in a moment that she was the person for me... If not for Elise, I could never have left Vienna. She was so strong, and she pro-tected me from Rudi."

"You felt as though you needed protection from him?"

Hanna thought about it for a time. "Only after we began the trip," she said. "I don't mean in the sense that I thought he would beat me, although there were times when I thought that was possible. What I mean was that he was very ... intrusive. He was always bursting in with one thing or another. I began to feel I could not breathe when he was near. Always with this schedule and that accompanist and what the acoustics were like in Philadelphia and where we would stay in New York. Sometimes I wanted to scream. Elise would see that, and very gently send him away, so that I could have some peace.

"Even so, it kept getting worse. I felt I was going mad. Rudi was always complaining about how much money he invested in me. I knew it was true, but at the same time I was never paid for my engagements. All I received was money for expenses, and very little of that. I was always supposed to be paying him back, paying him back, but he never showed me the accounts. And he was always complaining about how much the voyage cost, how much it cost to pay Elise to be my companion, how I was a very expensive little diva. Then it would seem that I could not breathe. Each day at sea, it was getting worse, as we got closer to North America."

We were in the kitchen. We had finished a light supper before we started talking, and the two candles we had lit were guttering. It was the time we usually went to bed, but I was reluctant. If Hanna wanted to go on talking, I was willing to listen, but after we sat in silence for a long while, she said that she was tired and wanted to sleep.

I had received four letters from Jem Doyle, asking if Hanna could clarify this point or that, above all if she could explain who the bloody hell it was we had seen on the table at Good King's, since it was certain that it was not Hanna – and by the way, would it be possible to bring her across the pond to testify in Montreal? I had to beg him to be patient. I was afraid that if I pushed too hard, she would pull back into her shell and never talk again. Hanna's well-being came first. Everything else, even the murder investigation, had to come after.

Elise also wrote to express her delight that her great

friend was alive, and to thank me for my persistence. "I did not want to believe too deeply in the possibility," she wrote, "lest the disappointment be too profound when it turned out not to be true. Yet it was always there, wasn't it? I sometimes think the truth can taunt us with its very tantalizing presence – there somewhere, but just out of reach."

Elise concluded her letters to both of us with the same paragraph: "Now you must come to visit me at the first opportunity," she said. "I know life in Vienna is very difficult. I must implore you to come take advantage of my hospitality. I am a wealthy woman now, through no fault of my own, and I must shower you with the largesse you both deserve."

CHAPTER 35

By Christmas of 1919, we were both feeling oppressed in Vienna and in need of a few days out of the city. The clean, cold air of Bad Gastein would do us both good and I wished to visit my grandfather, because it seemed that age was finally catching up with him.

We boarded the usual dilapidated train three days before Christmas. It left Wien Westbahnhof for Salzburg at three o'clock and before we had traveled much more than an hour we were already in darkness. Perhaps it was the darkness, or the hypnotic motion of the train, or the fact that we were fast approaching the sixth anniversary of the night Hanna first came to my apartment in desperation, but as the winter dark settled in, she began to talk, in a voice so soft that I had to bend almost to her lips to hear her over the roar of the train. She was in the seat nearest the window, her face against the cold glass, and we were huddled under my army greatcoat for warmth.

"What is the name of that place in Quebec," she asked me, "it sounds like the English word for *Hut*? Do you know it?"

"North Hatley," I said. "It sounds like *hat*. I know it only because I know you were there," I said. "When I was trying to understand what had happened, I read all the newspaper stories about you that I could find. One was in the society pages of the Montreal *Gazette,* and it mentioned that you had performed at a private estate in North Hatley."

"That was it. North Hatley. I thought it was a very funny name for a town."

"I suppose it is."

"That is where I met him," she said. "He was so kind to

me. He found me in a terrible state. I had left the grounds of the mansion where I was supposed to sing and taken a walk through the woods to calm myself before I sang. It was not successful. I needed Elise with me, but she had remained in the city because she wasn't feeling well. Rudi had accompanied me, but if I told him how anxious I was feeling, that would only have made it worse, so I was taking a walk alone, and crying a little, wondering how I could possibly sing on the great stages of North America if I couldn't even bring myself to perform at a small private event.

"Suddenly, there he was. This tall, very handsome, very confident man. About forty years old, I suppose, extremely well-dressed, with a very long stride. He lifted his hat and asked if I was quite alright.

"He said it in English, of course. I tried to answer, but my English was awful, and he saw immediately that I was German, so he asked, "*Geht es dir gut, fraulein?*" He spoke very good German. That alone made me trust him, immediately. He gave me his handkerchief, and I wiped my eyes, and he put his hand on my shoulder and walked with me. Before I knew it, I was unburdening myself to this total stranger, telling him about the anxiety I felt because I had to sing, how frightened I was of singing in New York, how my manager, Herr Mayr, simply did not understand – all of it. He listened very patiently, considering that he did not know me at all.

"When I had finished talking, he explained that he was a psycho-analyst, and that although he could not propose to help me in more than a superficial way at that moment, he felt that I might calm myself by breathing slowly and deeply. As we walked along together, he showed me how to breathe with him, each of us taking very deep breaths of the forest air with each slow step. It worked. I could feel my heart beating more slowly, the panic subsiding in my chest. By the time we returned to the grounds where I was to perform, I was mostly in possession of myself again. Before I sang, he gave me his card, and insisted that I visit him at his office as soon as we were back in the city. He said that he would make time for after-noon appointments for me, three times a week, so that we could deal as quickly as possible with all that was troubling me before I had to travel on to the United States."

The conductor came through the train, his uniform hanging off his shoulders like a coat on a hanger. I seemed to remember a time when all train conductors were broad-shouldered, imposing men. Now they all looked like scare-crows because they were half-starved.

"May I ask the name of the doctor you met?" I asked, although I already knew the answer.

"You know him," she said. "It was Dr. Percival Hyde."

Dr. Hyde had denied that he had anything at all to do with Hanna singing at the fateful reception at his mansion that August, yet he had encountered her during a forest stroll near North Hatley some weeks earlier. Moreover, Dr. Hyde himself had been the mysterious psychoanalyst she was see-ing in Montreal, during all those afternoons when she would slip away, with Elise Duvernay covering for her absence when Rudi Mayr posed uncomfortable questions.

I did my best to conceal all the confused thoughts run-ning through my mind. "I believe I told you the night we met that Dr. Percival Hyde was the reason I had come to Canada," I said. "Apparently he was knighted by the King for his service during the war. Now he's *Sir* Percival Hyde."

"So do we Austrians call him *Herr Doktor Sir* or *Herr Sir Doktor?*" Hanna asked. I was about to answer her seriously when I realized she was making fun of our national tendency to pile on titles at every opportunity. Hanna had too much sorrow within her to laugh or joke often, but when she did, she had a sly sense of humor.

"Yes, I remember," she went on. "I was pleased to know that you admired him, because I did as well. He had rescued me during that walk in the woods. I knew that it wouldn't last, but it got me through the performance that day, and for that I was very grateful. Rudi was furious. He had been looking for me and couldn't find me, and when he found me walking with a gentleman he was so angry his face turned red. But he couldn't start shouting at me in front of people, and I sang well that day, I think, so Rudi forgave me.

"Before we parted company, I had agreed to begin seeing Dr. Hyde in his office the following Wednesday, and to meet with him three times a week until it was time for me to depart for the American tour. It was embarrassing, but before I could agree I had to inform him that it would be impossible for me to pay, because Rudi never paid me. He laughed and said he was in the enviable position of a man who does not need the money and that he charged patients only so that they would make a serious commitment to the therapy. Otherwise, he said, patients tended to come when they liked and not make a real effort to take part in the healing process. I thanked him, and I told him that I would commit myself entirely to whatever it was he proposed to do, because time was short and I was in a constant state of the most terrible anxiety."

Hanna squeezed my arm and let her head rest on my shoulder. We sat in silence as the train rumbled on through the dark December night, and soon I realized that Hanna was fast asleep – while I could scarcely have been more awake. I was troubled by the fact that Dr. Hyde had not admitted to me that he had known Hanna and that she was a patient of his *before* she sang at the reception at his mansion where we first met. He had also failed to reveal to Jem Doyle that he had treated her – so he had lied to a police officer. He had an excuse, however – some in my profession consider their meetings with patients as sacrosanct as the confessional and believe it is wrong to divulge even the name of the patient. Still, when I asked him who had arranged for Hanna to sing that night, it had nothing to do with the fact that he was treating her, and still he had hidden the truth.

Once we arrived in Bad Gastein, we learned that the fanatically religious Frau Kachelmeier was so upset at the prospect of unmarried friends of opposite sexes staying in the house over the holidays that she went off on one of her pilgrimages, leaving Hanna and I to do the cooking for my father and grandfather, neither of whom could manage for themselves in the kitchen. We had fallen into the comfortable habit of cooking and doing the washing up together, so we did not hesitate to take over the chores, even if the Christmas goose was a rabbit grandfather had shot, and the turnips were moldy, and there was no *sachertorte* from Frau Kachelmeier's oven.

Still, I could plainly see that my ancestors were delighted to have the lovely and gentle Hanna as a guest, and to my surprise she sang three songs for them on Christmas Eve without being asked, and trudged through the snow the three miles to church for midnight mass. On the walk home after, we walked far ahead of the others and talked of the events that had brought us together on a very different Christmas Eve in 1913. Hanna put her arms around my waist and held me as tightly as she could.

"Maximilian, you know that if not for you, I would not be alive. You saved my life, and I shall always be grateful."

I noted that she had used my given name. I had never liked the clumsy "Maximilian," but Hanna had begun using it as a term of endearment, and now I had grown fond of it as well, simply because I loved to hear it on her lips. Oddly, I never thought that I might have saved her life when she came to me that first Christmas Eve. For too many years I thought she had died that night, and even after I learned the truth, I never thought of myself as her saviour.

After two more days of skiing and long winter walks, we were back on the train, returning to Vienna and its privations. I had hoped that perhaps Hanna would resume her narrative on the return journey, but she said barely a word. She was plainly wrapped up in her thoughts, and I did not intrude, although I could feel the emotions she was wrestling with through my hand, which she held the entire way without once letting go.

CHAPTER 36

The first thing we did when we returned to Vienna was to attend a performance of Tosca at the Vienna Staatsoper. Somehow, the music had never stopped in Vienna. Not during the war, not during those terrible years after the war, which in so many ways were worse than the war itself in terms of what those in Vienna endured.

It was the first week of January and bitterly cold. There was not enough heat in the cavernous State Opera, and we could see the musicians (all of whom were wearing their coats) blowing on their hands to warm them before they began the overture. We in the audience huddled together for warmth without removing our coats, hats and scarves or even our mittens. When the performance began we could see the breath of the singers on stage. It seemed impossible, but it went on, and it was as moving as any opera I have ever seen. When the soaring aria *"Vissi d'arte"* in Act II poured out over the audience, I could feel the emotion ripple through Hanna's body. She was with the singer on every note, her lips mouthing every word, and I was imagining the day when Hanna herself, once thought dead, would make her triumphant return to the stage and sing just such a role.

It was that night, perhaps moved by *Tosca,* that Hanna poured forth the rest of her story – or as much as she could remember. I was very tired, but we put more of our scarce coals on the fire, and lit a stub of a candle and she talked in the semi-darkness, her face in profile in the flickering candlelight more beautiful than ever. I was spellbound, I ached for her, yet I was bound by both profession and friendship to be her confessor and physician and to keep my own powerful emotions well in check.

It began when she asked whether I used hypnosis in my practice. "I do not," I said. "It was used by Dr. Freud for a time more than twenty years ago" I said. "I recall exactly what he wrote about it: *Treatment by means of hypnosis is a senseless and worthless proceeding.* I might not have put it so strongly myself, but I would not disagree, although I know that Dr. Hyde is still using it on occasion – or he was, before the war."

"Yes," she said, "he was still using it. He said it might be a good technique for me, because we needed to make rapid progress so that I would be able to perform in New York. The first time we met, we merely talked. Or rather I talked, and he listened, for the most part. I found him very magnetic. Very. I felt drawn to him. Even though he said very little, I felt he understood me. I was disappointed when the time was over and I had to go. That was when he told me that hypnosis might work. When I left he took my hand and there was a moment when I thought he might kiss me, but he did not. And if he had, I knew that I would have welcomed it. I felt flushed and warm all over – exhilarated and aroused."

Her words cut like a knife to the abdomen. It took all my willpower not to allow it to show on my face. I thought I had succeeded, but Hanna paused and reached out to stroke my face. "I know that you love me, Maxim," she said. "I can feel it in everything you do. I am sorry, I know this must be painful for you."

My first impulse was to deny that I loved her, but I had never been dishonest with Hanna, and I didn't want to start now. I simply nodded, and I reassured her that whatever had happened it was in the past, several years in the past now, and it would be absurd for me to feel jealous or hurt over things that happened before I knew her.

After some thought, she resumed. "I felt a little better after that first visit," she said. "But I wasn't really better, I was simply focused on something outside myself. All I thought of was Dr. Hyde. I was focused on him rather than myself. I knew he was married – he wore a ring, but something... I can't justify it. In any case, I went back very eagerly, and the second time he put me under hypnosis. He had warned me that I might not be a good subject, that it might not work – but he said afterward that I am extraordinarily susceptible to hypnosis. He felt certain that under hypnosis, he would be able to make suggestions that would have some force on my behavior. During that first session, he lifted my skirts and pinched the insides of my thighs. He showed me after what he had written. I had no recollection of what happened, but he had made notes: *Subject's skin flushed and hot... nostrils flared... breath very short... after one minute begins thrusting upward with her pelvis... would be easy to induce orgasmic contractions in this patient."*

Hanna broke off, shaking her head. "I was mortified," she said. "I did not understand why he had showed me his notes, but he said he wanted to prove to me that I had deep-seated erotic urges that I was pushing down, and the urges were part of the anxiety I felt."

I nodded. "When he was testing the uses of hypnosis, Dr. Freud had noted the same reaction in a female patient, Fraulein Elizabeth von R. He pinched her thighs during the examination and noted a distinct and immediate reaction on the part of the subject. Dr. Hyde obviously borrowed that little test from him. He professes great disdain for Dr. Freud, but he borrows many of his techniques – in this case, one that Dr. Freud tried and rejected."

"Yes. I am not surprised. Somehow... You will understand that I had very conflicting feelings. Physically, I know, I was very aroused, very attracted to this man. At the same time I was appalled and embarrassed that I had allowed a man to do that, to touch me like that. Yet I knew that I wanted more. I wanted him to do it again. Things progressed very quickly. It did not seem so to me, because I was in such a state of waiting for him, but after three or four sessions of hypnosis

I gave myself to him. I don't want to reveal more. I felt that I was in love with him, and for a time I thought he was in love with me. He was very ardent, Percy. He showered me with gifts. He sent flowers when I sang. He even sent perfume."

"*L'Heure Bleu,*" I said.

"Yes, how did you know?"

"I remembered it from the night we met. I thought I detected a trace of the scent in my apartment after you were there. Then I noted the same haunting scent when I was strolling in Cherbourg with Mlle Duvernay, so I asked her about it. She said you had received it as a gift from an admirer – that and a beautiful sable coat."

"Yes, I did. And the coat, both from Percival. That was quite extravagant. But it was a lovely coast. I thought he adored me. I think it was true for a time. He did not want me to go on tour. He begged me to remain in Montreal. He said that it was not wise for me to go without completing my treatments with him. ... And I listened. I thought he was sincere. I told Rudi that I was thinking of canceling the remainder of the tour, that I wasn't up to it.

"Rudi – well, you know how Rudi was. Enraged. I actually thought he might kill me. Even Percy was worried for me. He said that he was afraid Rudi might harm me. I was in the apartment on in Montreal where I was staying with Mlle Duvernay, and Rudi kept showing up at all hours, demanding that I change my mind and fulfil our contracts. And I refused. ... It was wrong of me, I know. But Dr. Hyde said the most important thing was my well-being, and for that I was better off remaining in treatment with him. He was still putting me under hypnosis three times a week, and I felt unable to refuse him anything... anything at all. If he asked me for something, I would give it, gladly. That was wrong, wasn't it?"

"You mean for you to give him anything he asked?"

"No, for him to ask it of me. That was wrong, wasn't it?"

"Yes. It was very wrong. You were very young, suffering from anxiety, under hypnosis – a subject very susceptible to hypnosis, as well. It was an opportunity for him to exert power over you. This is a problem Dr. Freud has identified – the attraction the patient feels for the analyst. It must be dealt with, not indulged in such a manner. But perhaps he was in love with you and incapable of restraining himself."

Even as I said it, the irony did not escape me. Here I was discussing the possibility that Dr. Hyde had been in love with Hanna and incapable of restraining himself when I was wrestling with the same conflicts. Was my own behaviour toward Hanna entirely proper? Was I capable of restraining myself? I had so far, but could I continue in this fashion when I wanted her desperately?

"Perhaps he could not restrain himself," Hanna was saying. "I don't know. I wonder about that often: did Percy love me? Does he love me still? Is he still mourning his murdered lover? Or does he not care at all? I don't know the answer to those questions. I have often thought of writing to him, but I simply did not want anyone in Canada to know that I was still alive, not even Percy. I felt safer that way, just as I felt safer in Montreal after Percy suggested I move into an apartment he had on Sherbrooke Street. He said that he kept it because it was near the headquarters of his shipping company and near McGill University as well. He said it would make things safer because Rudi would not know where I was and it would be easier for him to see me. By then we were lovers, very intense lovers. I wanted more of it, day and night. I did as Percy suggested. I left a trunk with most of my things in a storage room of the apartment on Greene Avenue and moved into his apartment one afternoon when Elise Duvernay was out and couldn't prevent it. I didn't even need my clothing, he bought me so many things. I didn't tell Rudi where I was going, and I didn't dare tell Elise because I was afraid she would tell Rudi. I just vanished from their world. They would go back to Europe, I didn't care – I had Percival.

"For a few weeks, everything was wonderful. I don't

know how long it was. I was in love, I was loved, I didn't care about anything outside that apartment. The only thing I disliked was Count Respighi. I don't know if you have met the count..."

"I have," I said. "Unfortunately..."

"Yes, unfortunately. In any case, I hated the way the count came and went as though he owned the place, and the way he looked at me as though he owned me. He would leer in the most suggestive way, and look me up and down from neck to ankle as though he were admiring a prize race-horse. He was always carrying a poor little kitten that he almost smothered, and I found it most revolting. When I told Percy that I did not like the count, he became very cross with me. He said that he owed a great deal to Count Respighi, and that I was to accommodate the man in every way. And he emphasized that again, *in every way...* I had no idea what he meant, but I soon found out."

I waited, sensing how very difficult this was for her. "What he meant," she said at last, "was that if the Count should ask for personal favours, specifically sexual favours, I was to comply and submit. I was to be submissive to his desires in every way. Nothing, absolutely nothing was to be *verboten.* Not even things I had never done with Percy, and I was a virgin when Percy first took me. Sometimes I had to do things with both of them at the same time, sometimes with Percy merely present during the act and directing things, like a stage director in the theatre. Then there were other men, and women too. You can't imagine ..."

I was aware that tears were running down my cheeks and I was fighting to hide the fact that my entire body was trembling with anger, but at that moment Hanna vomited profusely. She had no time to get to the lavatory or the sink. She vomited on the floor, and the carpet, and on herself, and some of it got on me. She vomited until her stomach was empty, and then she curled up on the floor, weeping and sobbing and trying to apologize. I assured her that I had seen far worse as a battlefield surgeon during the war. I got a mop and a bucket cleaned up, and when the floor was clean we changed our clothing, and I suggested that perhaps we should sleep.

"No, please. There is more I must tell you. Then we can sleep."

I nodded. I could not deny her at this point. She took a deep breath, sobbed a little, and began again. "I want to be clear, all I wanted was to please Percy, to keep his affection, to do whatever I needed to do to keep him. I don't know whether it was the hypnosis or whether it might have happened anyway, but he had complete control over me. I was unable to refuse him anything. For a time, I thought it would be alright. Then something happened, and to this day I don't understand it. I offended him, and after that things were never the same. We were in bed, Percy and I. It was early in the morning. I was completely naked under the blankets, and half asleep. Then I heard something and I realized the count had let himself into the apartment. He had a key – I hated it, but he did. I nudged Percy, afraid that some awful business was about to transpire, that the villain wanted to use me in his evil fashion, but Percy hastily put on his housecoat and went out to talk with the count. They were talking in English, but then the count said something and Percy began speaking to him very angrily in Italian. I could not understand what they were saying, but it seemed to me that Count Respighi was trying to soothe Percy..

"Then the count left, and I was relieved because it meant I would not have to please him. Percy came back into the room, and I asked what the count had wanted and of course he didn't tell me, because he never told me anything about his business. He was very angry with me. He dressed quickly, and I tried to ask what was wrong, but he would not answer. In ten minutes he was gone without saying goodbye, and he slammed the door on the way out.

"I was left to go over the conversation again and again, trying to understand what I had said that angered him so. He came back again the next day, just long enough to make love to me in a very violent, callous way. It was so brutal that it was as though he was punishing me for some crime. It was like that for perhaps a week. He would burst in at any hour of the day or night, and make love to me in a violent way that sometimes left me bleeding, and leave without saying a word.

"Then as he left the apartment one day, Percy said he would be out of town on business, and he did not know how long he would be away. His manner was kinder, more tender. He said that he had been under a lot of pressure, and he assured me that he would pay more attention to me when he returned. As he left, he reached into his wallet and gave me rather a lot of money, several hundred dollars, and told me to buy myself some nice things to show off for him when he returned. In the beginning, I had never wanted to accept money from him, but I knew that he was very wealthy, and I knew that my mother always needed money. Rudi owed me a great deal, but I didn't know if or when he would pay, so I accepted what Percy gave me and saved it for Mama. I felt sometimes that taking the money made me a prostitute, but I told myself that Percy and I were in love, so that was different.

"I still don't know what prompted me to do this, but I took the cash along with most of the money he had given me and that evening I returned to the hotel for women on Greene Avenue where I had been living with Elise Duvernay. There was a back entrance from the lane that led down to the storage room, and I knew that the woman who ran the hotel never locked it. I slipped down the back stairs without being seen, found my trunk with the heavy padlock, unlocked it and hid the money in the trunk. The trunk had a very heavy padlock, and I locked it carefully and returned the key to the old locket of my mother's that I always wore around my neck, because what was in the trunk was very important – the money, my passport, and a ticket guaranteeing me passage on a steamship traveling from New York to Hamburg in the spring. If I wanted to get away, I now had a means of escape. I wasn't yet at the point where I was ready to attempt to return to Europe, but I felt that I should be prepared in case I wanted to flee.

    "I had no way of knowing whether Elise remained in the apartment, but I did not want to see her in any case. By then I was feeling ashamed and embarrassed for my behaviour. If I had accidentally met up with Elise, I think I would have collapsed completely. To avoid it, I slipped out the way I had come and went back to Percy's apartment and waited for him to return, but he did not return. I never saw him again.

CHAPTER 37

The stub of a candle had guttered and gone out. Candles were expensive and hard to obtain, so we sat in the darkness, cold and shivering. I had passed through the point of absolute fatigue to where I felt numb. Her face now was lit by the moon. She squeezed my hand tightly on both her hands and went on.

"As I waited for Percy to return, I saw no one except the maid, a fat, unfriendly old woman from Brazil who spoke only Portuguese when she spoke at all. I think Percy had chosen her for that reason – because she couldn't communicate with anyone. The weather turned colder. When I went out, I wore my sable coat. It should have made me feel good, but it didn't, although it was very warm.

"I was dressed to go out one evening – I already had the coat on, and I was trying to find my gloves, when there was a very heavy knock at the door. It startled me. Percy had always been very strict – I was never to answer the door. The maid had her own key, as did Percy and the count, and in the event someone came to the door I was simply to remain silent and wait for whomever was at the door to give up and go away. I sat quietly to wait, but there was a second knock, louder than the first, and then a man's voice saying in English: 'Police! Open up!' I was terrified. Why would the police be at my door? What had I done?

"Again I tried to ignore the knocking, but the man's voice shouted, 'we know you're in there, Miss Goss. The doorman told us you were in. Now open the door or we're going to break it down!' Obviously, I had to open it. A heavy man in a grey suit was at the door, and beside him were two others who looked like criminals – one very large, and a smaller one who looked absolutely evil. None of them were in uniform and the two who weren't wearing suits didn't look like policemen at all. The one in the suit held up a badge. 'I'm Sergeant-Detective Cyril Leblanc from the Montreal Police. These two are Constable Sullivan and Constable Labrecque. We have here an authorization from your manager, Mr. Rudolf Mayr, asserting that you are not mentally stable and that you broke numerous solemn business contracts and committed assault on his person, and authorizing us to have you committed to a lunatic hospital for women for your own safety.'

"I... I can't even tell you how those words affected me. I was slow to grasp their meaning, and I had to think it through to understand the English, but the detective repeated every word, and I got it all the second time. Rudi had accused me of assaulting him, and he was having me committed to a lunatic hospital!"

"Cyril Leblanc is the name of the detective who investigated your supposed murder," I said.

"Yes. I saw that in the newspapers later. I assume it was a coincidence, but I don't know. Perhaps there is some connection. Anyway, I tried again to protest. 'I didn't assault Herr Mayr,' I said. 'He slapped me and I slapped him back. That was all that happened.' But this officer said that was an assault anyway, and a gentleman in a position of authority over me, namely my manager who was also my guardian, had signed the paper to have me committed to a lunatic hospital.

"He held up the paper for me to see – I recognized the signature. There was no doubt, it was Rudi Mayr's signature on the paper. He had a very elaborate, flamboyant way of signing his name, as you may imagine if you know him. His signature was unmistakable, all these large, jagged strokes. I would recognize it from across the room and it would be impossible to forge that signature. I stared at it. I simply could not believe that Rudi would do such a thing to me. We had quarreled, I knew he was angry, I knew that he had to cancel performances and all the rest, but for him to do this... I have never felt so betrayed. It was a betrayal of the worst kind. To commit me to an institution in a strange country, a place where I knew almost no one, when I did not speak English very well and French almost not at all – it was unimaginable. We had been friends. I had let him down, I knew that, but to do what he did to me... The pain of that betrayal was almost worse than what was happening to me.

"I had forgotten that when we first began traveling for performances, Rudi had my mother sign papers appointing him as my guardian, in case there were any awkward questions posed when we had to pass through customs. I was still not of age at the time, and Rudi being a man and all – well, you understand. So Rudi was my guardian and, according to this detective, he had the power to have me committed. I fainted. My legs gave way, and I was down on my knees, unable to stand. The next thing I knew this huge man, Officer Sullivan, was holding a glass of water for me and I was sitting on a chair. I suppose they had lifted me off the floor. They let me finish the water, and then I was ordered to pack one bag with my things, which I did while they watched and followed me everywhere.

"I told Detective Leblanc that this apartment belonged to Dr. Percival Hyde, and that Dr. Hyde was a very powerful man who would be very angry when he found out what had happened to me. He just shrugged. 'It's my understanding that Dr. Hyde is away on business,' he said, "and your guardian is Mr. Mayr, not Dr. Hyde. That was that. He told me to come along peacefully, or they would put me in handcuffs. What choice did I have? They took me down to the lobby and out the door to the police car, and I swear the doorman was smirking at me and almost laughing, while I was in tears. They had me sit in the back, between Officer Sullivan and Detective Leblanc, and the little one drove the automobile. While we drove, the detective took liberties with my person, touching me here and there in the most flagrant way. I tried to push him away, but I was afraid they would beat me if I didn't submit.

"Mercifully, it wasn't far, perhaps six blocks from the apartment where you once lived. I happened to see the sign for Aylmer street, and just then we passed a yellow house on the corner, and I was sure that was where you lived. I wanted to call out for you to rescue me, but I could not, so I tried to remember exactly where the house was. A few moments later, they were escorting me out of the car and into a big grey mansion on a side street, a building that had no sign or anything to show what it was. In one awful moment before we went through the big oak doors in front, I noticed that all the windows were barred. I screamed and tried to break away from them, but the one named Sullivan twisted my arm behind my back so hard I thought it would break, and he covered my mouth with an enormous hand and pushed me through the door.

"Inside, three large, heavy matrons were waiting. They must have known I was coming, because they were ready for me. They grabbed me very roughly from the policemen and led me down one hallway, and then another and another. It was a labyrinth of corridors, all of them long and narrow, and they were not well lit at all. All around me, shadowy women in grey smocks, some with their heads shaved, moved like wraiths along the walls, staring as I passed. They terrified me more than the matrons did. I tried to resist the matrons, but there were too many of them and they were much stronger than me, and Officer Sullivan was still there with his arm locked around my throat. I was pushed into a bare room with a cot and one lightbulb on the ceiling, a pot on the floor in case I had to relieve myself, and a small armoire where I could hang my coat. The matrons told me to hang my coat in the armoire, and then they led me down the hall to a bathroom. I was stripped and forced down into a tub of lukewarm water and scrubbed very hard with lye soap – to make certain that I didn't have lice, they said. Then I was toweled dry by very rough hands, and given one of the grey smocks to wear and taken back to my room. Someone had brought the suitcase I had packed into my room, and I was allowed to keep it. One of the matrons said that as long as I behaved myself I could keep my personal things, but that I had to wear the smock and slippers at all times and that no more screaming or fighting would be tolerated.

"One of them pinched my face in her hands and made me look at her. 'This is your very nice room,' she said. 'As long as you behave, you can have this nice room. But if you misbehave we have smaller rooms without beds. One of them is so small you can't sit or stand. That's for our incorrigibles. You aren't incorrigible, are you?'

"I stared at her. I didn't know what an incorrigible was, but I shook my head. 'Well that's good you're not an incorrigible, missy, because you might have gone to the Pinel with the rest of the incorrigibles, and they treat you something awful there. Here we run a genteel establishment for well brought-up young ladies, and we won't tolerate anything else, do I make myself clear?' My English was very bad then, but I understood enough. She was a huge, fierce-looking beast of a woman. I found out later she was the head matron and that the other inmates called her "the Toad." I felt that I had no choice, so I nodded, although I was so terrified I was afraid I might wet myself. She told me that I was to remain in my room for the night, and that breakfast would be at six o'clock the next morning, when I could meet the other 'guests.'

"Then they left, the door was closed and locked, and I was alone. You can't imagine the feeling. An hour earlier, I was a free woman, a celebrated singer able to go where I pleased, the mistress of a very wealthy and powerful man. Now I was a prisoner, and I had no way to tell him where I was. They might call it an asylum, but it was a prison, there was no mistaking that. I was in a strange country where I did not know the customs or the laws.

"I had been betrayed by Rudi Mayr, my own manager. It wasn't enough that he kept all the money I had earned, now he wanted to lock me away as well. To have such a thing done to me by a man I had considered my friend, it was beyond belief. I was certain that Percy could fix it – but how was he to know where I was? How could he help me if I had simply vanished? Perhaps he would think I had returned to Vienna or joined Rudi in New York, and he wouldn't attempt to find me. My only hope was to convince them that I was willing to do what Rudi wanted and to sing wherever he wished me to sing. Rudi had committed me to this place, surely he had the power to get me out.

"It was the most desolate night of my life, Maxim. I had no way to turn off the light from that single bulb on the ceiling. There was no switch, and the ceiling was so high I couldn't reach it even if I stood on the bed. There was no curtain on the window, but when I looked out there was nothing but the grey shadow of another building a few feet away. There was no doorknob on the inside of the door, so it opened only from the outside. There was one thin blanket on the bed, a set of grey sheets that had been washed too many times, and a thin pillow. That, the armoire and a bedpan were the only furnishings in the room. I had books at the apartment, three or four novels and some poetry in German, but I hadn't thought to bring them. The room was cold, and the blanket was not warm enough, so I covered myself with my coat and tried to sleep, but I could not. I have never been able to sleep with a light on, and in these conditions sleep was impossible. I had the horrifying thought that I might be here forever, that I might die in this room. No one except Rudi and the men who brought me knew I was here, no one could come to my rescue. I was doomed. The night was interminable. I heard a woman screaming and another sobbing.

"I was curled up in a ball and I cried most of the night. The light went off, I think at about ten o'clock. They must have had a switch that cut all the lights at the same time. I desperately wanted that light off, and then it was off and I was in complete darkness and I wished I could put it on again, because the darkness was worse than that bare white light. Any human would go insane in such a place, cut off from all contact, knowing no one, not knowing when the morning would come or whether I would be let out of this room when it did.

"The worst of it was knowing that my own manager, a man I thought was my friend, had committed me to this place, simply because I did not want to complete a tour he was forcing me to do. I have never been a violent person, but at that moment I wished for a knife to plunge into his throat."

"I am very angry with Herr Mayr," I said. "He professed such sorrow for you when we had dinner in Montreal. He made it sound as though he had nurtured and cared for you, and that he was genuinely grieving over your death, when the truth was that he had done such an awful thing to you. He is a great liar, Rudi."

"Yes, he is," Hanna said bitterly. "If you want to understand Rudi, I think, you have to understand that he cares for nothing but money. Once he knew I wasn't going to sing for him any more, he was determined to keep all that I had earned. He took the money and he left me in that place so that I could not pursue him for what was owed. It doesn't matter what his motives were. To commit a person who is not a criminal to such a prison is a vicious, horrible thing to do. I will never forgive him. Never."

"There is one thing I don't understand," I said. "How did they find you? When I had dinner with him in Montreal, Rudi claimed that he had searched for you for weeks and that he had even hired private detectives who were unable to locate you."

"I have thought of that," Hanna said. "I think it was the detective who came to the apartment, Cyril Leblanc. Perhaps the private detectives couldn't find me, but this man was a policeman. He must have had some way to find out where I was staying."

I was willing to let her go on, but Hanna was exhausted and had to sleep. We drifted off, wrapped as usual in our coats, and woke the next morning to see that Vienna was wrapped in a foot of fresh snow which hid the papers littering the ground and the sorrow and hunger of its people. Outside, children were already having snowball fights and making snowmen, and I rose to warm some bread for our breakfast.

"Her name was Ophélie," Hanna said when we had finished eating breakfast.

"Ophélie?" I asked, unsure to whom she was referring.

"My friend Ophélie," she said, "like in Hamlet. Ophélie Molyneux. She saved me from going mad in that place. Without her, I don't believe I would be here today. I met her the day after I was taken in. When they unlocked the door the next morning, I was so happy to be released that I dashed out of the room and ran right into another inmate in the hall. She grabbed my arms to keep us both from laughing. 'Well, look at you,' she said, 'another one with red hair!' It was true – she was a little taller and heavier than me, and we didn't look at all alike, but we had the same red hair. Then she took my arm. 'We redheads have to stick together,' she said.

We joined the line of women in their grey smocks shuffling along toward the large common room at the back of the building where we had our meals. She showed me where the plates were, and she grabbed an extra piece of toast for me to go with the lumpy oatmeal and bits of bacon we were served for breakfast, and she led me to a seat on one of the long benches where the women sat all in a row. When we were seated, she introduced herself. I tried to speak to her in French, but my French was not good enough, so we settled on English. She spoke bad English with a French accent, and I spoke bad English with a German accent, but we understood each other.

"Ophélie came from a poor neighborhood in the east end of Montreal. Her father worked as a laborer at a factory, but he wanted something better for her, his only child. She got her education and worked as a clerk at an insurance company, where she had fallen in love with the son of the owner. She became his mistress, but his father had forbade them to marry. When he became engaged to a wealthy young woman, Ophélie was angry and she made trouble for them. She went more than once to his office and even once to his home, where she made a scene. Then one day, the police appeared and told her that she was being committed to the asylum. They showed her the papers, signed by the man she loved. She had been there almost a year when I met her.

"Ophélie taught me how to behave in that madhouse. To keep my head down, never to make eye contact with the matrons. To talk softly and behave like a lady at all times, even when provoked. They would do everything possible to drive me mad, she warned, so I must pretend to be a lunatic in order to preserve my sanity. If I didn't there would be horrible ordeals – I would be wakened in the middle of the night and plunged into an icy bath, the light in my room would never be turned off, I might have my head shaved, or I could be stripped and beaten with hoses. It was barbaric, and yet they claimed we were there for our own health."

"All the most terrible, backward, medieval practices in psychiatric medicine," I said.

"Yes, exactly. Even in prisons, they wouldn't have been allowed to do such horrible things to us. And in countries like Canada or Austria, they would have to have a trial to put you in prison – but to have someone committed to an asylum, you had only to sign a paper."

I had to bite my lip and look away to conceal my emotions. The thought of young, innocent souls such as Hanna and Ophélie consigned to a virtual prison in the name of psychiatric medicine was sickening. I have spent many years now battling the worst excesses of my own profession, but I still remember my anger and frustration that day. I wanted to go to Montreal and tear this institution down with my bare hands.

At the first opportunity, I vowed to ask Dr. Hyde to join me in the effort to close it down. I was certain that had he known of its existence, he would not have tolerated such a thing.

"We had to be careful that we weren't seen talking too much," Hanna went on, "but Ophélie was very much desired by one of the matrons, and it had given her a certain freedom which she used, in part, to make my life a little easier. I don't know exactly what she was doing for that matron in exchange for her freedoms, but Ophélie was tough. She knew what she wanted, she had a plan, and she didn't hesitate to do what had to be done in order to make her plan work. I had plenty of time to get to know her. As long as we didn't raise our voices or quarrel, we were able to talk in the hallways, in what they called the 'recreation room' although there was nothing to do there except to knit, and at meals.

Perhaps half the women were quite mad – whether they arrived at the asylum already deranged or were made that way by the treatments, I don't know. A woman about fifty years old talked about her elementary school teacher and how she was making beautiful drawings to show the teacher when she went to school the next day. Another woman was constantly licking herself with her tongue, wherever she could reach, like a cat. One would rhythmically bang her head on a table. Others simply stared off into space and babbled. I had to work to keep from losing my own sanity, but Ophélie was always there, as sane as anyone I've ever known. If something disturbing was going on, I would look at her, and sometimes she would hold my hand, and I would feel that I could endure it another day.

"Still, there were terrible days and – well, not good days, but days when I thought I would survive. One of the most difficult things was not knowing how long I would be there. If you are a criminal sentenced to prison, you know that you will be there a year, five years, ten years. But we did not know if we might be released in a week, or never. There were times when I wondered if I would die there.

"Then about a week before Christmas, Ophélie told me that there was going to be a big party on Christmas Eve. We could get dressed up, and dance to the gramophone, and there was always liquor – lots of liquor. The inmates got drunk, the matrons got drunk, even those louts Sullivan and Labrecque got drunk. 'Sullivan and Labrecque – they're police officers!' I said. 'Oh, you believed that?' Ophélie said. 'They're not policemen, they're just thugs. They're always around, in case a woman starts acting up or tries to escape. They like to beat women, that's what they live for. They've given some of the women here the most awful beatings. One woman tried to escape, and when they caught her and brought her back, we could all hear her screaming. We never saw her again. We think she was beaten to death, but no one really knows.'

"Ophélie had to tell me all this in whispers, when she was sure no one was listening. At first I thought she was simply bitter because of what had happened to her, but I began to believe her. She said that we were all there simply because we were inconvenient to someone, usually a man. I was there because Rudi wanted to get me out of the way, Ophélie had been committed because she made trouble for her lover and his future wife. One very young woman had accused her father of violating her, another was a wife who made trouble over her husband's mistress, another was there simply because she refused to marry the man her parents wanted her to marry.

"But Ophélie had a plan. On Christmas Eve, we had a gift exchange. We were all allowed to give one gift to one friend. I thought about it a great deal, and finally I gave Ophélie my sable coat. She did not want to accept it, but I insisted. She had done so much for me, and I didn't feel the coat was really mine anyway. Dr. Hyde had given it to me at a time when I wasn't thinking very clearly. It made me feel like a prostitute. So Ophélie took the coat, and she gave me a beautiful necklace instead. I had two green gowns that my mother had sewn for me before the tour, and I loaned her one of those gowns and we had fun dressing each other up for the party. We had to let hers out a bit because she was larger and more curvaceous than me, but I helped my mother for years – I'm a good seamstress and I quickly had it adjusted for her.

"It seems silly but we were as excited as schoolgirls about the party. It was a chance to pretend that we were somewhere else, and that life was somehow normal. Before the party started, however, Ophélie whispered something in my ear: she said that no matter what, I should not get drunk. I could drink a little, and I could even pretend to get drunk, but it was important that I not get drunk. I have never gotten drunk in any case, but Ophélie would not tell me why I shouldn't on that particular night.

"The party started at five o'clock. Everyone was drinking heavily. The inmates were drunk, the matrons were drunk, even Sullivan and Labrecque were drunk. They were drinking beer and Irish whiskey, swallowing it like water. When they looked at me, the look was positively lascivious. I was sure that before the evening was out, they would try something. Ophélie was the life of the party. At the last minute, she had decided to wear the sable coat, and she refused to take it off. We danced to almost every song, with Ophélie dancing like a man. The matrons were dancing with some of the other women and the way they were dancing was – well, you can imagine what it was like. After a time there was a lot of kissing going on, women kissing women. Some were slipping away, going to the rooms to be alone. Even Sullivan and Labrecque disappeared somewhere, although I didn't see them go. There were three or four other guards who seemed to have been hired especially for that occasion, or maybe they were just there for the women, but they had disappeared too.

"The party was in the big common room where we ate our meals. It was at the back of the house. Beyond that there was a long, narrow corridor, and at the end of the corridor there was a lavatory. Ophélie said that she had to use the lavatory and disappeared for a few minutes, and when she returned her entire manner had changed. She no longer seemed drunk. There were several very drunken inmates still at the party, and two matrons who were so intoxicated they were almost in a stupor. Ophélie put her finger to her lips to warn me to be quiet and grabbed my arm so hard that she hurt me. 'Come!' she whispered, and pulled me back toward the lavatory.

"At the end of the corridor, the lavatory was to the right, and to the left was a set of heavy oak doors that were always kept locked. I saw right away that one of the doors was ajar. Ophélie eased it open a few inches and we slipped through. There was a key in the lock from the other side, and she locked it behind us. We were in a kind of foyer area. It was dark and hard to see, and I stumbled over a pair of men's work boots that had been left on the floor. At that moment, I realized that I had kicked off my shoes to dance, and I was in my stocking feet.

'Are you ready?' Ophélie asked me. 'We're going to escape!' My heart was pounding so fast that I thought I might faint. I thought of Sullivan and Labrecque beating to death a poor woman who tried to escape, and I was almost too frightened to take another step. But then Ophélie whispered to me to put on the boots that were on the floor, and I did as I was told. 'Where are we going?' I asked. She said that she knew a boarding house where they would take us in, no questions asked. It was about twenty blocks away, but we could make it. I pulled on the boots without taking time to tie them. They were a bit too large but they slipped on easily. When Ophélie opened the back door, I pulled back. I knew that I was making a decision that would affect me for the rest of my life, that might even get me killed. Then Ophélie tugged at my arm and we were out the door, slipping and sliding down the stone steps in the back of the building, then working our way through a narrow passage and out to the street.

"It was dark and it was snowing hard. We couldn't make out anything, and through all the twists and turns of the asylum building itself and the passage that led to the outdoors we had lost all sense of direction. We turned around helplessly, trying to figure out which way to go, until I noticed that the street sloped downhill, so that direction had to lead to Sherbrooke Street, while the other way would take us up to Mount Royal.

"I began leading the way, but it was very hard going in the snow. They don't clear the sidewalks properly in Montreal, and with all the snow there was nowhere to walk except a narrow track made by other pedestrians. I had no coat, but Ophélie was wearing party shoes with high heels, which I thought was worse. I was afraid she would break an ankle. We were holding onto each other for dear life, both of us terribly frightened, when I looked up and realized that we were walking directly past the front of the asylum. There was someone standing at a lighted window, looking out, and as we passed I realized that it was one of the matrons. An instant later, I heard her shout, and then an alarm bell went off.

"Ophélie tugged at my arm. 'Hurry,' she said, 'they're going to be after us!' I tried, but it was almost impossible in the snow. We went perhaps a block, and then we turned right on a side street, and as we did I heard a man shouting and cursing behind us, and then another one. Sullivan and Labrecque were on our trail. We hurried to the next corner and hesitated for a moment. 'We have to split up,' Ophélie said. 'They can't follow both of us. I'll go up toward the mountain, you go down to Sherbrooke. Get away and meet me at Windsor Station, alright? That's the train station, it's an easy place to find. I'll be there tomorrow morning. Now go!'

"I didn't even get to say goodbye. I shouted 'good luck!' over my shoulder and I tried to run, but it was impossible, so I kept plowing through the snow. At first I could hear the men cursing, but then their voices died away. I knew that I could not go far in that thin dress. It was bitterly cold and I would freeze to death before I made it to some warm place. Then I remembered the yellow house at the corner of Milton and Aylmer, and I remembered passing it on the way to the asylum.

I circled around and around again, but at last I saw a sign that said 'Aylmer Street' and a few moments later, I saw a light on in a window. I prayed that it would be your light. It seemed as though I pounded on the door forever, but at last you answered. You were so brave to go down and make them leave."

"I had no choice. I was lucky to be so sick. If I hadn't been able to convince them I had typhoid, I don't know what I would have done. I couldn't have kept the smaller one from forcing his way in, much less the big one. Do you think those two were Sullivan and Labrecque?"

"I'm sure they were."

"Those two fit your description – but they had scarves wrapped around their faces and I couldn't see them clearly. It's a good thing they were so frightened by a little vomit."

"Still, you were brave... you might have saved my life that night."

"You are resourceful. I think you would have gotten away."

"Not without you."

CHAPTER 38

I hesitated then, not sure if I should push Hanna to reveal more than she had already revealed, but my curiosity got the better of me.

"Where did you go that night, after you left my apartment?"

"I had a lot of time to think, sitting there watching you sleep," she said. "I knew I had to try to meet Ophélie at Windsor Station, but I needed money and my passport. I would have to get to the hotel and get the money out of my trunk. I decided it would be safer to do that while it was still dark. You had a bit of change on your table, so I begged your forgiveness and I took the change and borrowed your warm green loden coat and slipped out. I caught a tram on Sherbrooke Street and took it to Greene Avenue. I had the most awful time trying to find my trunk and open it in the dark, but I had kept the necklace and the locket with the key inside through all that happened to me, and I was finally able to find the trunk and open it. I took some of the money, enough to live on for several weeks if I had to, and the passport. When I locked the padlock I dropped the key on the floor of the storage room, and it took me several minutes to find it. I was desperate – without it, I could never get into my trunk again. At last my fingers found it in the darkness and I slipped it back into the locket.

"After I had the money, I thought of simply asking the woman who ran the hotel if I could have my room back – or a smaller room, since Elise would not be with me. But Rudi knew the address of that hotel, and if they contacted him, they might look for me there. I had to go somewhere no one would look, but first I had to wait for Ophélie at the train station. She would know what to do. I wandered down to St. Catherine Street, and then turned east and walked along, looking for a café that was open. But it was four or five o'clock in the morning on Christmas Day, everything was closed. I had a vague idea where the train station was, but I had to ask directions to find it.

"Inside the station, there was a little diner that was open and there were a few railway workers there. They all stared at me, but I was too hungry to let that bother me. I ordered a coffee and a pastry and paid for it, and then had another coffee and another pastry. It was all very delicious. I kept watching for Ophélie, praying that she had escaped. I stayed at the station until past noon that day, watching Christmas travelers come and go. When it was nearly one o'clock and Ophélie still hadn't appeared, I became very worried for her, but I was extremely tired and I needed to sleep. If I fell asleep in the station, I was afraid a policeman would get curious. I was a strange sight in a loden coat, a green gown and men's work boots.

"I asked the ticket agent, and he told me there were two or three small, inexpensive hotels near the station. I found one, rented a room with no questions asked, slept for two hours and went back to the station. For the next three days, that was all I did – sleep, eat small meals at the diner, watch for Ophélie. Then I learned about her death the same way you did. I found a French newspaper on a bench at the station and saw my picture on the front page, with a big headline informing the world that I was dead. I almost fainted. It's the most disorienting sensation, to read about your own death. I didn't understand all the French, but I understood enough to know what it was saying, and I saw the name of Cyril Leblanc, which chilled me to the bone. Of course, I knew that it had to be Ophélie who had been killed. She was wearing my coat, and I knew there was still an old letter from my mother in the pocket. I sat there with my arms wrapped tightly around me, grieving for Ophélie, grieving for my lost self. Poor Ophélie, doomed by the coat that had been my gift to her. I wished that it had been me who died instead!

"Finally, I stumbled back to my hotel, still carrying the newspaper, and fell on the bed sobbing. As much as I felt for Ophélie, I was terrified. Obviously, these people wouldn't hesitate to kill. They had beaten and murdered Ophélie, they wouldn't hesitate to do the same to me if I was caught. They knew that two of us had escaped and they had caught only one, so even if they thought I was the one they murdered, they would still be looking. I was awake most of the night, worrying, thinking, trying to decide what to do. I wanted to tell the police about Ophélie and point them to Sullivan and Labrecque, but Cyril Leblanc *was* the police. If I went near a policeman, I was afraid I would end up back in the asylum, or dead."

"You could have come to me," I said.

"Yes, I thought of that. I almost did. But I didn't want you involved in any way. That's why I broke in and stole the letter from your room, to keep you out of it and so that no one would know I was alive. To stay alive, I had to get away from Montreal. Finally I decided that I had to go to New York. I could take a train, and from New York City I could board a ship back to Europe and home. I went back to the train station and bought a ticket to travel to New York on New Year's Day. I found a friendly young man who drove a horse-drawn cab working near the station. His name was Jimmy. I gave him two dollars, and I told him that I would pay him five dollars more to take me to Greene Avenue on New Year's Eve and then bring me back to the station. Jimmy said he was free right then, but I said that New Year's Eve was better. I didn't tell him why, but I knew that on New Year's Eve everyone would be busy with parties and I could retrieve my trunk from the storage room without attracting attention.

"Jimmy turned up right when I told him too, at ten o'clock on New Year's Eve. We had a chilly ride and a difficult time getting the trunk out of the hotel basement, but Jimmy was young and strong and we managed to move it. I was able to get some traveling clothes from the trunk and change in the women's lavatory before I checked it at the station, but when I paid Jimmy, he tried to kiss me. I had to push him away, hard. I told him he had been a gentleman until then, and not to ruin it. He went away with his head hanging down and I felt badly for him, but after what I had been through, I was not going to be mauled by any man.

"My train left early the next morning for New York City. The agent at the border asked me a few questions, but I was able to show him my ticket to Hamburg and to convince him that I was only trying to get home to Austria. Once we were over the border into the USA, I began to breathe easier. I was away from Montreal, and I was sure I would never go back. As we got closer to New York, the more I thought of Rudi Mayr. I knew that he stayed at the Hotel Astor when he was in New York. I thought of going there to confront him but I was sure that if I did, he would call the authorities and have me committed again. I had my passage booked on a steamship to Hamburg in April, but that was too long to wait. I decided that I would have to find the offices of the shipping line and learn whether it was possible to exchange my ticket for a ship leaving for Europe as soon as possible.

"As it happened, I stayed almost a month in a little hotel for women not far from the train station in New York City. I kept to myself, but I found the city fascinating. I wished that I had simply overcome my fears to sing there. There was no difficulty in exchanging my ticket on the Hamburg Amerika line – I was even entitled to a refund. I sailed aboard the S.S. Pretoria. In six days, I was back in Europe, and in two more days I was in Vienna.

By then Rudi had informed my poor mother by telegram that I was dead. I arrived at night to find her dressed all in black and grieving. She was terrified at first, and I had to let her squeeze and pinch me all over before she was convinced that I was not a ghost. I told her some of what had happened to me, but never all of it. I begged her to keep my return a secret, because the fewer people who knew I was alive, the better. I did not think that they would trouble themselves to travel all the way to Vienna to kill me or to bring me back, but Rudi knew hundreds of people in Vienna, any one of whom might have informed him that I was alive and well and still a threat to him. Mama wanted to bring some kind of charges against Rudi, but I was able to convince her that could have a disastrous result as well. I was safe as long as they thought I was dead, so the best thing was to stay dead. And I did, until I saw you on the mountain during the war, then again at the cemetery. You are a relentless man, Dr. Maxim Balsano."

"That's because I love you very much," I said.

"I know, Max," Hanna said. "I love you, too. Completely. I am sorry there is so little of me left to give, because you deserve so much."

CHAPTER 39

Once she had revealed all that she had to tell, Hanna seemed rather drained and empty. It was good for her to share the full horror of this nightmare with someone, but it left her feeling rather desolate. Sharing her secret could not bring back her friend Ophélie Molyneux, nor could it restore the young Hanna Goss, the one who had left Vienna in 1913 with such a bright future, the rather shy but vastly talented soprano who had entrusted herself to Dr. Percival Hyde only to have him hypnotize her and use her for his own purposes, or the bruised but still buoyant and hopeful young woman who had been carted away to an asylum prison on the strength of a signature from her trusted friend and one-time manager, Rudolf Mayr. Add the war and all that she had seen working as a nurse in field hospitals, and a year of deprivation after the war, and Hanna in 1920 was not the woman I had met on that glowing August day in 1913, but she had not entirely lost her old self.

When she finished telling me her story, I told her of the fate that had befallen Sergeant-Detective Cyril Leblanc. "I had a letter from Jem Doyle after the war," I said. "It seems that M. Leblanc is in prison now. He was arrested for the theft of a certain sable coat from the stolen property room at the police station. He gave it to his mistress, and she was so foolish that she wore it to the Policeman's Ball."

Hanna stared at me with those lovely green eyes, and for a moment I thought she was going to berate me for making light of a serious situation. But then an impish smile played over her lips. She began to giggle, then to laugh, and finally she was laughing so hard that she was bent double, almost unable to breathe. Her laughter was infectious, and I laughed with her, and we laughed until we both had tears rolling down our cheeks. When we tried to stop and catch our breath, one of us would begin to chuckle and we would be off again in gales of laughter. Until that moment our relationship had been so serious, even tragic, that I had barely seen her smile. She had a wonderful laugh (as befits someone with a wonderful voice) deep and rich and heartfelt, and it was such a delight to hear her laugh that I felt almost as though we had both been released from that prison masquerading as an asylum where she had been held.

When we had finally calmed ourselves, I told her about the night I was so thoroughly beaten while on my way home that I ended up in hospital. She had no doubt that Sullivan and Labrecque were also behind the beating. "You see," she said, "I was right to try to keep you out of it – they are dangerous people. But you disobeyed my wishes, Maxim! I am glad you survived. I could not bear to have lost another friend."

"You did not lose me, Hanna. You will have me forever."

There was much more for both of us to learn, mainly details about what had happened during the six years we did not see each other, but we had time to catch up. Other things were more pressing: The first thing I had to do was to inform Jem Doyle in Montreal about the identity of the woman who had been murdered in Montreal on December 24, 1913: Ophélie Molyneux, a local woman from somewhere in the east end of the city. She was also certain of the names of Ophélie's killers: a M. Labrecque and and a Mr. Sullivan, men who had been working at an unidentified private asylum for women near McGill University and the Royal Victoria Hospital in 1913 and who also worked with Cyril Leblanc. It wasn't much to go on, but it was something.

Jem replied quickly. He was anxious to pursue Ophélie's killers and to learn the extent of Rudolf Mayr's involvement in her death – but he needed Hanna's assistance as a witness. Was there any possibility that she would be willing to travel across the Atlantic in order to give him the full story of the events of that night and to testify against the killers if they could be found?

I thought it over. It had occurred to me that I ought to take Hanna with me to Montreal. It was possible that she needed to confront it to put the nightmare behind her once and for all. I decided to consult first with Dr. Freud. He was curious about the health of the woman he had believed dead beyond a shadow of a doubt – a woman now suffering, in his view, of a trauma neurosis not unlike those that afflicted so many of the veterans in our care. I was invited to breakfast with him at 19 Berggasse, where he apologized repeatedly for the quality of the fare.

Since the war, my relations with the esteemed psychoanalyst had constantly improved. I knew that he was grateful for whatever insight I had been able to offer into the welfare of prisons of war in Italy before his son Martin was released, and he had come to respect my work. Beyond that, he seemed fond of me in a fatherly way, and I in turn had grown to respect him more. I was appalled when I thought of the cheeky young man who had journeyed to Montreal in 1913 because I didn't want to be just another disciple hanging on every word uttered by the great Freud. He liked that independence of mind, and he knew as well that I had grown more and more disenchanted with Dr. Percival Hyde, one of his chief rivals in the field.

In my conversation with Dr. Freud, I decided not to reveal Dr. Hyde's relationship with Hanna or his use of the discredited technique of hypnosis in her treatment. Whatever had happened between Hanna and Percival Hyde, it had little or nothing to do with either the murder investigation or Hanna's current state of mind, and to disclose the relationship would violate Hanna's privacy. Her imprisonment in the asylum on the authorization of Herr Mayr, however, was both pertinent. When I described the way she had been taken to the asylum and locked away, Freud slapped his palm on the table so hard that cups rattled.

"It is unacceptable that our profession is used as an excuse to imprison people," he said. "That is not why we are here. We are here to free minds from the coils of neurosis, not to create new ways to force the human spirit into captivity. If there is one thing I have learned, it is that no human benefits from being dragged into a virtual prison and held there. It accomplishes nothing, it is wrong, it is immoral, it is unethical and it ought to be illegal!"

I could only agree, as I imagined what a powerful witness Dr. Freud would make if he were asked to testify before a court about the practice of imprisoning people without trial on the flimsiest of excuse. I explained in some detail how it was that Hanna had escaped, and how the detail of the sable coat had caused the confusion about the identity of the murder victim – and brought about the murder of Hanna's friend. He thought that she was quite brave to set out on her own and travel to New York, Hamburg and home to Vienna entirely alone. The question before us now, however, was whether she would benefit from a return voyage to Montreal. Apart from the legal ramifications, did he feel that Hanna would benefit from confronting her past, or would it leave her emotionally crippled?

Dr. Freud toyed with a cigar and thought carefully before he answered. He knew the question was a weighty one for me, and that I wanted to follow the rule in the Hippocrate oath: "*Primum nil Nocere* – Do no harm."

"How fragile is your Hanna at the moment, in your estimation?" he asked.

"Far less than when I first found her. She is working, she doesn't feel the need to hide herself, she seems comfortable with me. And she is quite fierce when it comes to finding her friend's killers and putting them behind bars."

"Then what is the obstacle? She demonstrated considerable resilience and self-reliance in escaping from the asylum and getting herself home to Vienna, and she was much younger at the time. To play an active role in seeing the killers found and punished would do her nothing but good. More than six years have passed, she is more mature now, I see no reason why she should not return to Montreal, provided you are able to keep her safe, but I assume you will have the assistance of your detective friend in that aspect?"

"Of course I will. And Jem Doyle is quite the intimidating individual."

"Good, good. How, may I ask, are your relations with Dr. Percival Hyde? Are you able to ask him for assistance in this matter? As the foremost psychiatrist in Montreal, he surely carries considerable weight in the way private asylums conduct themselves, does he not? The one you described should be exposed and shut down. If Hanna can help in accomplishing that goal and in finding the killers, then good luck and godspeed. Ultimately, the decision should be left to her. Hanna is of age and highly intelligent. There is no harm in asking, so long as you do not press her too hard. She will know what is right for her."

We shook hands and I took my leave. According to my notes of the conversation, the date was 14 January 1920, a Wednesday. In six days' time, Dr. Freud would lose his beloved daughter Sophie, a mother with two young boys, to the Spanish Influenza. Sophie Halberstadt Freud died in Hamburg, where she had settled with her husband; it was typical of the times that Freud was unable to get space on a train to attend her funeral.

That evening as we sat in a tiny café near the hospital, drinking ersatz coffee and perusing the very short menu, I posed the question to Hanna: Would she be willing to travel to Montreal in order to assist Jem Doyle in his investigation into the death of Ophélie Molyneux?

Hanna didn't hesitate. "Of course I would. I am not afraid to go back now, so long as you come with me. Elise has thought of this. She said that I might find it necessary to return to Montreal in order to bring this to a conclusion, and she offered to pay for our passage – on condition that she is allowed to come along as well."

"I personally cannot accept her generosity as I have funds of my own," I said. "But if she wishes to come along, I would be delighted. It is my opinion that Mlle Duvernay has a very keen intelligence, and could only be of the greatest help to us."

Hanna could not contain her excitement. I had expected her to be frightened and hesitant, but she was like a huntress scenting her prey. Before we returned to the apartment, I sent a cable to Doyle: "Montreal-bound with Hanna. Must find a way out of Vienna first."

Within two days we were packed and ready to go. Hanna had wanted to sell her mother's house near Leopoldstadt. I convinced her that to sell now was not wise. The krone was falling daily, and speculators from virtually every nation in Europe with a stable currency were circling us like buzzards seeking bargains. Instead, I found a young Swiss psychiatrist who had come to study with Dr. Freud. He and his wife were looking for a home in Vienna, and he would not only pay Swiss francs to rent the house, he would also look after the property while we were away. We would simply vacate the apartment that had once belonged to Jan, leaving some things behind and taking only what we needed for the voyage.

All that was easy enough. What was nearly impossible was to locate a train that would take us at least as far as Switzerland, where we could board any number of swift trains that would take us to Paris and on to Cherbourg. We were unable to get a train out of Vienna for two months, although we went to the Westbahnhof seeking passage almost daily. Finally we left on the first day of spring for Linz, where we found another train to take us to Salzburg. We had to hire a horse-drawn cab from there to take us across the border into Germany, where we caught a similarly shabby train to Munich. There we spent three happy days in the company of Jan and Karine. Hanna and Karine got along wonderfully, and after finding Jan rather puffed up and proud of himself, we learned that Karine was expecting their first child in September.

The worst of the terrible inflation that would all but destroy Germany was yet to come, but all things German were nearly as shabby and run-down as Austria, and the people looked nearly as worn and hungry. It was not until we reached the French border at Strasbourg that we got our first taste of civilization, the almost forgotten joys of butter and pastry, real coffee, and clean trains with seats that weren't falling apart. The balance of the journey from Strasbourg to Paris and Paris to Cherbourg was splendid; we gorged ourselves on baguettes and fresh butter, tasted real, undiluted wine and arrived in Cherbourg at least a kilo or two heavier than we had been when we boarded the train in Vienna.

Elise was waiting to meet us at the station. Hanna ran to her as I searched for a porter and the two women embraced, both weeping, clinging to one another as though to life itself. I am not ashamed to say that I wept myself, seeing them together again at last, knowing all that had transpired since I had come to this same little city on the French coast during the last months of peace in the spring of 1914, a young man utterly unsuspecting of the events that were about to engulf us all. I joined the two of them in a lingering embrace, with many kisses on tear-streaked faces, until at last we were swept away by Mlle Duvernay's driver and taken to the splendid old château on the outskirts of the city that she had inherited from Madame Liais.

For the next month, our life was as unlike life in Vienna as it would be possible to imagine. We had traveled from want to plenty, from a cramped, cold apartment in a hungry city to a spacious château in France with servants at our beck and call. We walked every day along the sea and we took turns telling all that had befallen us in the intervening years.

I was anxious to board the ship but Elise had business to conclude and our surroundings were so pleasant that I could hardly complain. I took advantage of the interlude to work on a lengthy tract on my research into the war neuroses afflicting our veterans, a tract that would become my first book. We dined well, we slept in large, comfortable beds. My only sorrow was that Hanna now shared Elise's bed rather than mine.

Each evening, we took a lengthy stroll along the boardwalk before bed. Elise usually accompanied us, but she had a meeting one night, so Hanna and I walked together under a waxing crescent moon that winked in and out behind the clouds. Hanna took my hand and walked with her head almost leaning on my shoulder. Not for the first time, I was conscious of the warmth of her supple body, the fact that she was taller than me, the fresh scent that seemed always to emanate from her skin. I was about to make some innocuous remark about the sound of the waves when she stopped, turned my face to her, and kissed me full on the lips. I was so startled at first that I failed to respond, but her warm, pliable lips remained fastened to mine, and slowly I relaxed, wrapped my arms around her waist, and pulled her to me. The kiss went on and on for several minutes at least, the two of us releasing a hunger that had been there for years, unable to stop. Our tongues sought and probed and twined, mouths open, eyes closed, locked in a passionate embrace that might never have ended had we not been soaked by a tall wave that broke with the incoming tide and showered us with spray. We broke off, laughing, and went our way, holding hands.

I went to bed giddy that night, my head spinning. Until that moment, despite the comfort we gave each other, we had never kissed. Had things shifted between us, or was it a momentary impulse, sparked by the moonlight and the sea and the warmth of the night air? Whatever the reason, I was thrilled. Even if Hanna never kissed me again, I would have that kiss for as long as I lived.

Our departure was hastened by a letter I received from Jem Doyle. Enclosed was a short note and a clipping from the culture pages of one of the Montreal newspapers: the New York impresario Rudolf Mayr was expected to arrive in the city on May 10 with the full Russian cast of *Eugene Onegin*, which had just concluded its stand in New York. Rudi would be holding court at the Windsor Hotel for the length of the troupe's engagement in Montreal. Rudi was quoted at length in the story.

I showed the note and the clipping to Hanna and Elise. We agreed. It was time to set out for the New World, time to discomfit Herr Rudolf Mayr. We took great delight in imagining Rudi's reaction when he discovered that Hanna was alive and well.

"I hope Rudi's heart is sound," Elise smiled. "Otherwise, he's apt to expire on the spot."

Hanna laughed, but it was not a light-hearted laugh. You could sense the tension she felt at the thought of confronting Herr Mayr.

THE SPIDER'S LAIR

MONTREAL 1920

CHAPTER 40

On the first day of May, we passed through the magnificent Art Déco Hall des Transatlantiques in Cherbourg and boarded the Empress Eugénie for the voyage to Montreal, mindful that eight years earlier, the Titanic had called here after leaving Southampton and before setting out on its maiden voyage across the Atlantic. Elise, in her thorough fashion, had checked the number of lifeboats on the Empress Eugénie to make certain they were sufficient for the number of passengers before booking our voyage to the New World.

Somewhat against my will, I had agreed to let Elise pay for my passage. I would cheerfully have traveled second class, but she wanted to treat Hanna to a first-class berth, so if we were to associate aboard ship, I would have to have a similarly opulent cabin for myself. It was like a luxurious hotel on the water, complete with a gymnasium, swimming pool, surprisingly complete library, billiards room and spa. Other than the library, we made little use of the facilities. We had each other for company, we had the spacious deck for walks, and we had books. We felt little need for anything else. We also had ample time for talk during the crossing. On the second night out, we were conducting what we called "iceberg watch" on deck – which really meant lolling on deck chairs under blankets to watch the impossible splash of stars overhead and listen to the waves. Elise, who until then had only the sketchiest outline of what had happened to Hanna, persuaded Hanna to go through it all again. I listened intently, noting a change of emphasis here and there and one new detail – a second instance when Dr. Percival Hyde had become very angry with her, a week or two *before* he became so furious following the visit from Count Respighi that had somehow upset him.

"I was tidying up a little in the apartment, because I did not like to leave everything to the maid," Hanna said. "Dr. Hyde is frightfully messy. He's the sort of person who can walk into a room and everything is immediately in disarray, but he becomes frightfully angry if anyone attempts to straighten up the mess. The cleaning he leaves to the maid, everything else is supposed to remain as it is. I had thought all you doctors were obsessively neat, but that is certainly not the case with Percival Hyde."

"I cannot disagree," I said. "I'm afraid I'm one of those physicians who is ill at ease if anything is out of place."

Hanna laughed. "I know. Sometimes in Vienna, I couldn't resist leaving a chair pulled out from a table or messing up the books on the bookshelf. Then I would see how long it would take you to set it right after you came home. It was usually less than five minutes, and it was often the first thing you would do, even before you took your coat off. You weren't even conscious that you were doing it, but I was always grateful that you didn't get angry with me."

I had to laugh, trying to recall instances when I had compulsively tidied up as soon as I walked in the door. My mind drifted a little. Hanna was saying something about Lord Percival Hyde and his anger, but I didn't catch it all. I was back in the cramped apartment in Vienna, holding tight to Hanna through bitterly cold winter nights made colder by the lack of coal.

"I am fascinated with the horrible Percival Hyde," Elise was saying. "An untidy, morally unscrupulous, incredibly wealthy and brilliant man who is also irascible and quick to anger. Quite the portrait."

"In his defense, I must say that the brilliance is not faked," I said. "I have read some of his writings. That's what spurred me to cross the Atlantic to work with him in the first place – they're really quite brilliant. I tend to agree with his conclusions less and less, but his ability to pull together disparate strands of thought and research into a cogent argument is remarkable. I realize that doesn't make him a good or an ethical man, but his mental powers are extraordinary. I may add that he is obsessed with my mentor, Dr. Sigmund Freud. He detests Dr. Freud."

We were silent for a time, listening to the *thrum* of the ship's powerful engines, watching the stars overhead. The steward came then with nightcaps for the three of us. We toasted our mutual health and happiness, and as I gazed at Hanna's face in the moonlight, I thought that I had never seen a more beautiful sight in my life. When there were no strangers around, Hanna would occasionally sing for us. Sometimes a favorite aria, sometimes a lieder or two, occasionally a song like "Lili Marlene", which had become popular during the war. She would sing for a few minutes and then cease, smiling and embarrassed. Each time, Hanna seemed more confident. Would she return to the stage some day? I did not know, nor did I feel that it really mattered. What mattered was Hanna herself.

When you enter the Gulf of St. Lawrence from the Atlantic Ocean, it's so wide that you cannot see from shore to shore. It is only by degrees that the earth presses in, and you begin to make out a shadowy line of trees on the horizon. The motion of the ship eases to a slight wallow and then to nothing except a steady forward motion with the thrum of the great engines before you sight the steep cliffs of Quebec, where the daring British General James Wolfe sent troops up those impossible cliffs to surprise the French troops under Louis-Joseph, the Marquis de Montcalm, changing the course of North American history forever.

We endured customs formalities in Quebec City that were not especially long or onerous. Still, we were impatient. During the final hours of the voyage, we paced the deck ceaselessly, unable to contain our excitement. We were almost there, back in Montreal, where we would confront Herr Mayr and perhaps help to find and arrest the men who had pursued Hanna and murdered Ophélie Molyneux. While Elise shared my excitement, Hanna was now as apprehensive as she was eager, and she required some assurance that she would not be in danger. On the latter point, I felt that the mere presence of Jem Doyle would do a great deal to reassure her. Jem would be older now, but I doubted that he would seem any less intimidating.

At last we drew within sight of the magnificent Queen Victoria Bridge and the Port of Montreal. We were at the railing as we neared the dock, straining our eyes to catch a glimpse of
Jem and Sophie in the throng milling about on the quay: stevedores, newsmen, photographers, hawkers of everything from newspapers to sausages, friends and family members waiting to greet arriving passengers, uniformed police officers. I thought it would be impossible to spot them in such a throng, but then I saw a towering figure who loomed above the crowd – Jem Doyle wearing shirt sleeves and a big black hat. With the hat and his handlebar mustache, he looked like a sheriff in a western movie. I waved frantically, and when I pointed him out to Hanna and Elise, they waved too. Jem waved and resumed his position, like a soldier at attention. At last, I could make out Sophie standing in his shadow, fashionably decked out in a pink dress and a straw hat.

Once the ship was secure, the tumult began, with passengers pushing and shoving, anxious to be off the ship after too long a time at sea. We hung back, letting the mass descend the gangplank ahead of us and following after. I trailed behind the women, carrying three bags, feeling far too short to look for Jem in that mob. I needn't have worried. The multitude parted around him like the sea flowing past a rock, and soon Jem was engulfing the three of us in those powerful arms, treating Hanna and Elise like long-lost friends even though they had never met. I let the bags fall to the cobblestones and surrendered to Jem and Sophie, so delighted to see them that

I forgot myself completely and failed to make the introductions until Sophie stepped up and made the introductions in Hungarian, German, English and French. At last, Sophie threw her arms around my neck and showered my cheeks with kisses.

"Maxim, Maxim! Maxim, you are home!"

At that moment, in Sophie's motherly embrace, it felt like home. With all of us trying to talk at once in three or four languages. Jem scooped up the three bags I had been struggling with, tucked them under one arm, and led the way to his automobile. He had traded the old Model T for a 1919 Essex, which was parked three blocks to the west. The walk gave me ample time to observe the changes in Jem and Sophie. He possessed a bit more heft and she was thinner, but where Jem had only a few flecks of white hair in his black mustache, Sophie had gone completely grey. I didn't have to wonder why. Any mother with even one son in the war had grey hair by the time it was over.

Elise had reserved a room for herself and Hanna at the discreet women's apartment-hotel where they had stayed in 1913, while I was to stay with Jem and Sophie – but first we were all to go to Sophie's Café for a welcoming party. The café had been spruced up since the war, with a new sign outside and new tables, chairs and benches inside, but it exuded the same warmth, the same delicious mingling of scents and the same delightful memories. Sophie was right. It felt like home.

Hanna and Elise were delighted. All six of Sophie's boys were there: Joszef in his policeman's uniform, Lukacz, Erneszt, Tamas, Laszlo and Istvan – the latter two all grown up. Laszlo was twenty-two now, Istvan nineteen. Joszef and Lukacz had married sisters, buxom women who must have resembled Sophie when she was their age, and both had children. Over the next hour or two, members of the polka band filtered in, the palinka and beer began to flow, platters of fresh bread, sauerkraut and sausages were brought from the kitchen, and by nine o'clock in the evening there were at least fifty of Sophie's nearest and dearest friends on hand.

When the band struck up, even Hanna and Elise danced together. Watching Hanna's cheeks turn red as she danced and feeling myself enfolded at intervals in Sophie's embrace kept me from dwelling on the past. We were all here, we were alive, we were healthy, we were eating and drinking, dancing and talking. When Hanna took my shoulder and spun me into a polka, I felt as complete as I have at any time in my life.

I was anxious to talk with Jem, but it was not the time. Around ten o'clock, with Elise and Hanna visibly tired, Sophie's son Erneszt left to drive them to their hotel. By midnight I was tucked away in bed in the room Joszef and Lukasz had once shared. I thought I would have some difficulty falling asleep, but the next thing I knew I was smelling coffee and I could already hear Sophie and Jem in the kitchen. Five minutes later, I was seated at the table with them, enjoying the welcome accorded to a long-lost son and all the bacon, eggs, and coffee that went with it. When I had eaten my fill, Sophie began tidying up, and I went over the more significant details of Hanna's kidnapping and Ophélie's murder as I saw them. Jem, as usual, listened without saying much.

"I'll have to sit down with your lovely Hanna to go over the tale myself," Jem said when I finished. "I'm awfully sorry to put the lass through it. We've a pair of suspects, though. Them two orderlies at the asylum that never once emptied a bedpan nor changed a sheet. That would be a big fella named Bartley Sullivan, who hails from the Isle of Man, and a wee but savage Quebec fellow whose name is André Labrecque. They were both boxers at one time, before they threw too many fights and disappeared. We hadn't heard of them until they turned up working at the sanatorium where Eleanor Hyde was taken after she was found wandering the streets without a stitch. It's about eight blocks from your former abode on Aylmer Street, so we're reasonably sure that's where Hanna and Ophélie Molyneux were held as well.

"The sanatorium is buttoned up tight. We sent two detectives to ask some questions and they couldn't get through the front door. We were told to refer all requests, in writing, to the management – but of course they wouldn't tell us who that management might be. They've powerful connections on high, be sure of that. No one would dare to be so high-handed with the coppers if they didn't. But we're not all so sweet and gentle as myself. We're going through channels for the time being, but we're keeping an eye on the place and our two suspects, Sullivan and Labrecque, have not been seen. Maybe they were fired and moved on, maybe they're just lying low. Be that as it may, I'm more concerned with the gentleman that put your Hanna in that institution in the first place, Mr. Rudolf Mayr, the famous impresario."

"I have difficulty understanding Rudi," I said. "Was he simply angry with Hanna over the money, or was he seeking revenge because she had refused to continue the tour? Even Hanna concedes that he did a great many things for her. Eventually, though, she found the pressure he put on her seemed almost unbearable – but to have her committed to an institution..." I trailed off. Rudi's behaviour toward Hanna made me so angry that at times it was better to say nothing.

"I've got some questions for Mr. Mayr myself," he said. "I'm satisfied that the two thugs from the asylum killed Ophélie Molyneux. The thing is, someone put them up to it. They didn't take a sudden fancy to beat a young woman to death on Christmas Eve. Someone wanted her watched, and when she got away, they went after her. They must have been acting on Rudi's orders, and they knew that it was better to kill her than to allow her to escape. Or was Ophélie the target all along? This wasn't the kind of murder where a man simply lost his temper and went too far. That needle through the heart was the act of a cold-blooded killer."

"Can you arrest Rudi as soon as he gets off the train from New York?" I asked.

"We could drum up a reason, but so far as we know, there is nothing that would hold up in court. If he was her legal guardian, he had the right to have her committed. I know it's wrong, but what's wrong in fact is not always wrong in the eyes of the law. Makes me ill, but that's how things work. Unless he ordered those ruffians to kill her if she escaped, we have no cause to bring charges. Now a fellow such as Herr Mayr, he'll fold like a cheap tent if we twist his arm, but we have to tread softly. There are people in high places who take an interest in this case. I don't know who they are or why they're interested, but I know they're lurking in the background, and I don't want the investigation shut down a second time."

I asked Jem what else he knew about the Bethlehem Sanatorium.

"So far as we know, it's run pretty much like any of these asylums where women are tucked away when they get to be an inconvenience to somebody," he said. "It's more upper-crust than most, and it costs a pretty penny to keep a woman there, but it's still a very nasty business."

Jem ticked off some of the reasons a woman could be confined against her will: insanity caused by childbirth, insanity caused by anxiety, insanity caused by overwork, insanity caused by her husband taking a mistress. Somehow when there was a domestic issue, it was always the woman's fault, and if she did not behave as some male expected her to behave, she could be committed.

Sophie had joined us at the table. "When I come to Canada," she said, "they tell me it is a free country, everyone is entitled to a trial. Where was the trial when your Hanna was put away? There was no trial. They say, 'woman, you go to this place like a jail, and we tell you when you get out.' No trial, no jury. They can even put the wife of a rich man in this place. What is her name? Eleanor Hyde. They say she drinks. Maybe she has a reason to drink, no?"

"She was the envy of the town when she married her prince," Jem said, "but she'd have been better off with a pauper. A poor man would not have had the funds to have her put away like that. Although there was a story in the society pages

the other day saying that Eleanor Hyde hosted a gala to benefit the hospital, so I guess she has seen the error of her ways."

We sat quietly for a few moments, sipping our coffee
and meditating on the fate of poor Eleanor Hyde. Finally, Jem
broke the silence.

"You're in love with her, then," he said.

I looked at Jem in astonishment. "Eleanor Hyde?"

Jem laughed heartily and Sophie joined him, while I
looked from one to the other for some explanation. Jem
slapped me on the back so hard my bones rattled. "Nay, boy,"
he said. "Your lovely Hanna."

I blushed to the tips of my ears, but there was no point in
denying it. "I am. Deeply."

"And I would say she feels the same way. Have ye set a
date?"

"A date?"

"For a man with a medical degree in his pocket, you're
thick as two planks between the ears. A *wedding* date, ye young
fool. The two of you, pie-eyed over each other. It's plain as my
black mustache. That's the next step, ain't it? In the natural
progression of things? A wedding?"

"Oh, I don't know about that," I said. "I do believe that
Hanna loves me, I just don't know – I don't know that marriage
will ever suit her."

"Why ever not?"

"She received an awful shock here, and she went
through some terrifying moments in the war as well. I've been
studying war trauma in Vienna with Dr. Freud, looking at the
breakdowns that men suffer after they've been in battle. The
effect on Hanna was much like what we call war neuroses. She
trembles sometimes in the presence of men, she has terrible
nightmares and wakes up screaming, sometimes she feels as
though she's back in the asylum. If she is to be with someone as
man and wife, it's going to take time."

I left it there. It was reasonably clear what I meant. In
my opinion as both a medical professional and as a man who

loved her, I did not feel that Hanna was yet capable of normal relations with a man, and I wasn't sure that she ever would be. Nor was I one to pressure her in any way. We might have discussed it further, but the doorbell rang. Sophie went to answer it and returned with Hanna and Elise, who had walked from the hotel to enjoy the beautiful May morning. Sophie, fussing over them both to equal degrees, got them seated at the cheerful kitchen table and Sophie went to get them coffee and toast. Once they had eaten breakfast, Jem asked Hanna if she would be willing to talk with him about the events leading up to the death of Ophélie Molyneux. "I've heard some of it from Maxim," he explained, "but I need to hear it directly from you, and I have to know that you would be willing to testify in court, if necessary."

"I would like to help if it is true that I am able," Hanna said in English. "Ophélie's death is very bad for me. Maybe it helps me if you find who kill her? I will tell you all I know, but I must talk in German. My English is a big mess. Then someone must translate to you."

I was about to volunteer, but Elise said that she was accustomed to translating for Hanna, so long as she could translate into French for Jem. Jem answered in French and I was startled to discover that he was quite fluent in the language, although he spoke French with an Irish brogue. I thought of joining them in Jem's little nook of an office, but there wasn't room, so I asked Sophie if I might have another coffee. We sat and chatted while Hanna, for the first time since Ophélie's murder, unburdened herself to an officer of the law.

They talked for nearly an hour. I could hear Hanna's voice in German, then Elise in her beautiful French, with the occasional rumble when Jem asked a question. I had to concentrate to follow what Sophie was telling me. There had been some difficult years for the café during the war, she said, but things had improved considerably since. In Montreal, people had money and they were looking for a place to spend it. I told her about how difficult things were in Vienna, the shortages of almost everything from coffee to bread to shoe leather. Sophie had relatives in Budapest still, and they were suffering some of the same privations we endured in Vienna.

"It's hard to believe," she said. "Before the war, Europe was the future of the world. So optimistic, yes? Now it is smashed and poor. I feel very sad, but someday I will go to visit with Jem, to explore Budapest again, to see how it is. And you must be there with Hanna also. Some day when this business is over and when Europe is better again."

"Someday, Sophie. Someday."

Just then the door to Jem's office opened and the three of them came out to join us again. Hanna looked weary but relieved. Elise smiled and nodded to me to signal that the interview had gone well. Jem took his seat with a sheaf of very tidy notes he had taken during the interview. He drummed his fingers on the table and stroked his mustache, thinking things over.

"We must find the best way to approach Rudi Mayr," he said. "I have no doubt that if you gave me three minutes with the man and a rubber hose, I could get him to confess to anything, but that isn't the approach I want to take. We need to get at the truth, not to beat a confession out of the man. I would like to see how he reacts to the sight of Hanna, before he has time to make up a story."

Jem turned to Hanna. "He still believes you are dead, does he not?"

"Yes, he does."

"And unless I am mistaken, Rudi is a man of somewhat delicate disposition?"

Hanna didn't quite understand the question, so Elise answered for her. "He is, definitely.
I've seen him faint twice, once because of a tiny scratch on his thumb."

Jem nodded. "So, if he was confronted with the living presence of a woman whom he believed has been dead for nearly seven years, how would he react?"

"He might have a stroke," Elise said.

"Well, we wouldn't want that. What we want is to shake him to the core, make him want to tell the truth. But it would mean that Hanna would have to confront him, face to face. Are you able to do that, Hanna?"

"Absolutely! But you must promise never to let him have me put away again!"

"Never!" Jem said firmly. "You have my word on that."

"Rudi arrives tomorrow evening at eight o'clock," I said. "According to the papers, he's coming by train from New York City, along with the cast of *Eugene Onegin*. There will be newspaper reporters and photographers waiting, so the train station isn't the place to meet him. If I know Rudi, he's a man of habit, which means that he will be staying again at the Windsor Hotel. It seems to me that would be the place to confront him."

"Not in the lobby," Jem said. "That could cause an awful ruckus."

I thought it over. "Good hotels have an excellent staff, and their people have long memories. I know a concierge at that establishment, if he's still at work."

I laid out my plan. Jem was hesitant at first, but finally he agreed, as did Hanna and Elise, with a couple of minor adjustments. We were ready. There was nothing left except to wait for our quarry to arrive at the hotel.

CHAPTER 41

We rode down to Windsor Station in style in Jem's Essex. I rode up front with Jem, Hanna and Elise in the back. Sophie had wanted to come along, but she had a café to run, and I could sense that Jem thought it best if she stayed behind. Sophie had a temper and you never knew what might happen – she was apt to fly into Herr Rudolf Mayr the instant she saw him, making a fine mess of all our carefully calculated plans. It was a fine spring evening, but that didn't ease the tension we felt – all of us except Jem, that is. He delivered a running monologue on the attractions of Montreal along the way. I very much doubted that Jem had ever felt edgy or anxious in his life. If he did, he hid it well.

I was overwhelmed by the sheer number of automobiles on the street, the drivers more hurried and careless than any I had seen in Europe. The sidewalks were crowded with pedestrians, most of them looking well-fed and healthy, even the poor. Montreal was such a lively, vibrant, confident city, much as Vienna had been before the war. I thought of the starving wraiths of Vienna now, sliding along with their heads down and their hands jammed in their pockets, conserving energy, each behind a private wall of bitterness and frustration. Here in Montreal, people called out to one another across the street, shook hands, laughed freely as though they had not a care in the world.

Among these people, Jem moved like a king. The crowd parted to make way for the man with the handlebar mustache and the big black hat, and again I was reminded how much he looked like a sheriff in the western pictures at the cinema. We three followed in his wake like acolytes, waiting to obey his command. I had Hanna on one arm and Elise on the other, and I could feel the tension in Hanna.

Inside Windsor Station, we found a likely place on the edge of the lobby and settled in to wait for the train, which was scheduled to be right on time. We remained well back. Our only purpose was to verify that Rudi did indeed arrive on the train. If he was, then we would discreetly shadow him to his hotel next door.

There were at least twenty members of the working press on hand. They were easily identifiable by their notebooks, their ever-present cigarettes, their huge cameras being set up on
tripods, their noisy banter in both French and English. There was also a sizable crowd of ordinary folks, a mix of opera fans and the merely curious, all crowding the cavernous lobby of the station. Clouds of tobacco smoke rose from the mob, so much that my eyes burned. I had never acquired the tobacco habit, but there was so much smoke here that I might as well have joined them.

At last there was the hiss of steam and the squeal of heavy iron wheels on iron rails as the New York City Express braked into the station, a full ten minutes early. There was a mad rush forward as the reporters and photographers jockeyed for positions in front of the last two cars, where the opera stars and their impresario were riding. The crowd followed instinctively, until burly railroad guards and police officers hurled them back. The doors slid open along the length of the train, steps were put down, and the passengers began to disembark. Those at the front hurried away and the members of the opera company emerged last, stepping down like visiting grandees. They included the world-famous director, a towering baritone, a handsome tenor, a dark-haired soprano and, at the end of the procession, the impresario himself, Herr Rudolf Mayr wearing a purple Borsalino hat and a matching purple cape over a gold brocade vest and cream-colored trousers.

Herr Rudolf Mayr was a much more substantial figure

than when we last met, in both his dress and his ample belly, but he had the same neat little mustache, the round glasses, the dark curly hair cut just a bit too long. He was the very image of the successful impresario on the world stage, this time accompanying a famous troupe from New York. Next week it would be a dance company from the Bolshoi, or a risqué act from Paris. Rudi was connected everywhere, and the money was flowing in. I got a good look, and then he was surrounded by notebooks and cameras,
and I caught a last glimpse of his face with that sheen of success. He was a rich man now and he looked the part – rich and famous and atop the world.

As we had planned, Jem and the ladies slipped away before the crowd thinned. Rudi was near sighted and they were some distance away from him, but we didn't want to take a chance that he would recognize Hanna and panic. I waited among the hustling red caps carrying enormous trunks, suitcases and musical instruments, my hat pulled low over my eyes, until the last reporter had asked his last question and Rudi, accompanied by a slender blond man I took to be his secretary, made his way toward the exit from the train station and turned right toward the hotel. I gauged the distance perfectly and was just close enough to see Rudi tipping the bellhops as they headed into the entrance of the Windsor Hotel. Our quarry had arrived. The only possible delay now would come if he chose to have dinner immediately, but if I knew Rudi, he would first go upstairs and change into his evening clothes. I thought his slender companion might accompany him to his room, but they parted ways just as they arrived at the lift.

The only remaining obstacle was to find out what room Rudi was in without alerting him. I looked around and spotted the man I wanted, the concierge who had seen me waiting in the lobby after Hanna's funeral in January 1914, the one who told me not to worry because Rudi often ran late. I walked up to the concierge and removed my hat. *"Bon soir, monsieur,"* I said, knowing that any Frenchman believes that if you do not offer the customary greeting, it is a sign that you are an irredeemable savage.

"I doubt if you remember me," I went on. "I was here one night before the war, to dine with Herr Rudolf Mayr. He was very late, and when you asked for whom I was waiting, and I told you, you were kind enough to tell me that he often ran late."

The concierge peered at me intently. The war had marked me, as it had marked everyone, but it was still my misfortune to appear ten years younger than my actual age. He snapped his fingers. "The young Austrian gentleman," he said. "Dr. Balsano, isn't it? You had a schnapps or two while you were waiting, correct? Then you had a very long meal with Herr Mayr."

"Remarkable," I said, and I meant it. "I wish I had your memory. It would be useful in my profession."

He gave a slight bow. "I assume that you are here to dine with Herr Mayr again?" he asked. "Let me ring up and let him know you are here..."

"No!" I was rather too forceful, but I had to prevent a call that would have ruined everything. "No, please. I have two female friends with whom Rudi was once very close. We haven't seen him since before the war and he doesn't know we're here, so the ladies want to surprise him."

The concierge clapped his hands. "*Oh, j'aime les surprises!*" he said. "Rudi is in his suite, as always. Room 813. Shall I have someone escort you up?"

"That won't be necessary. The young ladies are waiting just outside. They didn't want to accidentally bump into him and ruin the surprise."

"Of course, of course."

I slipped back outdoors and found Jem waiting with Hanna and Elise in the shadows of a huge oak tree. "He's staying in room 813, and he's there now," I said. "I saw him take the lift. Give us three minutes, Jem. We shouldn't need more than that."

I took Hanna's arm. "Are you ready for this?" I asked. "You're certain?"

Hanna was very pale, but her jaw was set. She was ready. I led the way back through the lobby, where the smiling concierge bowed to us. We caught the lift just in time and asked the lift boy to take us to the eighth floor. The carpet in the hallway at the Windsor Hotel had that luxuriant thickness that makes it feel as though your feet are being massaged as you walk. That luxury also made it impossible to hear us walking along the corridor. We found room 813 halfway down. We paused at the door with Hanna in the middle, Elise to her left and me on her right. I nodded to Elise and we each stepped away a pace or two, leaving Hanna apparently alone. She took a deep breath and then another, gave each of us in turn a meaningful look, set her jaw – and knocked quite firmly at the door.

There was no response. She knocked a second time, louder, and then a third, louder still.

At last the door was opened a timid inch, and then another. Hanna gave it a firm push and they stood face to face, Rudi Mayr with his suspenders down and his shirt unbuttoned, Hanna staring at him from no more than a foot or two away. From the time she had moved in with me in November, Hanna had let her hair revert to its natural fiery red by letting it grow and then having it cut short so that only the natural colour remained. I could see her trembling ever so slightly, whether with anticipation or fear or anger, I could not say. Whatever her emotions, she managed to say in a loud, clear voice:

"*Guten abend, Rudi.* It has been a very long time."

Rudi's expression was one that I imagine most men wear the day they meet their Maker – or the Devil, whichever the case may be. His sanguine face lost all color. I thought for a moment, he was going to faint. Instead he dropped to his knees at her feet.

"Hanna! *Du bist ein Geist!*"

"Yes, Rudi. A ghost. Come back to settle things with you, in the town where you had me murdered."

"No, no! Where did you get such an idea? I didn't have you killed, of course not. Please, Hanna! What do you want from me? Why did you come back?"

I could hear the disgust in Hanna's voice. "I want to see you in prison," she said. "You tried to kill me, but you did not succeed. Your ruffians killed the wrong person. I am alive."

"Alive? It's a miracle!"

"It is not a miracle. I got away from the men you sent to kill me. Now I am back."

Rudi reached out and touched her foot. "My God. It's true. You are alive."

"Of course, I'm alive, you fool! Through no fault of yours. You tried to kill me!"

"No, no," Rudi said. "Hanna, I did not try to kill you. Why do you say that? This is a miracle. You must understand, I wanted the best for you, always, only the best..." Rudi's eyes filled with tears and he tried to wrap his arms around her legs. What happened next was so quick that I didn't see it coming. As Rudi groveled at her feet, Hanna drove a football player's kick directly into Rudi's nose. She was wearing durable mahogany walking Oxfords with a squarish, solid toe, and she had spent a good part of her childhood playing a rough brand of football with the neighborhood boys. Few men could have delivered a harder blow to poor, cringing Rudi, who fell back screaming, his broken spectacles dangling from one ear as bright red blood pumped from his shattered nose. Hanna was pitiless. Before I could move to intervene, she moved in to deliver a second kick squarely to his testicles, and a third kick caught Rudi in the solar plexus, knocking the wind out of him.

Hanna might have kicked the man to death right there, had Elise and I not pulled her away from him. Even then, she struggled to get at him and might have broken free of us, except that Jem came storming down the hallway to get between Hanna and her quarry. He took Rudi under the arms and dragged the bleeding man into the hotel room, while Elise and I led Hanna through the door and closed it behind us. Jem hoisted Rudi onto a divan in a semi-reclining position with his head thrown back, Elise fetched a wet cloth and held it to the wounded man's nose, and I managed to get Hanna seated next to me facing Rudi from a safe distance. She was still spitting fire, muttering Viennese curses half under her breath.

"She's going to kill me!" Rudi said, when he had recovered sufficiently to speak.

"It would be no great loss to humanity if she did," Jem said, "but there will be no killing done on my watch. I have some questions for you and if you don't answer truthfully, I shall unleash that woman over there and let her do her damnedest."

"You signed papers to put me in that asylum!" Hanna said, without waiting for Jem to begin asking questions. "I wouldn't do what you wanted, so you had me locked up! Why did you do that? It was because you wanted to keep my money, wasn't it?"

Rudi looked astounded. "I did no such thing! Why would I do that?"

"To get rid of me! I saw your signature! It was you, Rudi. No one else writes like that. The policeman showed me the paper. There it was. You think I don't know your signature?"

Jem held Rudi's head propped in one enormous paw. "Well, Rudi? What do you say to that? Hanna saw it. You signed the papers."

"*Hab ich nicht!*" Rudi repeated. "Why would I do that? Hanna was to be the greatest singer in my galaxy of singers. We could have made a fortune together!"

"Except that you had her put away."

"No, no... never. I was very angry with her for not making the American tour, but I would never do such a thing. You must believe me. Hanna was very dear to me. Is very dear to me. I was shattered when I thought she had been murdered." Rudi stared at me for a moment and seemed to recognize me as a potential saviour. "Dr. Balsano knows – tell them, Maxim!"

"I know only what you told me," I said. "I don't know if any of it was true."

Jem loomed over Rudi. "If you have an explanation, we need to hear it. Hanna was dragged off to a sanatorium because you signed a paper to have her committed. Another young woman was murdered, probably because she was mistaken for Hanna. You were paying for her incarceration, you put her there, you wanted her watched, and the watchers got a little too zealous. Or perhaps you meant it that way. If Hanna ended up dead, she could never ask for her money – and you would have your revenge for her decision to cancel the tour."

"No. No. I was never paying for her incarceration. I didn't know she had been locked away. The money... it is true, I have some money for Fraulein Goss, but it is not a great amount. I had obligations... the U.S. ... guarantees that were made, advances that had to be returned. ... Expenses. And revenge? Believe me, such revenge would hurt me more than anyone. If word got out that I had one of my own artists committed to a sanatorium, I would never get another client."

"Then how do you explain your signature on those papers?"

"I told you, I have no idea, none..." He paused, looking stricken. "*Oh, mein Gott im Himmel!*"

Jem leaned in closer. "What is it?"

"God in heaven," Rudi repeated. "I think I know what happened."

"Then you had better share it with us, before I get angry."

"I'd rather not say in front of the young ladies. It's... delicate."

"Hanna was a nurse in the war. Elise cared for an elderly woman. I don't believe you need to worry about their delicate sensibilities."

"It's frightfully embarrassing."

"Dammit, man!" Jem drove an enormous fist into the divan, deliberately missing Rudi's
ear by no more than an inch. "Quit dancing us around the block. Out with it! What is so damned embarrassing?"

Rudi sat up a bit, still dabbing at his nose although the blood had ceased to flow. "I was trapped," he said. "Followed and trapped. There was a rather enticing young blond fellow who caught my eye at the stage door after a rehearsal. You see I am... what the French call a *tapette*. I followed him, discreetly. He walked several blocks, and he kept looking back to be sure I was following. He led me into a public lavatory. I followed. There was no one else there. We were alone. He gestured to let me know what he wanted. We began... I must ask you to forgive me. There are ladies present, I can say no more. I knew it was dangerous, but I was... in the grip of lust, I don't know how else to explain it. Somehow the danger is part of the excitement. In any case, we had barely begun when three horrible men burst into the lavatory. I thought they were only thugs who prey on people like myself, but then one of them showed me a badge. He said he was a sergeant-detective. He slipped a dollar bill to the young blond fellow and told him to go away, and then the other two closed in on me. One of them was huge, the other a small man but very muscular, with rings on every finger."

Jem interrupted Rudi's narrative at that point. "Did they speak?" he asked.

Rudi paused. "It was a long time ago. I'm trying to remember. They did speak, but I don't recall what they said. Unspeakable things, most likely."

"English or French?"

"The big one spoke English, with an accent somewhat like your own. The smaller one spoke the sort of French the poorer classes speak in Quebec. Utterly incomprehensible to me, in other words."

"And the detective? Did he speak to you in French or English?"

"English, although he had a French name. Detective-Sergeant Lapointe, I think it was. I don't believe he told me his first name."

"Not Lapointe. Leblanc. Cyril Leblanc. Our old friend Cyril Leblanc."

"That's it."

"He's in prison now."

Rudi raised his eyebrows. "You don't say!"

"Let's get back to what happened to you in the lavatory. What did they do next? I still don't see what this had to do with the papers you signed to have Hanna confined."

"I'm getting to that. The next thing that happened was that the big one pinned my arms back, and the smaller one hit me in the stomach two or three times, very fast and incredibly hard, like a pugilist beating on one of those bags that they use. So hard that I vomited all over my shoes – a very fine pair I had purchased in Milan, ruined. I thought it was possible they might beat me to death right there in the lavatory, but this Leblanc person made them stop. He said he was arresting me for an indecent and immoral act, and it would go worse for me because the young blond fellow was only seventeen. It could mean a lengthy and very embarrassing sentence, one that would ruin my career even if I survived prison. I recall that he said it was unlikely I would live through the experience, as the prisons in Quebec were especially harsh."

Jem waited patiently. From his expression, I couldn't tell whether he believed Rudi or not. Hanna plainly did not believe him, her expression made that clear. Elise remained impassive. I was in an agony of indecision myself. Rudi's story, outlandish as it was, had the ring of truth. From my psychiatric work, I knew what homosexuals endured at the hands of the police in civilized Vienna; it was likely to be worse in corrupt Montreal. I found it almost unbearable to see a proud, sophisticated man such as Herr Mayr reduced to a bloody, sniveling wreck. At the same time, he had done horrible things to the woman I loved, and, directly or indirectly, he was responsible for the death of Ophélie Molyneux. More than anything, however, I simply wanted to know the truth.

Rudi asked for a glass of water, and Elise brought it from the tap in the lavatory. He drank it and resumed his narrative.

"I thought they were going to ask me for money. A common thing that men face when they suffer from my … inclinations. I was ready to pay them any amount, within reason. Anything but go to prison. Even a trial would have destroyed me – imagine the publicity? I am not Oscar Wilde, but even so, I was sufficiently known to make juicy reading for the gutter press. So here I was, beaten and bleeding, reeking of my own vomit, terrified. That's when Detective Leblanc offered me a choice. It was like being told that you've been granted immortality when you're at death's door. All I had to do was to sign a paper guaranteeing that I would not indulge in any such behavior again so long as I was in Montreal.

"I couldn't believe my ears. That was all they wanted? It didn't seem possible, but – what is it you English say? Do not look the gift horse in the mouth? Of course, I agreed! What else was I to do? The smaller one punched me on the back of the ear and told me to hurry up and sign. The detective drew a paper from inside his jacket, very official stationery, three or four pages. I reached for my spectacles in my vest pocket, but they had been smashed. The letters to me were just fuzzy squiggles. I couldn't make out a word, and I knew what these men would do to me if I asked them to read it to me before I signed.

"The detective pointed to where I was supposed to sign, and handed me a fountain pen. What else was I to do? I placed the document on the lavatory floor and signed. They snatched the papers away from me then, and that was all. Well, except for a farewell punch from that little savage. The detective warned me that if I should stray while I was on his territory, the punishment would be severe, because in addition to the offence, I would have broken a solemn vow not to offend. They stomped out and left me lying on the floor, knowing that now there was a signed document telling the world that I am a homosexual."

Jem remained skeptical. "Except that wasn't what you signed. You signed a document that would send your protégée to the asylum."

"I didn't know. You must believe me. I would never have willingly signed such a thing, committing Hanna to an institution." Rudi sat up straighter, trying to act dignified. "They could have beaten me for hours, I would never have done such a thing," he insisted. "Not to Hanna, my wonderful and talented Hanna."

"So you say, but you are a man of affairs, sir," Jem said. "Experienced in the ways of negotiation and the power of documents. You expect us to believe that you signed a document you had not read, in a language you did not understand?"

Rudi shrugged. "I did. It was absurd. I could have been signing away a fortune."

"Or a young woman's life," Jem snapped.

Rudi inclined his head toward Hanna by way of apology. "Or a young woman's life. I am very sorry, Hanna."

Hanna said nothing. Jem took a chair and sat twirling his mustache and staring at Rudi. "If what you say is true (and I'm not ready to believe that it is) then who put Detective Leblanc and those two thugs up to it? Why such an elaborate ruse to keep the true identity of the person who wanted Hanna locked up a secret? You were the one who had a motive, Herr Mayr."

"I'm sorry, but what possible motive did I have?" Rudi asked.

"You had a good deal of money that belonged to Hanna, and you didn't want to part with it, and she had embarrassed you by cancelling the American portion of the tour."

"I assure you, detective, I was angry with her, but not to

the point where I would do such a thing. As for money, I stood to make a good deal more by persuading Hanna to return to the stage."

"Perhaps. But if you didn't have Hanna put away, who did?"

"I have no idea," Rudi said.

Jem paused, drumming his fingers on his thigh, thinking it over.

"Let us say I believe you, at least for the moment," he said. "There is still the matter of a substantial sum owed to Hanna from her appearances during the time you acted as her manager. I will give you one week to give her a full accounting and see to it that she is paid in full, with interest. If you fail, I will see to it that you face legal proceedings, and that some friendly newspaper reporters have every juicy detail of the manner in which you cheated one of your own clients. Do we understand each other, Mr. Mayr?"

"If you do that, I will be ruined!" Rudi protested.

"Precisely. That is why you must do as I have instructed. The same thing will happen to you if you choose to bring charges of assault against Miss Goss – she was acting under duress. Now I will ask you again, Herr Mayr: do we understand each other?"

Rudi hung his head. "We do," he muttered.

We took our leave, Elise rather more gently than the rest, and left Rudi to tend to his wounds. On the way out, the concierge asked me if Rudi had enjoyed his surprise visit.

"Oh yes," I said, "I think he enjoyed it very much."

We lingered outside the hotel for a time, enjoying the fresh night air and comparing notes on our varying reactions to what Rudi had said.

"I've heard Rudi lie many times," Elise said. "Always for business. He would tell someone that he had many offers for one of his singers, when in fact he had none. He would make up the most outlandish excuses. But I could always tell when he was lying. Tonight, I did not feel that he was. I believe he told the truth, or most of it. How could he have known of this Sergeant-Detective Leblanc if it did not happen as he said?"

Hanna shook her head rather fiercely. "I too have listened to Rudi's lies," she said in English. "He is one who lies when there is no reason to lie, because with him, it is habit. Perhaps he hired this Leblanc to put me away, then he made up this story so that I do not kick him some more. He is a coward, Rudi. He is afraid even of me, and with Jem, he is shaking. I am surprise he do not wet himself."

Jem looked at me. "Maxim? What did you think?"

"I felt some sympathy for the man, although I don't blame Hanna for kicking him."

"But did you believe the man?"

"I rather did, I'm afraid," I said. "I know that homosexuals can have a very rough time of
it. It sounded like something that could happen, being arrested in a public lavatory."

"It does happen," Jem said. "But it could have happened to Rudi in other circumstances.
Here, Vienna, New York – anywhere. Perhaps he had been through it before, so it made a convenient story to explain his signature on the document."

"What about this Leblanc character? How would Rudi know about him otherwise?"

"He could have hired the man. It's plausible. Cyril Leblanc was for sale. That was pretty generally known. If you were looking to employ a dishonest cop, you could ask around in the criminal milieu. Sooner or later, you'd be directed to Cyril. He's both corrupt and stupid."

"What about you?" I asked. "Did you believe Rudi?"

"I try not to believe any witness unless I can corroborate what he says from another source. I do know one fellow who might settle it all with a word or two."

"And who might that be?"

"My old friend, the former Sergeant-Detective Leblanc, now just Leblanc the convict. He's not difficult to find – he's still in prison. He knows whether Rudi's story is true, and if it is, he knows who wanted Rudi's signature on that document, and for how much. I think I will pay old Cyril a visit tomorrow. You might tag along if you wish, Max."

"Would I be admitted? In what capacity?"

Jem chuckled. "I have the feeling that Cyril might require a visit from a trained psychoanalyst. I have friends at the prison. It shouldn't be a problem. Ladies, I'm afraid I can't think of an excuse that would gain admittance for you."

Elise smiled. "Montreal is a lovely city," she said. "I think we can find a way to pass our time that is more congenial than a visit to a prison. Although I would like to treat this Leblanc fellow the way Hanna treated poor Rudi!"

Now it was Hanna's turn to blush. "I am sorry, I did not plan it. Something about him just made all the anger come..."

"It's quite alright, Hanna," I said. "Even if he wasn't directly responsible for sending you to the asylum, he treated you abominably."

Hanna smiled ruefully at me and leaned her head briefly against my shoulder. I caught the scent of her perfume. Elise had replenished Hanna's supply. Almost instantly, I was transported to a state bordering on ecstasy, with nothing more than her smile, a whiff of her perfume, the ticklish sensation of a breeze blowing her red hair against my neck.

CHAPTER 42

I t was three days before Jem could arrange a visit to Cyril Leblanc. In the interval, the weather had changed. It was chilly and raining so hard that the side streets were already a river of mud. It took us nearly an hour to make it from Sherbrooke Street to Gouin Boulevard, where Bordeaux Prison had been constructed shortly before the war. The architecture was such that it might have been a nunnery or a monastic retreat, if not for the barbed wire atop the brick walls. Jem had telephoned in advance and he was clearly well-known by the prison staff. He was greeted everywhere with a tip of the cap and a cheerful "bon jour, M. le detective!" or "Mr. Doyle, sir! Good morning to you!" My passing was scarcely noted, although I had gotten thoroughly wet and muddy while trying to wrestle the Essex out of a mudhole along the way, and I looked more like a drowned rat than a psychiatrist. We were waved through one heavy iron door after another. As they clanged shut behind us, I was overcome by an irrational fear that the doors would never open again, and I would be swallowed up by this place.

At last we were shown to a rather dark and oppressive little room with no furniture except a bare wooden table and four uncomfortable, stiff-backed wooden chairs without cushions. Someone fetched us each a cup of tepid coffee that was as nearly undrinkable as any concoction I have ever tasted. I had armed myself with two cups of Sophie's wonderful coffee before we left, so I left mine untouched after the first sip. We waited half an hour for Cyril Leblanc to be led in and Jem was uncharacteristically silent, wrapped in his thoughts, while I could barely force myself to remain seated. We heard the footsteps coming from far down the hall and Leblanc was brought into the room in handcuffs, flanked by two prison guards. Somehow, I had imagined him as a slender young man with a thin mustache and dark hair. All that was wrong. He was about Jem's age, with a pudgy physique running to fat, a sallow complexion and pock-marked cheeks, thinning blond hair that wanted cutting and a rather prominent scar on the side of his neck. A cigarette dangled from his bottom lip, and I had the sense that he was likely to be cooperative.

"Doyle, you bastard," Leblanc said when he saw the big detective awaiting him. "Are you still shacked up with that fat Bohunk who runs the café? What's her name, Sylvie?"

I was taken aback. I half-expected Jem to take the man's head off, but he didn't blink. The guards led Leblanc to a stiff-backed chair opposite us, where they had to push him down before he would sit.

Jem waved them away. "That's okay, boys. I can handle this one without help."

The guards stepped out and Jem and Leblanc sat staring at one another. Leblanc smoked the cigarette down to where it was nothing more than a hot coal burning on his lip before he stubbed it out on the table and then flicked the remnants toward Jem.

Finally, Jem spoke. "Cyril, this young fellow is a psychiatrist. Dr. Maxim Balsano. Just so you know. He's here to monitor your state of mind."

Leblanc shifted his stare to me. He had eyes cold as a dead fish. "They'd love you in here, pretty boy," he said.

Jem ignored the remark. "We came all the way up here in a rainstorm to ask you about one thing," he said. "This goes back to before the war. You and a couple of your pals roughed up a fellow named Rudolf Mayr. You accused him of being a homosexual and you forced him to sign some papers. You told him the papers were a promise never to repeat the offence, but they were to commit a woman named Hanna Goss to the Bethlehem Asylum. Not only did you blackmail Rudi Mayr to sign the papers, you also showed up at the apartment where she was living and dragged her away."

Leblanc shrugged. "I've had memory problems since you bastards locked me away," he said. "Sometimes, I can't remember what I had for breakfast."

"You had lumpy oatmeal and some cold, greasy bacon with a lot of gristle. I've seen it." "Seen it but not eaten it."

"That's correct. And I don't plan to. You have to find yourself a better class of mistress if you ever get out of here, Cyril. If she hadn't been so stupid as to wear that sable coat to the Policemans Ball, you might be on the outside yet, beating up homosexuals, covering up murders, dragging young ladies off to the asylum."

"I didn't cover up no murder."

"Maybe not. You're probably the dumbest cop on the force, so it's possible you just did not do a good job investigating the murder of Ophélie Molyneux."

The ex-cop glared at Jem. "Never heard of her."

"You and your boys thought she was Hanna Goss. The singer. The same one you dragged off to the sanatorium. Hanna was the one they were supposed to watch. They got confused with the coat and the snowstorm and they killed the wrong woman."

"I don't know nothing about that. It was a robbery gone bad, like I said at the time."

"A robbery where they left the only valuable thing the woman had with her – the coat. Here's the thing, Cyril. With just a little more scrutiny, I might connect you with that murder."

For the first time, Leblanc had a reaction that was other than a sneer. "Me? I had nothing to do with it. I was the investigating officer."

"Were you? Damned convenient to be Johnny-on-the-spot, and on a Christmas Eve at that, when most police officers are home with their families. I checked, Cyril. You weren't scheduled to be on duty that night. There was nobody walking a dog in that snowstorm. That was bull. You were out hunting for the women who escaped from the asylum during that storm. You probably got a call from the sanatorium, telling you their prize inmate had escaped. The two thugs caught her and beat the hell out of her, then you came along and stabbed her."

"Stabbed? She wasn't stabbed."

"Oh, yes she was, Cyril. Good King found it. A very narrow blade to the heart. Easy to miss when you aren't thorough, but that was what killed her. If you bothered to read his report, you'd know that."

Leblanc leaned back in his chair. "That doesn't make me a killer. You've got nothing."

"What do you think it would take to get those two thugs to turn on you? They could hang for this. If I squeeze them a bit, they'll point the finger right at you, the ex-cop. You're already a convict. It shouldn't be too difficult to get a jury to believe you're capable of murder."

"Except I had nothing to do with it. I didn't kill that girl."

"Convince me. Tell me who sent you to get Rudi Mayr to sign those papers."

"I don't know."

"So you're admitting that you threatened the man and got his signature on a document,
but you're claiming you don't know who put you up to it?"

"It's the truth."

"Cyril, you wouldn't know the truth if it rose up from its wormy grave to strike you dead. You know that I am not a gullible person, and yet you try to lead me down the primrose path. Who put you up to it? That's all I'm asking."

"I don't know."

"I don't believe you. Who paid you? Because I know you, Cyril. You don't break wind unless someone pays you two bits to expel gas. Who paid you?"

"I can tell you who paid me, but that isn't the person behind this. I was paid by the Toad."

"Never heard of him."

"It isn't a him. The Toad is a woman. Runs the sanatorium, or did, and a crueler old biddy you never laid eyes on. There are killers in here with sweeter dispositions."

"The Toad paid you, then?"

"Yes. Like clockwork. I did some work for the sanatorium, and on the first day of every month, she handed me an envelope of cash. But I never knew the source. Nor did I ask, long as it kept coming regular."

"And she gave you your instructions?"

"Not always. Sometimes I would get a typewritten envelope, delivered to me at home."

I thought immediately of the typewritten notes sent to M. Bourgie at the funeral home and to the Mount Royal Cemetery, asking them to arrange the funeral of the woman we thought was Hanna Goss.

"And in this case? You received a typewritten note asking you to follow Rudolf Mayr, to catch him in a compromising position and get him to sign that document?"

"That isn't how it worked. They tell me to get a signature, I get a signature. Don't matter how we do it. We followed the guy for a couple of days. He was a lurker. Hung around places homosexuals were known to frequent. That made it easy. We figured it was only a matter of time until we caught him in the act, but I decided to hurry things along by hiring the blond boy."

"Someone you had worked with before."

"Oh, yes. We caught the boy at it once, brazen as you please. Let him go with an understanding that he was to help us any time the police force needed assistance. You know how it works."

"I do. Except in this case it wasn't the police force, it was Cyril Leblanc and two thugs. Would you mind naming them for us, Cyril, just to be certain we're looking for the right fellas?"

At that point, it seemed Leblanc would do anything in his power to avoid the threat of the noose. "They're a couple of ex-pugs," he said. "Manx Sullivan and Pepper Labrecque. Sullivan is big, but Labrecque is the evil one. You'll want to give him a wide berth."

"You must have some idea who's behind this, Cyril. You're not much of a detective, but someone is handing you regular cash, you have to know who it was."

Leblanc shook his head. "I swear, I have no idea. There were women in that place who were connected to a couple of dozen rich, powerful men. Judges, businessmen, politicians. It could have been any one of them that wanted this Hanna Goss out of the way. Wasn't none of my business. Long as I got paid regular, I did what they asked."

Jem looked puzzled. "Once you had Rudi Mayr's signature, how did you figure out where to find the woman? Seems to me that's beyond your slender powers of deduction, isn't it?"

"I showed the signed document to the Toad at the asylum, and she wrote an address on a
tiny scrap of paper, told me to memorize it and then forget it, and threw it in the fire. An hour later, we had the songbird in her cage."

"Very poetic," Jem growled.

"Ain't it, though."

"This woman they call the Toad. She have a name?"

"Well, the girls that work at the asylum call her Madame Marie-Ange when she's in
earshot. Ain't that a hoot? There isn't a thing about that woman that has to do with the Virgin Mary or angels neither."

Jem noted it carefully in block letters in his notebook: Marie-Ange.

"Write it down if you want, Doyle," Leblanc said. "Won't do you a bit of good."

"Why's that?"

"Because that old fright passed onto the next world. Dropped dead over breakfast about a year back. And I doubt there was a soul on this earth who wept for her."

Jem closed his notebook and slipped it into his pocket along with the stub of a pencil he always used.

"So am I in the clear now?" Leblanc asked. "You're not going to bring up that murder thing again? Because I might be a lot of things you don't like, Doyle, but I don't kill. Not even for money."

"You'll never be clear of it, Cyril. Never. I can't charge you, maybe, but there was a young woman who was murdered on Christmas Eve, and you were in it up to your filthy neck. It's a nasty business all round, and when you're out of here, I'm going to take you down to the docks and thrash you to within an inch of your miserable life for bringing dishonor to the profession. Something for you to look forward to, once you've been inside a few more years."

Jem put his notebook away, summoned the guards and Cyril Leblanc was taken back to his cell. We wound our way once more through the labyrinth, along corridor after corridor with the heavy iron doors clanging shut behind us. I hoped that Jem wouldn't notice that I was breaking out in a cold sweat and I had to fight the urge to sprint to the gates. Once through the last barrier, I took great gulps of moist, rain-damp air.

Behind me, I heard Jem chuckling. "It can be a tad oppressive in there, lad. Especially the first time. I ought to have warned you. Breathe all you need. I dislike it myself, the whole idea of caging men for their sins, yet I've not been able to think of a better way to enforce the law."

If anything, it was raining even harder on the way back to Sophie's Café.

"Are you really going to thrash Cyril to within an inch of his miserable life?"

"Nope. I've never done such a thing and I don't plan to start now. But it won't hurt the man any to contemplate the possibility, will it? He'll be fear-ing the day he gets out and looking over his shoulder every day after. Think of it as an extension of his sentence."

I had to smile. Jem Doyle could be devious when the circumstances warranted. He was quiet after that, steering through the mud and the driving rain, avoiding horse-drawn milk carts and brick wagons and a great heavy truck that was hogging most of the road.

At one point, Jem laughed to himself and smacked my shoulder so hard he left a bruise. "Nothing like a wee so-cial call to brighten a man's day, now is there, lad?"

I had to smile with satisfaction. Even if he hadn't killed her, Cyril Leblanc had a great deal to do with the death of Ophélie Molyneux, not to mention the suffering Hanna had endured. Whatever suffering lay ahead for him, it was richly deserved.

CHAPTER 43

I rose early the next morning, but Jem had already left. Sophie was in a buoyant mood, even for her. Elise and Hanna arrived as Sophie was starting breakfast. The streets were still muddy, but they wanted to go for a walk on Mount Royal – and they wanted to know what had transpired when Jem and I met with Cyril Leblanc. They wanted to leave immediately, but Sophie wouldn't hear of it. First we had to have one of her royal breakfast feasts.

It was a full hour before Sophie was persuaded that we couldn't possibly eat another bite. We thanked her profusely and left to take an east-bound tram as far as Peel Street, where we disembarked for the hike up to the mountain. We were halfway up when it occurred to me that from the right spot, we would have a superb view of Hyde House. We found a spot where the trees were cleared and looked down. From there we could clearly see the gargoyles that dotted the roof, the wide driveway leading to the front door and the spacious slope of the great lawn behind the house, with the vast, glassed-in conservatory a lengthy rectangle along one side and the red brick carriage house in the rear.

Hanna pointed to the bandshell where she had performed on the August night when we first met. I was flattered that she recalled the spot where I had been standing as she sang, and the wooded area on the east side of the vast lawn where we had strolled when I first began to fall in love with her.

Like Sophie at breakfast, Hanna seemed unusually buoyant. She and Elise had packed a picnic lunch, which we ate on the opposite side of the mountain, and we dozed for a time in the sun before we began to make our way down toward McGill University. We paused on Aylmer Street to ring the bell at the yellow house. To my surprise, Mrs. Guterson herself answered the door and burst into tears at the sight of me.

"Maximilian! I am so very pleased to see you. You naughty boy, you have not written to me in a very long time. I didn't even know if you had survived the war. You do know that you were one of my favorites, don't you? Perhaps my very favorite. You were always so responsible and so polite – those wonderful European manners. Europeans might be about to invade your country, but they will bow politely before they inform you of the fact, isn't that so, Maxim? I'm afraid we don't often see those manners on our rough Canadian boys and the Americans are much worse. But now you must exercise those manners, young man, and introduce me to your female friends. Is one of these beautiful creatures your wife?"

I introduced Hanna and Elise. My former landlady insisted that we have tea at the table in her cozy kitchen, while Battling Billy the cat curled his way back and forth under our feet. Battling Billy had picked up more scars, proof that he had used more of his nine lives, but he had outlived many of the humans that I had known, including, sadly, several of the young men who had been boarders at Mrs. Guterson's and had died in the war. It was gratifying to see Billy still alive, if not quite lively.

The school year had finished, so most of the rooms in the boarding house were unoccupied, including my former apartment. Mrs. Guterson opened the door and I stepped aside to let Hanna and Elise precede me into the room. As I followed Mrs. Guterson I saw Hanna collapse into a chair and bury her face in her hands. The emotional reaction I thought she might have had at Hyde House had not occurred, but the sight of my old apartment had overwhelmed her. Elise went to console her immediately.

Mrs. Guterson looked to me for an explanation. "Whatever is wrong? Is she suffering from the heat?"

I shook my head. The landlady could hardly expel me from my lodgings now, so I decided the truth was best. "Hanna is my fellow Austrian. We met when she sang at a reception for medical students and she remembered that I lived in the yellow house on the corner. On Christmas Eve in 1913, she came to the door because she was being pursued by two horrible men who wanted to do her harm. I was able to offer her protection, but that same night, they murdered a friend of hers not far from here. That is the reason for our presence in Canada. We want to see that those responsible are found and punished."

"Oh, the poor thing!" Mrs. Guterson said. "And you, Maximilian, you ought to have told me the truth at the time. I found some long red hairs in this room when I came to clean it and I thought you had been up to something mischievous! I am not as old-fashioned as you think. You had only to explain the circumstances."

"Yes. There was nothing... immoral. I was very ill. I was able to persuade the men I had typhoid to get rid of them and Hanna left the same night and eventually made her way back to Vienna. Now we are trying to determine what was behind it all."

Hanna, her face streaked with tears, looked up at us. "I'm sorry, I'm sorry," she said. "I did not expect to react as I did. That night... the way I felt. Such terror. And so grateful to Maxim for taking me in."

Mrs. Guterson knelt at Hanna's side and took her hand. "Please," she said. "I'm glad he did. I would have been most unhappy with Maximilian if he had not offered you his protection. It's only a pity I was not here. I have my husband's old shotgun in my quarters, and it has two barrels – one for each of those creatures. I grew up on a farm in Sweden. I am most familiar with shotguns."

Hanna laughed at that, and I saw that she was recovering from the shock of seeing the apartment again and remembering that terrible night. She opened the window to show us where she had crawled through the night she returned for the letter, and we went back downstairs for tea and pastries before we left, with many promises to return for another visit.

Elise and Hanna wanted to change at their hotel, so we caught the tram to their hotel, where they took an unconscionably long time getting dressed. When at last they came down the stairs, they were both wearing their newest finery, including a new green dress that Elise had purchased for Hanna the day before, while Jem and I were paying a call on Cyril Leblanc. Elise looked stylish as always in yellow, but Hanna took my breath away in her green dress. They were both carrying rather cumbersome packages, which they said were surprises for Jem and Sophie, and when I offered to help with the packages they wouldn't hear of it.

Even then, they dawdled along so slowly that we did not arrive at Sophie's Café until after six o'clock in the evening. I was so absorbed by Hanna's loveliness during the walk that it didn't occur to me that something might be afoot, and it was not until we opened the door of the Café and fifty people shouted "Happy Birthday, Maxim!" in unison that I recalled that it was my thirty-first birthday. Elise and Hanna had a wonderful laugh at how obtuse men can be. Neither the obvious packages nor the way they lingered at the hotel had alerted me to the fact that it was my birthday and that something was planned. I had been so absorbed in the details of the murder investigation that it had quite slipped my mind – or perhaps, at age thirty-one, I had simply reached that stage in life when birthdays become something best forgotten.

Sophie was at the front of the celebrants awaiting my arrival, ready to scoop me up in one of her unforgettable bear hugs, followed by Jem and Sophie's sons, who stepped up one by one to shake my hand. Soon the wine, beer, Irish whiskey and pálinka were flowing, the polka band was tuning up, and Hanna and I were off on the dance floor together, she with her cheeks glowing and her feet very nimble while I tried to follow along. At some point I was forced to sit on a chair and open a pile of gifts, more than I had received on all my previous birthdays combined.

Sometime after midnight, Elise and Hanna said their goodbyes and were about to walk back to their hotel when Jem intervened and had one of his sergeants drive them back. The gesture might have been taken for simple politeness, but I thought something else was behind it. Jem recalled the terrible beating I had absorbed on my way to my Aylmer Street apartment and he was being cautious. I was fairly inebriated, but I still felt a tremor of unease and I wondered if we should not have insisted that the two women stay for the night.

CHAPTER 44

My first thought, when Jem shook me awake not much more than two hours later, was that something terrible had befallen Hanna and Elise, but that was not the case. "Blind Pig in the Point," Jem growled, forgetting I hadn't the slightest idea what either a blind pig or the Point might be. "One of my officers rang. Manx Sullivan is at the bar. You've got two minutes to dress if you want to be in on this."

Roughly three minutes later, we were driving downhill toward the Montreal neighborhood known as Point St. Charles. A blind pig, Jem was kind enough to explain, was an illegal establishment that remained open after drinking hours. Before I was fully awake, we were bumping our way along a rough and muddy track in the Point. It was a dark night and there was not a streetlight to be seen. If not for the headlights of Jem's automobile, we would have been driving blind. I could just make out rough shanties on either side of the street, wooden structures piled atop one another, most of them looking as though they would collapse in the first strong breeze. Now and then we heard shouts and screams along the dark street. I had no idea how Jem could make out where we were. Finally, he let the car roll to a stop.

"Stay directly behind me and don't try to get involved, whatever you do," he whispered. "We'll handle this."

We went another block on foot, almost feeling our way along as our eyes adjusted to the near-absolute darkness. There was a stench of rotting garbage, and when I stumbled over something I first took to be a man asleep on the sidewalk, I heard the squeal of a hog and a sizable spotted beast grunted as it lumbered off into the darkness, setting off the neighborhood dogs, which barked lustily. As Jem started up a rickety flight of stairs, shadowy figures closed in on us from either side. I thought we were being attacked, but Jem paused just long enough to issue a few orders. The men who now flanked us on either side were cops, all of them big and burly, two of them Irish friends of Jem's still tipsy from my party.

When Jem knocked, someone inside asked him for a password.

"It's Jem Doyle. Open the fecking door Reg Curran, or I'll I kick it down."

The door opened to the reek of whiskey, tobacco and vomit. A portly man whom I took to be the proprietor took Jem's arm. "No troubles now, captain," he said. "We've been making our payments regular, like clockwork."

"I'm not on your payroll and this ain't a raid. We're here to collect Manx Sullivan and we'll be on our way."

"Thanks be to God. He's been at the bar since before midnight, in a foul and nasty mood. Scared off most of the paying customers. The men I pay to look after the place are afraid to ask him to leave."

"I'll have a wee word with Manx and he'll leave, right enough," Jem said. He turned to me. "You stay here, at the back. I don't want to see you get broken in two. Manx Sullivan is likely to be a handful, and this place is as foul a doggery as you're likely to find."

We turned to the left and in the dim light, we could see a dozen customers, including three or four women, drinking at tables. A Black piano player who was as good as any I've heard was thumping out a ragtime tune, drowning out what conversation there was. The four policemen who had been flanking us moved to either side of the bar, and two more policemen who had been keeping an eye on Sullivan from a table in the shadows also moved in. Jem was in the middle of the floor, with three cops on either side. He took two steps and kicked the barstool out from under the massive individual who was seated there. Manx went down heavily, his beer glass crashing along with him, but he jumped to his feet and charged at Jem with a roar. Jem stepped aside and clipped him on the side of the head as he went past, but Manx threw a hard right that caught Jem in the ribs.

I wanted to scream at the other police officers, who were standing with their arms folded, calmly surveying what was turning into a real battle, with Jem facing off against a one-time professional boxer. Watching him work, however, you would have taken Jem for the professional and Manx for the dangerous but raw amateur, perhaps because Jem was more or less sober, while Manx had (as Jem put it later) "caught the Irish flu from a wretched excess of whiskey."

The fight didn't last much longer than a single three-minute round, but it seemed like thirty minutes to me, hearing the crash of those mighty blows finding the target. Even the piano player had stopped and was standing on his chair to get a better view of the action. Jem was perhaps the taller of the two men by an inch or so, but Manx clearly outweighed him by thirty or forty pounds and Manx knew how to set himself in order to get all his weight behind his punches, any one of which might have killed a man like me.

Jem took his share of punches but he was the quicker and smarter fighter, and he hit Manx Sullivan five times for each one that he absorbed. After a series of powerful right hands that were like watching a lumberjack fell a tree, the fight ended with Manx's face a bloody mess, the big hooligan lying face down in a puddle of his own puke. Jem ordered a double whiskey, poured half of it on his skinned knuckles and downed the rest. He was breathing hard, but otherwise you would have thought he had done no more than climb a flight of stairs. He gestured for his men to get handcuffs on Manx.

I was exasperated with him. "Why did you invite all these men along if you were going to fight him by yourself?" I asked.

"In case I lost."

"Then why didn't they help you?"

"Because they know I need a little exercise once in a while."

The semi-conscious Manx was dragged to his feet. He tried to head-butt one of the constables and received a kick in the groin for his troubles. Then they were dragging him down the steps, and not worrying too much about what parts of his anatomy were hitting the stairs. Jem supervised while they stuffed him into a squad car and drove away with Manx in the back, flanked by two big cops. We found our way back to Jem's automobile, which to my surprise had not been stolen while we were otherwise occupied.

CHAPTER 45

The interrogation room at the police station was far worse than the one at Bordeaux Prison. It had yellowish walls that looked as though they hadn't been painted since the turn of the century, and it reeked of sweat, urine, vomit and feces. Above all, it smelled of fear – I knew that scent intimately from the war. There was rust-colored spatter on several spots on the walls that had to be blood – blood spatter looks the same whether it's on the walls of a battlefield surgery or an ugly little room in a police station. Jem, however, looked completely at ease with his surroundings. I knew his thoughts on the subject, and I knew that he didn't believe in beating confessions out of a subject, but he had been a copper for so long that I don't think he even noticed the blood on the walls.

Manx Sullivan had already done his bleeding. By the time he was brought in, you could see that all the fight was out of him. Under the bright bare light bulb of the interrogation room, trying to peer through the battered slits of his eyes, the man was enormous. He had gone to fat, but after what I had seen, I knew that Jem would have beaten him even in his boxing days. Sullivan appeared to think the same, because he sat with his head down, looking every bit the beaten man. He wasn't shaved, he had obviously slept in his clothes for several days, and he stank.

Jem looked him up and down. "You're Irish, aren't ye, Bartley?"

For a moment, the prisoner looked confused. "Aye, Bartley," he said. "That's me given name. Bartley Sullivan.

Them as knows me calls me 'Manx.' Manx Sullivan. Grew up on the Isle of Man, I did, speaking Manx Gaelic. That's why they calls me Manx. Or Sully, from time to time."

Jem said something incomprehensible which I took to be in Gaelic. Manx Sullivan understood and laughed a rueful laugh.

"So, Manx Sullivan," Jem said in English, "ye've got your fat Isle of Man arse in a predicament, haven't ye?"

Manx stared at him, uncomprehending. "I don't get it," he said. "What's it I'm supposed to've done? I got a drunk and disorderly on New Year's Eve, but I've kept me nose clean since."

"Oh, this ain't about drunk and disorderly," Jem said. "Ye wouldn't be in here talkin' to a captain of detectives if it were only drunk and disorderly, now would ye, Manx?"

"I expect not."

"You expect correctly. The problem we have goes back a while, y'see. To Christmas Eve of 1913, and the rather brutal murder of a lady named Ophélie Molyneux."

"Never heard of her," Manx growled.

"Oh, you have, right enough. She was once in your charge, along with another young woman named Hanna Goss. You thought the woman you killed was Hanna, but it was Mlle Molyneux."

Manx furrowed his brow. "Hanna Goss, now that name rings a wee bell," he said. "Songbird, weren't she? She were in the papers? Got herself killed, as I recall. Was a big to-do for a few days, then it all went away, didn't it?"

"Murder never goes away," Jem said. "Murder sticks with you forever. But you killed the wrong girl, Manx. It wasn't Hanna Goss you murdered on Christmas Eve, it was Ophélie Molyneux. It may have been a case of mistaken identity on your part. They both had red hair, and Mlle. Molyneux was wearing a sable coat that had belonged to Hanna Goss. You went after the wrong woman, and you killed her."

Manx managed to look genuinely offended. "I did no

such thing!" he protested. "Never murdered a human being in my life. Knocked a fella or two around, maybe, in the course of the job, but murder? Not Manx Sullivan!"

"Knocked a fella around?" Jem asked. "From what we hear, you're handier at knocking women around at this asylum where you work. We have information that says you beat at least one woman so badly that she never came back."

"I never! Was that damned Labrecque..."

Manx clamped his mouth shut, wishing he could bite off what he had said.

Jem rose up out of his chair and loomed over the prisoner. "Now we're making progress, Mr. Sullivan! That's a good fella! Tell us about your partner. Pepper Labrecque, right? Ex-pugilist known for what they call *peppering* his opponent with blows? The two of you have been working for the asylum for what? Ten years now? That's why I couldn't locate you, y'see. I had feelers out all over town, looking for a couple of thugs. One of 'em short and squat and French, the other big as a redwood and dumb, and either English, Irish or Scottish. I figured it would be easy enough, but I stuck my nose in every dive in town, twisted the arms of every informant I have and came up with nothing. That's because you and Pepper hid behind your respectable employment, isn't that right? You were on the books as orderlies at an asylum, but your real job was to beat the hell out of women, wasn't it?"

"I didn't beat women, I swear," Manx said, staring disconsolately at the floor. "That was Pepper. I held 'em. I'll give you that. But he did the hitting, on account of he liked it. Men or women, didn't matter to Pepper. He'd beat his own grandmother if there was two bits in it."

"So, it was Pepper that beat the Molyneux woman to death, is that it?"

"Nope. I don't know nothing about no Molyneux woman."

Jem rapped his knuckles on the table, then went to pacing back and forth. I could see the prisoner flinching, expecting to be hit, because that must have been his experience of police stations – but Jem had a different way of interrogating a prisoner. He stopped pacing, glared down Manx, then tried a different tack.

"What is it you weigh, Manx?" he asked. "I'm guessing twenty-five stone, is that right? So about three hundred and fifty pounds?"

"That ain't my fighting weight," Sullivan said. "If I was at my fighting weight, you wouldn't have waltzed me around like you done. I would break up a pup like you."

"If it soothes your mind to think it, Manx, I'll not begrudge ye. Dreams are free. But you've gone to fat, like many an old pug. The upshot of it is, you're a sizable man, near three times the weight of my friend Dr. Balsano here. I'm near twenty stone myself, I know what it's like. But here's the rub. The problem for big fellas is, we don't hang easy, if ye get my drift."

Manx stared at him with those beady eyes. "Can't say as I do."

"I'll spell it out for you, Manx. If it helps, I can bring in some pictures. We've lots of photographs that make the result real clear. Big fellas like us, we present a problem to a hangman because of the weight, see. If the hangman gets it just right, your neck snaps and it's over quick. That's what you pray for, that the hangman knows his business. If he gets the drop wrong, if it ain't deep enough, then you're up there on the business end of that rope, strangling real slow. I've seen it take fifteen minutes or more. Terrible sight. Then there's the other extreme, when he gives you too much drop. That's the tendency with a heavy fella such as yourself. A really big drop, and the head is yanked right off the shoulders. The trapdoor falls, see, the body drops, there's this terrible sound of the head being ripped right off the body, and your head rolls way over there, while your body falls straight down in a headless heap. I imagine it takes a while for the brain to die, so you're lying there helpless, eyes still open, contemplating the sorry sight of your headless body until such time as the Lord takes you."

Manx shook his big shaggy head. His pallid face, through the cuts and bruises and the three-day growth of dark beard, had taken on a greenish hue. He stared miserably at the floor, saying nothing.

Jem lowered his voice. "Prison is something we can't avoid in this situation, Manx. Prison is in your future. What you can avoid is a thick hangman's rope yanking your head clean off. We know you were after that poor woman. We have an eyewitness. All we need is to know which of you done it. Was it you holding and Pepper hitting, like you said? Or was it Pepper holding and you hitting? Was that how Ophélie Molyneux died?"

I noticed that Jem did not mention the sharp object that had penetrated Mlle Molyneux's heart, but I refrained from comment. I was feeling a little green myself after that description of a botched hanging.

When Manx looked up, there were tears in his eyes. "What's it you want from me?"

"Only the truth," Jem said.

"Uh-huh."

The prisoner fell silent and for several long minutes, the only sound was his heavy breathing and a clock ticking somewhere. Finally, he cleared his throat.

"We was drunk the night them two women ran off," he said. "Drunk as skunks. Christmas Eve and all. The women was all drunk too, every last one. We knew how this was likely to end – we'd grab a lady for ourselves, or maybe two, and we'd have sport that would last half the night."

Jem said nothing. He was leaving a void the suspect would feel compelled to fill. It's a technique that sometimes works for psychoanalysts as well.

"Them two redheads was the pick of the crop, but we had strict orders: no messing with the songbird. She was special. We was to watch her at all times, which wasn't hard because she was a treat to the eyes – but we wasn't to touch. Orders."

"Whose orders?" Jem asked.

"The Toad, but it was somebody else telling her what was wanted. She took orders from him, or maybe it was a her, and passed 'em on to us. We never dealt with nobody but the Toad. Or your pal Cyril, as the case may be. If there was a job outside, like bringin' the songbird in or getting that queer fella to sign the papers, then we worked for Cyril."

"Fair enough. Go on."

"So, we're drunk, and we're watching all them ladies. One thing and another, Pepper and I are trying to decide which one we'll bed that night, but Pepper wants the two redheads that are dancing with each other. I tell him we ain't allowed to touch the songbird so maybe we'll both have a go with the other one. Then we notices that the two of 'em, the redheads, they're gone. Vanished. Like a magic trick – poof! Pepper and me, we knew it was our jobs if they'd took off and us watching them, so we starts nosing around the place quiet-like, because we don't want to upset the party. We check the lavatory, nobody there. We're about to check their rooms when somebody yells up front of the house. The redheads is on the run, and the Toad has her fat ugly face about three inches from mine, hollering that there's been an escape, and me and Pepper has to get after them. Pepper tries to tell her that there's a blizzard out there, that you can't see your hand in front of your face and the women are likely to freeze to death before they go a hundred yards, and it's not a fit night for man nor beast, but she won't have none of it. She's on the telephone, and I hear her telling somebody that the songbird is on the loose.

"When the Toad hangs up the telephone, she turns to us and says that we're to find them and bring 'em back, but not to come back without the songbird. I asks her what about the other one, and she says if we can only find one, get the songbird first and worry about the other one after. Then I say it's dark out there and it's a blizzard and they look alike, how are we supposed to know which one is which? She calls me a fat Manx fool then and says the one we want is wearin' that damned fancy fur coat, and even a dumb palooka like me ought to know a fur coat when I sees one. The other one, the one who *ain't* in the fur coat, we got permission to shut her up for good, and we know what that means.

"I want to hit the old bitch square between the eyes, but I know which side my bread is buttered on, so me and Pepper, we pull on our galoshes and overcoats and such and then we're out in the blizzard trying to find these two shebas. It ain't hard to follow the tracks, but with heavy snow to plow through and us drunk as skunks and not being able to see twenty feet ahead, we ain't makin' much headway. We're following them west toward McGill, see, but then we comes to a place where the tracks split up in the snow. One of them turns left down toward Sherbrooke Street, and goes the other way, up toward Pine Avenue.

"We're trying to figure out which way to go, but just then there's a break in the snow and Pepper sees the one in the coat about a hundred feet up the hill. She's down and it looks like maybe she's hurt some way, because she can't get up. It's hard going uphill, and I'm way behind when Pepper gets to her, and I see him pull the coat off her and then he goes to work, slamming her with both fists. He's got rings on every finger, does Pepper, and by the time I catches up her own mother wouldn't know that more woman, he's beat her so bad. She ain't fightin' back at all, and I drag Pepper off her and feel her throat and there ain't no pulse. 'She's dead!' I tells Pepper. 'You killed her, you damned fool.'

"Pepper, he says he ain't killed nobody. She was dead when he got to her. So I asks him why he had to beat on a dead woman, and he says it's on account of she drug us out on a night that ain't fit for man nor beast. I looks around and there ain't nobody else on the street, not in that storm. I can see a set of tricks that came down the hill to where the dame was, then went back up again, but the way it's snowing they'll be gone in five minutes. I says to Pepper that we got to leave this one where she is and find the other redhead and shut her up good. He wants to take the coat but I tell him not to be stupid. That is gonna be the hottest coat in town and we don't need to be packing that around in a blizzard."

Manx had run down. Jem looked at me and I nodded wearily. The story he was spinning was just strange enough to be true.

"So if somebody else killed her, you didn't get a look at him?" Jem asked.

"Not at all," Manx said. "Whoever done it was gone in the storm. He might have been a hundred feet away but we couldn't see him."

"And she wasn't on Prince Arthur when you left her?"

"No. She was on up. About halfway to Pine, I'd say."

"But that wasn't where the body was found."

Manx shrugged. "Maybe somebody moved her," he said, "or maybe Mr. Cyril Leblanc wasn't strictly telling the truth about where he found her."

Jem carefully noted everything Manx had said, and for a while the only sound was the scratching of pencil on paper. Whether it was fatigue or the nightmarish quality of all that happened from the time Jem roused me out of a warm bed, I shivered rather violently. Jem had to prod Manx to go on with the story and explain what happened next. Abruptly, Manx switched his attention to me. His black eyebrows met in the middle of his forehead. He stared at me the way a wolf looks at a lamb. I could see him trying to make out where he had seen me before, squinting at my face intently until he had it.

"You're the runt what had the typhoid! When we was after the other bitch! We followed her right to your door. You puked on my boots."

"Yes, I did," I said. "But I had the flu. It wasn't typhus."

Manx glared at me. "She was there, weren't she? At your digs? The other dame. You was probably having it off with her, and us stomping through the snow, hither and yon, near frozen to death trying to find her, when the tracks led right to your door. I ought to claw your liver right out from your gut and eat it right here."

"That's enough, Manx," Jem said. "You're in enough trouble as it is without issuing death threats in the presence of an officer of the law. I take it you gave up trying to find the second woman after your encounter with Dr. Balsano here?"

"For that night, we did. We went back to the asylum, found everything all stirred up. But there was fresh instructions. The one that mattered, that is the songbird, she was dead. How she died was none of our affair. We was to head back out the next day to look for the other one, because she might be a nasty witness if you coppers got to her first – but quiet-like, not making any waves. Only we never found her, because this little bastard had her hid away."

Jem asked a dozen more questions, mostly about the whereabouts of Pepper Labrecque. Manx insisted he had no idea where his erstwhile partner had gone, only that Pepper had many friends in the underworld and he was good at hiding. When Jem was through, he nodded to the two burly officers in attendance and they each took an elbow to escort the miscreant back to his cell. He shuffled off in his handcuffs and leg-irons, looking as woebegone as any man I have seen.

CHAPTER 46

The next evening, Jem was downing a Guinness as I sipped a palinka in the café and Sophie made herself pretty upstairs. We were all to go out to dinner at a fine French restaurant that evening as guests of Elise Duvernay, who wished to repay Sophie and Jem for all they had done. Jem was grousing a little, saying he didn't feel comfortable in a joint that didn't have pig's knuckle and steak-and-kidney pie on the menu, but I knew that he secretly fancied the idea of eating with the swells.

As we waited for Sophie, Jem said that he had an assignment for me. He wanted me to go by the Hyde House and pay a social call on Eleanor Hyde.

I was stunned. "Whatever for?"

"Well, she was recently a guest of the Bethlehem Sanatorium, was she not?"

"She was. I hardly think she's going to discuss it."

"Perhaps. Perhaps not. When you talked with her at that dinner party before the war, did it seem that she was trying to tell you something? All that talk of terrible things going on?"

"Yes, it did, but that was six years ago..."

"And we never learned what terrible things she was referring to, did we?"

"No, we didn't, but..."

"It would just be a social call."

"If that's all it is, why don't you go?"

"Because I'm a great oaf of a clumsy Irish cop, that's why. You have the manners. You say please and thank you. You won't crush a teacup in your fist or use a priceless vase as a spittoon. And you've been a guest in the house before. She can hardly turn you away."

"What reason will I give for the call?"

"You haven't caught up with Dr. Hyde since you came back to town, have ye?"

"No, but…"

"So you came round hoping to find him in. Upon encountering the lady of the house, you get her to invite you in for tea. Surely they have tea."

"I believe they do, yes… But what am I trying to learn?"

"What goes on at Bethlehem Sanatorium, since she was recently a guest. And what she was trying to tell you six years ago. I would also like to get some notion as to her mental state – and you happen to be the only psychiatrist I know personally. Perhaps you'll learn nothing at all, but I think there's good reason to make the visit. If I was to go blundering in there, the big, scary Irish copper with the black mustache, I would be delayed just long enough for them to form an entire phalanx of lawyers from the Hyde Shipping Company. I'd be asked my motives for harassing Lady Hyde, told to put my questions in writing, and thrown out on my Black Irish arse."

After a wonderful dinner in the company of four of my favorite people, I spent a nervous night thinking about it, tossing and turning, trying to imagine what I would ask Eleanor Hyde.

The next day, I approached the gates on foot at fifteen minutes before three o'clock in the afternoon, presented my card, and asked to see Lady Hyde.

The footman at the gate squinted at me suspiciously. "Is she expecting you?"

"No, she isn't," I said. "We've known each other since before the war. I've just arrived from Austria and I'm paying calls on some of my former acquaintances, including Lady Hyde."

As I had anticipated, he looked undecided. "You may

have seen me here – it was February of 1914, I think."

The footman obviously didn't remember me, but he couldn't possibly turn away someone who had previously been a guest. He led me to the front door, where a completely bald butler named Stephens appeared. I was sure I had not seen him before. He took my card and vanished into the house. I stood waiting politely, trying not to fidget, still watched by the footman.

Stephens was gone a good ten minutes. When he returned, he bowed politely. "My lady recalls your previous visit," he said. "Lord Hyde is away, but Lady Hyde will receive you in the drawing room."

The house was very dim inside, and strangely cold for the month of June. I wondered how they kept it so cool. He led me through the maze of the great house to the drawing room, where a fistful of daffodils in an overly large vase had been left to die under an Old Masters portrait so dark I couldn't tell whether the subject was a man or a woman. Stephens bowed his way out and left me there to peruse the portrait, along with an antique harpsichord, a vast armoire and some very uncomfortable looking straight-backed chairs. The curtains were drawn, and the room was more like a mausoleum than part of a living household. I had envisioned us having tea in a gazebo on that expanse of lawn overlooking the city where Hanna and I had first walked together, but it was not to be.

At last, Eleanor Hyde was led in by the butler. It was hard to tell in that dim light, but it appeared that she was wearing a violet dress. Her hair was beautifully coiffed and although I could not see her shoes, I guessed that the heels must have been high, because she was half a foot taller than me. As she stepped forward to greet me, I noticed that her appearance was essentially unchanged, except that she was not visibly inebriated. She was six years older than the first time I had seen her, but she had the same erect carriage, the same raven hair and blue eyes, no doubt the same appealing sprinkle of freckles across her pretty nose, although they were invisible in the drawing room. She was still the same elegant, ravishing beauty who could reduce a man to jelly with a glance, and the effect was enhanced by the fact that she was sober. Either she had given up the drink, or she was no longer drinking before three o'clock in the afternoon. There was more than sobriety about her, however – something watchful and suspicious. When I bowed and brushed my lips over the back of her hand, it was cold as marble. It was not surprising that her hand would be rather chilly because it was frigid in the house, but there was a coldness about her that made it seem as though she was not quite human, as though she had been taken apart and put back together in some subterranean laboratory.

"Dr. Balsano," she said, "I remember you quite clearly from our last encounter. I must apologize. I was nervous about the dinner and I'm afraid I had a bit too much to drink on an empty stomach that day."

I had not anticipated that she would make any reference to our previous meeting. I simply bowed my head by way of a response, unable to think of anything to say. If Jem had hoped that my surprise visit would discomfit her and throw her off in any way, he was wrong. She was in control of the situation.

"Stephens is having tea sent in," she said. "I usually take tea in my chambers or skip it all together, but then I don't usually have company in the afternoon. I am so very sorry Percy is not here."

"Yes," I said. "I had hoped to come earlier. Unfortunately, things in Europe were rather confusing. It's quite hard to get out of Austria these days. The trains simply aren't running."

"So I've heard," she said. "I haven't visited, but I have acquaintances who have been to Germany and they tell me life there is quite brutish. But then you did start the war and you did lose it, didn't you?"

"It's unfair to say that we started it," I protested. "It began when the Serbs assassinated our Archduke Ferdinand.

On the front where I worked as a surgeon, it was the Italians who attacked us, not the other way around. In any case, you are correct: we did lose it."

"Is that true?" she seemed genuinely interested. "I had not realized Italy was in the war – or perhaps I thought they were on the other side. Your side."

I was about to reply when a maid came in with tea and a type of pastries I had never tasted before. I asked what they were, and Lady Hyde replied that they were something called "scones," served with clotted cream and strawberries, a delicious confection. I had skipped lunch because I had been going over the anticipated conversation in my mind, and I was famished. I'm afraid I rather dove into the scones and strawberries, but Eleanor did not seem to mind. After I had polished off considerably more than my share, we resumed our conversation.

"So, I assume that your presence here would indicate that you are about to take the position working with Percy?"

"I'm not certain," I said. "I would of course have to discuss it with Dr. Hyde. My visit has another purpose."

"And what might that be?"

"I am trying to solve a murder."

I watched her reaction carefully, but she betrayed not the slightest sign of surprise or discomfort. "Oh, really?" she said. "I don't recall any murder case in the papers that might prompt a young man to come all the way from Austria to help us solve it."

"Oh, this case goes back some time. Christmas Eve, 1913, to be exact."

"Oh, was that your friend the singer – what was her name? She performed here once. Anna something…"

"Hanna Goss."

"That's it. What a pity. She had a superb voice, although to be truthful, I dislike opera. I was very sad when I heard that she had been murdered, however. A robbery, they said."

I was watching her carefully, trying to discern whether she was sincere. There was something so mechanical about her conversation that it was hard to tell.

"Yes, well it's not as simple as all that. Actually, she wasn't murdered. A friend of hers was the victim, a young woman named Ophélie Molyneux."

Eleanor Hyde appeared genuinely surprised. "Is that true? How could the police have gotten it wrong? You must be mistaken. I'm sure I read in the papers that it was the opera singer who was killed."

"That's what they believed at the time. We have since learned that Hanna Goss survived, but the other young woman sadly did not."

"We...?"

"My friend Jem Doyle and I. He's a detective."

"But you're not a policeman? Why would you be interested, Dr. Balsano?"

"Because Hanna and I are both Austrian. Because we have a friendship and her friend was murdered, after they had both been committed to the Bethlehem Sanatorium."

"Oh, the sanatorium! I've been there. It's very nice. It belongs to my husband, you know."

Now it was my turn to be surprised, although I attempted to hide it. "Does it? Dr. Hyde is the owner of a private asylum? I did not know that. Was that always the case?"

"Oh, yes. He founded the asylum after he returned to Canada. He found there was a lack of private institutions to give real care to women dealing with nervous conditions. You know Percy, he's always looking to do good in some way. He and Count Respighi started the sanatorium together."

"I don't think that's generally known," I said.

"It isn't. It's a very private place. Some of the guests there are extremely wealthy, so everything about the asylum must be completely discreet. But I still don't understand what this has to do with your friend and the other woman, Ophelia..."

"Ophélie Molyneux,"I said. "The two of them escaped together, but Ophélie was wearing Hanna's sable coat and they were both redheads. After they split up, someone must have mistaken her for Hanna. She was killed just around the corner from here."

Eleanor Hyde looked at me coolly. "Are you insinuating something, Dr. Balsano? That the murder of this obscure woman had anything to do with this household? Because if you are, I must ask you to leave."

"I'm sure Dr. Balsano wasn't insinuating anything at all, Eleanor."

The voice came from directly behind my chair. I whirled around. I hadn't heard a sound, but Count Ottavio Respighi was standing there, so close he could have strangled me. He was wearing a cream-colored suit and vest with a purple cravat, and he held in the crook of his arm a grey kitten who looked exactly like the grey kitten he had been holding the last time I saw him. I wondered if he had an inexhaustible supply of grey kittens, and what happened to all the kittens that had grown too large to carry about in that fashion?

Count Respighi came around from behind my chair and bowed. I rose and bowed stiffly in return. I have encountered very few people in my lifetime whom I despise on sight, but the count was one of them. As I faced him, I noted that he was wearing his usual cape – this one cream-colored like his suit, with a purple lining to match his cravat. As usual his black hair was pomaded, and his pointed black beard neatly trimmed, and he smelled very strongly of some kind of gentleman's cologne.

I said nothing, but I was furious. How long had Count Respighi been standing there, listening? How could a man who must weigh three hundred pounds creep about without making a noise? I had let slip a couple of facts I would not have chosen to share with him had I known he was there, like the fact that Hanna was still alive and that the real victim of the murder was Mlle Molyneux.

Still, one had to keep up appearances. As soon as Count Respighi appeared, I knew that my interview with Eleanor Hyde was over. Just as he had once crept up to put an end to the encounter between Eleanor and myself outside the lavatory, now he was cutting off our conversation for a second time.

"Dr. Balsano," he said, taking my elbow, "I must take you on a tour of the grounds. We have done a great deal of work since the war, especially on my pet project, the conservatory. You will find it very different than it was before. Come with me, please."

I took my leave of Eleanor Hyde, who had little more to offer than a wan smile. Reluctantly, I allowed myself to be shown to the huge conservatory where, in another time, I had admired the lemon trees and the airy beauty of flowering plants reaching toward the glass ceiling of the brilliantly lit greenhouse. Now, it was oppressive, dark, humid, and so hot that I had to remove my jacket immediately. A tangle of plants covered the floor so that it was difficult to find a path, and vines above all but blotted about the light from the panes of glass overhead.

"We have created our own private jungle here," the count said, "or rather I have. Percy doesn't have the time or interest for such things. I have been quite meticulous about assembling the same sort of plants and ferns you would find in the jungle. And like the jungle, it's actually quite dark in here."

In another mood, I might have been content to explore the conservatory for hours. But all I wanted to do now was to escape from Count Respighi's clutches. The greenhouse as it was now I found dark, oppressive, and almost unbearably hot, and when at last we burst through into the open, I was gasping for air. The count dabbed at his face with a handkerchief.

"Not a place where one would want to spend a night, is it?" the count asked. "I've even equipped it with several specimens of an especially deadly species of spider."

It crossed my mind that the most dangerous spider in the conservatory was the one I was looking at, but I kept it to myself. All I wanted was to escape, and I did, after the count issued a veiled warning.

"I shouldn't disturb Lady Hyde again if I were you," he said. "She has been through some difficult times, and Lord Hyde prefers that she be allowed to rest and recover."

I simply nodded. I had no intention of allowing Count Respighi to tell me what to do, but there was no point in forcing a confrontation now. I bade him farewell and he saw me to the front gate and closed it rather more firmly than necessary after I had stepped through.

CHAPTER 47

T hat evening, Jem did his best to convince me that my interview with Eleanor Hyde was not the utter failure I had taken it to be. I had, after all, discovered that the Bethlehem Sanatorium was run by Percival Hyde and Count Respighi in some form of partnership, so Dr. Hyde himself had been in charge of the institution where Hanna had been committed. I had learned that Eleanor Hyde was more in possession of her faculties than she had been the first time we met (or at least that she was more under control) and that Count Respighi was sufficiently concerned about our conversation to eavesdrop, and then to warn me off with his not-so-subtle hint about poisonous spiders in the conservatory.

"If nothing else, we've reason enough to concentrate on them," Jem said. "That's Lord Hyde and Count Respighi. I'll wager someone at Hyde House knows what really happened to Mlle. Molyneux and why Hanna was committed to the sanatorium in the first place. It could well be that Percival Hyde simply wanted her out of the way."

I nodded sadly. It seemed that might be the case, but why commit murder? The wrong person had been killed, but we knew that she had been killed because she had been mistaken for Hanna Goss. The connections were still a mystery to me. Somehow, Lord Hyde and Count Respighi were involved – but how? Surely men of such wealth and power had no reason to attack a young singer who could not possibly pose a threat to them?

Hanna and Elise arrived for dinner at seven o'clock, and Jem and I steered the conversation away from the murder

investigation. Sophie joined us for a delicious meal of pep-
pery goulash and home-made dumplings washed down with
Irish beer, and we talked, laughed and sang snatches of various
songs until nearly midnight. One of us would launch into an
off-key tune and sing a few bars, and then Hanna would catch
on and take the melody for us, and with her leading the way
we sounded like a well-drilled choir.

When it came time for the women to leave, Jem
offered to drive them back to their hotel. Elise insisted that
they would be fine on their own. It was a beautiful June evening, they had only to walk a few blocks along Sherbrooke
Street, and Jem faced an early morning. He agreed somewhat
reluctantly, and we all went off to bed. I tried to go over the
events of that afternoon in my mind, the conversation with
Eleanor Hyde and its aftermath, but I could not focus, and in
less than a minute I was fast asleep.

Somehow, through my sleep, I heard the telephone
ring and Sophie answer it, then her voice calling to Jem. I
pulled the curtain back slightly and peered outside; it was just
beginning to get light outdoors, so it was past four o'clock in
the morning. I heard Jem on the telephone for a few moments,
and then his heavy stride coming my way. He opened my door,
and the light from the hallway hurt my eyes.

"Are ye awake, Maxim?" he asked.

"I am now."

"Well, get your pants on and your boots on. I've bad
news: Mlle Duvernay is in the hospital after a terrible beating,
and Hanna is missing."

Never have I gone from sound asleep to fully awake so
quickly. I dressed with my heart pounding and my hands shaking so badly that I had to make four attempts to buckle my
belt. In the kitchen, Sophie already had coffee percolating and
bread in the oven. I splashed cold water from the sink over
my face and choked down a cup of coffee so hot that it burned
my tongue. I had to apologize to Sophie, though, because I
couldn't face the toast she buttered so carefully.

In the automobile, Jem's jaw was set, and he drove much too fast. We jolted over potholes and cobblestones as we raced to the Royal Victoria Hospital. "I should have driven them home," he said over and over. "This was no time to get careless."

"How much do you know?"

"Only that Elise was found unconscious a few yards from the entrance to her hotel," he said. "It seems that she revived in the hospital, and she was able to talk enough to tell them to contact me. She had heard Hanna screaming, but she has no idea what happened to her."

We parked at the entrance to the hospital, leapt out of the car and raced inside. We found Elise Duvernay on the second floor, in a private room guarded by a uniformed police officer. As soon as I got a look at her, I knew what had happened to her. She had cuts on her face similar to those I had suffered when I was beaten, similar to the cuts on the face of Ophélie Molyneux. It was the work of Pepper Labreque, with those vicious rings on his fingers.

Elise wept when she saw us. "I'm so sorry," she said through swollen lips and teeth that had been knocked loose. "I should have known better. It's my fault, and now Hanna is gone."

Elise told us what she knew, which was very little. They were strolling along, talking happily, when they passed by the entrance to a dark lane near the hotel. The attackers came from the side and from behind; one of them struck her in the face and she went down.

"I shouted to Hanna to run, but I don't think she had time," Elise said. "I heard her scream, and I saw that it looked as though she was trying to fight off two men. Then she was gone. The third man kept hitting me in the face. He had rings on his fingers."

I took Elise's hand. "It's not your fault," I said. "If anything, I dragged the two of you into this. Now we have to find Hanna."

"Did you by chance hear an automobile?" Jem asked.

"I can't say for sure," Elise said. "It seems that I heard something, maybe a car door opening and closing, but I don't know for certain. Then everything went black and when I woke up, I was in this hospital bed and Hanna was gone."

I was frantic. I wanted to run around the city searching for Hanna, but Jem convinced me that there was no point going on a wild goose chase. The police had their sources and their methods, and he would see to it that the entire force was engaged in the search for Hanna Goss.

"I think it's best if you stay here with Mlle. Duvernay," he said. "I've got a search to run."

Jem rushed out and I sat down next to Elise's bed, suddenly exhausted. Elise had been given morphine, and for the next twelve hours, she slept on and off, and I slept on the chair beside her. When she was awake, I tried to reassure her that Hanna would be found, but I spoke with a confidence I did not feel. I made it quite clear that what had happened was my fault, not hers. My visit to Eleanor Hyde was behind this attack. In the process of trying to get information from her, I had revealed too much. Eleanor might not have understood the significance of my words, but it was all but certain that Count Respighi had been eavesdropping. It was then that he learned that Hanna was still alive, and that she was in town. It was even possible that the count had me followed to Sophie's Café.

In the afternoon, Sophie came to visit. She brought a message from Jem: the entire police force had been mobilized and they were systematically searching the city. The press had gotten hold of the story, including the fact that the missing woman was the soprano Hanna Goss, once thought murdered. It was a frenzy, and Jem was at the hub of it, although that didn't prevent him from stationing officers outside the hospital room to make sure Elise was not disturbed. It was not a good day to be a young woman with red hair; several were stopped by the police on the street and asked if they might be Hanna Goss. Warehouses were searched, blind pigs were raided, every informant the police had was rounded up and questioned about Hanna's whereabouts, without success.

Jem also had police searching for Pepper Labrecque, because the beating Elise had received had to have come at his hands. His reasoning was that if the police located Pepper, they could surely find Hanna. When Jem came to visit that evening, I asked if it might be worthwhile to visit the Hyde mansion. Jem had already thought of it and had made the visit himself. He had spoken with Lord Hyde, who professed that he had no knowledge whatsoever of Hanna Goss or her whereabouts. Jem had asked to speak with Count Respighi, but he was told that the count was not at home. Lord Hyde had insisted that he did not know the whereabouts of his friend and partner, but he promised to have the count get in touch when he returned.

"If that lot is somehow behind this," Jem said with barely suppressed fury, "they're not going to let on. I tried to get the chief to authorize a search of the premises, but he just laughed. I can't blame him. With no more than we have to go on, one call from Percival Hyde and the chief would be out of a job – and so would I."

I had to agree. With great wealth came enormous political power. Even Jem Doyle had to be careful in his approach to people as powerful as Lord and Lady Hyde and Count Respighi.

The search for Hanna went on for three days without success. Through most of those three days, I remained at the hospital with Elise. She had multiple injuries, including broken ribs and bruised kidneys. She was in a great deal of pain and although she feared addiction to morphine, there were times when she couldn't bear it any longer and begged for an injection. When she was reasonably alert, she tried to think of something that might help the search for Hanna, but like me, she was drawing a blank.

Twice I returned to Sophie's for a few hours' sleep

and a change of clothes, but I could never really sleep. I was haunted by Hanna's face, by my fears as to what men like Pepper Labrecque might be doing to her, by horrid images of Hanna's body dumped down an elevator shaft or buried in a shallow grave. I was furious with myself for bringing her back to Canada, furious that I had failed to protect her once she was in Montreal, furious that I hadn't at least walked the women home the night they were attacked, furious that I had let slip the fact that she was still alive while conversing with Lady Hyde.

On the afternoon of the third day, I must have nodded off in the chair, listening to the sound of Elise Duvernay's ragged breathing, worn out from the tension, bitterly discouraged by the unsuccessful results of the search. When I woke, I had been dreaming about a scene aboard the ship on the way from France. It was the night Hanna had repeated the entire narrative of her experience with Dr. Percival Hyde, the manner in which she ended up in the asylum, her escape and the murder of Ophélie Molyneux. While Hanna was speaking, my mind had drifted for a moment into selfish concerns of my own, and I missed something Hanna had said to Elise.

Or rather, I should say that my *conscious* mind had missed it: Somehow it imprinted itself on my subconscious, and it surfaced in the dream I had while seated in the chair in Elise's hospital room. I could hear Hanna saying it, almost word for word. She was talking about a photograph she had found at Dr. Hyde's apartment one afternoon when she was dusting – a picture that was tucked into the back of the frame of a larger photo that was on display. She had been talking about how he was a naturally untidy man, but he did not like any of his things to be disturbed by herself or the maid, and the fact that she had stumbled on the photograph on the back of the frame marked the first occasion when Dr. Hyde became very angry with her. The second time was when he was speaking with Count Respighi and the count said something that made Percy very angry. He had berated the count in rapid Italian that Hanna was unable to grasp, and yet when she asked about it he became angry again, and this time things between them seemed to change in a fundamental way. Twice Dr. Hyde had lost his temper, but how were the two events linked? I sat watching Elise breathe in her hospital bed, thinking it over.

Abruptly, it all fell into place. The last bit of the puzzle – a name. A name Hanna had heard, although she wasn't aware of it. That's what had caused Dr. Hyde to address the count in furious Italian. The name he had spoken was the clue and somehow it had surfaced in my dream. Elise was still asleep. I rose, grabbed my hat and hurried out the door, so quickly that I almost bumped into Sophie, who was coming to visit Elise.

"Sophie," I said, "can you reach Jem?"

"He's working, but I can call him on the telelphone."

"Here's what I want you to tell him," I said. I told her where I was going, and then I was off. I ran down the stairs and out, dodged the traffic to cross Pine Avenue from the Royal Victoria Hospital, and sprinted west.

CHAPTER 48

I ran every step of the way to Hyde House. There was no guard at the gate, and the gate was open. I ran right on through and up to the front door. It was unlocked, so I didn't bother to knock. I burst into the house, shouting at the top of my lungs: "Hanna! Where are you, Hanna? Tell me! Has anyone seen Hanna?"

I almost fell over a housekeeper who was down on her knees dusting a small collection of ceramics, skirted a maid who tried half-heartedly to block my way – and ran almost headlong into Stephens, the butler.

"I beg your pardon, young man," he said. "Why are you charging around the house like an angry buffalo?"

"I am looking for Hanna," I said. "Hanna Goss. Where are you keeping her?"

"I'm sorry, I know of no such person."

"She's here. I know she is. Don't lie to me. Where is Dr. Hyde? Lady Hyde? Where are they? I must talk with them now."

"They are attending a function. They left thirty minutes ago. Now I must ask you to leave..."

"Count Respighi? Where is Count Respighi?"

"I'm sorry, he is not here either. Now I must..."

I darted around Stephens and sprinted up the steps, shouting for Hanna. I ran from room to room, throwing doors open and shouting. "Hanna! Hanna, where are you?" On every floor, members of the household staff stopped to stare at this strange, wild-haired man bursting into one room after another and screaming like a maniac.

I descended a staircase at the back of the house and had reached the last flight of stairs when I saw Stephens again, now with two husky young footmen waiting to bar the way at the bottom of the steps. On the landing there were crossed swords in a glass case over a coat of arms. Never in my life have I been a man of action, but desperation gave me strength. I shattered the glass with my elbow, tore one of the swords out of the case and waved it around wildly as I hurried down the last flight of steps. "Don't try to stop me," I warned the footmen. "I'm not leaving here without Hanna."

They stepped back cautiously, as did Stephens. They might be loyal employees of Dr. Hyde, but they were not going to risk their lives in a confrontation with a sword-wielding madman. I had reached the long corridor that ran through the center of the main floor when it hit me – I knew exactly where they were holding Hanna. I ran out the door onto the back terrace, leapt a low marble wall, sprinted across the expanse of lawn and opened the door to the conservatory.

Once inside, I was immersed in the dark, steamy world of Count Respighi's *ersatz* jungle. If anything, the conservatory seemed more densely overgrown than it had on my previous visit – and hotter. No sooner had I slipped through the door than I was drenched with sweat. I wanted to tear through the place at top speed, but it was impossible. The plants had grown into such a dense tangle that it almost required a machete to hack your way through. I still had the sword, and I tried to use it like a machete, cutting down anything that got in my way – but I found that the blade was very dull and the sword very heavy, especially in that heat. I tossed it aside and pawed at the plants with my bare hands until my palms were slashed with tiny cuts.

All around me, plants fought for light in the struggle that has been going on for millions of years. The only sound was that of dripping water. The heavy, cloying odor of earth and greenery was unleavened by the lighter notes of floral growth one normally encounters in a conservatory. Here it was all leaf and tendril, root and vine and mold, the suppressed fury of imprisoned plants seeking to impose their will on their rivals.

I kept calling Hanna's name, but there was no response. I was breathing heavily, bathed in sweat, barely aware of what an odd spectacle I must make. By now, the household staff would have alerted Lord Hyde and Count Respighi to the presence of a madman on the grounds. I prayed that Sophie had been able to contact Jem. If she had reached him, he would soon be on his way.

After searching for twenty minutes in that enervating heat, I had almost given up when I caught the scent through all that tangled greenery. Light, feathery, caressing, very different from the jungle heaviness of the conservatory. Almost undetectable, yet as distinct as a rose is distinct from a lily. It was l'Heure Bleu, Hanna's perfume. I sniffed again, and the odor vanished. I took a step forward and sniffed again, once more caught the merest hint. I was now like a bloodhound on the trail, inching forward, sniffing to the right and left, trying to pick up the scent again, calling out to her. "Hanna? Hanna?" She did not answer, but the scent of her perfume grew steadily more distinct.

I came around a curve in the narrow, winding path. There was an opening a few feet wide, with the narrow stone bench I had seen when Count Respighi took me through the conservatory. There Hanna sat. My Hanna. Lovely in a pale green dress I had never seen before, a filmy dress that clung to her body in the heat. Tears streamed down her cheeks and she was shivering despite the heat, but she was otherwise immobile, staring at me as though she couldn't see me.

"Hanna!" I said. "Thank God I've found you! Are you alright?" I started to move toward her, but she shook her head violently and held up a hand as though to warn me away. "No, Maximilian. Please! You must go."

"Come with me. We've got to get you out of here."

Hanna remained immobile. Her lower lip was trembling, but her eyes were unfocused. I couldn't understand what was wrong with her. She wasn't bound or restrained, so why wasn't she responding to me?

Suddenly, I knew that we were not alone. I hadn't heard a sound, but I sniffed the mingled odor of sweat, cigars, overpowering cologne and hair pomade. I was about to whirl around when I felt something cold and metallic pressed against the back of my neck – a pistol, surely.

"Dr. Balsano," said Count Respighi. "How thoughtful of you to come join us."

"Let her go," I said. "You have me, let Hanna go."

"But we have plans for her. So lovely she is. So pliable, given the right suggestions. Naturally rebellious, I would say, but also very susceptible to hypnosis. In the right hands, she is very willing, it turns out."

"Let her go!"

"Don't you see?" the count said. "She is not restrained. She isn't bound. She isn't gagged or blindfolded. Why does she not run? Why did she not call out to you? Look at her. What do you see in her face? Terror, that is what you see. The poor creature is so frightened that she has wet herself several times during our training sessions, I'm afraid. Mercifully, Eleanor has taken her own lessons very well, so she was able to assist in changing Hanna's clothing when things became unpleasant. It's a pity, but Hanna had forgotten most of the schooling we gave her before the war. She was inclined to resist, but she understands now to whom she belongs, don't you, Hanna?"

It's a pity you didn't choose to work with us, Dr. Balsano. Percy assures me of your brilliance, and we could have used a young man like you. It's a terrible waste, because now I shall have to shoot you, and you could have assisted us in our experiments. Dr. Hyde assures me that we have only scratched the surface, using a combination of hypnosis, sensory withdrawal, isolation, sleep deprivation and drugs. In Hanna's case, we were supplied with an unexpectedly effective method. Hanna is pathologically afraid of spiders – did you know that,

Dr. Balsano? And I mentioned, did I not, that there are poisonous spiders loose in our jungle, for the sake of authenticity?
You can't see them, but there are some very near poor Hanna
at the moment – and she has been warned that if she moves
abruptly, she may provoke an attack that could prove fatal.

"In the course of our experiments, we have discovered
that it is the *anticipation* of pain rather than the actual pain
that reduces a subject to the state in which your Hanna now
exists – isn't that so, my dear? Like your fear of spiders, which
is certain to be worse than their actual bite. Once a subject has
experienced the *actual* pain, the mind begins to adjust, to fight
back. Shall we give Dr. Balsano a little demonstration, Hanna?
Has he ever had the pleasure of hearing you scream? Extraordinary voice, truly extraordinary. I believe we shall allow him
to hear it – there is a particularly fat spider about to descend
on your neck at this moment, Hanna."

Count Respighi was wrong. I had heard that scream before, when she found a common and very harmless spider in
the lavatory in our apartment in Vienna. Everyone is afraid of
something – it was only that Hanna gave voice to hear fear in
spectacular fashion.

"You are a scoundrel and a fraud," I said.

"In the eyes of small-minded *bourgeoisie* such as yourself, perhaps. That's because you lack the vision to imagine
the things Dr. Hyde and I can imagine. You have the intelligence to do great things, but you are restrained by an exagger-
ated sense of propriety, decorum, ethics, morality, whatever
you choose to call it. All that *bourgeois* claptrap with which
you have been indoctrinated. If you could free yourself, you
would see that we are making great discoveries. You have already seen the result of our most successful experiment."

"What would that be?"

"Why, Eleanor Hyde, of course. She was young and im-
pressionable and weak when Percival was foolish enough to
marry her (the poor man is susceptible to this romantic weakness for the opposite sex, I'm afraid) and Eleanor went through

a phase during which she fought us to an unreasonable degree. We had to confine her to the asylum on three separate occasions, and I'm afraid I had to draw out my little tool bag of devilish instruments in order to bend her unfailingly to our will.

"Didn't you find Eleanor a shining example of the perfectly trained wife? My wife late Celeste, may she rest in peace, was another. I perfected the techniques I used on Eleanor and Hanna by training Celeste for years. Now you see Eleanor as the mistress of the mansion, performing her duties without a hint of the drunken young woman who so embarrassed herself in your presence before the war. Hanna will be much like her when we are through – completely obedient, the ideal, submissive mistress, bent only on fulfilling our instructions to the letter. Since poor Celeste regrettably departed this life during a little reminder session with my implements, I require a new wife, but she must be flawlessly trained first. I shan't permit Hanna the honour of marrying me until she is docile as a lamb."

At that instant, I almost did a very foolish thing and attacked a man holding a pistol to my head. "How can you possibly think you can get away with this?" I asked. "Too many people know. Captain Jem Doyle is on his way. It's only a matter of time."

"Your police captain is a threat, but we'll dispose of him as well. That is Pepper Labrecque's task. Pepper is a limited and violent little man, but he is a born killer. He'll get to Jem. I know you found his partner Manx Sullivan, because Sullivan is a fool and a drunkard, but you'll not find Pepper so easily taken. As for you, my friend Dr. Balsano, you will be buried here, in the conservatory, so that when we visit our plants, we can think of you rotting beneath our little make-believe jungle. Hanna and I will sit on this bench after our nuptials, within sight of your grave."

It was now nearing dusk. There was still some light at this time of year, but it was *l'heure bleu,* the same enchanted time of the evening when Hanna and I had first walked on the lawn outside the conservatory. It was time to face the truth. It was growing dark, and I was about to die. I looked at Hanna, my lovely Hanna. Great tears streamed down her cheeks, but she remained immobile, paralyzed with fear, unable to move. I had wanted so much to help her, first to find the men I thought had murdered her, and then to help bring her back from what she had endured, and all I had accomplished was to lead these vicious men back to her. I wanted to beg her forgiveness, but all that came to mind was a meaningless jumble of English and German and I could not sort out the words.

I was still facing Hanna but turned slightly so that I could also keep an eye on the count. I thought for a moment that I saw a looming shadow behind him, but in the fading light it was impossible to tell. The grey kitten, as always, was clawing at his arm, trying to escape, and it seemed that the animal's claws must have gone through Count Respighi's white silk shirt and into his forearm because he cursed in Italian and rapped the animal sharply on the head with the barrel of the pistol. In doing so he lost his grip. The kitten sprang free and scurried into the darkness under the plants. The count fired a single shot at the kitten, and the noise of the revolver going off in that enclosed glass room was like the explosion of a mine on the battlefield.

A pane of glass shattered and fell. Hanna screamed. I shouted. The combined noise provided all the cover that was needed. The shadow I had seen in the background now closed the distance to Count Respighi, two powerful hands grasped the arm holding the pistol and wrenched it backwards and upwards so that the arm broke with a distinct snap and the revolver clattered to the floor. The count uttered a gurgling scream as Jem Doyle kicked him violently in the back of the knee, wrapped a powerful left arm around his throat and took him down hard, fact-first. I darted over to retrieve the pistol where it fell and pointed it at the two enormous shadows struggling on the floor, but I couldn't risk a shot. They rolled this way and that, cursing and grunting. Somehow, the count got his left hand into a pocket of his waistcoat, and I saw a flash of something metallic.

I tried to warn Jem. "He's got a knife!"

The warning came too late. The big Irishman roared in pain. He had been stabbed in the thigh. Jem clubbed Count Respighi in the back of the ear with a mighty fist. On blow and the count collapsed face down in the dirt and lay still. Jem rolled over onto his back, holding his thigh high up in the groin area and cursing. There was already a quantity of blood darkening his trousers. I feared that the count's knife (or whatever weapon he had used) had pierced the femoral artery.

"Hanna!" I said. "Help me!" Hanna stared at me, uncomprehending and unmoving. She was still under the influence of Percival Hyde's insidious hypnosis techniques, and I didn't have time to ease her back into complete consciousness. I barked a wartime command, in what I hoped was a voice of authority: "Krankenschwester! Schnell! Helfe mir!" "Nurse! Hurry! Help me!"

Who knows how many hundreds of times Hanna had heard that command during the war? Still, I had to repeat it three times before she rose like a woman sleepwalking and came toward us.

"Hanna, do you understand me?" I asked.

She simply stared. "This is very important," I said. "We have to stop the bleeding, or he'll go into shock."

Hanna simply stood and stared. It was maddening. I barked the command in the manner of the German sergeant abusing his men during the war: "Krankenschwester! Macht schnell!"

She nodded slowly, then more definitely. She began to do as she had been trained during the war. She ripped the silk shirt from the back of the obese and unconscious count, wadded it into a ball, and placed it under Jem's hip to elevate the wound. I removed my own shirt and used it to apply pressure, with Jem using an encyclopedic mix of Gaelic and English curses to tell me exactly what he thought of me and of the whole process.

"Aren't ye going to apply a tourniquet, man?" Jem asked.

"I'll be happy to use a tourniquet," I said as calmly as I could, "so long as you don't mind losing the leg, because that's what will happen. You are the detective. I am the physician."

Jem cursed me. I cursed the darkness. It was getting darker by the minute and without light I could not possibly see what I was doing. I had worked in many dim operating theatres on the Italian front, but I could not work in absolute darkness.

"Is there a light switch somewhere?" I asked Hanna. "I must have light."

She nodded without saying anything and rose to look for one, but just then the powerful lights of the conservatory came on overhead and an entire squad of police officers rushed to my assistance. Sergeant-Detective Bryce O'Doul, a man I knew from Sophie's Café, took in the situation at a glance and slapped handcuffs on the unconscious, moaning Count Respighi.

"Touchette!" he said to another detective. "Get to the house and call an ambulance. The hospital is only five blocks away, they can get here quickly."

"We'll need two ambulances," I said. "It won't do to put Jem and the Count in the same vehicle."

Touchette sprinted off to call for two ambulances.

"Anything I can do?" Sergeant O'Doul asked.

"Keep the pressure on the wound until the ambulance gets here. I need to look after Hanna."

Near the back entrance to the conservatory there was a fountain, with a jet of water flowing constantly from the mouth of a cherub. I took Hanna by the hand and led her to it. At first, she tried to hang back.

"Maxim," she said, "the spiders. I'm afraid of the spiders."

"The spiders are a myth," I said, with more conviction

than I felt. "The count couldn't have poisonous spiders in here without risking his own life and the lives of anyone who came to tend the plants. That was simply a technique he used to control you."

"But I saw one... He held it in his hand. I saw it."

"Then it wasn't poisonous. Count Respighi is a master at manipulating the mind, but he can't control the mind of a spider in his palm. It's over now, Hanna. The Count is in handcuffs. He will never be allowed to harm you again, do you understand?"

Hanna nodded. "But Percy can still hurt me," she said.

"Percy is out at a function with his wife," I said. "The moment he returns, we will have a long conversation with Dr. Percival Hyde, and then he will be arrested. He will never be allowed to touch you again, I assure you."

I took cool water from the fountain in my palms and used it to bathe Hanna's face and neck. She stood gratefully, letting the cool water flow over her. I could not contain myself.

"Hanna," I said, "I am so relieved. I love you so impossibly much. You are my entire world."

"I know, Maxim," she said. "I love you as much, perhaps more. It was terrible. The worst part was that I thought I would never see you again. The count is a monster, and so is Percy. They are monsters."

"Yes, they are. They are evil men. I should never have let you out of my sight. But now they will both spend the rest of his life behind bars."

Hanna nodded, but I could see that she didn't quite believe that she was safe. Not yet. She was another traumatized soldier, the victim of another kind of war, the war that a certain kind of men wage against women.

A wounded police officer provokes a quick reaction in the emergency services in any country. The ambulance crew arrived on the double. I gave them quick instructions. We were only five blocks from the Royal Victoria Hospital and the bleeding was under control with the constant pressure Sergeant O'Doul was applying. All they had to do was to get Jem to the hospital where the wounded artery could be sutured. From the quantity of blood, it appeared the artery had only been nicked. I wanted to accompany the stretcher to the hospital, but the ambulance men seemed competent, and I had a more urgent patient to care for. Hanna stood before me, looking stunned and weary. I helped her back to the bench where she had been sitting and sat next to her. We watched as Count Respighi sat up groggily and was hauled to his feet by four burly police officers just as a second ambulance crew arrived.

"Is this the bastard what stabbed Jem?" O'Doul asked.

"That's him. I saw him do it. And he's done a whole lot more."

O'Doul brought his beefy face to within an inch of Count Respighi. "If Jem dies," he said, "you won't have to worry about them hanging you. I'll cut your bollocks off and let you bleed to death."

Something on the ground caught O'Doul's eye. He took out a handkerchief and wrapped it around the sturdy wooden handle of some sort of implement with a four-inch blade as thin as a needle.

"What is that?" I asked.

O'Doul shrugged. "I don't know," he said. "It's too thin to be an ice-pick."

Detective Touchette peered at it. "That's a sailor's awl," he said.

"A what?"

"A sailor's awl. Like a long needle but with a solid handle. See? It has an eye at the tip, just like a sewing needle, only bigger and stronger. Sailors use it to patch their sails, but it's sharp as hell because it has to punch through canvas."

"Sharp enough to kill?"

"Absolutely, if you hit the right spot. Wouldn't leave much of a wound, either."

I recalled the discovery made by the Italian poet, Signore Traversini, in his research into the death of Adrian Howell. Howell was thought drowned during preparations for the regatta on Lago di Garda, when in truth he had died in exactly this fashion, with an almost undetectable stab wound to the femoral artery. Thirteen years after Howell's death, Ophélie Molyneux had been murdered with a quick stab to the heart with the same weapon (or at least the same type of weapon) the one that had now stabbed my dear friend, Jem Doyle. Only one man had been present on all three occasions: Count Ottavio Respighi.

As the Count regained consciousness, he became aware of the terrible pain in his shattered arm. He gave a terrible groan and glared at me: "You're a doctor," he said, "do something! Give me morphine, man!"

"Let me see," I said, and probed the arm hard where I knew it would hurt most. Respighi screamed.

"Does that hurt?" I asked.

"Of course, it hurts, you cretin! Does no one here have morphine?"

"In good time. First I have to determine the nature of your injury." I probed the arm again. This time, Count Respighi turned positively green.

"Oh, my," I said. "I believe you have a broken arm. It's likely to be quite painful unless they take you to the hospital and give you morphine."

"Take me to the hospital," he ordered. "Immediately!"

"One moment. I have a question to ask you first."

"I don't have to tell you anything," he said.

"No, you don't. We can stay here, and I can manipulate your arm in a number of interesting ways. It should fascinate you, the expert in pain." I gave him a sample, tugging the arm down and back. The count screamed. Like most sadists, he was a coward when it came to his own pain. "No, please!" he begged. "I will answer your questions."

"I have only one," I said. I turned to Sergeant O'Doul.

"Sergeant, could you come here for a moment? I want you to hear this."

The sergeant knelt beside us.

"Tell me what happened the night Ophélie Molyneux was killed," I said.

The Count sneered. "How should I know?"

I tugged on his arm. "Alright! Alright! I received a telephone call from the sanatorium, telling me these two foolish women had escaped. There was a function underway here at Hyde House, with a hundred guests in attendance. I feared that Hanna might make her way here and create a scene, so I went out to aid with the search. I had barely left the house when I saw the woman walking toward me. I didn't hesitate – Dr. Hyde's weakness for this woman had put everything we were trying to do in jeopardy. I wanted to put an end to it."

"So you stabbed her?"

"I did. But it was dark and it was snowing hard. I didn't know it was the wrong woman. Now morphine, please. Please."

"Not yet. We aren't finished. And the murder on the lake twenty years ago? What was said to be the drowning of Adrian Howell? That was your work also, wasn't it?"

Count Respighi nodded feebly. "Now. Please. Morphine."

"One more question and they will take you to the ambulance. I leaned forward to within a few inches of his ear and asked my question. Count Respighi shook his head furiously. "You fool! I'm not going to answer that!"

I grabbed his arm and twisted, hard. This time I thought the scream was going to tear his throat open. When it subsided, and he caught his breath, I asked the question again. When he hesitated, I gave the arm the slightest tug. "No!" he shouted. "Please!" I repeated the question for a third time, and this time he answered clearly.

"Did you hear that, Sergeant O'Doul?" I asked.

"I did," O'Doul said. "The bastard!"

CHAPTER 49

L ord Hyde was standing near his chauffeur-driven automobile on the curved driveway in front of the house,
where by now there were a dozen police officers and
two ambulance crews at work. Hyde stalked back and forth,
talking to this officer and that. Every phrase he uttered began
with the words, "I demand..." but no one paid him the least
attention. "I demand an explanation... I demand that you tell
me what is going on here... I demand that you explain why
Count Respighi is under arrest..."

Eleanor Hyde, looking more dishevelled and unfocused than on the afternoon I visited her, stood at the top
of the steps that led to the house, watching it all in some confusion, as though she were at the cinema and had stumbled
in halfway through the picture – which, in a sense, was true.
Hanna clung to my arm and would not let go, and Eleanor
stared at us but seemed unable to grasp who I was or why we
were there.

I managed to pull Sergeant O'Doul aside and to explain, very quickly, why it was that I needed to have a conversation with Lord Hyde, and why it was important that O'Doul
himself and (if possible) other police officers be present. I
saw at once why Jem placed such faith in the burly detective: O'Doul immediately assigned three of his men to accompany us and deftly took charge of the irate Lord Hyde, guiding
him toward the house with only the slightest pressure on his
elbow.

Once inside, with Eleanor Hyde, O'Doul asked if there
was somewhere in the house where we could converse in pri-

vate. "Third floor," Hyde said. "My private office."

He led the way and we trooped up the stairs. I asked Hanna if she wished to wait below, but she shook her head. "No," she said firmly. "I must come with you."

We followed the police officers up the steps, with me keeping a close eye on Hanna. I was not at all certain that she should be present, but then it was Percival Hyde who had put us all in this situation, so she had as much a right as anyone to witness his interrogation.

Lord Hyde led us into his spacious, book-lined private office, which was lined with Impressionist paintings, rare books and Oriental sculptures of elephants, panthers, and the Buddha. The desk itself was Chinese in origin and a dozen feet wide. Lord Hyde's chair sat behind it, and behind that was the balcony that extended the length of the east side of the house and looked down on the terracotta terrace below.

When Dr. Hyde saw Hanna enter, he looked at her sharply. "Does she have to be here?" he asked in irritation.

"She does," I said. He turned his back on us and stared out the window.

There was a thick Oriental carpet on the floor, so he was unable to hear my footsteps. The inspiration hit me then, and I acted on it before I could consider the ethical implications of my unorthodox approach. I walked up directly behind him before I spoke.

"Adrian Howell!" I said, in a loud, firm tone.

Dr. He spun around like a boxer facing an expected threat from behind. There was nothing congenial or in his manner now. "What did you say ?" he demanded.

"Adrian Howell. You are Adrian Howell. You are not Percival Hyde at all. You are Adrian Howell. You murdered the real Percival Hyde twenty years ago in Italy and you assumed his identity in order to inherit a fortune. Then you tried to have Hanna murdered to cover up what you had done. She had overheard when Count Respighi forgot himself and addressed you as 'Adrian.' You and the count were afraid she would make the connection and realize your real identity. That was why you had her committed to the Bethlehem Sanatorium. She was a danger to you both."

I heard Hanna gasp, but I kept my eyes on Howell/Hyde. He didn't flinch. In fact, he laughed uproariously. "I must congratulate you, Balsano. That is the most outlandish thing I have ever heard. Highly inventive on your part. You dare to burst in here with a story like that? I would have you arrested if it weren't so amusing. You ought to be a writer of fiction."

"It is not fiction, and you know it. Your partner in crime, Count Respighi, told us as much just now, before he was taken to hospital. He confirmed what I suspected. The Count has a broken arm. He was in a great deal of pain, and eager to get a shot of morphine. We detained him just long enough to get the truth. Sergeant O'Doul heard him quite clearly when he admitted that you are indeed Adrian Howell."

I saw Howell waver ever so slightly. Now he understood why so many police officers had accompanied us upstairs. Still, he tried to brazen it out.

"I can't imagine how you reached such a preposterous conclusion," he said. "I am Dr. Percival Hyde. Everyone knows who I am. I am the man who invited you to this country in the first place, I might add."

"Yes, you did – under false pretenses, because you are neither a medical doctor nor a psychiatrist. Your medical career is as fraudulent as your status as the heir to a shipping fortune. I will grant that you have learned a great deal for a man who was expelled from his university. You might have made a huge impact on psychiatry, but you also used your knowledge of hypnosis and drugs to bend young women to your will, and to establish a sanatorium that exists only to confine women who have become troublesome for a variety of reasons. Beyond that, you have become a sort of pimp to wealthy men in your circle, allowing them to rent women under your control for their pleasure – including your own wife. The first time I came here, she tried to tell me about 'terrible things' that were afoot here, but she was inebriated, and I didn't believe her. Now I know she was telling the truth."

Hyde leaned briefly on the desk, trying to collect himself. "I can't imagine what led you to this absurdity," he said.

"Hanna came to me the night of her supposed murder. It was Christmas Eve, 1913. She had escaped from the Bethlehem Sanatorium (an institution owned and founded by yourself and Count Respighi, I might add) and she was fleeing for her life with a friend named Ophélie Molyneux. They both had red hair, and Hanna had given Ophélie the sable coat you purchased for her. Your thugs caught up to the wrong woman and beat her, but it was your partner Count Respighi who killed her with a sailor's awl that pierced her heart – the same instrument he used to stab Jem Doyle tonight, the weapon that killed the real Percival Hyde twenty years ago. Respighi is an assassin who favours a particular weapon.

"Of course, you didn't know that Hanna had survived, and the wrong woman had been murdered. Hanna didn't know who was behind her incarceration in the sanatorium or the murder of Mlle Molyneux, but she was so frightened she had dyed her hair and changed her name after she returned to Vienna. She had come to my apartment fleeing your ruffians and spent part of the night with me, then vanished, leaving me with an enduring mystery. I knew that she had been in my apartment at three o'clock in the morning on Christmas Day, but all the newspaper stories said that she had been murdered the evening before. How could that be? Either I had been visited by a ghost, or Hanna was still alive.

"Eventually, I found her in Vienna and I learned what had happened: Before she vanished in the fall of 1913, Hanna had been your mistress. She was living in your apartment. Two things happened while she was living there, both of which made you irrationally angry. First, she found a small photograph tucked into the back of the frame holding another photograph. The small photo showed you with another young man when you were both in your young teens. The two of you looked so much alike that Hanna thought you might be twins. When she mentioned that to you, you became very angry and ordered her never to clean the apartment again.

"Then Hanna happened to be in the bedroom one morning when Count Respighi paid an early-morning visit. She wasn't really paying attention, but she heard the Count call you a certain name; she couldn't recall what it was. You became very angry and berated him in Italian. Then you turned your fury on her, though she couldn't understand why – she didn't realize the significance of the name she had heard when the Count forgot himself and called you "Adrian." Two weeks later, she was dragged off to the sanatorium by Cyril Leblanc, a corrupt detective in your pay. He used threats and blackmail to get a signature from Rudolf Mayr, Hanna's manager, committing her to the asylum. You were making sure no one could connect you to this dirty business – and it worked. Hanna blamed Rudi for having her committed.

"The day you became so furious with her, it was because Count Respighi called you 'Adrian,' was it not? The count had forgotten himself and called you by your real name, the name you bore when the two of you first met in Italy. You feared that Hanna would guess that you were, in fact, Adrian Howell, not Percival Hyde, and that you murdered your friend Percy to gain access to his inheritance and a vast fortune. You are a complete fraud, Adrian. You are not a doctor, nor a psychiatrist, nor a shipping heir. You are a thief and an impostor. You may not have done the killing yourself, but you are an accessory to murder."

Howell remained as haughty and aloof as ever, staring down his nose at me, the little Austrian fool who had blundered into the spider's web and somehow survived. I held his gaze for several long moments, refusing to back away. At last, something inside him seemed to give way. He was surrounded by police officers. His closest confederate had already confessed his secret. After successfully maintaining his fraudulent identity for two decades, he had run out of time, and he was shrewd enough to know it. He sat down at his desk, drumming his fingers on it as he peered round at his tormentors: myself, Hanna, Sergeant O'Doul, the other police officers. I am sure he was calculating his chances of maintaining the fiction that he was in fact Percival Hyde, or, failing that, to make his escape. Finally, he seemed to realize that neither option was possible. He took a deep, shuddering breath, and for a moment he looked utterly weary.

"You don't know what a delicious drug power can be, Dr. Balsano," he said. "It's intoxicating. I don't mean the power of a man who owns a thousand ships. The money meant nothing to me. I had no interest at all in the dreary task of running a shipping company. But psychiatry and hypnosis could grant me absolute power over another human being, especially a woman. The power to debase that woman, to be able to compel her to do absolutely anything to remain in your affections, to do things she would have found utterly disgusting only a few weeks before – don't tell me you don't know that intoxication, Balsano. Isn't that why we become psychoanalysts in the first place? So that we can completely dominate another mind?"

"Not for an instant," I said. "We become psychoanalysts to *heal* other minds, and perhaps ourselves. I'm afraid you missed that part, Mr. Howell. You failed to heal yourself, and now you've chosen to inflict your own inner darkness on innocents. How many unfortunate women have you subjugated? How many people have died so that you can cover your tracks? More than just Percy Hyde and Ophélie Molyneux, I'm sure. You have perverted everything we have worked to achieve. You despise my mentor, Dr. Sigmund Freud, but you're not fit to carry his cigar case. You may be brilliant, I'll give you that, but you have perverted everything we set out to do. You use what you have learned to corrupt the innocent, not to help the unfortunate, patients whose own minds have become a living hell. Instead, you create for them a hell far worse than anything they had endured before they met you, all to satisfy your own lust for power. Then you discard them like used handkerchiefs and move on to your next victim. You and that Italian count are a murderous pair. When you aren't killing someone outright, you're destroying a mind and leaving a husk of a human behind."

Howell looked at me scornfully. "Hasn't it occurred to you," he said, "that some of the people we dominated were never much more than husks to begin with? Like Percy Hyde. Poor, dim Percy. We were very young when Percy came under my spell, you know, at the boarding school where we both began our education. The only thing we had in common was that we were both orphans, but I was a poor orphan on a scholarship, while Percy had millions behind him. Percy fell head-over-heels in love with me, perhaps because there was some facial similarity between us, although I was always taller and stronger and infinitely more athletic. The poor fool was absolutely besotted. I used to give him impossible tasks, and he would go to any length to carry them out. I loved to force him to do risky things after lights out. 'Percy, old boy,' I would say, 'I have a craving for a tin of caviar. Could you fetch one for me?' Off he would go, risking a terrible beating to steal a tin of caviar out of someone else's locker. He would come panting back and hand it to me, and sometimes out of pure meanness I would say, 'Hyde! You brought me caviar! I distinctly asked you for sardines and biscuits!' Off he would go, apologizing because he had forgotten his errand and disappointed me.

"Oh, it was great fun, tormenting Percy. Now most boys outgrow that sort of thing, but not Percy. As we got older, he craved his little physical satisfactions. Occasionally, just often enough to keep him on the hook, I would grant him a sexual favor. Allow him to subjugate himself to me even more, to literally get down on his knees or bend over for me, because that was what he craved. It meant nothing to me, but to him, it was everything – he would be in ecstasy for a week after each encounter, but I granted my favours sparingly. It was best to keep him panting for more. It was very useful to have a chum with so much money at his fingertips, but Percy was always a dreary fellow. No imagination, no daring. I looked forward to the day I would be free of him, all that smothering attention and petty jealousy.

"When I was turfed out of Cambridge for a minor dalliance with a village girl, I thought I had seen the last of Percy. I left England and I went walking in Europe, met Count Respighi, spent some time in Tangiers, sailed to India and Ceylon and back. Meanwhile, Percy kept plugging away at medicine and got by somehow, even without me to help him. I would get a letter from him every week, but I wrote back only when I needed money. By the time he had completed his medical training, I was back in Italy, sharing a rundown villa with the count and trying to decide what I wanted to do next. Percy wrote, proposing to join us for a short time to kick up his heels, as he put it, before settling into a medical career.

"I wanted to sail in the regatta on Lago di Garda, but our boat was hopelessly inadequate. I knew that Percy had the means to acquire a far better racing boat, so we invited him to join us. He purchased the boat I wanted, and we began practicing seriously, because I wanted to win that race. We were thinking of nothing else, but then Percy received a telegram from Canada, informing him that he was no longer restricted to living on an annuity: he was now heir to the Hyde Shipping Company and the entire family fortune, including Hyde House. Immediately, Percy's entire manner toward us changed. He was going to be a proper Canadian and a shipping magnate; it wouldn't do for him to hang around with raffish sorts such as the count and myself, nor could it be known that he had a male lover. I didn't mind in the least, in fact I would have been glad to see the last of him. All I asked was an annual stipend of a hundred thousand English pounds – not a great deal of money for a man who now had millions upon millions at his fingertips. But when I made my little request, Percy was shocked. He called it blackmail and said that he would not start his new career by being blackmailed.

"When it became clear that he intended to abandon me to begin his new life, it was Count Respighi who came up with a plan. In Canada and at the headquarters of Hyde Shipping, Percy was as much a stranger as I was. The few individuals who remembered him recalled a very young boy, not the adult he had become. The Count knew a man who could alter Percy's passport in an afternoon, replacing Percy's photo with mine. We looked so much alike in any case – that's what Hanna noticed when she found the photograph of the two of us together. But Percy's passport photo bore little resemblance to me, so it had to be changed. After that, there was simply the matter of disposing of Percy."

I saw it all clearly now. "And the storm on Lago di Garda while you were practicing for the regatta was the perfect situation," I said. "That's why you went out on the lake that day. It wasn't because you were determined to sail despite the weather."

"Yes, it was. I thought we were simply going to hit him over the head and throw him overboard, but Count Respighi is fond of that sailor's awl because it leaves so little trace. One quick strike to the heart or the femoral artery when Percy was looking the other way, and it would all be over. In the event, Percy saw what was coming and there was a bit of a struggle, but I was able to overpower him until the count did his work with that needle. Then we tossed him into the lake."

"How could you possibly believe that you could get away with it?" I asked.

"What do you mean? We have gotten away with it for twenty years. If your little friend Hanna hadn't stumbled onto my secret, we may never have been caught."

"But she didn't stumble on your secret. She never knew why your manner toward her changed so dramatically. Had you simply left her alone, nothing would have happened, and Ophélie Molyneux would be alive today."

"Ah, but I had no way of knowing that, did I? And I could hardly question Hanna to find out how much she knew without tipping my hand. Look at the choices: Remain in control of Hyde Shipping and a vast fortune, not to mention my growing fame as a psychiatrist, or go to prison for fraud, and possibly be extradited to Italy to face a murder charge. I could not take that chance. Even if I wished to take the risk, Count Respighi would not have permitted it and I had to bow to his wishes. He knew too much."

"Surely someone must have recognized you in all these years?"

"It was easier than you think. No one on this continent had seen Percy Hyde since he was seven years old. I may have looked somewhat different than he did, but we were often taken for brothers and a person changes a great deal between the ages of seven and twenty-seven. I was recognized only once, at a board meeting in England. An old school chum who had known both of us as teenagers kept insisting that I was indeed Adrian Howell, not Percy. I told him that he was sadly mistaken, but he persisted, and in fact he came to my hotel room that evening to persuade me to confess that I was an impostor. Fortunately, Count Respighi had accompanied me on that voyage. He took care of our little difficulty."

"Meaning that you have another murder on your hands?"

"Not I. I have never murdered anyone. The Count enjoys killing. He had learned the uses of that sailor's awl as a teenager in Naples. He didn't require encouragement. He always knew what to do without consulting me."

"Perhaps you didn't wield that awl, but at least three people are dead because of you. Including Ophélie, who had nothing to do with you."

"It's your fault she died," Howell said, glaring at Hanna. "You should have been wearing that sable coat I gave you, not this damned Molyneux woman. Because I had a weakness for you, I ended up paying for that woman's funeral, along with a very expensive casket that was meant for you."

It came back to me then: a tall man who seemed somehow familiar, who had been standing on a rise surveying the funeral on that frigid January day. "Why did you feel compelled to do that?" I asked. "Rather a strange act, isn't it? To have someone killed and then pay for the funeral?"

"Ah, that was my weakness," he said. "Love – that disgusting emotion. The first time I heard Hanna sing out in North Hatley, I fell in love with her. Had to have her. The fact that she was suffering from rather acute anxiety because of her North American tour made it all too easy. Soon I had made my conquest, and I was looking for some convenient way to divorce Eleanor so that I could marry Hanna. Hanna is so much more intelligent and talented than my wife. Poor Eleanor, her only talent is her beauty and that will fade. Everything was going according to plan until Hanna overheard Count Respighi calling me Adrian. After that, the Count convinced me that it would have been foolhardy for me to go on. Hanna had to be put away where she couldn't expose us. I was genuinely grieving after her death. I felt I had to do something, so I paid for her funeral. But I swore to myself that I would never be so foolish as to fall in love again."

Hanna, who had remained silent all the while, could contain herself no longer. "You!" she spat, and I thought she might attack Adrian Howell as she had attacked Rudi Mayr, "you don't know what love is. Love creates, but all you do is destroy! You are filth, and you are going away to a very filthy prison. You will never be free!"

"You don't know that. I retain some very excellent lawyers."

"You have just made a full confession to a room full of witnesses, including four police officers," I said. "I don't believe there is a lawyer in the world who could extricate you from this."

As Adrian Howell spoke, we felt the storm building outside, a full-fledged summer thunderstorm with attendant drama. The wind picked up, rain lashed the window panes. There was a flash of lightning nearby, followed by the sharp crack of thunder.

"Oh, I love a thunderstorm, don't you?" Howell said. He jumped up to fling open the windows behind his desk and a gust of wind blew the rain into his face. He stood rather dramatically before the open window, arms flung wide as though daring the storm to do its worst. The narrow balcony outside had only a low iron railing that barely came to the knees of a man as tall as Adrian Howell, and far below was that terrace, surrounded by a marble wall. We stood watching him – Hanna, myself and four police officers, allowing him a last look at freedom. Sergeant O'Doul dangled the handcuffs in his hand, waiting for the right moment to make the formal arrest.

O'Doul and I sensed what Howell was about to do at the same moment – an instant too late. We both shouted in alarm and rushed to hold him back, but Adrian Howell was still the athlete, and he had a head start. He took three steps and sailed over the railing into a graceful swan dive. A flash of lightning caught him at the peak of his leap before he fell, down and down into the darkness. We heard the thud as his body hit the marble wall below, sounding for all the world like a sack of potatoes thrown from a great height.

Hanna nearly collapsed then, but I was able to catch her and ease her into a chair before I joined Sergeant O'Doul on the balcony. Down below, three or four members of the household staff ran out to attend to the man now sprawled and broken on the terrace wall. Stephens the butler was one of them. He bent over the lord of the manor for a few moments, then looked up at us.

"I believe Lord Hyde is dead," he shouted up at us.

"Yes," I said. "Lord Hyde has been dead for some time."

CHAPTER 50

I spent that night at the Royal Victoria Hospital, rushing back and forth between the room where Jem Doyle was offending his nurses by smoking a cigar while he recovered from his wound, the room where Hanna was taken to rest and recuperate from her experience, and the room where Elise was anxiously demanding to know more about Hanna. At about four o'clock in the morning, I persuaded the physician in charge to put the two women in the same room, and I stood by awkwardly as Hanna and Elise held each other and wept.

Near dawn, Sophie arrived and ordered me to go home and rest. I did as I was told and slept until late afternoon. When I woke, it took several cups of Sophie's strong coffee to revive me fully. The events at Hyde House came back to me in flashes, like fragments of a dream. After living with this thing for so long, it was over, but it would take many months before I would fully grasp that truth.

When I was fully awake, I decided to walk to the hospital. It was a beautiful early summer evening, and I should have been content. Hanna had been found, alive if not entirely well. Elise had survived the beating she endured. The stab wound from the sailor's awl had, as I suspected, nicked Jem Doyle's femoral artery, but two deft sutures were enough to close the wound. (The surgeon, I learned, had served during the Great War in battlefield operating theaters in France. Ironically, it was our combined experience during that murderous war that had saved Jem's life.)

All had turned out as well as could be expected, apart

from the death of Adrian Howell. There would be a great deal of work for the civil courts and the lawyers, a family fortune that would now, presumably, pass to Eleanor Hyde – although since she had never been married to the actual Percival Hyde, would she still have a claim? It was more than I could unravel, but I sensed the lawyers would be building mansions of their own before it had all been sorted out. My more immediate concern was the physical battering Elise had suffered, and the psychological damage done to Hanna. Hanna had already been through this once, and I had been able to bring her only part way back. Would she recover after being seized a second time, and abused by Adrian Howell and the count? Or would she forever be like some of the war veterans I had studied in Vienna, the *zitterers* who would live out their lives as broken men. All that I knew for certain was that I would see to it that Hanna had all the help she needed to recover.

By the end of the week, Hanna, Elise and Jem had all been released from the hospital. The following week, an alert police officer at the train station spotted Pepper Labrecque trying to board a train to Halifax. He had tried to grow a beard as a disguise, but the rings on his fingers gave him away. Pepper was a tougher nut to crack than Manx Sullivan, but in the end, he corroborated Manx's story: Ophélie Molyneux had been alive when she was left in the snow. Pepper hadn't actually seen Count Respighi murder the young woman, but all the circumstantial evidence pointed to him. Pepper and Manx Sullivan were with assaulting Ophélie, but they also faced murder charges in connection with the death of Anne McCleod, the young woman who had been beaten to death after she tried to escape the sanatorium.

The Count was duly charged with murder in the first degree. The Italian government, however, immediately issued a formal request for Count Respighi's extradition to Italy to face charges in the murder of Dr. Percival Hyde. The matter had to be settled at the highest levels of government; there was a *quid pro quo* of some sort and the Count was sent back to

Italy to stand trial for the murder of Percival Hyde.

Not two weeks after the death of Adrian Howell, I was approached by the head of the medical school at McGill University to become the first head of a new department of psychiatry. It was a wonderful offer, even if it came only because of my ties to Dr. Sigmund Freud, but I had to refuse. I discussed it briefly with Hanna, but I already knew her feelings – too much had happened to her in Montreal. She could not bear to remain in the city much longer. Hanna encouraged me to accept McGill's offer and to remain in the New World to further my career, but I had to refuse. My place was as near to her as she would allow me to be. If she returned to Europe, then I would return to Europe as well. If it were possible, I would never again allow her out of my sight.

We remained another six weeks after the fateful night at the Hyde mansion in order to give Hanna and Elise time to heal. Before we left, we had one last party at Sophie's Café with her sons and their wives and children and a dozen police officers, including Sergeant O'Doul. Even in such a crowded room, I had eyes only for Hanna.

On the first day of August 1920, we took ship for Cherbourg after a long and tearful goodbye with Jem and Sophie, and only after they promised to visit the following summer. On August 4 Elise and I ordered a bottle of champagne, and we celebrated Hanna's twenty-eighth birthday as she thrilled to the sight of a school of flying fish keeping pace with the ship, soaring through the sparkling waves of the Atlantic Ocean.

Elise took to her bed early that night. I thought Hanna might want to join her, but she lingered with me instead. We found a deck chair, wrapped ourselves in a blanket with her head resting on my shoulder, and lay watching the slow wheel of the stars overhead. What, I wondered, was to become of us? I could not imagine a world without Hanna, but how did she feel?

The answer came in the form of a question. Hanna raised herself onto her elbow, looked down at me, and placed a finger on my lips.

"Maxim," she said, "I have a question for you."

"Yes?"

"You know that it will take me a long time to become whole again, right?"

"I do. I understand completely. I want to help you heal. I want to be with you every step of the way."

Hanna bit her thumb for a moment, as she often did when she was thinking.

"Very well then," she said. "Dr. Maximilian Balsano – will you marry me?"

AFTERWORD

by Dr. Lukas Balsano

D r. Maximilian Balsano was my father, and I adored him extravagantly. He was a gentleman of a type that is now almost extinct, firmly Old World in his manners but New World in his outlook, although he rarely returned to North America following the events recounted here. He was kind, thoughtful, so gentle of manner that it was sometimes taken for weakness, but when courage was called for, he possessed more than most of those who make a great show of their superficial toughness. It has been my great good fortune, following my own retirement from a career as a psychoanalyst, to spend much of the past fifteen years translating his work from German into English. I began with the five pioneering works my father wrote on his specialty, the field of psychiatry. I then translated his two-volume History of Psychiatry, a memoir on his long association with Dr. Sigmund Freud, and the brief and modest account of his efforts to help Jews escape from his native Austria between 1938 and 1945.

After that labor, I thought my work was finished until the day I was cleaning the attic in our old summer home (a modest cabin on Lake Léman in Switzerland) when I came across a small wooden trunk with leather handles. Begging my father's forgiveness, I broke the rusty lock and opened the trunk. Inside, perfectly preserved, I found a fairly lengthy manuscript written on sheets of unlined foolscap paper at its full size, seventeen by thirteen and one-half inches. I could see at once that it was written in my father's hand, the cursive script Austrian school-boys were once taught.

This work was titled *The Woman in Green*, and it was his account of a period in his life about which he had always been uncharacteristically secretive, beginning with a mysterious episode that occurred in Montreal in 1913. I began to read, and many hours later, I had fallen asleep with sheets of foolscap paper all around me, halfway into a mystery that seemed to deepen with every page.

As I was going through my mother's things after I had completed this translation, I found a photograph taken at Bad Gastein in June 1921, nearly a year after my parents left Montreal. I knew they had been married by the ship's captain the previous year, but this was a wedding photo. My mother, Hanna Goss Balsano, was in white. She was posed next to my father at the center of the photograph, which had been taken by a gentleman who ran a studio in the village. All around them were the people I had gotten to know so well while translating Papa's book: There was my grandfather, great-grandfather and the dour housekeeper, Frau Kachelmeier. There was the distinguished, white-haired poet, Signore Amedeo Traversini, with his buxom Carlotta. There was a tall, cadaverous looking gentleman whom I took to be Dr. Jan Muršak standing alongside his dark-haired wife Karine, who was holding a baby while two older children clung to her skirts. Next to my mother was an elegantly dressed woman who could only have been Elise Duvernay, and beside her was the short, squarish Sophie Szitva and a towering fellow with a fierce black mustache who had to be Jem Doyle. Somehow, Sophie and Jem had been enticed to come all the way from Canada for the ceremony.

At the bottom of the photograph was an inscription in my mother's hand. It read, "the day I truly became Maxim's wife." Now that could mean that it was the day the marriage was sanctified by a church wedding with a priest officiating, or it could mean something else; I shall draw a veil over the rest and leave my mother and father their privacy. In any case,

JACK TODD

another decade would pass before my birth, a first and only child born rather late to his adoring parents. I now have this precious photograph, newly framed, on the wall of my study here in the old house in Bad Gastein. All around it are photos of my mother and father together; in Rome and Budapest, Vienna and Lugano, even Hong Kong and Tokyo, but never in Montreal.

When I reached the end of my father's narrative, the point at which Hanna, Elise and Maxim had taken ship for Cherbourg from Montreal in 1920 (the end of our narrative, in other words) I had many questions but no answers. The tale stopped there, with the clear two-word marking my father put at the end of everything he wrote: *das Ende*.

Das Ende und der Anfang: the end and the beginning, because returning to Europe meant starting a new life. That was the life I knew. Until I began this translation of my father's work, I did not know that my mother had ever been anything more than a singing teacher. I knew that she taught generations of singers, but I did not know anything of her own brief but brilliant career.

Inside the same small trunk that contained this manuscript were the two ten-inch discs containing concert recordings from the Deutsche Gramophone-Acktiengesselschaft company that Elise Duvernay had given to Maxim in 1914, one with the recording of my mother singing the Hugo Wolf lieder "Vergeborgenheit", the other the "Caro Nome" from *Rigoletto*.

I was fortunate to locate a shop in Vienna where I had the old recordings copied in digital form. I have now heard them played on an antique gramophone, and on the newest modern technology, and in truth I prefer the gramophone. On either recording, however, that voice is unmistakable. It takes me back instantly to one of my fondest memories: Summers on Lake Léman in Switzerland, when late each afternoon, I played or fished from the dock in front of our cottage where we kept our little rowboat. We ate very late and at dusk (the time I now think of as *l'heure bleu*) my father always sat reading in his favorite chair outside the cottage, keeping an eye on me and gazing out at the lake while my mother made dinner.

Once her concoctions were in the oven, Mama would emerge onto the little balcony outside the kitchen in our cottage, and she would sing to my father. Sometimes she sang arias from various operas, sometimes she sang my father's favorite *lieder*, especially those by Hugo Wolf. Sometimes she sang popular songs, and when she was in an especially sentimental mood, she would often sing *Lili Marlene*. For the most part, there was no one but us to hear her impromptu recitals, but now and then a lone fisherman in his boat on the water would ship his oars and pause to listen while that rich, pure voice poured over the water. My father would sit very still, as though any sudden movement might cause her to stop, and listen intently with tears coursing down his cheeks as she sang.

When it was over, the last notes always seemed to linger, shimmering in the air.

ABOUT THE AUTHOR

Jack Todd

Jack Todd is the author of four previous published novels and the memoir Desertion in the Time of Vietnam. As a columnist for the Montreal Gazette, he has written about the city for thirty years, including two interactive mysteries. His memoir was shortlisted for the Governor-General's Award and won the Mavis Gallant Prize for Non-Fiction. He lives in Montreal.

BOOKS BY THIS AUTHOR

Desertion In The Time Of Vietnam

A memoir describing Todd's moral struggles over the Vietnam War and his journey from Fort Lewis to Mexico and back to Canada.

Sun Going Down

The first volume of the epic saga of the Paint family on the American frontier in South Dakota, Wyoming and Nebraska, based loosely on diaries and letters left by the author's family.

Come Again No More

The second volume of the Paint Family Saga takes the story as far as the Great Depression. Based on the author's parents and their struggles to survive during some of the hardest times Americans have known.

Rain Falls Like Mercy

The third volume of the Paint saga follows multiple generations of the family through heroism and hardship to the end of World War 2.

Rose & Poe

The story of the indomitable Rose Didelot and her giant, ungainly son Poe as they attempt to scratch out a living in the mythical Belle Coeur County, Vermont, in a time much like our own – surviving and thriving until a vigilante posse comes looking for Poe.

Acknowledgments

If you have read the splendid old Wilkie Collins tome called *The Woman in White*, you will no doubt have noticed certain similarities between it and the current work, beginning with the title. This is not a coincidence. This is my homage to that work and to others like it, the great English (and I refer here to the nation, not the language) tradition of the mystery novel. You will not find otherwise many similarities, beyond a couple of characters and a similar theme. If reading *The Woman in Green* sends you back to read *The Woman in White*, all the better. For the sections set in Vienna before, during and after World War I, I am much indebted to the two great Austrian novelists, Stefan Zweig and Joseph Roth. For a full history of the cultural life of the time, I cannot recommend the two volumes by Frederic Morton: *A Nervous Splendor: Vienna 1888-89* and *Thunder at Twilight: Vienna 1913-1914*. Finally, I could not have written of the much-neglected war on the Italian front without the magnificent *The White War: Life and Death on the Italian Front 1915-1919*, by Mark Thompson. Thanks to my friend and partner in this venture Dr. John X. Cooper for his reading and insights, to Eugene Marc and Peter Vaillancourt-McIver, the first to lose an entire night's sleep reading this book, and Hilary Stanley for her wise advice. Finally, without the help and support of my friend Magnolia Kahrizi from start to finish, this book would not exist.